Praise for *New York Times* bestselling author Sharon Sala

"Well-developed secondary characters and a surprise ending spice up a familiar story line in Sala's latest romantic intrigue."

—*Publishers Weekly* on *Snowfall*

"A wonderful romance, thriller, and delightful book."

—*USATODAY.com*'s *Happy Ever After* blog on *Life of Lies*

"In Sala's latest page-turner, staying alive is the biggest challenge of all. There are appealing characters to root for, and one slimy villain who needs to be stopped."

—*RT Book Reviews* on *Race Against Time*

Praise for *USA TODAY* bestselling author Rita Herron

"Herron understands the bonds between mother and child and presents a touching and terrifying tale of evil and redemption."

—*RT Book Reviews* on *Unbreakable Bond*

"A slick plot combined with riveting characters and unyielding suspense make Herron's latest a star attraction for fans."

—*RT Book Reviews* on *The Missing Twin*

"This story will totally captivate the reader. A tale packed solid with suspense and excitement with a new surprise at the turn of every page… An absolutely fascinating read that is definitely recommended. Rita Herron is an extremely gifted writer."

—*FreshFiction* on *Forbidden Passion*

NEW YORK TIMES BESTSELLING AUTHOR

SHARON SALA

FAMILIAR STRANGER

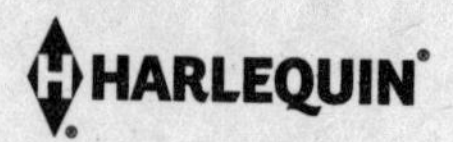

Recycling programs for this product may not exist in your area.

ISBN-13: 978-1-335-40999-7
Familiar Stranger
First published in 2001.
This edition published in 2021.

Special thanks and acknowledgment are given to Sharon Sala for her contribution to the A Year of Loving Dangerously series.

Collecting Evidence
First published in 2009.
This edition published in 2021.

Special thanks and acknowledgment are given to Rita Herron for her contribution to the Kenner County Crime Unit miniseries.

This edition published by arrangement with Harlequin Books S.A.

For questions and comments about the quality of this book, please contact us at CustomerService@Harlequin.com.

Harlequin Enterprises ULC
22 Adelaide St. West, 40th Floor
Toronto, Ontario M5H 4E3, Canada
www.Harlequin.com

Printed in U.S.A.

CONTENTS

Sharon Sala is a *New York Times* bestselling author. She has 123 books published in romance, young adult, Western, women's fiction and nonfiction. First published in 1991, she's an eight-time RITA® Award finalist. Industry awards include the following: the Janet Dailey Award; five Career Achievement Awards from *RT Book Reviews*; five National Readers' Choice Awards; five Colorado Romance Writers Awards of Excellence; the Heart of Excellence Award; the Booksellers' Best Award; the Nora Roberts Lifetime Achievement Award presented by RWA; and the Centennial Award from RWA for recognition of her 100th published novel.

Books by Sharon Sala

Secrets and Lies

Dark Hearts
Cold Hearts
Wild Hearts

Forces of Nature

Going Gone
Going Twice
Going Once

The Rebel Ridge novels

'Til Death
Don't Cry for Me
Next of Kin

Visit the Author Profile page
at Harlequin.com for more titles.

FAMILIAR STRANGER

Sharon Sala

Chapter 1

Rain thumped against the small, thatched roof like soggy bullets. The familiar sound of an incoming Huey rocked the air as it passed overhead, but Private David Wilson was deaf to everything but the panic.

Blood...so much blood. Don't look at Frank. Don't think about what he's done...what he made you do. Destroy the evidence before it's too late.

The scent of gasoline was everywhere now. On the walls, on the bodies, saturating the money that his brother, Frank, had been willing to die for.

Stupid. Stupid. Stupid. Money for guns. Brother for brother. Honor for sale. Stupid. Stupid. Stupid.

Match. Need a match. Don't look at Frank. Just think about what has to be done.

Jonah rolled from his belly to his back and kicked in his sleep, unconsciously sending his covers to the foot of the bed. Even though the second-story window beside his bed was open, there was little breeze stirring. It was unseasonably warm for the Colorado mountains this time of year, but the sweat on his body wasn't from the heat of the night. It was from the hell in his dream. And even in that dream, he still couldn't control his own warning.

He looked. And saw the dead gunrunners...and the money, now saturated with rain and mud and gasoline... and the blood pooling beneath his brother's body.

A muscle twitched near Jonah's mouth, a reflex to the scream echoing inside his mind as the match was struck. A word slipped from between his lips, too faint to be heard, although it hardly mattered. He'd been alone for so many years he wouldn't have known how to share his thoughts if he'd had the chance.

In the space of one breath, the dream jumped from 1974 and Vietnam to two weeks ago in New York City, bringing with it the same sense of desperation and leaving Jonah writhing in torment.

From the air, New York City appeared as a vast but inanimate object, with only a small cluster of land and trees they called Central Park embedded within the mass of concrete and steel.

He banked the chopper toward the unwinding ribbon that was the East River, and as he did, his heart began to pound. Only a few more minutes and this hell would come to an end.

Below him was a dark blanket of land peppered with thousands and thousands of lights. Almost there. With the desperation in Del Rogers's voice still ringing in his head, all he could think was, no more. Too many innocents have been caught in this crazy man's revenge to bring me down. Please, God, just let Maggie and her baby still be alive. Let us get them out of all this still breathing and kicking.

Unconsciously, Jonah's hands curled into fists, as he relived the descent of the black stealth helicopter he was piloting, all the while knowing that Simon was holding a woman and child between himself and destiny.

A faint breeze came through the open windows, blowing across his nude body, but Jonah was too deeply asleep to appreciate the sensation. The muscles in his legs twitched as he relived landing the chopper.

In the landing lights, the fear on Maggie's face was vivid, overwhelming Jonah with a renewed sense of guilt.

The cowardly son of a bitch, using innocent people just to get to me.

The force of wind from the descending helicopter whipped Maggie's hair and clothes and sent a shower of grit and dust into the air around them. He saw her trying to use her body as a shield for the hysterical baby in her arms, but the man holding her hostage gave her a yank, making sure she still stood between him and the guns aimed in his direction.

As the helicopter landed, Jonah could only imagine what was going through Maggie's mind—all this hell—all the danger to her family—and for a man she didn't even know. He slid open a door in the side of the chopper and flashed a bright light in Simon's face.

In that moment, Jonah's mind shut down. Before his senses could wrap around the truth of what he was seeing, Simon's body jerked. He had been shot by Del Rogers.

After that, everything seemed to be happening in slow motion.

SPEAR agents firing from surrounding rooftops.

Simon taking another bullet.

The play of emotions moving across Simon's face—a face that was aged with hate as well as passing years, bearing scars both old and new.

The impact of the bullet as the shot tore through Simon's body.

The desperate lunge Simon made toward the East River in a last-ditch effort to escape.

The way the water parted to let him in.

The knot of dismay in Jonah's belly when he realized that Simon was gone.

Jonah woke with a grunt and sat straight up in bed. It had been two weeks, and he still hadn't gotten over the shock of seeing Simon's face. The guilt of all these years—of thinking he had killed his brother—had been for nothing.

"Ah, God… Frank. I thought you were dead."

He shook his head and then massaged the tension in the back of his neck. As he did, the powerful muscles in his shoulders bunched and rolled. The misery of these nightmare-filled nights was getting to him. He needed to work it off, but not in the weight room, as he normally did. He wanted the air against his skin and the ground beneath his feet. He needed to run until he set his muscles on fire.

It was 5:10 A.M. as he rolled out of bed and strode to the bathroom. Even the shock of cold water on his face was not enough to wash away the horror of what he'd been dreaming. With a curse on his lips, he strode into his bedroom, moving through the darkness with the confidence of an animal that well knew its lair.

Every motion was deliberate as he dressed—grabbing

a pair of shorts and a clean T-shirt from the top drawer of the dresser, then lacing his running shoes and fastening the holster of a small-caliber handgun at the waistband of his shorts. Five minutes later he paused at the kitchen table, fingering the single page of a letter he'd received less than twenty-four hours ago. Although the room was too dark to read the words again, he didn't need to read them to remember.

I know who you are. Your time has come. I'll be in touch. Frank.

Jonah shuddered. Ghosts. He'd never believed in them until now. He dropped the letter and moved onto the deck. Daybreak was less than an hour away, but he didn't need light by which to see. He stretched a couple of times to ease tense muscles, then he stepped off the deck and began to walk toward the trees. Within moments, he'd moved to a jog, and by the time he disappeared into the tree line, he was running, only now there were no demons to outrun. He had a face and a name to go with it and only a short time left before the inevitable confrontation. Only God knew how it would end, and in a way, it almost didn't matter.

Almost.

He wanted this over. All of it. Being Jonah. Hiding secrets. Telling lies. Just over. He wasn't the first man to give up his identity for the good of his country and he wouldn't be the last. But he'd given up more than an identity, and that was what dug at him in the wee hours of the mornings when sleep eluded him.

He'd given up Cara.

Unconsciously, he increased his speed as the memory of her face crept into his mind. So pretty. So young. And they'd been so much in love. Looking back, he would say crazy in love.

He ducked on the path to avoid a low-hanging branch and swiped his arm across his forehead, catching the sweat before it ran in his eyes. His calves were starting to burn. The pain felt good—a reminder that he was more than just a machine for Uncle Sam.

Cara.

My God, what had he been thinking? They were only sixteen years old and he'd begged her to run away with him. What had he thought they'd do? Better yet, where in hell would they have gone? The fact that she'd pleaded with him to wait until they were out of college said something for the theory that girls matured faster than boys. In their case, she certainly had. She'd known what he'd refused to consider, and because they'd fought and then been too stubborn to admit they were wrong, their lives had turned upside down.

A large bird flew across his line of vision, and he could tell by the absence of sound at its passing that it was an owl, probably on its way home from a night of hunting.

If only he'd had the sense to go home after their fight, but no, he'd had to show the world—and maybe himself—that he was a man. And what better way to do that than to go fight a war?

His older brother, Frank, had signed up months earlier and was already somewhere in the jungles of Vietnam. The family had gotten one letter from him in all that time, and their mother had cried herself to sleep when it came. But that hadn't occurred to David then. All he'd wanted to do was prove that he was man enough for Cara to love.

When he told her he'd enlisted, he hadn't expected her to like it, but he'd expected her to wait for him to come back. Instead, she'd cried hysterically, claiming that he'd chosen the army over her. Unable to undo all the choices he'd made, he got on the bus and never came back, although at first, that hadn't been his plan.

He'd written to her religiously, but to his dismay she never replied. Over a year and a half later and a world away in Saigon, it had all come undone. Receiving a package containing all of his letters unopened was rough, but it was the two accompanying newspaper clippings that nearly killed him. One was the announcement of her wedding, the second the birth of her first child.

He knew Cara, and he'd done the math. The baby was his. He had a daughter back home in the state of New York, and someone else was going to raise her.

After that, short of turning the gun on himself, he'd tried to die. So many times. In so many ways. It should have been simple. Everyone else around him was dying in combat, but it was as if he'd become immortal. Nothing could hurt him.

Then he'd discovered Frank's treason, and bloodshed had followed. After that, he'd quit on everything, including himself. Just before the war was over, he was recruited by SPEAR. By then, giving up David Wilson was simple. His parents were dead. Cara had given her life and their child to another man. A man who slept with her and laughed with her and raised the baby David had put in her belly.

And David had left her alone—until now. With no way to know what the future would hold, he needed to make peace with his past. Cara was a widow these past three years. Their child was grown. Hell, he was a grandfather and had never set eyes on his own daughter. It, by God, wasn't fair.

Daybreak was hovering on the horizon by the time he reached the edge of the cliff. His heart was still pounding from the run, his clothes dripping with sweat as he lowered himself down into a sitting position on the lip of a rock, as he had so many, many times before.

The air was beginning to stir, promising a stiff breeze before the day was out. He sat with back straight and legs folded, his hands resting lightly on his knees, staring at the crack of light appearing over the mountain. The sky was changing now, wrapping itself in pale, dusty blues intermingled with threads of hot pink and gold.

As he watched, the anger in him slowly stilled. He'd seen just such a sunrise many times since he'd come to this place, but it never failed to instill in him a feeling of awe—a gentle and vibrant reminder of Who was really in charge. The vista blurred and he told himself it was nothing but sweat in his eyes.

Moments later, the sun made itself known—the first rays catching and then holding in the silver wings of hair at his temples. With a deep, heartfelt sigh, he stood. It was time to go home. But not just to the cabin. Thanks to the chaos Frank Wilson had created, his days as Jonah had to be over. His guess was, the President was probably already in the process of choosing his successor, but would wait until his formal request for retirement. And before that came, he had the final showdown with Frank. The way he saw it, he owed it to himself to make peace with his past, and to do that, he had to become David Wilson one last time and see Cara—the girl he had left behind.

Finger Lakes Region, New York State

Cara Justice swatted at a bee that kept pilfering about her flowers as she knelt at the side of the flower bed.

"Get back, you little beggar. Just let me get these weeds out of the bed and then you can have at the blossoms."

The bee, of course, didn't answer, and Cara, of course, expected none. But it felt good to be talking aloud, even if there was no one to hear. She tossed aside the last handful of weeds and then stood, brushing off the knees of her slacks and straightening the collar of her shirt. The day was warm, but not unbearably so. She stood for a moment, surveying the landscape of her backyard, and smiled. She loved this time of year. Everything was new and green, flowers in varying stages of buds and blooms, birds nesting.

Renewal.

That's what it was. Everything was new all over again. *Except me*, she thought, and then thought of her youth and sighed. Those had been sad times and nothing she would ever want to relive. She'd suffered, endured and prevailed. After that, she'd made herself always look forward, never dwelling on the past. Truth be told, she didn't want to be young again. It had hurt too much the first time around. Turning fifty had been a plateau she'd welcomed. Her oldest daughter, Bethany, who lived just down the road, was grown and married, as were her two youngest children, Tyler and Valerie, although they lived out of state.

She bent to pick up her hoe, and as she did, her blond chin-length hair brushed the sides or her face. She straightened, tossing her head to get it out of her eyes, and made a mental note next time she came out to tie it all back. As she started toward the gardening shed, a stiff breeze came out of nowhere, molding her clothes to her body and momentarily outlining her slender, willowy build. From a distance, she could easily have passed for a young, thirty-something woman. It wasn't until one looked closer that the tiny wrinkles at the corners of her eyes and the small laugh lines framing her mouth were evident. Her stomach growled as she put up the hoe and tossed her gloves in the basket. She glanced at her watch, surprised that noontime had come and gone.

As she started toward the back door, she heard the sounds of an approaching car. It couldn't be Bethany. She and her family were on vacation and weren't due back for several days. Maybe it was the mailman with a package, she thought, and hurried toward the front of the house, anxious to catch him before he left.

It wasn't until she rounded the corner of the house and saw the tail end of a dark sedan that she knew it wasn't the mailman. She paused in the shade beneath the cluster of maple trees and watched as a tall, middle-aged man emerged from the driver's side of the car. His shoulders were broad, his belly flat beneath his white polo shirt. He walked with a military bearing—head back, chin up. His hair was short and dark, but winged with silver above his ears. In reflex, she touched her own hair, aware that the same silver threads lay there among the taffy-colored strands, only not as evident as those on the man.

He didn't see her at first, and so she allowed herself to stare, trying to think why he seemed so familiar. She was certain she'd never seen him before. She would definitely have remembered. And then the stranger suddenly stopped and turned, as if sensing her scrutiny. She waited for him to speak.

David didn't have to look at the map to Cara's home that he'd downloaded from the Internet. It was burned into his memory. Even though he knew how to get to her house, he felt lost. As Jonah, he'd done something unheard of by seeking out any part of his past.

But it wasn't as if he'd just walked off the job. There was enough equipment in the trunk of his car to connect him with everything from spy satellites to the President of the United States, should the need arise. For all intents and purposes, he was still in charge of SPEAR, but in his heart, he was already pulling away.

Frank had set the ball rolling in this direction the day he'd kidnapped Easton Kirby's son. After the last incident with Maggie and her baby, David had mentally called it quits. There would be no more people assigned to risk their lives on his behalf. Not for an issue that was technically personal. The President knew David's feelings on this, and although David had not said a word about looking for Cara, he made sure the President knew things were going to change.

As he came around a curve, his heart started to pound. He was almost there. He began slowing down, then turned the steering wheel, guided the car into a long, graveled drive and pulled up to the house. He killed the engine and then sat for a moment, absorbing the structure.

It was a long, rambling two-story brick home with a porch that ran half the length of the house. A chimney rose from the center of the roof, evidence of warm fires on cold winter nights. Ancient trees threw large patterns of shade upon the lawn while flowers in bloom abounded everywhere.

He sighed. It looked so beautifully ordinary. Would a woman who lived in a home like this be able to accept what he was going to say? Then he took a deep breath and got out of the car. Hesitation would gain him nothing. Centering his sunglasses comfortably on the bridge of his nose, he started toward the house.

More than halfway up the walk, he caught a movement from the corner of his eye and paused, then turned.

God in heaven, it was her—standing beneath a cluster of maples with a curious look on her face. Once he'd seen her, his feet moved of their own accord. When he was only yards away, he said her name, and as he did, he saw confusion and then panic as it registered on her face.

"Cara."

She gasped, then in spite of the heat, shivered.

He took a step toward her, and then another. Cara started to shake.

"Cara, don't be afraid."

"No," Cara moaned, and covered her face. "No ghosts. No ghosts. I don't believe in ghosts."

Suddenly his voice was right beside her. She opened her eyes.

"I'm not a ghost."

"David?"

His stomach knotted. After all these years, hearing his name from her lips was more painful than he would have believed.

Before he could answer her, she shook her head in vehement denial.

"You're not David. David is dead."

This was harder than he'd imagined. "Cara… I'm sorry…so sorry."

He reached for her hand. When he touched her, she shuddered once, then her eyes rolled back in her head.

He caught her before she fell.

"Damn, damn, damn," he muttered, as he carried her unconscious body to the shade of the porch.

Choosing the nearest chair, he sat down, cradling her carefully as he looked at her face, trying to find the girl that he'd known in the woman he held in his lap, but she was gone.

It wasn't until her eyelids began to flutter and he saw the clear, pure blue of her eyes that he found the girl he'd left behind.

"Are you all right?" he asked.

Her hands cupped his face—her eyes wide with disbelief.

"David? Is it really you?"

A car drove past on the road beyond the house, and David looked up, suddenly aware of how public their reunion had become.

"Let's go inside. We need to talk," he said, and started to carry her inside when she slid out of his lap and threw her arms around his neck.

"How? Why? Did you—"

He put a finger across her lips, momentarily silencing her next question.

"Inside…please?"

Cara grabbed him by the hand and led him inside the house. The moment they entered the hallway, she shut the door behind them then stood, staring at his face with her hands pressed to her mouth to keep from crying.

David ran a shaky hand through his hair, then gave her a tentative smile.

"I don't know quite where to start," he said. "Do you want to—"

Tears rolled down her face, silencing whatever he'd been about to say.

"Oh, honey, don't. You know I never could stand to see you cry."

And then her hands were on his shirt, moving frantically across the breadth of his chest, then up the muscular column of his throat, then tracing the outline of his features. He grabbed her fingers, trying to put some distance between them so he could think. But there had already been forty years of distance, and for Cara, it was forty years too much.

His name was just a whisper on her lips as she wrapped her arms around his neck. Before he could think, she'd kissed him—a tentative foray that went from testing ground status to an all-out explosion. It was instinct that made him pull her against his body, but it was need that kept her there.

"If this is a dream, I don't want to wake," Cara muttered, and then pulled his shirt out of the waistband of his slacks.

His stomach flattened as he inhaled sharply. The feel of her fingernails against his skin was an aphrodisiac he wouldn't have expected. Then her arms were around his waist as she lifted her lips for his kiss. David was broadsided by the sexual tension erupting between them. He'd planned for everything—except this.

"Cara… God, Cara, we shouldn't be—"

"Since when did shouldn't become part of your vocabulary?" she asked.

She caught him off guard, and he laughed. And the moment the sound came out of his throat, he wanted to cry. He couldn't remember the last time he'd known joy. His eyes narrowed hungrily as he began pulling at her clothes, undoing buttons and shoving aside fabric. Her hands were on him, as well. Somewhere between one moment and the next, his shirt was on the floor and his slacks were undone. He lifted her off her feet and then spun around, pinning her between his body and the wall. Her arms were around his neck, her legs around his waist and she threw back her head and laughed when he slammed into her.

One hard, desperate thrust followed another and another, as if they were trying to destroy all the bad memories with this sexual act. Somewhere between one breath and the next, it began to change—turning into a dance between lovers.

Cara's eyes were closed, her lower lip caught between her teeth as she followed the rhythm of his body and was taken by surprise by the force of her climax. While she was still riding the high, David spilled himself within her in what seemed like endless, shuddering thrusts.

The silence that came after was as abrupt as their mating had been. David's hands were slick with sweat as he eased her down, and when she moved away and started rearranging her clothes, David followed suit. He could tell that she was as shaken by what they'd done as he, and was afraid she'd withdraw in embarrassment before he had a chance to explain. He touched her shoulder, and when she turned, he cupped her face in his hands.

"Look at me," he said.

Cara hesitated, then lifted her head, meeting his gaze straight on. Again, disbelief came and went as she stared at him. Then she touched the swollen edges of her mouth, as if needing the reminder of pain to assure her what had happened was real.

"I see you," she said. "Oh, David, there are so many things I have to tell you. After you left, I found out I was pregnant. We have a—"

"I know," he said. "Bethany."

A look of shock came and went on her face and then her eyes narrowed sharply.

"You knew we had a daughter?"

He nodded.

The timbre of her voice rose a notch. "You knew and you still didn't come back?"

David felt as if he'd been sucker punched. He should have seen this coming, and yet after what they'd just done…

"It wasn't like—"

"No. Wait. Let's start this meeting all over again."

The anger in her voice was blatantly apparent now, and he knew there was no going back.

"David Lee Wilson, just where the hell have you been?"

Chapter 2

"Cara, please…can we do this somewhere else?"

She made no attempt to hide her pain. "Maybe we should adjourn to the bedroom to talk, since we just had sex in my hall."

David inhaled slowly, using every mental skill he had to remain calm.

For Cara, his silence was stronger than any denial he might have made. Courtesy demanded she apologize. She lifted her chin.

"I'm sorry. That was uncalled for. What happened just now was more my fault than yours. If you don't mind, I'd like to change my clothes. The guest bathroom is just down the hall if you'd like to…uh… I'm just going upstairs now and…"

"Ssh," he said softly, and lifted a lock of her hair with one finger, gently pushing it into place. "Go do what you have to do. I'll be here when you get back."

The tenderness in his voice was her undoing. Tears filled her eyes, but she refused to let them go.

"You'll pardon me if I have doubts about that," she said. "I seem to remember telling you the same thing about forty years ago and look what happened."

She walked away, leaving him with nothing but a cold, hard truth. He had walked out on her—twice. Once when she wouldn't run away with him and then again when he left for Vietnam. He headed for the bathroom, feeling a lot less optimism than he had when he walked in the door with her earlier.

Cara barely made it to her bedroom before she started to cry—huge, gulping sobs that shattered her all the way to her soul.

Tearing off her clothes as she went, she staggered into the shower and then turned the water on full force, standing beneath the stinging spray until her mind was numb and her skin was burning.

One minute led to another and then another until she lost all track of time. The adrenaline rush of making love to a man she'd long thought dead was fading, leaving her shaken and weak. If it hadn't been for the slight discomfort between her legs, she could have made herself believe it was nothing more than a dream.

She flinched as the water began to run cold and reached down and turned off the faucets. She pushed back the curtains only to find David sitting on a small stool by the door.

He handed her a towel.

"I got worried."

She clutched it in front of her nudity like a shield, and as she did, realized any show of modesty was like closing the barn door after the horse had escaped.

"If you'll give me a few moments..."

He stood up and quietly closed the door, leaving her alone to finish drying.

Cara's hands began to shake as she swiped erratically at the moisture clinging to her body. It wasn't until she was completely dry that she realized her clothes were in the other room, with him. She grabbed her bathrobe from a hook on the back of the door and quickly put it on, wrapping and tying it firmly before making another appearance. To her relief, he was nowhere in sight.

As she began to dress, she glanced at the clock. It was almost three. It had been just after one when she'd come around the corner of the house. No wonder he'd come looking for her. He probably thought she'd gone to her room and slit her wrists.

She snorted lightly as the thought came and went. If ever there had been a day when that thought had crossed her mind, it was long since over. She'd survived a lot more than this with a hell of a lot less reason. Except for their child. After she'd known about Bethany, everything had changed. David Wilson might have walked out on her, but he'd left a piece of himself behind that he'd never get back. With that thought in mind, she gave herself the once-over in the mirror, nodding in satisfaction at the simplistic style of her clothes. No need dressing like this was any kind of a celebration, because it felt more like a wake. But as she started down the stairs to face the ghost from her past, she had to accept the fact that she didn't want to bury him again.

David was lost in thought, staring at the array of family pictures displayed on the mantel and trying not to resent the picture of the short, stocky man with his arms around Cara. Ray Justice. They had been laughing when the picture was taken. He took a deep breath, making himself accept the reality of her life. She'd done just fine without him. Maybe being here was another selfish act on his part and he should never have come back. Before his thoughts could go further, he heard her footsteps in the hall and turned to face his accuser.

She saw him by the mantel. Her gaze slid from his face to the pictures behind him, and she realized what he'd been doing.

"She's beautiful," David said.

Cara's lips trembled, but she nodded. "She has your coloring. All that pretty dark hair and your eyes."

"But she has your smile."

Cara caught back a sob, determined not to fall apart again.

"Oh, David…where have you been? We were told you were dead, you know."

"Yes, I know."

Cara tried not to stare as she sat down on the sofa, but it was difficult not to do so. Her memories encompassed a young, gangly sixteen-year-old boy, not this powerful, secretive man.

"Won't you please sit?" she said, as she seated herself on the sofa.

"I think better standing."

She sighed and then smoothed her hands down the legs of her navy slacks.

"I couldn't form a rational thought right now if my life depended on it," she said.

David shoved his hands in the pockets of his slacks.

"I know this is going to be difficult for you to understand, but you've got to believe me when I tell you that what I did, I did *for* you, not *to* you."

Cara's eyes teared again, but she remained firmly in her seat.

"Letting me think you were dead was doing me a favor?" Her voice started to shake. "Even if I didn't matter to you anymore, how could you father a child and then ignore her existence?"

"No…no…not that. Never that."

"Then explain," Cara begged. "Make me understand."

He took his hands out of his pockets as he began to pace, and Cara couldn't help but stare at the animal grace of his movements. And then he started to talk and she became lost in the sound of his voice.

"It began with the letters."

"What letters?"

"The letters I wrote to you."

"I didn't receive any letters."

"Yes, I know…at least, I knew after a while, but before I found out, I kept wondering why you didn't answer mine. There were dozens and dozens. I wrote almost every day for about three months and then as often as I could after that."

She stiffened. "I don't believe you."

He strode to a chair and picked up a packet he'd gotten from his car while she had been dressing.

"See for yourself. I carried the damn things all over Nam after they came back. Half a dozen times I thought about chucking them, but I couldn't bring myself to get rid of them. Even though you hadn't opened them, they were the last link I had to you."

Cara's brows knitted as she dumped the contents of the packet into her lap.

"That's not all of them," David said. "But enough for you to know I'm telling the truth."

As she turned them over, she started to shake. The evidence was there before her eyes. Water-stained papers. Ancient postmarks. All addressed to Cara Weber and all unopened. But it was the two newspaper clippings, yellowed with age, that startled her. One was of her wedding, the other an announcement of her baby's birth.

"Where did you get these?"

"Your parents sent them to me, along with all of the letters I'd written you."

She gasped.

"The message was plain," David said. "I had no place in your life anymore. You had a husband and a child." He tried to smile, but the pain of saying what he'd lived with all these years made it impossible. "Only, I knew the child was mine. I knew you would never have cheated on me before, and the baby came too soon after your wedding."

"But, David…why let everyone think you were dead? I would never have refused you the right to know and love your own child."

"I know, but you have to understand. It was hell over there and Frank died about a month after I got the package. After that, I guess I pretty much went out of my head. I tried so many damn ways to get myself killed, but it didn't work. I volunteered for mission after mission, and each one should have been my last. When my tour of duty was up, I reenlisted. I was there when Saigon fell."

Tears slid down Cara's face as she sat with her hands clenched tightly in her lap.

"Why didn't you come home then? Why did you let me…let everyone…think you were dead?"

He shrugged. "I don't know. Hell… I felt dead, I guess

I was just waiting for my body to catch up with my mind. Only thing was, Uncle Sam beat me to it."

"I don't understand."

He hesitated, trying to figure out exactly what he could say without giving too much away.

"I can't tell you everything," he said. "But I got recruited by a Special Forces unit and became involved in some covert missions for the government. One thing led to another and now, let's just say that my years with Uncle Sam are coming to an end."

"Are you telling me you became a spy?"

"Don't ask me anything more, honey… please. I've already said more than I should have."

"My God," Cara muttered. She stared down at the unopened letters in her lap and then covered her face with her hands.

David dropped to his knees and took her hands in his. "Cara?"

Forced to look at him, she realized that, for the first time, she was really seeing the man—and his secrets—and his scars.

"Why did you come back? Why now, after all these years?"

He hesitated again, still carefully choosing his answers.

"Because I needed to make peace with myself and with you. I needed to look you in the face and tell you that when I left for Vietnam, I had every intention of coming back and making a life with you. I couldn't go to my grave knowing you still believed I'd walked out on you, leaving you pregnant to raise our baby on your own. I swear to God, Cara, I would never have done that to you. I loved you."

"What do you mean, go to your grave? Are you ill?"

He slid into the seat beside her, reaching for her hands.

"No, no, I didn't mean it like that. I'm fine."

Cara looked down at his hands, so gently worrying the knuckles of her fingers, wondering if it was safe to give so much of herself away. And then she shoved the worry away. They'd already lost too many precious years. Whatever he had to give her, she was willing to take.

"What are your plans?" she asked. "I mean...can you stay awhile? Maybe a few days? I want to show you things...and oh, David, you have to stay and meet Bethany. She and her family are on vacation, but they'll be back at the end of the week. Five or six days. You can stay that long...can't you?"

He heard himself answering and knew he was making a mistake, but there was no way he was going to lose her again, at least not yet. There was every reason to believe that his final showdown with Frank could be his last. He didn't want to give Cara false hope, but on the other hand, he couldn't deny himself this little bit of heaven.

"Yes. I'll stay. At least for a while."

For the first time in a very long while, Cara felt a sense of anticipation.

"Are you hungry? I was coming in the house to make myself some lunch when I heard you arrive."

The lilt in her voice only deepened his guilt, but he found himself agreeing. "That sounds good. I can't remember when I last shared a meal with anyone."

Cara pulled out of his embrace. "Can't remember when you last shared a meal? My God, David, what kind of life *have* you been living?"

"You don't want to know."

* * *

It was the dripping faucet in this excuse for a kitchen that finally sent Frank over the edge. He picked up a pan and began hammering on the fixture until it broke off in the sink. Water shot up like a geyser, spraying the ceiling and cabinets alike. A string of virulent curses filled the air as he reached for the shut-off valve beneath the sink. Finally, the water ceased to flow and Frank was left with a bigger mess than before he'd started. But it wasn't the condition of his decrepit hideout that was pushing his buttons. It was the fact that, once again, he had failed to reach his goal. The water pooled around his pant legs as he leaned back against the cabinets and closed his eyes. He'd been close, so close.

He'd seen the stealth chopper coming in and knew in his bones it was David. Who else would have access to such state-of-the-art military equipment but the infamous Jonah?

As he thought of David, the muscles in his wounded shoulder gave a twinge and he shifted, easing his back to a more comfortable position against the cabinets. It was nothing but a flesh wound. He'd had worse. And the wound on his ear was almost well, too, although it would never be the same. Then he ran his hands through his hair in mute frustration, absently fingering the ancient burn scars on the side of his face. Hell, nothing had been the same since the day his own brother tried to burn him alive.

Disgusted with the mess in which he was standing, he went to the phone to call the manager to fix the sink. It didn't occur to him that, like the sink, all of his troubles stemmed from something he'd done, rather than something that had been done to him. Afterward, he strode into the bedroom to change his clothes, absently stepping on a cockroach as he went. As he crossed the threshold, he caught a glimpse of himself in the cracked and dusty mirror across the room and froze. In that moment, he saw himself as others saw him, a tall and aging man with a glass eye and a bitter expression. His gray, thinning hair was brushed back, baring his scarred face for anyone who chose to look. Oddly enough, the look seemed to appeal to a certain type of woman, although he rarely took advantage of the fact. He still mourned his beloved Martha, his wife of so many years.

As he thought of her, pain shafted. He turned away, moving to the closet to get a fresh change of clothes. As soon as his shoulder was better, he was going after David himself. No more trying to get to him through the agents who worked under him. He was tired of this game. He wanted it over.

He dressed quickly, his mind shifting from one scenario to another, imagining the pleasure of watching the life drain out of David's body. There was no future for him beyond that fact. His daughter had ceased to exist for him when she'd defected to the other side by falling in love with one of the agents. If only Martha was still alive. She'd been his reason for living. Then he blanked out the thought. There would be time later to wallow in memories. Right now, he had murder on his mind.

Night had come when Cara wasn't looking. One minute she was cleaning up their supper dishes and tidying the living room and the next thing she knew it was dark. The idea of sleeping under the same roof with David Wilson was almost frightening. She'd known the boy, but she didn't know this dark, brooding man. Then she reminded herself that his persona hadn't bothered her enough to stop her from making love to him in her hall. Surely they could sleep beneath the same roof without incident. It wasn't like he was going to murder her in her bed.

And the moment she thought it, her sanity took a hike. He'd all but said he was a spy. Spies killed people. Then she shook off the thought. He'd also been a soldier, and they killed people, too. It didn't make them heinous. It made them heroes.

Having settled that in her mind, she began to rearrange the magazines on the coffee table, unaware that David was watching her from the doorway. It wasn't until she straightened and started to leave that she saw him standing in the shadows.

"Oh! David! You startled me."

"Sorry. I didn't mean to."

"Was there something you needed?" she asked.

Yes, my life back...with you. "Not really. I was just watching you, thinking how very beautiful you are."

"I'm a middle-aged grandmother," she muttered, and gave the coffee table a final swipe with her dust cloth.

"With a damned fine body and a face that could still break a heart," he added, and then walked into the room and took the dust cloth out of her hands. "We need to talk."

Her heart fluttered, then settled back into a normal rhythm as she reminded herself there was no need to be nervous. The man was the father of her child. But when he took her by the hand and pulled her close to the light, she felt naked all over again beneath his gaze.

"I frighten you, don't I?" he asked.

Cara blushed then sighed. Finally, she nodded. "A little."

"My life has been ugly, I'll admit, but I would die before I'd hurt you."

The tenderness in his words was shattering. Before she knew it, her hands were on his chest, her face tilted toward the light—and him.

"I didn't mean it like that," she said quickly. "I wasn't thinking physical harm. It's just that I've been alone for almost three years now and just starting to learn to live without the sound of someone else's voice. It's hard to become accustomed to loneliness when you've shared your life with another."

"I wouldn't know."

Again, his answer pulled at her emotions.

"What I'm trying to say is…you were my first love, David. I gave the truest and best part of myself to you."

He groaned and started to take her in his arms when she stopped him.

"No…wait…let me finish." She took a deep breath. "The only thing that kept me going after you left was knowing that I carried your child. My husband was a good man. He loved Bethany as if she was his own and never made a difference between his affections for her and our other two children." She ducked her head and then made herself look at him. "But I'm ashamed to say that I never gave him what I should have because I'd already given it to you. Dead or alive, you had my heart. Now he's dead and you're back and I'm afraid. I'm afraid to get to know the man you've become. I'm afraid I'll love him as much as I loved the boy." Her voice trailed off into a whisper. "And I'm afraid that if I do, I won't get over losing you again. So…what I guess I'm asking is, why did you really come? Was it just to assuage what you perceived as guilt, or were you looking for something more?"

He wanted to assure her, but he couldn't lie. As long as Frank was loose, his life wasn't worth a damn.

"I'd be lying if I said I'd only come to say hello. But there are a lot of loose ends to my past that have to be tied, and until that happens, I don't have the luxury of making plans."

Cara felt the blood draining from her face. That wasn't what she expected to hear.

"That sounds fatal," she said, trying to fake a laugh.

He didn't answer, and the laugh became a sob.

"My God…tell me I'm wrong."

"I can't make promises…but if I could, then I'd be giving you fair warning that I wanted back in your life."

Her voice trembled. "How far?"

"As far as you'd let me go."

"Ah… David…you always were a hard sell," she said, and then wrapped her arms around his neck.

The weight of her body against his chest was a gift.

"So, are you saying it's enough?"

She shook her head. "No, I'm not saying that, but I am saying that I'll take what you're willing to give. I asked for too much the first time and lost you. I'm not willing to make that mistake again."

He wrapped his arms around her, pulling her close.

"God…woman, you don't know how many years I've dreamed of this."

She pulled back to look at him. "Oh, but yes, I do. And while I would like the luxury of being wooed and courted, I'm not willing to waste our time on the ritual."

"What are you saying?"

"I want to fall asleep in your arms and wake up the same way. I want to laugh with you and cook for you and play with you. I don't want to think about loose ends. Whatever time you have to give me will have to be enough."

He tunneled his fingers through her hair, taking her kiss without asking, ripping her emotions to shreds with the anguish on his face.

"I don't deserve this," he said.

"No, you don't," she said. "But I do."

He laughed softly, then swept her off her feet and into his arms.

"Are you going to make love to me?" she asked.

"Hell, yes," he muttered.

She sighed. "It's about time."

"If you don't mind," David whispered, nuzzling the side of her neck, "I'd rather do this in a bed this time."

"Down the hall, third door on the right."

As he carried her there, he had to remind himself that this wasn't a dream. Cara was really in his arms.

When they reached Cara's room, he set her down by her bed and kissed her. Tentatively, then gently, then with a low, muffled groan.

Cara tangled her arms around his neck, clutching him desperately. When he began to take off her clothes, her knees went weak. This was happening, she knew, but it was all so surreal. She couldn't count the number of times in her life when she'd imagined such a scene. David striding through the door and sweeping her into his arms and then carrying her off into the sunset. The fantasy had lasted through her twenties and her thirties, and somewhere around the middle of her forties, she'd given up on fantasies.

Now this was happening and it wasn't a dream.

It wasn't a fantasy.

It was David—a rock-solid, flesh-and-blood man who wanted her as much as she wanted him.

When he began pulling off her clothes, then his, her pulse accelerated. Seconds later, she was flat on her back in the middle of her bed and he was hovering above her.

"You are so very beautiful," David whispered, and then rolled over onto his side and began tracing the contours of her body with one hand, fingering the curve of her chin, cupping the shape of a breast, mapping the plains of her belly, then testing the juncture between her thighs.

Cara's heart was pounding, her mouth slack with desire. She wanted to touch him, too, to test the strength of his muscles against the tenderness of his gaze, but she was too distracted by what he was doing.

"David?"

He shook his head and leaned over her, taking license with everything that he chose while leaving her breathless and aching for more.

One minute passed and then another and another and the coil that had been winding within Cara's belly began to throb. She moaned, then moaned again. This time louder. This time longer.

David's head was pounding as the blood rushed through his veins. The need to be inside her was strong, but he was waiting for that breaking point of coming undone.

Then he heard her gasp and saw her eyes lose all focus. When she clutched at his arms, his name a prayer on her lips, he made his move.

"David…oh…oh…please."

He was above her and inside her before she took her next breath. Her climax shook him, coming within three strokes of entry, and it was all he could do not to follow. But when she started to cry in soft, happy sobs, he couldn't hold himself back. The joy of knowing he'd given her this pleasure was an aphrodisiac he couldn't control. He rode the feeling with all the strength he could muster, and when it was over, thought he'd died in her arms.

Cara woke abruptly, as mothers always do when sensing something wasn't right in their world. Only this time, it wasn't the high-pitched wail of a frightened child that woke her, it was the man beside her. She lay motionless, listening to the labored rhythm of his breathing, and fought an urge to cry. His skin was clammy and he kept muttering something she couldn't understand. She raised up on one elbow, staring intently into the shadowed contours of his face, then let her gaze drift down his body. She'd seen the scars. Bullet holes. A shrapnel wound. A thick, ropy scar along the back of his leg. Dear Lord, what had happened to him? What hell was he reliving in his dreams?

Suddenly, he sat straight up in bed and she fell back in surprise.

"David?"

At the sound of her voice, his body went limp.

"I forgot where I was," he said.

"You were dreaming."

"Yes."

"Can I get you something? A glass of water? Some aspirin?"

He crawled out of bed and walked across the room to where his suitcase was lying.

"Where are you going?" she asked, as she watched him dig a pair of shorts from the case.

"I need to run it off," he said shortly. "I'll be fine. Go back to sleep."

"Run what off, David?"

He turned then, nothing but a mass of shadow and shape on the other side of the room, but the tone of his voice was image enough.

"The past."

"But, David, you can't run away from the past."

"I know, but I can damn well wear it out. Now go back to sleep. I'll let myself in when I come back."

"You'll need a key," she said, and started to get up.

"No, I won't."

Then he was gone.

She lay there for a moment, absorbing the last thing he'd said and then started to tremble. What kind of man had she let into her bed?

Chapter 3

David ran without thought, focusing only on the impact of foot to ground and the mind-numbing relief that exhaustion always brought. Leaving Cara had seemed cowardly, especially after he'd come all this way to see her. But he was too ashamed to let her see his weaknesses—to admit that something as innocuous as a nightmare could undo him to this extent.

When he'd first run into the woods behind her house, he'd gone without a destination other than to forget. But a short time later, when he realized he had no idea where he was, he paused in a clearing and looked at the sky, reading the heavens like road map. The North Star was a constant that he quickly sought out. Once he found it, he realigned himself with the world and wished it was as simple to do that in his own life. By the time he'd outrun the demons, he had begun to circle back and was less than a mile from her home. Now it was simply a matter of getting there before exhaustion hit.

He came out of the trees, his steps dragging, his feet numb and burning. As he started up the gentle slope behind her house, he looked up and then stopped.

Lights.

She'd turned on the lights so he could see to come home.

There had been so many times in his life when he had not allowed himself the luxury of shedding a tear. He had no way of knowing that the simple act of lighting his way home was all it would take. But now…

He shuddered, then swallowed around a lump in his throat. Not once since he'd begun this lonely journey that had become his life had he had someone to come home to.

Dear God, if only he did belong here—to Cara and what was left of her world. He needed it—deserved it. He'd given up so damned much. Surely he would be allowed some joy on this earth before his days were over. He took a deep breath and then shook off the thoughts. As long as the showdown with Frank still loomed, he couldn't allow himself to dwell on the future. He threw back his shoulders and started to walk.

Cara saw him come out of the trees. Her shoulders sagged with a relief she wouldn't voice. He paused at the bottom of the hill, and although she couldn't see his features, she was struck by the stillness of his posture, as if he'd become a part of the scenery. Then he started toward her, his steps slow and dragging.

She stood up from the chair in which she'd been sitting, then stayed within the shadows, struggling with the urge to run to him. Still uncertain where she fit into his life, she watched, waiting to take her cue from him.

David felt her presence before he saw her, and when she stepped out of the shadows to the edge of the porch, a weight lifted from his chest. This was just like a dream he'd had so many times before. Coming home to find this woman awaiting his arrival was nothing short of a miracle.

"Cara."

"Are you okay?"

"Yes."

"I made some coffee. There are fresh towels and a washcloth in the bathroom." She hesitated, then added, "Do you need anything else?"

He swallowed around a lump in his throat. "Just you."

"I've been here all the time."

"I know. I'm the one who's been lost."

She walked off the porch and took him by the hand. "Then welcome home, my darling," she said softly, and led him inside.

David went silently, knowing that simple act had done more toward saving his sanity than anything else she could have ever done.

When he came out of the shower it was close to four in the morning. The lights were out in the rest of the house, with only a small ginger jar lamp lighting the area beside Cara's bed. He stood in the doorway, watching her sleep. So still. So beautiful.

He wondered how many times Ray Justice had done this very same thing, maybe in this very same place—watching his wife in their bed. Jealousy burned low in his gut but he shoved it aside. There was nothing left to be jealous about. The man was dead, and he was here.

But there was Frank.

The possibility existed that he might never have another chance to do this—to stand within the quiet of a home and watch the woman he loved as she slept. This time, it was regret that drew him to the bed. He pulled back the covers and slipped in beside her, selfishly taking everything she had to offer now.

When she sighed and turned, snuggling her cheek against his chest, his arms tightened around her.

God...don't let this end.

Then he closed his eyes and let exhaustion claim him.

David smelled coffee and rolled over in surprise. Most of his adult life had hinged on being cognizant of his surroundings, even in his sleep, and yet Cara had arisen from this bed and dressed without him knowing it. And from the scents wafting down the hallway, she'd been up for some time. Not only did he smell coffee, but if he wasn't mistaken, also bacon and the aroma of baking bread. He rolled out of bed and grabbed a clean pair of shorts and a shirt, unwilling to waste another moment of this day. After a quick trip to the bathroom to brush his teeth and comb his hair, he padded barefoot down the hall. The television was on in the living room and he stopped, taking a moment to listen to the announcer.

"Talks between the Irish Republican Army and Great Britain have come to a halt. Reports from unnamed sources tell us that the recent bombing in Trafalgar Square has been attributed to a renegade faction of the IRA and that until this has been sorted out, negotiations will cease."

"Damn," David muttered, and made himself a mental note to check on the status of the situation. When the announcer continued, he lingered another moment, although he was torn between his duty to SPEAR and his longing to be with Cara.

"On the local front, hit-and-run robberies are continuing within a three-county area of upstate New York. Just last night, a liquor store in Three Corners was held up, and the clerk on duty was shot and robbed of more than six thousand dollars. The woman, a thirty-four-year-old Asian mother of two, is still in surgery. More on her condition later."

David sighed, sorry for the woman and her family, but his focus had to be on the larger picture. Even though it was on a limited basis, terrorism had already made its mark in the United States. It was part of his job to make sure it didn't escalate.

When the station broke for commercial, he turned to other issues—namely breakfast with Cara.

When he entered the kitchen, Cara was washing her hands at the sink. He walked up behind her, slipped his arms around her waist and nuzzled the back of her neck.

Cara gasped with surprise.

"David! You startled me," she said, then she leaned back against him and closed her eyes as his hands moved up her belly to her breasts.

"Then we both got a surprise this morning," he said, as he turned her in his arms and kissed the smile on her lips.

"How so?" Cara asked.

"I never heard you get up."

She shrugged. "I was trying to be quiet. You were sleeping so soundly I thought you must need the rest."

"That's beside the point," David said. "There were lots of days and nights I went without sleep and I still stayed alert. It made the difference in my ever seeing another sunrise."

She cupped his face with her hands. "Yes, but that was when you were in danger, right?"

"Yes."

"So...subconsciously, you knew there was nothing here to fear. End of story. Now come sit down. Breakfast is almost done."

She was right, and the answer was so simple, he didn't know why it hadn't occurred to him first. Maybe he'd spent too much of his life in hiding to be able to do this normal-guy stuff.

"Need any help?" he asked.

"No, but thanks."

He took a seat, thinking he couldn't remember the last time he sat down to a meal with flowers on the table. Then he saw the basket of hot blueberry muffins and his heart skipped a beat. He felt Cara's hand on the back of his neck.

He looked at her. She was smiling.

"You remembered," he said softly.

"How could I forget," Cara said, and then brushed a brief kiss across his mouth. "We had breakfast together at Flanders' Deli the morning you left for basic training. I was so mad at you and I still came to say goodbye."

David sighed, unwilling to think about the negative aspects of their parting. "It was blueberry muffins with some kind of sugary stuff on top."

"Streusel. It's called streusel."

David touched the corner of her mouth. "You had it stuck right here."

Cara smiled. "And you removed it with your tongue. Caused quite a scene there in the deli, as I recall." Then she frowned. "Someone told my parents. When I got home, there was the proverbial hell to pay."

"Sorry," David said.

"I'm not. Even though they've been gone for several years, after knowing what they did to us, David, I don't think I can ever forgive them."

"Holding on to grudges isn't healthy," he said, thinking of Frank. "Let's just focus on here and now."

Cara sensed he was alluding to more than what her parents had done, because that dark look was back in his eyes. Determined not to talk about anything negative, she handed him a muffin and made herself smile. "Start on that while I get the rest of our food."

The bread was warm against his palm, and when he broke it open, the scent of sugar and blueberries made him feel like a kid of sixteen all over again. Ignoring the butter and jam, he took a big bite, savoring the taste as well as the thought behind it.

"What do you think?" Cara asked as she set a plate of bacon and scrambled eggs at his place.

He swallowed. "I think Ray Justice was a damned lucky man."

At first, the mention of her deceased husband was startling, until she began to accept the compliment in the manner in which it had been made. She smiled.

"Why, David...what a genuinely dear thing to say."

He arched an eyebrow. "I have my moments."

She laughed and then went to get her own food, leaving David with the sound of her laughter echoing in his ears and the knowledge that whatever happened later, he'd been right in coming.

They finished their meal in near silence, each absorbed in the simple wonder of sharing food. For Cara, the whole experience seemed surreal. Day before yesterday, David Wilson was a heartache from her past, and now he was sitting in her house, at her table, eating the food that she'd prepared. But this David was nothing like the boy who'd left her behind. He was hard and secretive and rarely smiled. She wanted her old David back. Not only that, she wanted more—so much more. But she kept remembering an old saying about being careful of what you wished for. Her life was settled. If he stayed, could she live with a man with so many secrets—a man who had to wear himself out physically to be able to rest? She sighed. God help them both, because she had never wanted anything so much in her life and she was afraid she wouldn't be up to the task.

David got up to pour himself another cup of coffee. "Want a refill?" he asked.

"No, I've had enough."

Her words wrapped around his senses, reminding him that he would never have enough of her. The smile he'd been wearing stopped at the corner of his mouth as he sat the cup down on the counter, unfilled. Then he walked across the room, pulled her up from her chair and into his arms.

"You sure?" he asked, his voice husky with promise.

She smiled. "Maybe I was a little hasty."

"If you come back to the bedroom with me, we can take all the time you need to decide."

A shiver of longing rolled through her as she slid her arms around his neck.

"The way I'm feeling right now, it won't take any time at all."

A rare smile broke the somberness of his face as he scooped her up in his arms.

"I *can* walk," she said, as he carried her down the hall.

He laid her on the bed and then crawled on top of her, straddling her legs. There was a gleam in his eye as he began to undress her.

"Tell me that again afterward," he said.

Breath caught in the back of her throat as his hands tugged her shirt from the waistband of her slacks. From where she was lying, he seemed indomitable. And then he leaned forward and centered his mouth across her lips. She moaned.

He leaned even closer, his mouth against her ear as he whispered something dark and promising that sent her sense of self into a tailspin. Could she do something like that—even with a man she loved?

Clothes came off, flying in every direction.

Her slacks.

His shorts.

Her bra.

His shirt.

When there was nothing left between them but his promises, he turned her over on her stomach.

Cara shivered as his hands encircled her ankles. After that, nothing in her life would ever be the same.

Cara stepped out of the shower to find David waiting on her. She smiled slowly, gazing her fill of his strong, naked body and the look in his eyes.

David returned her grin as he wrapped her in a towel. "What?" he asked.

"It would have been an absolute tragedy if I'd lived my whole life without experiencing that."

The corner of his mouth tilted, but not much. "That,

as you call it, is one of the most interesting pages of the Kama Sutra."

"Oh? And here I thought you'd learned that from some Mata Hari type during your world travels."

"Hell, honey, it wasn't a James Bond type of life, I can tell you that. I could count the number of women I've slept with in the last twenty years on one hand and have fingers left over."

"Oh, I wasn't speaking from jealousy," Cara said. "Quite the reverse. I was going to suggest that if I'm ever with you and you see any of those women again, please introduce me."

"Why?"

"I want to thank them for whatever they added to your expertise."

His eyes widened in surprise and then he threw back his head and laughed as he swung her off her feet.

Cara wrapped her arms around his neck, grinning at his delight.

"God, woman, you unman me," he said, as he set her on her feet.

"Not for too long, I hope. Now let me get dressed. I can't stay naked all day."

"Why not?"

Her grin widened. "Because I have things to do."

He frowned. "What kind of things?"

She shrugged. "Normal, everyday things, like picking up some clothes from the cleaners, buying groceries, washing the car. You know…just stuff."

David followed her into the bedroom and sat on the bed as she began to dress. He didn't want to admit that he *didn't* know. *Stuff* hadn't been on his agenda since the day he'd left for Vietnam.

"Can I come?"

Cara turned, surprised by the hesitant tone in his voice.

"Of course you can. I expected you to."

"Is there a dress code for this kind of *stuff*?"

She started to laugh and then realized he was serious. Her hands fisted as she struggled to keep the anger out of her voice.

"I keep wanting to ask exactly what the hell the United States government did to you in the name of peace, but I'm afraid of the answer. You can wear shorts or any kind of pants. Jeans…slacks, whatever you like. A shirt of any kind is fine with me. There's this great little restaurant where we can have lunch." She frowned, then added, "Actually, it's more like a tearoom, but the dress code is casual."

"Okay," David said, and took a pair of chinos from a hanger, then stood for a moment, choosing a shirt that would match.

Cara paused, watching the play of muscles across his back. Her gaze fell on the multitude of scars on his body as it had so many times before. Suddenly blinded by tears, she turned before he could see them and began digging through a dresser drawer.

It occurred to her then that she'd taken her freedom for granted, never considering the countless men who sacrificed on a daily basis so that she would never live in fear. She turned abruptly.

"David."

"Yeah?" he muttered, as he bent over to tie his shoe.

"Thank you."

He looked up. "For what?"

"For the years you spent in the service of this country. For the nights you didn't sleep and the pain—"

He stood and put his forefinger in the center of her mouth, gently stopping what she'd been about to say.

"You don't have to say this," he said.

"Yes…actually I do," Cara said. "I spent a lot of years feeling sorry for myself because my life didn't work out the way I'd planned. And then I see you, like this, and what you suffered while I was warm and safe and—"

Her voice broke and she looked away.

David's expression was shuttered. How did he respond to a brutal truth?

"Come here, honey. It's okay."

"No," she muttered. "It will never be okay."

"It's almost over," he said.

She frowned. "That's not the first time you've alluded to unfinished business. What is it, David? Why can't you tell me?"

He tried to grin. "You know the old spy joke. If I told you, then I'd have to kill you, and we both know I couldn't do that. So…"

Cara turned away, muttering something beneath her breath as she finished dressing.

David arched an eyebrow as he smiled. "Those are pretty salty words for such a pretty lady."

She purposefully ignored him, which made him smile even more. This woman was a far cry from the girl he'd left behind. He was falling in love all over again.

"I'll finish dressing now," he said.

She almost glared. "Are you making fun of me?"

"No, ma'am."

She sighed. "Yes, you are."

"What would it take for you to change the subject?" he asked.

She lifted her chin, refusing to smile. "I'm going to the living room. When you're ready, I will be waiting." Then she marched out of the bedroom, leaving him on his own.

David hesitated briefly, then grabbed his wallet and keys before following her exit. This might be new and uncharted territory for him, but damned if he wasn't looking forward to it.

Tearoom, indeed.

Two hours and a half dozen errands later, they walked into the restaurant. Almost immediately, Cara saw people she knew. They waved a hello, and she could tell by the looks on their faces that their curiosity was raised by the man at her side.

Earlier, she'd almost lost his company when she had gone into the hair salon to pick up a bottle of her favorite shampoo. One of the stylists had flirted, which he'd calmly ignored, but when the shampoo girl came by and pinched his behind, Cara thought he was going to bolt. Cara had calmly told the girl to go molest someone else, which had made everyone laugh, including David. After that, the rest of the morning had been fairly innocuous. But now there was this. She glanced at David, judging his expression. To her surprise, he was looking at her.

"What do you think?" Cara asked.

"It smells good in here," he said.

She smiled. "The food tastes as good as it smells."

"Then I think you made the right choice, and I think those people at the table near the window are trying to get your attention."

Cara sighed. "Yes, I know. What do I do...about you, I mean?"

An eyebrow arched. "What do you want to do...about me, I mean?"

She grinned. "One thing has certainly changed since I first knew you. You have a wicked sense of humor. Now be serious. Is it, uh, safe to introduce you as David or should I—"

David slid his hand along the length of her spine and gave her a gentle push in their direction.

"I am who I am. If it was dangerous for me to surface, I damn sure wouldn't have brought it to you."

She looked startled, and he realized she hadn't considered that aspect of his life having a negative impact on hers.

"Cara! Dear! How wonderful to see you."

Cara smiled. Obviously they'd stood too long at the door waiting to be seated. Her friend Debra Shay had been too curious to wait.

"Good to see you, too," Cara said.

"Well...aren't you going to introduce me?" Debra asked, and then glanced coyly at David.

Cara smiled. "If you promise not to pinch him on the backside, I will."

Debra giggled and patted David's arm in commiseration. "Oh, no! You must have been at Ream's Salon. That Janis female is lethal around good-looking men."

David smiled. "I'll take that as a compliment," he said smoothly. "I'm David Wilson. It's a pleasure to meet one of Cara's friends."

"David, this is Debra Shay," Cara said. "Ray worked with her husband, Roy."

David nodded congenially while thinking that he felt

like he was playing a part. Normal chit-chat, ordinary people, having lunch in a tearoom in Chiltingham, New York. It was a far cry from subterfuge and espionage. And then the hostess arrived and the moment ended.

"I'm sorry for the delay," she said. "Please follow me."

"Nice to meet you," Debra gushed, giggling again as David and Cara were shown to their table.

David seated Cara, then took the chair beside her. As soon as the hostess left, he took Cara's hand.

"That wasn't so bad, was it?"

She made herself smile. "No."

"Why do I feel like there's a but just waiting to come out?"

She sighed. "Because there is."

"Then what?"

"This doesn't feel real."

He started to smile, which was the last thing Cara would have expected him to do.

"What's so funny?" she asked.

"I'd forgotten that we used to think alike."

"What do you mean?"

"Just a few moments ago I was thinking the very same thing. I feel like I'm acting a part and any minute now someone is going to yell cut and I'm going to turn back into—"

He caught himself before he said the word *Jonah* and looked away, but the message was clear. Cara put her hands over his and gave them a squeeze.

"It's all right, darling," she said quietly. "If you're uncomfortable, we can go home. I'll make us some sandwiches and we can—"

"Hell, no. I'm not fragile, just out of practice," he said, and then handed her a menu. "Now, tell me what's good."

The smile on her face was worth every uncomfortable moment he'd had thus far. When she bent her head to study the menu, he watched her changing expression as devoutly as he'd watched the sunrises over the Rockies. He didn't know how this journey was going to end, but he would never be sorry he'd made it.

"How hungry are you?" Cara asked.

He blinked. Telling her the truth about what he really hungered for would probably embarrass her, but when she started to blush, he figured she'd just read his mind.

A small grin tilted the right side of his mouth, then as quickly disappeared.

He leaned across the table until their foreheads were almost touching. "I'm starving," he said softly.

Her blush heightened. "Just don't lick the corner of my mouth again until there's a really good reason."

His eyes glittered warmly as he sat back in his chair. "You're safe for now," he promised. "Now, since you're the expert here, why don't you order for me?"

"Really?"

"I think I'm secure enough as a man to let a woman order for me without feeling threatened. Besides, I'm curious as to what you think might appeal to me."

"What if you don't like it?"

He thought of the times he'd eaten grubs and insects to survive and decided against mentioning it.

"I'll still eat it."

She beamed. "My kind of man."

The teasing disappeared from his eyes. "Sweetheart, I was always your man."

Unprepared for the gentleness in his voice, Cara's eyes teared, but she blinked them away.

"Just for that, you're going to get their famous dessert, too," she said.

"What's that?"

She grinned. "Cake. It's called Better Than Sex."

David thought she was putting him on until she pointed to the dessert portion of the menu.

"No way," he muttered, wondering what else had changed in this world while he'd been hiding behind the generations of Jonahs who'd gone before him.

"Oh, yes, and when you've finished your meal, I'll prove it," Cara said.

At this point, David's sense of justice got the best of him. He'd never had a bite of food in his life that was better than making love to Cara—not even when he'd been starving.

"You just do that," he whispered. "And I'll be a really good boy and eat everything on my plate, but when we get home, I'm going to prove to you that there isn't anything better than sex, especially when it's with the right person."

"May I take your order?"

Startled, Cara looked up. The waitress was grinning—proof that she'd overheard, at the very least, the last thing David just said. Cara glared at David and then rolled her eyes. This would be all over the tearoom before they'd been served their first dish.

The waitress waited, her pen poised above her pad.

Refusing to look at David, Cara gave their order. As soon as the waitress was gone, Cara glanced up, but he seemed preoccupied with a couple across the room. She turned to look and then sighed. It was Ben and Katie Murphy and their new baby girl. Probably their first outing since the baby's arrival last month. She looked at David again. The pain in his eyes was unmistakable. Despite the fact that everyone in the room would see and put their own interpretation on the action, she reached for his hand.

Startled by her touch, David blinked, then turned his focus to Cara.

"I'm sorry," she said softly.

He sighed. So she'd read his mind again. So what else was new?

"You have nothing to be sorry for," he said briefly.

"Don't, David."

"Don't what?"

"Don't deny your feelings…not to me."

"Okay then. What do you want to hear first?" he asked, his voice barely above a whisper. "That I envy that young couple the life ahead of them, or that I want things I know I can never have?"

"I can't give you back your youth, but I can give you a daughter…and grandchildren." She held her breath, afraid to say the rest of it—that she would be his wife if he wanted it.

David made himself smile, unaware that the action never reached his eyes.

"You've already done that," he said. "And I can only hope that they will forgive me as quickly as you have."

"There's nothing to forgive," Cara said, refusing to admit her disappointment that he had mentioned nothing about the future of their relationship. "When they get to know you, they will love you."

Before David could answer, he saw a woman approaching their table. From the look on her face, the curiosity was eating her up. He gave Cara a nod and then braced himself, thankful he was sitting down. This one looked as if she wouldn't settle for a simple pinch on the behind.

"Ooh, Cara, who's this big hunk and where have you been keeping him?"

Cara flinched and David saw it, identifying the woman as someone other than a friend. Whoever she was, she'd just become his enemy, too.

"Macie, I thought you were in Reno."

"I just got back, and look, I'm a free woman again." She wiggled the empty fingers on her left hand as proof.

"I'm sorry to hear that," Cara said.

"Don't be! I don't know what I was thinking when I married that Glen Harvey."

"That he owned his daddy's business?" Cara muttered, too low for anyone but David to hear.

"Well," Macie said. "Aren't you going to introduce me?"

It was the way Macie Harvey leaned over, displaying her more than ample charms in David's face, that pushed Cara's buttons. That plus the fact her husband, Ray, had confessed to having a brief affair with Macie between husbands three and four. Although she had finally forgiven Ray, she had never confronted the woman. Suddenly, now seemed like the perfect time to yank her chain.

She turned in her seat, giving Macie a beatific smile. "Macie, this is David Wilson. He's not only my childhood sweetheart, but also Bethany's father. David, Macie Harvey. Elizabeth Taylor has nothing on our Macie for shedding husbands. I believe Glen was number seven… or was it eight?"

David was surprised but secretly pleased that she'd admitted their relationship. He stood and held out his hand.

"Mrs. Harvey, my condolences on your recent divorce, but as I'm sure you must know, time *does* heal all wounds, except those that kill you, of course."

Macie blinked. She didn't know whether to be insulted first, or run to spread this juicy bit of news. She opted for the news.

"Yes…well…thank you, I'm sure," she said, giving Cara a fierce glare.

Cara returned the look, still wearing her smile. Macie was the first to look away.

"I'd better get back to my table," Macie said. "I think my order has arrived."

"Enjoy," Cara said.

Cara's eyes were glittering as she turned to David.

"Cara, honey?"

"What?"

"Remind me never to make you mad."

She started to grin. "Why?"

"Because you shed blood better without weapons than anyone I've ever seen."

She tossed her head and then smiled primly. "Thank you. It's part of the gift of being a woman."

"Old enemies are often the most difficult to dispatch," David added, thinking of Frank.

"She had an affair with Ray. They thought I didn't know."

David's heart twisted. So many things she'd had to endure, and all because he hadn't come home. This time, he was the one reaching for her hand.

"This time, it's me who's saying I'm sorry."

She shrugged. "You didn't do it. You have nothing to apologize for."

"Oh, but you're wrong," he said softly. "It's what I didn't do that has caused the most hurt."

Before she could answer, their food arrived and the tension of the moment dissipated.

"Hot beef sandwich and tuna salad, coming up," the waitress said, setting the hot plate of thinly sliced roast beef on toast points with thick brown gravy in front of David and the plate of cold tuna salad on lettuce in front of Cara. "Eat hearty, folks, but remember to save some room. You don't want to forget that dessert."

David laughed.

It filtered through Cara's anger, leaving her weak and breathless. It had been so long since she'd heard that remarkable sound.

"This looks great," David said. "I don't remember the last time I had this."

He dug in with relish, rolling his eyes in appreciation.

Cara smiled and tucked into her own food, all the while thinking about cake and sex with the marvelous man at her right.

Chapter 4

Frank Wilson slammed the phone down in disgust. So far, no amount of money had been able to buy him any pertinent information on where his baby brother had gone. David had disappeared as thoroughly as he had when he'd first come back from Vietnam. He frowned as he stared across the room. He didn't like not knowing where his enemies were. It left him defenseless, and he didn't like being weak.

Abruptly, he strode to the window overlooking the street below. East L.A. was an easy place to get lost in. Cash bought anonymity here. Identification was unnecessary for renting rooms or cars if enough money changed hands. Despite all that, the fact that he was still in the United States was dangerous. He'd messed with Uncle Sam's elite, and even though he'd gotten away, he'd ruffled far too many feathers to think they'd brushed him off.

His frown deepened as he absently stared at the people on the street below. There were too damned many people in this world and not a one of them knew their hand from their ass. The longer he thought about it, the more convinced he became that that was what was wrong with his plans. No more trying to get to David through other people. He'd taken eleven runs at the man and come up empty-handed every time. The next time it happened, it would be himself and David—face to face.

Next time.

In frustration, he suddenly slammed his fist against the window ledge, and in doing so, jarred his shoulder, sending a barrage of pain up his neck and to the back of his head. What if there was no next time?

Cursing the infirmity that caused him pain, he turned away from the window and moved to the bed to lie down, telling himself that he would find David. It would happen—when he was ready. He had no desire to face him again until his gunshot wounds weren't so tender. Another day or so and he'd be raring to go.

He closed his eyes, letting his thoughts drift. Outside, the squeal of a police siren came and went, while down the hall, he could hear a man cursing and a woman's shrill cries for help. He rolled over on his good shoulder and pulled the pillow over his head. Crazy. The world had gone crazy. Within a few minutes, he was snoring. Sometime later, he began to dream.

"Frankie, go find your brother and tell him supper is ready."

Ten-year-old Frankie Wilson rolled his eyes, then peeked over the kitchen counter to the pies cooling on the rack near the sink.

"Okay, Ma, and can I have seconds on dessert?"

"If you eat good."

"I will," Frankie said, exiting the kitchen on the run. He jumped off the porch and ran around the holly bushes toward the side of the house where his six-year-old brother, Davie, had been playing. But when he got there, the yard was empty.

"Dumb kid," he muttered, thinking of the dessert awaiting him inside. "Hey, Davie! Supper!"

No one answered and no little kid came running. He began to circle the house, thinking that Davie must have moved to the shade tree in front. But when he got there, his little brother was nowhere in sight.

"Hey, Davie! Davie!"

No answer. He frowned. Frankie Wilson considered himself almost grown, but Davie was just a kid, and he knew better than to leave the yard without permission.

He jogged toward the sidewalk, and as he did he heard the unmistakable cry of someone in pain. A few feet farther, he rounded the lilac bush and saw his little brother sitting on the curb, holding his knee. His bicycle with training wheels was lying on its side in the street.

"Hey, kid, what happened?" Frankie asked, as he knelt in front of Davie.

Davie sniffed loudly, then wiped a dirty hand beneath his nose.

"I fell and skinned my knee," he said.

Frankie looked. Sure enough, the kid was missing a good chunk of skin and bleeding all over his shoes.

"You weren't supposed to be in the street. If Ma finds out, she'll whip your butt."

Davie's eyes widened. Not only had his brother used the B word, but he was right about their mother. She would whip him for riding his bike in the street.

"Don't tell on me, Frankie. I don't want a whipping."

Frankie sighed. Being a big brother carried a lot of responsibilities. He patted Davie on the head and then helped him to his feet.

"Come on, kid. I'll get your bike in the yard and Ma will just think you fell off there, okay?"

Davie nodded. "Okay." Then he smiled through his tears. "Thanks, Frankie, you're the best brother ever."

"Yeah, I know," Frankie said. "Now hurry. Supper is ready and we got cherry pie for dessert."

A car backfired and a motorcycle revved before taking off, leaving a single trail of rubber behind on the L.A. street. Frank jerked in his sleep, but he didn't awake. Instead, the sound shifted his dream from childhood to Vietnam.

David came out of nowhere. The stupid little bastard. He was going to mess everything up. Then Frank's shock turned to panic when he realized the gunrunners were reaching for their weapons.

"Don't!" he yelled. "He's my brother."

"Get rid of him," one of them snapped, "or we'll do it for you."

Before he could react, David stepped between them, yanking the money out of Frank's hands and throwing it on the ground.

"What the hell do you think you're doing?" Frank yelled.

"Saving your stupid ass," David said. "Now let's get out of here."

"What's going on?" the gunrunner asked.

Frank spun, his eyes blazing with anger. "Leave this to me," he said, and shoved David aside as he reached for the money.

But the kid stepped on his fingers, stopping his intent. After that, everything became a blur. Before he knew it, both of the gunrunners were dead and David was staring at him as if he'd never seen him before.

Time blurred the memories of what came next. All Frank could remember was pointing a gun in his brother's face and then pulling the trigger. After that, he remembered coming to on the floor of the hut, smelling gasoline and feeling the heat of the fire against his face. He'd crawled through fire, living with one purpose only, and that was to make David pay for what he'd done. Over the years, Frank had chosen to forget that he was the one to fire the first shot. His entire purpose for living was revenge.

And that same revenge had kept him alive in Vietnam, hiding in an empty village under the nose of the Vietcong until he was healed, then smuggling himself into Indonesia and stowing away on a freighter bound for New Zealand. He strangled the man who helped him on board, stole his identity, then hid in the hold among the freight until they docked weeks later. Within a year, he was working the opal mines in Australia and saving every penny he could get his hands on. Through every tough, hungry day and night of his life, one thing had kept him going—the knowledge that some day he would find David Wilson, and when he did, he would kill him.

Finally, Frank slipped into a deep, dreamless sleep. As he did, he rolled onto his back, his arms flung out. Asleep, his scars gave him a look of vulnerability, but they were deceiving. He'd gone into this vendetta with nothing to lose. His beloved Martha was dead and his only child, like his brother, had turned into a traitor. There was nothing helpless about Frank Wilson, and everything to fear.

* * *

It was three in the morning when the nightmares started. Cara woke abruptly, her senses on an all-out alert. David was still asleep, but curled up in a ball with his back to her. The muscles in his arms were jerking, and every now and then he would kick, as if fighting off an invisible foe. She reached for the lamp, quickly turning it on and illuminating their corner of the room with a soft, yellow glow. A thin film of sweat covered his skin, and the sheet that had been over his body was twisted around his ankles.

Cara got up from the bed, untwisted the sheet and pulled it up to his waist before crawling in beside him. Then she spooned herself against the curve of his back, slid an arm around his waist and held on.

He moaned.

"Ssh, David, ssh. Everything is all right, darling. Everything is all right."

The softness of her voice seemed to penetrate his subconscious. He stiffened momentarily and then ever so slowly began to relax.

Cara pulled herself closer against him, and as she did, he turned over and pillowed his cheek against her breasts. His face was streaked with sweat, his features twisted into a grimace. As she looked, she felt like crying. Instead, she held him close. Only after she heard the even tenor of his breathing did she close her eyes.

David was no longer the fearless young man who'd first gone off to war, convinced of his immortality. This man who'd come back to her had been forged in hellfire and was holding himself together by nothing more than sheer will. He was hard to the point of brittle, and his smiles were far too rare for her peace of mind. He existed by day and suffered by night. And her rage for the injuries he'd sustained grew with each passing day. The only thing she had to give him was her love. She prayed it would be enough.

Dawn finally broke, bathing the couple in the warm fingers of light slipping through the curtains. David was the first to stir, and as he did, he realized that something of a miracle had occurred. He'd slept the entire night through without waking up. And then he felt Cara's arms around him and realized she must have held him while he slept. A great wave of peace fell over him, leaving him weak and humbled. Dear God—he didn't deserve this woman, but he wasn't going to give her up. Not now. Not when he'd finally found a reason to live again.

He shifted slightly so that he could see her. The morning light was soft, shadowing the fine lines that time had etched on her face. So beautiful. She was so very, very beautiful. He thought of Frank and knew that he couldn't put off their meeting too much longer. If Frank had even an inkling of Cara's importance in David's life, he would kill her just to see David weep.

He shuddered, and as he did, her arms instinctively tightened around him. Even in her sleep, she seemed to sense his despair.

He raised up on one elbow. She opened her eyes. For a moment, it was as if they'd seen into each other's soul. Then David cupped her face and kissed her. She sighed as he levered himself above her body. He kissed her again. She shifted, making room for him to come in. He took her there, in the early morning light with her hair in tangles and love in her eyes.

By mid-morning, Cara was in the kitchen packing a picnic lunch while David was rummaging in the storage shed out back, looking for Ray's fishing equipment. Despite his claim to the opposite, Cara suspected it had been years since he'd done something as innocuous as fishing, especially for fun.

The day was warm with a line of white puffy clouds in the distance, the wind almost nonexistent, making it a perfect day to go to the lake. She was putting the last of the sandwiches into the cooler when the doorbell rang. She wiped her hands and then frowned as it began to ring again. Someone was certainly insistent. She hurried through the house, peeked through the window before answering the door and then groaned.

It was Harry Belton.

He'd been trying to court her for more than a year now. She didn't know how much plainer she could be without being terribly rude, but she wasn't interested. Masking her irritation, she opened the door.

"Cara! How are you, dear?"

"Harold?"

"I know I should have called, but I was in the neighborhood and couldn't bring myself to leave without saying hello."

She frowned. He was lying, and they both knew it.

"You really should have called," she said. "I was just going out."

Ignoring the hint she had just given him to make a graceful exit, he stepped inside the door and then peered over her shoulder.

"I see by the car in the driveway that you have company. I hope I'm not intruding."

"Actually, that's what I was trying to—"

"There's the silliest rumor going around Chiltingham that there's a stranger staying in your house."

Cara's eyes flashed angrily, although she maintained her calm.

"No. There's no stranger staying in my house," she said.

He smiled and put his hands on her shoulders. "There now! I knew when Macie said it that she was just telling tales. Even though Ray has been gone these three years, you just aren't the kind of woman to—"

Cara watched his eyes widen and his mouth drop. The fact that he'd forgotten what he was saying told her that David must have come in the house.

Harold glared at her, and the tone of his voice changed from happy to accusing.

"I thought you said you were alone."

"No. I didn't say I was alone. I said there wasn't a strange man in my house. David isn't a stranger."

Harold's face turned a dark, ugly red, his eyes narrowing angrily.

"If I hadn't seen this with my own eyes, I would never have believed it."

Suddenly, David was standing at her back, his voice dark and full of unleashed anger.

"You've never seen a fishing pole?" David asked, and then thrust a rod and reel in Harold's face. "Then here, take a real good look before I shove it right up your—"

Cara stifled a grin as Harold dropped the rod and bolted for the door. Only after he was on the porch with the screen door between them did he stop and turn. It was a mistake, because David was right behind him. Now the only person still in the house was Cara.

"Don't touch me!" Harold screeched.

"Don't ever raise your voice to her again, do you hear me?" David asked.

There was a look in the man's eyes that Harold seemed afraid to challenge. He nodded.

David continued. "And you better hope I don't hear one denigrating word being said about Cara Justice or I'm coming after you."

"But what if I'm not the one who said it?" Harold muttered.

"Then I suggest you pray."

"My word!" Harold gasped, and bolted for the car, leaving dust and gravel in the air behind him as he drove away.

Cara came outside and slipped her hand in the crook of David's arm.

"My hero."

David looked at her and then shrugged. "He ticked me off."

She smiled. "I could tell."

"Are you mad at me?" he asked, suddenly aware that he might have run off someone she actually cared for.

She laughed. "For getting rid of Hasty Harold? No way!"

"Hasty Harold?"

"It's an unfortunate nickname, but one he's certainly earned. He's the first man on the doorstep when a woman gets divorced and the first one to express his sympathy when there's a new widow in town. I've been fighting off his advances for three years now. Thanks to you, I think I've just seen the last of the pest."

"You're welcome," he said, and then slipped his arm around her shoulders. "Are we still going fishing?"

"Oh, yes," Cara said. "I wouldn't miss this trip with you for anything. Let's load up before we have any more uninvited visitors."

They were on their way within the hour, and for David, everything seemed surreal. He had the love of his life at his side, a picnic lunch in a cooler in the back of Cara's SUV, along with a couple of fishing poles and tackle. The sky was a pale blue-white with a few scattered clouds upon the horizon. All they needed to finish the postcard image was a couple of kids screaming in the back seat and a dog poking his head out the window. He glanced over at Cara, who was talking about something that had happened in her past. He was so fascinated by the fact that he was actually here in the moment that he lost track of what she was saying. Suddenly, a shiver of foreboding ran up his spine. The day was almost too perfect. He shrugged it off as a hangover from the life he'd just given up and concentrated on his driving and the directions Cara was giving him to the lake.

"Look!" Cara cried, as they came around a bend in the road.

It was a magnificent buck, momentarily spellbound by their oncoming vehicle.

"Wow, a sixteen pointer," David said, admiring the rack of antlers on the animal's head.

Cara was scrambling in the glove box when the buck suddenly came to itself and bounded into the surrounding woods.

"Darn it," she muttered. "I was going to take a picture."

"You brought a camera?"

She nodded, holding up a compact 35mm camera with a telescoping lense. Her expression of joy suddenly stilled, as if she was afraid of his reaction.

"What's wrong?" David asked.

"Nothing."

He frowned and then pulled off to the side of the road and turned to face her.

"That look on your face is not nothing," he said. "Talk to me."

She looked away, afraid he would read what was in her heart. "It's no big deal. I just wanted to take a few pictures to remember this day."

It wasn't what she said but what she omitted that hit him like the proverbial rock. God. It was just like before. She didn't trust he would come back and was making memories for the day that he would leave. What hurt him the most was that he couldn't promise to return. He could say he wanted to. But that didn't mean he would live through his confrontation with Frank.

It was at that moment he made up his mind to quit thinking negatively. He, by God, *was* going to come back and he *was* going to spend the rest of his life with her. He brushed the side of her cheek with the back of his hand, then gave the lobe of her ear a gentle tug.

"That's good. We can look back on them when we're old and gray and remember that I was the one who caught the most fish."

Cara turned her head, saw the challenge in his eyes, and in spite of her fears made herself smile. Two could play at this game of pretend.

"The most fish? You're already telling me this is going to be a competition in which you're going to win and you haven't even wet your hook?"

He grinned as he pulled onto the road. "So I like a little challenge now and then. What's so wrong with that?"

"Absolutely nothing," she said. "And I'm going to add a little something to the pot, okay?"

"Why not? I know how to be a good sport. Name your something."

"The loser has to clean the fish."

He wrinkled his nose. "I don't know. I don't want you hurting yourself."

She laughed. "My word! The utter gall of the man. Not only have you announced yourself winner before the game even starts, but you're already concerning yourself with my inability to clean a fish."

"Not *a* fish, my darling woman. Lots and lots of fish."

"Fine. I accept your challenge."

He nodded in satisfaction. "Good. Now…is this the turnoff you told me to take, or do we take the second one posted on that sign?"

"This is it," Cara said, pointing toward a narrow blacktop road leading off to the right of the highway. "Caribou Lake, dead ahead."

It was late afternoon before Cara showed signs of wearing out. They'd shared a picnic and taken pictures and reminisced about so many people that David's head was flooded with things he had spent years trying to forget.

To his delight, she'd caught the most fish, and her pride had been obvious. His claim to fame for the day was that he'd caught the smallest, which she had promptly recorded for posterity with a demand for a pose. Laughing, he'd held up the four-inch fish on the line, measuring it with his thumb and forefinger for the camera as she snapped the shot.

He glanced at her again, as he had so often during the day, smiling about the smear of dirt on her forehead and the faint hint of sunburn on her reddening nose and cheeks.

"Don't you think it's time to call it quits?" he asked.

She looked at him, her eyes snapping with challenge. "Only if you're the one who's saying uncle."

"Then uncle…and aunt, and cousin Joe, and Uncle Bob, and whatever the hell else it takes for you to admit you're as tired as I am."

She grinned. "All right then, just one more cast and I'm yours."

"Now you're talking," he said, and then watched as she made a perfect cast into the lake.

"Good one," he said. "Where did you learn to fish like this?"

"My son, Tyler. He demanded his time between ballet lessons and cheerleading practices."

David nodded, wondering where Ray Justice had been during those years. So far, Cara rarely mentioned his presence in their everyday lives. Then her next comment answered his question without being asked.

"Ray was always working," she said. "Someone had to do the guy stuff with our son." Slowly, she reeled in the line, skillfully playing the lure in the water as she talked. "I got pretty good at it, too. In fact, there for a while, spending the night at Tyler's house was all the rage because his mom wasn't squeamish about worms."

David grinned.

Suddenly, Cara's line jerked.

"I've got one!" she shouted, and began backing up as she reeled.

The pole was bending, the line quivering and taut. When it was less than five feet from the shore, they could see the shadowy shape of the fish beneath the water.

"It's a big one," she squealed. "Just look at him fight."

David glanced toward the water just as she took another turn on the reel. In that moment, the fish slipped the hook. The tension went from constant to nothing and the hook came up and out of the water like a pronged bullet, heading straight for Cara's face.

David reacted without thinking, spinning between her and the missile, then flinching in pain when the hook set itself deep within his back.

Still blinking from an impact that never happened, Cara saw David reaching over his shoulder, feeling his way around the wound. When he removed his hand, it came away bloody.

"David?"

"It's in my back," he said. "If I had a pair of needle-nosed pliers, I could pull it out."

"Oh, my God," she moaned, and made him turn around. "I saw it coming and just froze. If it hadn't been for you, it would have been in my face."

"It's nothing," he said. "Lord knows I've had worse. Now go look for the pliers, will you?"

"I will not," she stated firmly, and took a pocketknife out of her tackle box and quickly cut the line. "We're going to the emergency room. You're going to have that taken out like a decent human being, not ripped out of your flesh like some barbarian."

"But I am a barbarian," he muttered.

"Not in my world, you're not."

"Damn it, Cara, it's a little bitty hook."

"That's imbedded in your back," she retorted.

He glared.

She frowned.

He sighed.

She began gathering up their things.

"Give me those," David said, taking the heaviest of their gear out of her hands. "I'm not crippled."

"No, just difficult," she said, and then started to cry.

"God…don't do that," David said, as he followed her to the car.

"I have to," Cara said.

"Why?"

"Because I'm a woman and because if I don't cry, I might say something stupid. Trust me. It's better if I cry."

In spite of the burning pain in his back, he had to grin.

When they reached the SUV, she opened the back door and slid the rods inside.

"Is this something I should start getting used to?" David asked.

Her cheeks were streaked with tears, her eyes still brimming, but she managed a weak smile as she took the tackle boxes from him and put them in the floorboard behind the front seat.

"What? You mean crying?" she asked.

"Um…that and being bossed around."

This time her smile was genuine. "Was I bossing?"

"Oh, yeah."

"How did you feel about it?"

He grinned back. "Scared?"

"Oh, right," she muttered, and held out her hand. "May I please have the car keys?"

"And you're driving, too? Dang, Cara, I'm not dying."

"Do you know where the hospital is?"

"Oh."

"That's what I thought. The keys, please."

He handed them to her without further argument and got into the passenger side.

"What about the fish that we caught?" he asked.

"Drat," Cara muttered, as she realized she'd left her stringer of fish in the water. "Wait a minute. I'll be right back."

David watched her sprinting toward the lake, her long, slender legs making quick work of the distance. When she reached the shore, he saw her kneel and lift the stringer out of the water. But to his surprise, she didn't bring it to the car. Instead, she gently removed each one and released them into the lake.

When she got to the car, she tossed the empty stringer into the back seat with the rest of the tackle and brushed her hands on the seat of her pants.

"So, I'm not going to have to clean them after all," David said.

She looked at the bloodstained portion of his shirt and the hook still protruding from his back, and her eyes filled with sympathetic pain.

"I just realized how the fish must have felt when they bit the bait. I thought it was only fair that I let them go."

David's heart twisted. Her empathy for suffering was humbling. He thought of all his years in the military and then his years with SPEAR and wondered, if she knew what he'd done in the name of freedom, would she still be as sympathetic to his pain?

Chapter 5

They walked into the emergency room, still arguing. The nurse at the admitting desk looked up, saw the blood on the man's shirt as well as some of the same spots on Cara's arms.

"Cara! My word! What on earth is going on? Are you hurt?"

"I'm not, but he is," Cara said. "He's got a fishhook in his back."

"Goodness gracious," the nurse said. "Come this way. We'll get that taken care of immediately."

In a town as small as Chiltingham, it stood to reason Cara would be recognized, but for David, a man who'd spent most of his adult life pretending to be someone else, it was a bit disconcerting.

"How did this happen?" Frances said, as she reached for a pair of scissors and began cutting David's shirt down the middle of the back.

"I liked that shirt," David muttered.

"You can buy another one," Cara said. "Now quit fussing and let her do her thing."

David wanted to glare, but the damned hook was really starting to throb. If he had to give up a good T-shirt, then so be it. Anything to get a little relief from the pain.

"There now," Frances said. "I'm going to get Dr. Edwards. I'll be right back."

Cara bit her lower lip. Now that the shirt was gone, she could actually see how deep the hook had gone.

"If that had hit my eye, it would have blinded me. I can't believe you just stepped in front of it like that."

"It was reflex," David said. "It didn't amount to anything much."

"It's much to me," she muttered through tightly clenched teeth. "If I say you're a hero, then you're a hero."

At that point, a tall, skinny man who looked to be on the far side of sixty walked up to the side of the examination table where David was sitting. If it wasn't for the white lab coat he was wearing over a Grateful Dead T-shirt and jeans, David would have doubted the man's authenticity. This, he supposed, would be Doctor Edwards.

"Well, now, Cara, who do we have here?" he asked, looking at Cara instead of the man on the examining table.

David frowned. They were acting as if he was dumb, as well as bloody.

"My name is David Wilson," he said, answering for himself.

"He's my friend," Cara said. "And if he hadn't moved as quickly as he did, that hook would have been in my face, not his back."

Now Marvin Edwards looked at David, looking past the bloody condition of his clothes to the anger on his face and offered his hand.

"Then on behalf of the residents of Chiltingham, let me be the one to thank you. Cara is a much beloved member of this community and it seems you have averted a tragedy. I like to fish myself, and know how these things can happen. One minute a fish is on the hook and the next it's not. Those hooks can come flying, especially if there is a lot of tension on the line. How did you react so quickly?"

David wasn't in the mood to explain that it had been the same instinct he'd had a thousand times before in the jungles of Vietnam.

Knowing a sniper was hidden somewhere up a tree.

Knowing there were booby traps on the trail up ahead although nothing could be seen.

Knowing that the smiling old man who appeared on the trail in front of him was holding an unpinned hand grenade beneath the sheaves of rice.

It was an ingrained sense to survive. Or in this instance. to protect.

"I don't know. I just did," he said.

Marvin Edwards smiled, satisfied with David's reticent attitude. He could respect that. There were plenty of times when he didn't much want to talk. Unfortunately, in his line of work, he didn't have the luxury of clamming up.

With the shirt off his patient's back, Marvin ran his fingers across the multitude of scars on David's body without comment, then waved at Frances.

"Get me a syringe, Frances. We're going to need to deaden this area first."

The nurse busied herself at a nearby table while David fidgeted beneath Cara's worried gaze.

"Look," David said. "Trust me, Doc, this is nothing. I've been hurt enough times in my life to know the difference."

"Then humor me so I can humor our friend Cara Justice. What do you say?"

David grimaced. "Fine. Look and dig. It's just a hook."

Marvin Edwards grinned. "Look and dig? I spent all those years and all that money on medical school just so I could look and dig?"

The older man's sarcasm almost made David grin. "Sorry. Figure of speech."

"Apology accepted," Marvin said, as he closed the curtain around the examining table and took the syringe the nurse handed him.

"Here goes nothing. Please don't move."

David sighed, barely aware when the doctor shoved the needle into his back, but he winked at Cara, who looked as if she was going to cry.

"Honey, why don't you go find a bathroom and wash that blood off your hands?"

"Are you saying you don't want me here?" she asked.

"No. I'm saying you don't need to be here. You're going to cry again and it's really not a big deal, okay?"

"Promise?"

"I promise."

"I'll be right back," she said.

"I figured that."

She slipped out of the curtained area, leaving the two men alone.

"So... David, is it?"

David nodded.

"Exactly what line of business are you in?"

"I'm semi-retired," David said.

"Um, I see. But before...what did you do?"

David didn't respond.

Marvin Edwards glanced up. The expression on the man's face was closed, so he tried another topic.

"Are you just visiting, or planning to stay?" he asked, as he reached for a small scalpel.

David didn't answer.

Marvin grunted. So the man wasn't a talker. That was all right with him.

"This might sting a little," he said, as he made the first cut. "Frances, swab that for me, will you?"

The nurse caught the instant flow of blood as he lifted the scalpel from David's flesh.

He made another small cut and then laid down the scalpel and picked up an instrument that looked to David a whole lot like the damned needle-nosed pliers he'd wanted in the first place. With a couple of tugs and one small sideways twist, the hook came out.

"That's got it," Marvin said. "Flood it with disinfectant, Frances, then I'll stitch it up."

David felt cold fluid running down his back, but nothing more. That would come later, when the shot wore off.

In between stitches, the doctor watched David's face, absently noting the military-straight set to his shoulders and an unflinching stare. It reminded him of a drill sergeant he'd known and hated.

"Who are you?" he asked.

David sighed. How the hell did he answer that one? Then he remembered what Cara had done yesterday and took his cue from her.

"David Wilson."

"I knew Cara and her husband for years. I never heard either of them mention you before."

"I don't doubt that," David said.

This wasn't the answer Marvin was looking for.

"Look, I'm not being nosy." Then he sighed. "Well, yes, maybe I am, a bit. Cara's a widow. Sometimes widows can be very vulnerable. I would not like to see—"

David took a deep breath and jumped in with both feet. "Do you know Cara's daughter Bethany?"

"Sure do. I delivered all three of her children."

"I'm Bethany's father."

Marvin Edwards's jaw dropped, but only momentarily.

"I'm sorry. I never heard them mention—"

"They thought I was dead."

"For all these years?"

David shrugged. "It seemed like a good idea at the time."

Suddenly, Marvin Edwards began to see things in a different light. The horrific scars on this man. The secrets. The military bearing of a man who was supposed to be dead. His gaze sharpened.

"I was a medic in Nam," Marvin said softly.

David shifted. "You must have been pretty young."

"Yes, a lot of us went in too young, didn't we?"

David resisted an urge to look around lest they be overheard. And then he realized it no longer mattered. Lots of people were veterans, which is exactly what he'd become. Finally, he nodded.

"So, did you die on your own, or did Uncle Sam help you?"

Again, David was surprised by the man's perceptions.

"It's no longer a factor in my life," David said.

"You planning to stick around?"

David sighed. "I would like nothing better." He refused to acknowledge, even to himself, that there was still a huge obstacle between him and a normal life.

Marvin grinned and held out his hand. "Then, welcome home, soldier."

David knew he was shaking the doctor's hand, but he couldn't feel it. He could tell that the man was still talking, because he could see his lips moving, but he couldn't hear what was being said. All sound had faded except Marvin Edwards's last words. He'd never thought of himself as a man without a country, because he'd given a good portion of his life in helping keep it safe, but it was true. Until this moment, David Wilson had never truly come home from Vietnam. The emotion of it all almost nailed him. His hands were shaking as the doctor continued to talk.

"So," Marvin said, as he took his last stitch. "Do you golf?"

It was the most benign question David had been asked in over forty years, and he didn't know how to answer it. Coping with the innocence of everyday life was more difficult than he would have believed.

"No. Can't say that I do."

"Shame," Marvin said. "I'm always looking for a buddy to play the front nine."

"I thought doctors were supposed to be notorious for their eighteen-hole games," Da- vid said.

Marvin shrugged. "Not doctors in towns this size. We're always on call and it seems as if I always get paged before I get to the back nine."

Before David could respond, Cara returned.

"Is he okay?" she asked.

"Ask me," David muttered. "I'm the one to whom he shoved a knife in the back."

Cara blinked, then grinned as Marvin Edwards calmly ignored David's petulance and answered.

"Right as rain," Marvin said. "And he'll be just as pretty as he was before. My stitches are as good as my grannie's quilting stitches were."

David resisted the urge to roll his eyes. Quilting stitches? Have mercy.

Marvin Edwards put a small bandage over the stitches and then gave David a thump on the thigh. "Don't forget what I said about that golf."

David nodded. "I remember… I remember everything you said." He hesitated, and then impulsively shook the doctor's hand. "And I thank you."

"For what?" Marvin asked.

The words "welcome home, soldier" were still ringing in his ears, but he couldn't bring himself to admit how much they'd meant. Instead, he just shrugged.

"For everything."

"You'll get my bill," Marvin said, and handed him a prescription for pain pills.

"What's that?" David asked.

"Something for the pain."

"I won't need it," David said.

Marvin Edwards arched an eyebrow, purposefully letting his gaze linger on the big scar on David's chest.

"Oh, right, what was I thinking?"

Cara ignored them both and took the prescription from David before he could protest.

"We'll get it filled at the drive-through pharmacy," she said.

"Better yet, take these instead," Marvin said, and handed Cara some pharmaceutical samples from a drawer.

"Thank you, Dr. Edwards."

"You're welcome," he said, than waved a finger in David's face. "Mind that woman, you hear me, boy?"

David didn't answer, but a smile teased the corners of his mouth as they left the hospital.

"I'm still driving," Cara said.

David didn't argue.

"I like that," Cara said.

"Like what?" David asked, as she started the car.

"That smile on your face. You should wear it more often."

David thought about waking up beside Cara each morning and sleeping beside her each night. Of buying groceries and getting haircuts and playing golf with a friend. Yes, it would be easy to smile about a life like that.

"You think?" he asked, and gave her a wink.

"Yes, I think. Now make yourself comfortable, darling. We're going straight home."

Home.

God. His fingers curled in his lap as Cara accelerated the car.

Frank stood before the bathroom mirror, adjusting his wig and running his fingers over the mustache he'd affected, testing its position. Everything seemed stable enough. He straightened the collar of his white Gucci shirt, checked one last time to make sure it was tucked neatly into his navy blue slacks, then picked up the sunglasses from the back of the commode and slipped them on before looking up.

Perfect! The man in the mirror was a stranger.

He grinned, and as he did, the movement puckered the burn scars on the side of his face, giving him a slightly demonic expression. If she'd still been alive, his own mother would not have recognized him.

Frank was a master at disguise. It had kept him alive all these years without detection. He had no reason to suppose it would fail him now. The wound on his shoulder was almost well. Only now and then did he feel a real twinge of pain. The fact that he was missing most of the top half of one ear was hidden nicely by the hairstyle of the wig.

Convinced that all was well, he strode out of the bathroom, picked up the suitcase he'd packed last night and then paused at the door, giving the apartment a final look. Satisfied that he'd left nothing of himself behind, he opened the door and walked out. No more roach motel. It was time to move up and on, which meant once again changing his persona.

When he passed through the lobby, he tossed the room key on the desk and kept on walking. The clerk didn't bother to look up, which was just as well, because he wouldn't have recognized the man as the former resident of room 413.

Frank was on the street less than a minute before hailing an empty cab.

"Where to, buddy?" the cab driver asked.

"LAX, and step on it," he said. "I've got a flight to catch."

David lay on his side on the bed. At Cara's insistence, he was supposed to be resting, but in truth, he had a lot of thinking to do. Before he'd come, his expectations of seeing Cara had not included a future. All he'd wanted to do was see her—ask her forgiveness—and, if possible, make a place for himself within his daughter's life. Not as a father, of course. He didn't deserve that much consideration. But he wanted to know her—and he wanted her to know him. That had been the apex of his dream. Making love to Cara within minutes of his arrival would never have occurred to him, not even in his wildest imagination. But it had happened and he had accepted the fact that she'd been making love to the boy he'd been, not the man that he'd become. However, that didn't account for the other times since, or the fact that Cara had openly admitted she wanted him to stay. And he wanted to, desperately so. He wasn't going to lose her again.

Somehow, he had to find a way to stop Frank for good without losing his life in the process. Frustrated with the mess he was in, he rolled over on his back, wincing slightly as the pressure caused a slight pain, then he closed his eyes. In spite of himself, the pain pills were having their way.

He didn't know how long he'd been sleeping when the phone rang. He woke abruptly, waiting for Cara to answer, but she didn't. On the fourth ring, he thought he heard water running from the faucet outside and realized she must not be in the house. He reached for the phone and answered as it rang again.

"Justice residence."

There was a soft gasp on the other end of the line and then a young woman's voice, hesitant and suddenly anxious.

"Who's speaking, please?"

David hesitated briefly, then opted for minimal introduction.

"This is David."

"Um… David, this is Bethany. Is my mother there?"

David stood abruptly, his heart pounding against his chest. All he could think was, *My God, I am hearing my daughter's voice.*

"Hello? Are you still there?" Bethany asked.

David felt like crying. Instead, he took a deep breath and then exhaled slowly, making himself focus.

"Sorry. Yes, I'm here, and so is your mother, but I think she's outside. Do you want to wait while I check and see?"

"Yes, please," she said.

David didn't want to break the connection, but was not about to explain his reluctance.

"Okay. You'll hang on?"

"Yes."

He hurried through the house and then ran into Cara as she was coming in the back door.

David held up the phone. "It's Bethany. She wants to talk to you."

Cara's eyes widened. She could tell from the stricken look on David's face that he had been sideswiped by the call.

"You didn't say anything about who you are?" she asked, keeping her voice low.

He shook his head.

Even though she wanted to tell Bethany everything about David's arrival, it wasn't news to be told over a phone.

"Hello? Bethany?"

"Mom, are you all right?"

Cara rolled her eyes at David, who was pushing her toward a chair.

"Yes, I'm fine, sweetheart. How's the vacation going?"

Now David was the one rolling his eyes at her as she struggled to make conversation.

Cara made a face at him, and they both smiled.

"So… Mom?"

"Yes?"

Cara heard an exasperated sigh and knew Bethany wasn't anywhere near satisfied with what she'd been told.

"Who is David?"

Cara looked at the man sitting across the kitchen table from her.

"He's a friend."

Bethany snorted. "I've never heard you or Dad mention anyone by the name of David. When did you meet him?"

"Years ago," Cara said. "Enough about me. How's the vacation? Are the kids having fun?"

This time Cara could hear noise in the background and deduced that the rest of Bethany's family was just returning to the hotel room.

"Yes, they're having a ball. Actually, we're all having a wonderful time. We've got to come here again and when we do, you have to come with us. You would love Disney World as well as Epcot Center."

Cara smiled. "I'm glad everything is going well."

Bethany continued, "I didn't really have a reason to call other than to say hello and to tell you we'll be home Sunday. I think our plane lands around two in the afternoon. We should be home before dark. We'll talk more then."

"I can't wait to hear all about the trip," Cara said. "Oh, by the way…when you get home, we need to talk. It's important."

David flinched. Just the thought of facing his daughter and trying to explain why he'd absented himself from her life made him sick to his stomach.

"Mother! It's about the man who answered the phone, isn't it? I knew it! You haven't been out with a man since Dad died. Who is he? Is this serious?" Then she shrieked. "It can't be serious. We've only been gone for eight days. Please tell me you've known him longer than eight days!"

"Much longer than that," Cara said. "Now calm down. We'll talk when you get home."

"How much longer?" Bethany asked. "Weeks? Months?"

"Years, darling. Years and years. Now have a safe trip home and call me when you get in."

"Mother, you're not telling me what I want to hear."

"I love you, Bethany. Take care and give my love to Tom and the girls."

"Mother! Don't you dare hang up until you—"

Cara calmly punched the off button and then laid the phone down on the table beside her.

"Our daughter is in a panic," Cara said.

"Why? Because I'm here?"

Cara nodded.

"Are you okay with this, because if my being here is going to cause you trouble, then I'll leave. I won't want to, but I'll do it for you."

Cara got up from her chair and sat in David's lap. Relief hit him fast and hard as she wound her arms around his neck, careful not to touch his stitches.

"If you weren't wounded…"

He grinned. "It's not fatal," he said, as he began unbuttoning her shirt.

"But your stitches..."

"Are not in the way," David said, finishing her sentence for her.

She grinned. "That's not what I was going to say and you know it."

He stood up and then grabbed her hand, giving it a tug.

"Today, I was a hero, remember? No one gave me the keys to the city, so I'm taking you instead."

He didn't have to ask her twice. In spite of her better judgment, she let him pick her up in his arms and carry her all the way to her bed.

"We seem to be doing an awful lot of this lately," Cara said.

David paused in the act of removing his shirt, his eyes dancing with mischief.

"What? Undressing?"

She blushed. "No. Well, yes, but not that specifically."

David tossed his shirt and then reached for his belt. "Are you referring to the fact that I keep taking you to bed?"

She arched an eyebrow. "You know exactly what I mean."

"Ah...well then," David said, removing his right shoe. "I look at it this way. I have forty years of making up to do and not a long time to do it, so if I'm ever going to catch up..."

She laughed and threw a pillow at him.

He dodged it neatly then kicked off his other shoe, shed the rest of his clothes and pounced.

Cara was still laughing when he slid into her body.

The laugh turned into a groan and then a sigh. After that, it was downhill all the way.

Later, as they lay quietly in each other's arms, talking and savoring the pleasure of what had just happened, Cara could feel David starting to withdraw. She raised up on one elbow, looking at him.

"Is something wrong?" she asked.

He started not to answer, then sighed. "Not with you…or with us. It's just that I need to…uh…check in at the office."

"Of course," she said, and reached for the phone. "Please feel free to use my phone anytime you need. I'll get dressed and give you some privacy."

David grabbed her arm, stilling her intent.

"Thank you, Cara, more than I can say. But I can't use your phone."

"Why? I don't—" Understanding dawned. "Oh."

He kissed the side of her face. "It's all right. I have everything I need in the trunk of my car. However, it will take a while to set up and I don't want you to think—"

This time, she was the one to silence him.

"David. Enough. You don't explain to me. You do what you have to do and just stay in one piece. I'll be satisfied with that, all right?"

He smiled. "Thank you, baby."

"Use any room in this house that you need. I have plenty of things I need to do outside. Just let me know when you're through."

David thought about it and then shook his head.

"No. I don't want to bring any part of that life into this house, and I don't need to necessarily be inside. I think I'll drive back toward the lake."

She nodded, frowning as she tried to picture a place at the lake where he could stay unobserved.

"You remember where we turned to go to the landing?"

He nodded.

"If you skip that turn and take the next one instead, it will take you to a very wooded area of the lake. There aren't any campsites or boat docks there. I think they have plans to develop it, but so far nothing has been done."

David smiled. "Sounds perfect."

Cara looked pleased. "Good, and while you're gone, I'm going to do some laundry. Do you have anything you need washed?"

"No, baby, but thanks," David said, and gave her a quick kiss before he rolled out of bed and headed for the bathroom.

When he came out a few minutes later, Cara was already gone. By the time he dressed and left the house, he'd left more than Cara behind. David Wilson wasn't the man who got into the rental car and drove away toward the lake. It was Jonah.

By the time he reached the area that Cara had mentioned, he had completely refocused. There was nothing in his head but duty. In less than thirty minutes, he had everything set up and running. With a laptop and modem, some prototype chips in his Global Positioning System and a couple of other gadgets from technical research that had yet to be named, he had logged into his site and retrieved his messages.

Within an hour, he had two agents en route to Illinois to investigate death threats against the President, another dispatched to the border between Mexico and Texas and had restructured a list of agents on foreign soil to insure their identities stayed anonymous.

Out of curiosity, he checked a site reserved for personal messages between him and the White House. To his relief, there were none. He checked another site, hoping that there was some sort of message on there that had been intercepted from Frank, but again, there was nothing.

Convinced that he'd done all he could do, he logged off, packed the stuff back in the trunk and then strolled to the edge of the lake.

The day was calm, the water so still it looked like glass. Only the smallest of ripples could be seen as the water lapped at the shore. He stood for a while, absorbing the peacefulness of the day while mentally letting go of Jonah before he returned to Cara.

A trio of gulls circled high over his head. Curious, he watched for a while, thinking that they were quite a distance from the sea. Probably blown here with the last storm to pass through and just stayed—so symbolic of the path his own life had taken.

He'd set out on one path and had been war-tossed into another. And, instead of finding his way back home, like the gulls, he'd stayed. Had it been a mistake? If he'd come back after the war, what kind of a husband and father would he have been? He thought of the hell he'd lived with, thinking he'd not only killed his own brother but had hidden the truth about Frank being a traitor. In that moment, he accepted his life without regret. He would have been hell to live with, would have ruined whatever chances he and Cara might have had for a happy life, and they would have been divorced before they were thirty.

He sighed, remembering something his mother had said, that things always happened for a reason. It wasn't always easy to understand, but that with time, understanding always came. She'd been right. Now, looking back on what he'd done and his mental state at the time, he'd done the best thing for both of them.

The water beckoned.

Impulsively, he shed his clothes where he stood and then walked into the water until he was up to his chest and then started to swim. The water was cool against the heat of his skin. He swam until his car was little more than a black speck beneath the trees before he turned and went back. By the time he emerged from the lake, he was tired but renewed.

Within a very few minutes, he was dry enough to put on his clothes. As he walked to his car, he began to smile. It had been a long time since he'd done anything so innocent as skinny-dip. Maybe he was actually getting the hang of being a normal guy, after all.

By the time he got to Cara's house, it was mid-afternoon. When he drove up and parked, she looked up from the flower beds in front of her house and waved, but then continued to weed. He had no way of knowing how many prayers she'd sent up in his name, or that she'd cried more than once, fearing he would not return. All he saw was a woman confident within her life, waving a hello.

"Looks like you've been busy," he said, tweaking the end of her sun-stained nose. "You're about to get a sunburn, honey."

She rocked on her heels and put the back of her arm against her cheeks and nose, only then feeling the emanating heat.

"Ooh, you're right," she said. "And I forgot to put on sunscreen before I came out." She stood, dusting off her gloves and pushing her hair away from her face. "I've done enough anyway. Let's go inside. Are you hungry?"

He realized that he was.

"Yes, starving."

She smiled. "Good. How about a ham and cheese sandwich?"

"How about two?"

She laughed. "I think that can be arranged."

She went inside, leaving the door ajar for him to follow. As he stepped over the threshold, he sighed.

David Wilson was home.

Chapter 6

Sundown had long since come and gone. The evening had passed with remarkable simplicity. It was as if the time David had spent away from the house had somehow settled some of the turmoil he'd brought with him. They'd watched television together like a couple who'd been married for years. David sat with an open book in his lap, sometimes reading, other times watching the program in broadcast, while Cara shelled some peas she'd bought from a nearby truck farm.

The gentleness of the evening had rolled over into their bedtime. Now, Cara lay naked beneath David's gaze. The love she felt for him was there in her eyes for him to see. All he had to do was look. Silently she watched as he undressed beside the bed. He moved in the darkness as if he had lived here all his life. She could tell he was far more comfortable within the shadows than the light.

"David."

He dropped the shirt he'd just taken off and turned. "Yes?"

"That bullet scar on your back."

"What about it?"

"How did you get it?"

He frowned. "I thought you wanted to make love."

"I do, but I also want to know who I'm making love to and there is a huge gap between the boy who went off to war and the man you are today."

"If you knew, you wouldn't want me in your house, let alone your bed."

The defeat in his voice surprised her. She got up on her knees and then pulled him down onto the bed beside her.

"That's not true," she said. "I didn't ask because I feel a need to judge you. I asked for the same reasons I see in your eyes when Ray's name is mentioned."

David pulled her into his arms and pressed her cheek against his chest.

"It's not jealously, baby, I swear," David said.

"I know, but we lost so many years… wonderful years we could have spent together. I just have this overwhelming urge to fill myself up with your life. Maybe because it's the only way I have left to share it."

David bowed his head, pressing a soft kiss against her cheek, and then eased her back onto the pillow.

"If I talk, will you promise to lie still?"

She sighed. "Are you turning down my rather blatant request?"

He grinned. "Not by a long shot…just postponing it a bit."

She made a face.

He tweaked her nose. "Okay, you wanted to know about the scar on my shoulder?"

"Yes, please."

He thought of the searing pain from Frank's gun, spinning him around and knocking him off his feet.

"Vietnam."

"And the one on the side of your neck?"

"Afghanistan. Don't ask me why I was there."

"What about the long scar on the back of your right leg?"

"Disagreement with a sniper in Beirut. He ran out of bullets and I jumped him. I didn't know he had a knife."

Cara's eyes were huge, her lips slack with shock. He was telling these horrors in such a calm voice, and she felt like throwing up. She laid her hand on the sickle-shaped scar above his heart.

"And this one?"

He hesitated, and suddenly Cara put her hand on his mouth before he could answer. "I don't think I want to know."

"Now you're getting the picture. They don't matter anymore, baby. That part of my life is almost over."

Cara looked away and then closed her eyes.

David could tell she was fighting tears. He cupped her cheek gently, then kissed the side of her face.

"What, honey? Don't shut me out now."

"Oh, God, David. Don't you understand? It's the *almost* that undoes me." She ran a finger along the surface of the old scars. "I can live with these. It's the ones you have yet to receive that scare me most."

There was nothing he could really say that would reassure her and still be truthful. And he wasn't lying to Cara—not ever again.

"Look at it this way," he said. "I was always outnumbered and survived. This time it's only one man."

"Why do you have to do this alone? Aren't there people you can call on? Isn't there anyone in authority who will stand beside you?"

David hesitated. "It's not that. It's just that the man wants me and only me. He's spent the better part of a year trying to destroy me and damned near took a huge chunk of national security and my best agents along with him. We can't afford…no… *I* can't afford to waste any more time. He has to be stopped." His voice changed to a deep, warning growl. "How much do you value your life and the lives of your children and grandchildren?"

Cara's mouth parted, her lips slack with shock.

"If he knew about you…about Bethany and her family…their lives wouldn't be worth dirt. In the past eleven months, he's kidnapped, lied, stolen and killed, and all in the name of trying to get to me. I am resigning from my post because I can't let another person fight what was ultimately my battle from the start."

"Dear God, David, what manner of man is he? Why you? What did you ever do to him to make him hate you this way?"

Silence hung between them, shrouded in secrets and guilt. He preferred not to answer, but if they were ever going to have a chance at any kind of a future, she had to know part of the past.

"He's a man gone crazy. It started years ago in Vietnam. He shot at me. I shot back. In fact, I thought I had killed him."

"Who is he, David? What kind of man hates like that?"

"You know the old saying about blood being thicker than water? Well, hate within a family is just as strong."

Cara frowned. "I don't understand. Your parents are dead. Your brother died in Vietnam. Who else is—"

Even though the room was in darkness, she saw enough of his expression to realize what he'd been trying not to say.

"Oh…my… God. Please tell me it's not what I'm thinking. Frank's dead…isn't he?"

His silence rocked the room.

She inhaled sharply. "What can you tell me?"

"Nothing that will make any sense."

Her gaze went straight to the scar on his shoulder. She touched it in disbelief.

"He did this, didn't he?"

David nodded.

She started to cry.

"We all tried to kill you, didn't we, darling? Deception. Lies. Betrayals. My God, you must have thought there was no one on your side. Not even me."

"Don't say that," he muttered, and took her in his arms. "I never once blamed you. You did what you had to do."

"I will forever blame my parents for the lies they told me about you."

"And they did what they thought was right, too. Let it go, Cara. I'm here now."

She buried her face against the curve of his neck. "I'm scared."

His arms tightened around her. "I'm scared, too, but not *of* Frank…only what he can do if he isn't stopped. You understand, don't you?"

Her voice was shaking, her face streaked with tears.

"Yes, as much as I hate to admit it, I do. I promise I won't talk about this again. We have now and we have each other. And when you come back, we'll have the rest of our lives."

Now David felt like crying. Instead, he laid her down and began to kiss her. Gently at first and then with desperation, until they were lost in the passion.

After a day of traveling in his new disguise, Frank Wilson was comfortable in his skin as he tossed a handful of bills onto the counter, picked up the sacks containing his new wardrobe and sauntered out of the Denver, Colorado store. The day was almost balmy. One of those clear, robin's-egg blue skies that made a man feel as if he could take on the world. He paused at the curb before swaggering down the street. More than one woman gave him a second look as he passed, and in spite of his scars, and his long ponytail wig, he knew it was not in disgust. There was a bad-boy air of danger about him that never failed to attract the women. Granted, they were always the wrong kind of women, not like his beloved Martha, but they were always there just the same.

He stopped at a crosswalk, waiting for the red light to change, and thought of what he had lost. His identity was unimportant. He'd lived so long in the shadows that another assumed name would be a small price to pay for peace of mind. After his confrontation with David was over, maybe he'd find himself a good woman and settle down again. Despite the fact that his sixtieth birthday had come and gone, he had the body and constitution of a much younger man, and he knew it. It wasn't too late to make a new life for himself. He would have the time, and he already had the money.

The light changed, and he started across the street, losing himself in the crowd of pedestrians. By the time he got back to his hotel, he'd made up his mind to head south after he rid himself of David. Maybe the Florida Keys. He liked the sun. It was why he'd settled in Australia, but he'd had enough of the outback. This time, he wanted to be where there was water. A whole lot of water.

Inside his room, he tossed the bags with his purchases onto the bed and began to go through them, searching for certain items. A few minutes later, he had changed into khaki-colored cotton shorts and a navy blue T-shirt. He put on a baseball cap with the Denver Broncos logo and then transferred a number of items into a medium-size fanny pack, patted his pockets to make sure he had his wallet and room key, as well as some other identification, and headed out the door. He had an appointment he didn't want to miss.

A half hour later, a cab dropped him off at a public firing range. He sauntered inside as if he owned the place.

The clerk at the front desk looked up. "Can I help you?" he asked.

Frank nodded, flashing a badge. "Detective Ferraro out of New York City. I'm here on vacation. Thought I'd get in some target practice while the little woman spends all my money."

The clerk grinned. "Yeah, I can identify with that, buddy," he said. "Sign in here. I'll get an escort to take you into the range. He'll get you all set up."

"Great," Frank said, signing his fake name with a flourish.

A few minutes later, he stood within his cubicle,

safety glasses and headphones on, his 9mm Glock loaded and waiting for the first target to appear. Someone tapped him on the shoulder. He turned.

"Are you ready, sir?"

Frank nodded, took aim and waited. About fifty feet in front of him, a paper target appeared. He squeezed off a couple of rounds, taking satisfaction in the weapon's kick against the palms of his hands. The muffled sounds of gunfire, the smell of burning gunpowder, the surge of adrenaline—everything combined within his senses and sent his memory into overdrive. David's face suddenly appeared on the target, taunting him like the ghost that he'd become, and when it did, Frank snapped, emptying his gun into the target. Moving in robotlike motions, he ejected the empty clip and slipped a full one in place before pressing the button on the wall beside him to bring the paper target up close.

Yanking it from the wire, he grunted in satisfaction. Every shot he'd fired had hit within a three-inch radius of where a man's heart would be. He dropped it onto the floor beside him, hit the switch, then adjusted his safety glasses as he waited for a new target to appear. He'd done fine, just fine. But he could do better.

He set the distance on the new target at fifty feet farther back than before and took aim. Again, David's face appeared before him. He squeezed the trigger in rapid succession again, this time peppering the head until there was nothing left of the target above the shoulders and no bullets left in the clip.

Muscles in his healing shoulder protested, but he ignored the painful twinges as he took off the headphones and goggles, then mopped the sweat from his face with his handkerchief.

A passing attendant glanced into Frank's cubicle and whistled softly.

"Good job, sir. Whoever he is, he's definitely dead."

Frank turned abruptly, still holding his weapon and making sure that he'd never seen him before. Luckily for the attendant, he was a stranger to Frank, or he might never have lived to see another sunrise. Then Frank smiled, pulling the scarred side of his mouth into a grimace.

"Yeah...he's that, all right," Frank said, and headed for the exit.

Morning dawned on a gray, overcast day. It looked like rain. David stood at the living room windows staring out into the yard, but he wasn't looking at the view. His thoughts had gone inward, mentally plotting out a course of action. The scent of coffee still permeated the air from their breakfast. Cara had scooted David out of the kitchen, claiming she was making him a surprise. Then she'd argued he should be resting in bed and he'd retaliated by ignoring her.

Now, although they were but a room away from each other, the distance between them couldn't have been further. He wasn't thinking like David. He'd become Jonah again—planning the best way to trap and dispose of a killer.

Happy with the pie she was baking, Cara never knew when David went out the front door and checked the contents of his trunk. He needed to check in with his agents and the powers that be again. If God had been listening to his prayers, maybe they'd already fished Frank's body out of the East River, but he wasn't betting his future on that. At least not yet.

He looked at the house. He wasn't in the mood to go to the lake, but no way was he ever going to destroy the sanctity of that home by bringing any part of his old life into it. Anxious to get things in motion, he set the bag in the front seat of the car and ran into the house.

Cara heard the front door slam, then the sound of running footsteps. She turned just as David entered the kitchen.

"What's the hurry?"

He hesitated. "Something smells good."

She frowned. "David. I raised three children and I've heard just about every excuse in the book. That's not what you came here to tell me."

He grinned. "Damn, you're good."

"Yes, and don't you forget it," she muttered. "So, what's up?"

"I'm going to take another little drive. I won't be gone long, okay?"

Her fingers tightened around the handle of the knife she was holding. It was the only outward sign of her unease.

"Okay. If you get as far as Chiltingham, would you mind bringing back a gallon of milk?"

His eyes widened, then a genuine smile spread across his face. He hadn't done anything that ordinary since before he'd left for Vietnam.

"No, I don't mind. I don't mind at all," he said, and then suddenly swooped, swinging her up in his arms and dancing her across the kitchen with her feet dangling above the floor.

"Be careful of your stitches," she cried.

"To hell with the stitches. I'm going to kiss you."

Cara laughed from the joy in his eyes and from the

silliness of it all. By the time he stopped moving, she was dizzy from all the spinning.

"You're a crazy man," she said, and planted a hard kiss in the center of his mouth.

"That kind of behavior will make a man crazy," he muttered, and kissed her back. Then he turned her loose with a reluctant groan. "I won't be long," he said.

She eyed him cautiously, afraid to say what was in her heart, but David read the expression on her face.

"I swear I'll be back," he said softly.

"I knew that," Cara said. "Now get. This pie won't be ready in time for supper if I don't get it in the oven."

But David didn't move and he wouldn't turn her loose.

"Cara..."

"Yes?"

"I love you very much."

Quick tears blurred his face. It had been forty years since she'd heard him say those words and yet her heart still skipped a beat. She cupped his face with her hands, fingering the silver strands of hair above his ears and then smiling.

"Thank you, my darling. I love you, too."

He laughed and then hugged her fiercely before bolting out of the house. Only after Cara could no longer hear the sound of the car's engine did she sit down and cry.

Still riding on an emotional high, David drove with focus, searching for the same road that he'd taken before. The radio was on, but turned down low, little more than background noise for bigger plans. But when he heard the disc jockey giving a brief update on a breaking story, he turned it up, then began to frown. Another business had been robbed, presumably by the same three thieves who'd been terrorizing the area.

"They'll make a mistake," he muttered. "They're getting too cocky."

A few miles down the road, he saw the cutoff he was looking for and swerved. The car bumped and bounced along the graveled road before he had a chance to slow down. Just like before, no one was anywhere in sight, not even on the water.

A few minutes later, he was set up and running. As he dialed the first number, he felt himself slipping back into the Jonah mind-set, and as he did, realized that it felt uncomfortable. Just these few days with Cara were easing forty years of scars from his military service. Seconds later, his call was answered. He gave a one-word code, which instantly connected him to another line, then another. Finally, his call reached its final destination.

"Hello, Jonah, this is the President. How have you been?"

"Better, sir," David said briefly. "Has there been any word on our quarry?"

"No, I'm sorry to say there has not. It looks like your assumptions were correct after all."

David slumped in disappointment and was glad the President couldn't see his face.

"Yes, sir. I'm sorry, too, sir."

"Is there anything you need?"

"Not at the moment, sir. I'll let you know when it's over."

"Thank you, Jonah. I appreciate that."

"Oh…sir?"

"Yes?"

"About looking for my replacement."

"Yes?"

"I suggest you start the process."

"It's your call," the President said, and then added, "I hope you know how much I regret it had to come to this."

"Yes, sir. Thank you, sir, but it was inevitable. We don't last forever in this job."

The President's chuckle rumbled in David's ear. "Longer than I do in mine, I can assure you."

David grinned. "Yes, sir." Then he added quickly, "I'll be in touch."

The line went dead in his ear. Satisfied that was done, he dialed another number. Seconds later, a woman's voice answered.

"MailBin, Birmingham branch, Jennifer speaking."

"Hello, Jennifer, this is David Wilson."

"Oh, hi, Mr. Wilson. Long time, no talkie," she said, and then giggled at the joke she'd just made.

"Yes, it has been a while," David said. "I need you to do something for me."

"Are we forwarding your stuff again?" she asked.

"Yes."

"Okeydoke. Even though I recognize your voice, I need your password."

"Fourth of July," he said.

"All righty, then. Where do you want your stuff sent this time?"

"I'll be in Washington D.C. by Monday. Please send the contents of the box to the Wardman Park Hotel. Here's the address."

A couple of minutes later, he hung up again, satisfied that whatever mail had been accumulating for him would be awaiting his arrival at the hotel. Then he dialed another number, checked upon the situation at the

Texas/Mexico border and deployed another agent to help the one already on-site, then sent another agent to assist the two in Illinois who were investigating the death threats on the President.

Once he'd finished with the business of SPEAR, he dialed one more number, this time his last.

"Marriott Wardman Park, how can I direct your call?"

"Reservations, please," David said.

"One moment, sir."

A couple of rings later, David was connected.

"Reservations, how may I help you?"

"This is David L. Wilson. Number fifty-one. I will be arriving Sunday afternoon."

The moment the name was typed into the hotel computer, it automatically opened into a security file with a predestined room ready at his disposal.

"Yes, Mr. Wilson, I have entered you into the system. Will you be needing a driver at the airport?"

"Not this trip," David said. "I'll catch a cab. Oh… there will be a package arriving for me within a couple of days. That is to be held for me to pick up upon my arrival."

"Yes, sir. Have a safe flight."

David hung up, set the laptop aside and crossed his arms upon the steering wheel then leaned forward. The sun was close to setting, giving the glassy surface of the lake a mirrorlike appearance. It seemed almost impossible to believe that only the day before yesterday they'd been here, fishing and laughing and pretending that they were normal people with normal lives.

Although he sat without moving, his thoughts were in constant motion. He'd done all there was to do from this end. There was nothing left to do but get to D.C. and wait for Frank to contact him. And he was in no doubt that it would happen. His brother had obviously invested a lifetime in tracking him down with full intentions of destroying him. All David had to do was make sure it didn't happen.

A simple thing, actually. Just stay alive. It was an instinctive act that shouldn't pose a real problem. The only thing was, Frank was most likely set on the very same thing.

David said a brief but fervent prayer. It wouldn't be the first time brother had fought brother on American soil. He just hoped to God the outcome of their meeting would lie in his favor.

When he looked up, the sun was slipping behind the treetops. He packed up his equipment and then started the car. He had a gallon of milk to buy and a woman to come home to.

By the time he got into Chiltingham, the streetlights were on. The charm of the little town was amazing to him. Everywhere he looked was a picture postcard scene. Perfect little houses with perfect little lawns and perfect little flower beds to accentuate their beauty. He pulled into the parking lot to the supermarket and caught himself whistling as he walked toward the door.

Lord, when had he last done something so innocuous as whistle? Then he grinned. Too damned long, that's what.

As he strolled inside, he grabbed a shopping cart and began to wheel it down the aisles.

What was it Cara wanted me to buy? Oh, yeah...milk.

He headed toward the back of the store, knowing that was where most of the cold storage items were kept, but got sidetracked by the cookie aisle and then sideswiped by a woman he knew he'd seen before. It wasn't until she started to speak that he remembered her name. Macie. The woman with whom Ray had his affair.

"Why…if it isn't Cara's sweetheart," she said, and slid her hand up his arm. "Isn't this cute? I just love to see a big, strong man doing these thoughtful little chores."

David reached for a package of cookies, well aware that as he did, she had to step back.

"I'm sorry, but I've forgotten your name," David said, knowing that wasn't something she would appreciate. From the frown that appeared on her forehead, he was right.

"Macie. My name is Macie."

He nodded. "Now I remember. Sorry. Nice seeing you again," he said, and pushed the cart a little farther down the aisle. Unfortunately, she followed.

"I see you have a sweet tooth," Macie purred, and then lowered her eyelashes to half mast.

David assumed she thought it was sexy, but he could see they were false and wondered if she knew one was coming unglued.

"You know what they say about men who love their food," she whispered.

David grinned. "Yeah, they get fat. Listen, it's been nice talking to you, and I'll be sure and tell Cara you said hello."

Macie looked irritated. "Yes, well…you do that," she muttered, and then walked away.

David didn't bother to watch. He'd spied a box of cereal that he might want to try and tossed it into the cart.

"Milk. Milk. Remember to get milk," he muttered, and kept on going.

By the time he got to the checkout stand, he'd covered the entire store. He now knew where the toilet paper was shelved and where he could find aspirin and cinnamon, as well.

The checker, who couldn't have been more than nineteen or twenty, rang up his purchases, eyeing him curiously as she did. When he handed over a ten and a twenty to pay for his purchases, he caught her staring at him and he winked.

She blushed all the way to the roots of her hair and dropped a dime of his change.

"I'm sorry," she mumbled, as she dug another out of the drawer and handed it to him. "Thank you, and come back again."

"Yes, thanks, I will," he said.

"Do you need any help carrying those out?" she asked.

"Are you offering?"

She blushed even harder. "Why, no, sir, but I could call a—"

David grinned. "No, thanks. I don't need any help. I was just teasing you."

She grinned then, a little more sure of herself.

"Well, I *was* staring. I suppose I had it coming." Then she added, "Are you new here, or just passing through?"

He hesitated and then smiled. "New."

"Then welcome to Chiltingham," she said.

The innocence of her remark took him aback and then touched him greatly.

"Thank you. The longer I'm here, the more certain I am that it's just where I belong."

As he left the store, he had the feeling that he'd just made another friend. Dr. Marvin Edwards had welcomed him home from Vietnam and now this girl, barely past her childhood, had welcomed him to the town. Damned if he wasn't taking a real liking to normal living.

He put his purchases in the trunk and then drove out of town, anxious to get back home. He thought of the pie that Cara had been baking when he left and wondered what other surprises she had in store for him. Whatever they were, they were bound to be good.

Chapter 7

David pulled into the driveway of Cara's house and parked. Before he could get out of the car, she came out the door to meet him. He waved as she circled the car and gave him a welcome-home kiss.

"I got the milk," he said, as he popped the trunk of the car.

Cara peeked over his shoulder and stifled a grin.

"It's sort of difficult to see it among all the other stuff you bought, so I'll just have to take your word for it."

"Do not chide the hunter who brings home sustenance," David said.

This time she let her grin show.

He handed her one grocery sack and then took the other two himself, closed the trunk lid with his elbow and shifted the sacks to a safer position within his grasp.

"Lead the way," he said. "I'm right behind you."

All sorts of wonderful scents assailed David as they entered the house. He could definitely smell that apple pie she'd been baking when he left.

"Smells good in here," he said, as he sat the grocery sacks on the counter.

"I haven't had this much fun cooking in I don't know when," Cara said.

David took the grocery sack from her and then took her in his arms.

"Yeah, and I don't know when I've had this much fun, period."

She smiled and combed her fingers through his hair.

"You're too easy to please," she said softly.

"It's not that. It's the woman who's doing it."

She gave him a quick kiss. "Save that for later. I want to see what the *hunter* has bagged."

"Just stuff," he said, and dug the milk from a sack and put it into the refrigerator.

"Is there anything else in these that needs refrigerating?" Cara asked.

"A couple of things, I guess."

"Like what?" she asked, as she started digging through the sacks.

"Well…like this…and for sure this, and I think this would spoil, too."

Her eyes widened, then she started to smile as she watched him pull out a half gallon of Rocky Road ice cream, a package of hot Polish sausage and a carton of dip to go with the enormous bag of chips in the other sack.

"This looks like the groceries Tyler used to bring home."

"He's the youngest, isn't he?"

Cara nodded. "And my only son. He'll be thirty on his next birthday. You'll like him."

David stilled, watching as Cara began putting the items away that he'd purchased.

"Saw Ms. Macie at the supermarket. She said to say hello."

Cara turned. "And you would be lying to me now."

He nodded. "Well...she definitely said hello to me."

"She's a snake," Cara muttered.

"More like a barracuda," David offered.

The simile made Cara smile.

He handed her a couple more items from the grocery sacks, which she put on the refrigerator shelves, then moved to the pantry to store the rest.

As she worked, she realized David had gotten very quiet. She turned and looked at him, trying to judge what he was thinking against the expression on his face. As usual, it was impossible to tell.

"Well," she said. "Are you going to tell me, or is this going to be another game of twenty questions?"

"This life is so simple—so ordinary. I keep worrying if I'll ever fit in. And your children... I'm trying to put myself in their places when confronted with someone like me. I'm not so sure this is going to be good. If I was them, I don't think I would like me."

"Well... I like you, which is all that matters. Besides, you don't know them or you wouldn't be worrying," she said, and handed him the ice cream. "Put this in the freezer, please."

He did as she asked.

"Now go wash up, super shopper. Supper is ready."

David sighed and then headed for the bathroom. For a

man used to being the one giving orders, this was a definite change in his routine, but one he could get used to.

He paused at the doorway and looked back. Cara was already at the stove, dishing up the food.

So beautiful. Then he shook his head and then hurried down the hall, anxious not to waste another moment of his time with her.

By the time he returned, she was carrying the last of the dishes into the dining room. He followed, his eyes widening with appreciation as he entered. The cherry wood table was set with china instead of the stoneware she used every day. There was a bouquet of her own flowers in the center of the table and lit candles on the mantel as well as on either side of the flowers. He thought of all the lonely days and nights of the last forty years and words failed him. When Cara turned, she saw him standing in the doorway and held out her hand. He took it, kissing it twice—once on the back, then again in the center of her palm.

"For you," Cara said softly. "For all the meals you ate alone."

He took her in his arms, too overwhelmed to speak. Cara was the first to move.

"Let's eat before it gets cold."

He seated Cara and then himself, missing nothing of the elegance. Everywhere he looked he saw beauty, and all for him—all in the name of love. Cara handed him the carving knife, indicating that he carve the roast she had cooked.

He looked at the long, thin-bladed knife, trying to relate it to serving food, but the images it evoked were deadly and ugly. Almost immediately, he laid it down.

"There's something I need to do first," David said,

and took her by the hand. His thoughts flashed to Frank, lying in his own blood, and he shook his head as if clearing away the ghosts.

Cara waited.

David bowed his head, uncertain how to proceed, but the need to acknowledge a greater power was, at that moment, overwhelming.

There, in a deep, quiet voice, David Wilson asked a blessing for the food and the woman who had cooked it, ending his awkward plea with a soft amen.

Cara squeezed his hand. "Thank you, my darling, that was wonderful. Would you carve?"

This time when David picked up the carving knife, it didn't feel lethal in his hands.

"I would be honored."

After that, time passed in a series of moments that would forever be in his heart.

The flickering candlelight softening the passage of time on their faces.

The dark, blood-red wine as he filled their crystal goblets.

The purity of the *clink* as they toasted their future.

The look of joy in Cara's eyes when he took his first bite of roast.

The sensation of crisp, sugary crust, warm, cinnamon apples and the cold, silken sensation of vanilla ice cream as they ate the dessert, apple pie à la mode.

Finally, David pushed back his dessert plate with a groan.

"I have never had such wonderful food in my entire life."

Cara beamed, then held out her hand. "Come with me. The evening isn't over yet."

He groaned again. "Whatever it is, I better not have to eat it."

She laughed. "Come on. You won't be disappointed. I promise."

They got as far as the living room when Cara ordered him to take a seat.

"Just remember to save room for me," she said, and headed for the television across the room.

While David watched, she slipped a video from a case and put it into the VCR, then took a seat beside David on the sofa and punched the remote.

He grinned. "What's playing?"

"Your daughter's life."

The grin slid sideways. "They're videos of Bethany?"

She nodded. "And later Valerie and Tyler will be in them, too."

He looked at the screen, his expression fixed. When the first images appeared, she heard him grunt as if someone had just kicked him in the belly. It was easy to see why. Ray had taken it the day of her release after giving birth to Bethany. A nurse was wheeling her out of the hospital with the baby in her arms.

"Oh, Lord, I always forget how long my hair was then," Cara said, but words were beyond David.

He saw the sadness of her smile and knew it was because of him. Then the camera panned to the baby she was holding. The focus was bad and the picture kept bouncing, as if the photographer was walking as he filmed, but there was no denying the tiny little face peering out from the blankets, nor the dark wisps of hair framing her features.

"Even then, she looked like you," Cara said. "It was at

once a blessing and a pain. She was a constant reminder of how much I loved you and how much I'd lost."

"Lord," David muttered.

Cara rubbed her hand across his shoulder in a comforting motion.

"It's okay, honey. Just watch. If you have questions, ask. Otherwise, most of the stuff is self-explanatory."

He leaned forward, his elbows resting on his knees. For the next two hours, he was virtually mute. When that video was over, he looked up with a start, like a man who had been rudely awakened.

"That's not all, is it?"

He'd only seen the first year of her life. She had just been learning to walk.

Cara was already up and changing the tape.

"Oh, no. There are far more than you could possibly watch in one night. You haven't even gotten to the part where she finally gets a whole spoonful of cereal into her mouth without spilling it."

"You have that on tape?"

"Yes, thanks to Ray."

He swallowed around the lump in his throat. "It seems I have a lot to thank Ray Justice for."

"Don't be sad, David. I couldn't bear it if this hurt you. I only wanted you to see the little milestones in her life. They weren't all caught on tape, but enough were so that you will see part of her growing up."

"Not sad. Just so damned sorry."

She hesitated before putting the next tape in the VCR.

"No regrets, remember?"

He sighed. "I remember."

"Okay. Then here goes."

And so David sat, reliving his daughter's life in silence, from birthday parties and swimming lessons, to learning to ride a bike. When the camera caught her taking a spill, David flinched. He watched her get up crying—saw a tiny trickle of blood on her knee and the pain in his chest was so great he thought he would die. She'd hurt and someone else had wiped away her tears.

He saw her hit a home run at a softball game and the joy on her face as she rounded third base to home made him laugh aloud.

Cara hugged him, her cheek against his shoulder, but she remained silent, answering questions only when he asked, letting him see and accept this in his own way—in his own time.

Bethany's life unfolded beneath his gaze, from the gap in her smile when she lost her first tooth to her first date. He saw it all, unaware that Cara had fallen asleep beside him. When the tape in the VCR ran out, he glanced at his watch, then at Cara. She was asleep on the sofa beside him, and no wonder. It was ten minutes to three in the morning.

He switched off the TV then picked her up and carried her to their bed. As he laid her down, she roused briefly.

"Ssh, just sleep," he said softly, as he took off her shoes.

She rolled over with a sigh. He pulled a sheet over her shoulders, not bothering to help her undress. He'd slept many nights in his clothes and it hadn't changed the gravity of the earth. She could surely do the same. But when he started to undress and get into bed beside her, he hesitated, then stopped. Knowing himself too well, he knew there was no way he would be able to sleep. Not after the evening he'd just had.

Instead, he moved quietly through the house and

began to clear the dinner dishes from the table. There in the quiet of the house with the memories of his baby girl's face in his heart, he washed the dishes from the meal that Cara had prepared. The hot soapy water felt good on his skin, cleaning the ugliness of his past just as he cleaned the china. Uncertain where to put the things he had washed, he left the china in neat stacks on the kitchen counter instead, then hung up the dish towel and turned out the light.

As he exited, he stopped in the doorway and turned, looking back at the room to make sure he'd left nothing undone. The table was clean. The dishes were shadowy stacks against a darkened counter—the curtained windows like judgmental eyes looking back at him. He shuddered, and as he did, sensed he wasn't alone in his inability to sleep. Somewhere, his brother was also awake—and thinking of ways to kill him.

Frank Wilson was a haunted man. The past year had been one disappointment after another, and with each failure to get to David, his frustration had risen, multiplying into a dozen different symptoms.

Spicy food made him nauseous and he couldn't remember when he hadn't had a headache. He had intermittent bouts of insomnia that would often last for days and when his body finally gave out and he could sleep, it wasn't rest. Instead, he seemed destined to relive the failures of his past.

Inevitably, the dreams always spiraled into one horrible, recurring nightmare—of fire and burning flesh, of the mind-bending pain that came afterward. His brother's traitorous face was etched in his brain and he would know no peace until David was dead.

Tonight wasn't any different. The silhouette of the Colorado Rockies were visible from his hotel room. They rose above the landscape like jagged rips in the horizon. But the grandeur of the presence completely missed him. He rubbed a weary hand across his face and wished for peace.

At night, without his wig and mustache, he couldn't hide from himself. The face looking back at him in the mirror was the same man who was on the run, not the cocky New York cop he was pretending to be. He hated that face. He hated the man behind it.

He paced before the windows, ignoring the traffic on the street below for the blanket of star-littered sky. It was nights like this that he missed Australia. It seemed that the sky there was larger and the stars closer. Martha had loved to camp out with him, lying on their bedrolls beneath the wide open spaces and sleeping beneath the stars.

His chin jutted angrily as he slammed a fist against the windowsill.

Get over it, sucker. Those times are gone forever.

"Damn it," he muttered, and sank onto the side of the bed, then covered his face with his hands, unconsciously tracing the road map of burn scars with his fingertips.

A car horn sounded on the street below, and in the distance, he could hear approaching sirens.

God, but he missed the quiet of the outback. Maybe retiring to Florida wasn't such a good idea after all. Quiet would be the last thing he'd find in such a place.

Swamps and alligators—oranges and hurricanes.

Hundreds of thousands of people whose first language was not English.

Old people who'd moved there to live out what was left of their lives.

He sighed. Damn it all to hell, wasn't there a place left on earth to which he could belong?

He laid back on the bed and closed his eyes, and while he was feeling sorry for himself, exhaustion came and wrapped him in a blanket of deep, dreamless sleep.

The unexpected night of rest had given Frank a whole new outlook on life. He awoke with the feeling that he could conquer the world. For the first time in months, he was confident of what he was doing. As he dressed, he began to lay out his plans for the day. Maybe another round of practice at the firing range, a good meal around mid-afternoon; after that, find a good travel agent. Another night or so here in Denver and it would be time to move on.

This hotel suite was a far cry from the roach motel he'd been at in L.A., but then, he'd had few options. It had been easier to disappear into the seedy life of a city than to explain away the bandages he'd been wearing at the time. Now that they were gone, his lifestyle had taken a big change for the better.

He sat down on the sofa, opened his laptop, plugged in the modem and logged on to the Internet. His hands were steady as he opened his e-mail, but his heart was pounding. He'd been sending the same message to the same mailbox each day, certain that he would eventually get the answer he wanted. It began to download, zapping one message after the other through a medium he still found amazing. He'd seen a lot of things in his lifetime, but in his opinion, the public availability of the Internet was the most life-altering one of them all.

The little You've Got Mail logo centered on the screen. He scanned the contents rapidly, deleting any and everything that didn't have David Wilson's name on it. Thirty-nine messages later he leaned back with a frustrated sigh. Still no answer.

He shrugged. It didn't matter. It wasn't like he was on a time schedule. Hell. Time was all he had. He could wait.

He typed in the same message that he'd been sending regularly each day and then pressed send. When the process was finished, he shut down the computer and set it aside. His stomach was growling and he had a need to feel the sun on his face and the wind in his hair.

A few minutes later, he exited the hotel and strode to the curb to hail a cab. As he did, he heard the shrill and strident voice of an insistent child. He looked out of curiosity and suddenly found himself on the receiving end of a little girl's delight.

"Ganpa! Ganpa!"

He froze. The little girl, who couldn't have been more than two or three, had wrapped herself around his leg.

"Up!" she shrieked. "Want up!"

Before he could react, a young woman emerged from a doorway, her expression frantic.

"Martie! Martie! Where are you?" she shouted.

Frank turned again, this time waving to get the woman's attention.

"Lady…is this your kid?"

"Oh, my God!" the woman cried, and then bolted toward them. Seconds later she was on her knees, unwinding the child from Frank's leg. Then she stood and picked her up in her arms. "Bad girl! You ran away from Mommy."

The baby's lower lip slipped forward in an instinctive pout.

"Ganpa!" she muttered.

For the first time, the woman got a good look at Frank's face, and as she did, a smile of recognition replaced her frown.

"Oh, my goodness," she said. "No wonder Martie ran to you."

"I'm sorry?" Frank said, certain that he'd never seen them before in his life.

"No, I'm the one who should be apologizing," the woman said, and then held out her hand. "My name is Beth Stalling. This is my daughter, Martha. We call her Martie, for short. You look enough like my father-in-law to be his twin." Then she hugged her daughter to her. "And Martie loves her grandpa Jules. She must have thought you were him."

Frank shook her hand, but he had quit listening to what she was saying after hearing the little girl's name. Martha. Martha of the blue eyes and platinum blond hair. And this little girl had blue eyes and almost cotton-white hair, just like *his* Martha.

"…so I hope you understand," the woman finished.

Frank blinked, suddenly realizing that she'd still been talking.

"Of course. No harm done," he said briefly, and then something—maybe the last good part of his soul—prompted an action quite out of character. He reached for the little girl's hair and lightly fingered the soft, cottony whorls.

"I'm thinking Grandpa Jules is a very fortunate man."

The woman beamed. "Why, thank you."

Suddenly uncomfortable with the whole incident, he

muttered something about being late for a meeting and headed for the curb. Saved from having to make further conversation by the immediate arrival of a cab, he slid into the back seat and actually breathed a sigh of relief as the door slammed behind him.

Unwilling to be reminded of a life he'd chosen to forgo, he wouldn't look back. Yet the farther they drove, the heavier his heart became. He even toyed with the notion of walking away now. Just quitting on the idea of revenge and losing himself in America. He could do it. He'd done it before. Everyone knew that you could buy anything in America for the right amount of money. It would be cheap to buy a new identity and live out the rest of his life in relative comfort. But as he glanced at the window, he caught a glimpse of his reflection and realized it was not his own. With his mask in place, the man beneath did not exist. But night always came and the mask always came off.

The notion of forgive and forget quickly disappeared. David had wronged him. He had to pay.

"Let me out here," he told the cabby, tossed him a handful of dollars and all but bolted from the cab.

His steps were hasty as he started down the street, as if he was trying to outrun a new enemy. But the farther he went, the more he realized that there was no escape for him as long as David still lived.

Once the thought was firmly in his mind, he began to relax. His steps slowed, his thinking cleared. He spied a travel agent on the opposite corner of the street. Now was as good a time as any to make his plans. But as he stood at the corner, waiting for the light to change, he knew it would be a long, long time before he forgot the silken texture of baby hair against the palm of his hand.

By the time night came to Denver, Frank Wilson was long gone. As his plane landed in Chicago, he had security of knowing that the next four days were securely mapped out in his mind. This time when he got to a hotel, he was digging in until he heard from David.

Cara came out of the kitchen with a vase of flowers in her hand, heading toward the dining room table. Every wood surface in the house gleamed from the polishing she'd given it, and wonderful scents were coming from the kitchen. In spite of the enticing aromas, David knew they were not for him.

Last night, just as Cara had come out of the shower, she'd glanced at the calendar and gasped. The planning committee for the annual fall church bazaar was being held at her house. And the meeting was going to be tomorrow! She'd known about it for weeks. But with all the excitement of David's arrival, she'd completely forgotten the date and that she was expected to serve lunch in the process.

He'd laughed and told her not to worry, that he'd help her straighten up the house, but that was before he had completely understood.

Twelve women were coming to her home. Twelve women who had husbands and children and homes of their own. Twelve women who would be judging Cara's worth on this earth by how clean she kept her house and how tasty and unique her menu would be.

She had set the alarm for six-thirty and was up before it went off. And she hadn't just straightened the house. In David's opinion, she'd done everything short of rebuild it. Wisely, he'd chosen a simple bowl of cereal for breakfast and then when he was finished, washed and dried the dish and put it back where it belonged.

By the time she had moved into the kitchen to begin preparing the food she would serve, he'd made another wise decision and dragged the lawn mower out of the shed and begun mowing the front yard. Her pleasure at his choice of occupation was obvious when, an hour later, she brought him a cold drink and gave him a kiss that rocked him back on his heels.

"The yard is looking wonderful," she said. "I've got to run. The oven timer is about to go off."

"I may not get through in the back before they come. Is that all right?"

"Oh, sure. It won't matter if you're still mowing."

He sighed with relief. If he was still working in the back, he would have a very good excuse to absent himself from their presence.

By the time he had finished in the front and come in the back door for another drink, the food in different stages of preparation looked like something from a five-star restaurant. The elegance of the presentation was surpassed only by the aroma.

"Wow, Cara. I didn't know you could do stuff like this."

She gave him a harried smile and shrugged.

"You'd be surprised what a female can do in an emergency."

He shook his head without comment. This church bazaar had taken on the undertones of a life-and-death situation. Her emergencies were certainly different from the ones that he'd faced, but something told him that it would be easier to deal with an international terrorist than to face these twelve women.

"I made you some food," Cara said. "Although you are certainly welcome to sit and eat with us at noon."

"No," David said, and then countered the abruptness of his answer with a smile. "But thank you for inviting me."

She sighed. "I wouldn't want to eat with us, either. I can't believe I'd forgotten this."

David shoved aside her hair and kissed the back of her neck.

"I'll eat later, after I've finished mowing the back yard, okay?" Then he added, "And, if you're not finished with your meeting by that time, I'll be eating in the kitchen."

She laughed and tweaked his nose.

"Coward."

"Devout and proud of it," he said, and then turned at the sound of a car coming up the drive. "Looks like your first guest is already arriving."

Cara turned to the window and peered out.

"Oh, Lord! It would be Hillary. She's the most critical of the lot."

He put his finger under the edge of her chin and lightly pushed up.

"Chin up, baby. Just remember that all the time they're looking at you and the house, you've got a man in your yard who likes to jump your bones."

Having said that, he gave her a devilish grin and winked, then walked out the back door just as the front doorbell began to ring.

David's words were still in her head as she rushed to the front door. Thankful that thoughts were not visible, she smoothed her hair and then straightened her blouse before opening the door.

"Hillary! You look gorgeous as always. Come in."

Hillary Redford sauntered into the house. Cara knew that Hillary was well aware her friends dreaded her arrival and she liked it that way. It gave her a sense of importance to think they valued her approval enough to be worried.

"How nice everything looks," she said, raking the gleaming wood and fresh flowers with quiet approval.

Cara resisted the urge to snort beneath her breath. Nice? It looked great and she knew it.

"Have a seat, will you? I need to take one more thing out of the oven and then I'll be right back."

Hillary sat, tentatively testing the cushions of the sofa and finding the one that suited her best. Within moments, Cara was back, and one by one, the other eleven women began to arrive. The noise level rose with each arrival until the front part of Cara's house was as noisy as a Saturday night at the local bar.

Cara flitted among them, serving dainty little appetizers and flutes of white wine, knowing that each time she left the room, they resumed their conversation, which was all about her.

As they nibbled and talked, Cara finished carrying the last of the food to the dining room where she'd set up a buffet on the sideboard. With one last glance to make sure she'd forgotten nothing important, she went to the living room to call them to eat.

"Ladies, the food is ready. Let's adjourn to the dining room where you can continue your discussion about my life and if somewhere in the midst of it someone should happen to remember we are planning a bazaar, then that would be wonderful."

There was a moment of embarrassed silence and then everyone laughed while Hillary felt the need to explain.

"Oh, Cara, you funny thing. We weren't really talking *about* you, just curious about the new man in your life. After all, you can't really blame us for that."

Cara smiled and then led the way into the dining room, comfortable with the fact that she'd taken the wind out of their sails by acknowledging the gossip and then ignoring it.

"Mm, everything smells wonderful," one of them said, while Hillary Redford silently applauded the elegance of the dishes she'd fixed.

"Thank you," Cara said. "Although they're really simple, they are some of my favorite recipes."

As they began to round the buffet and fill their plates, their chatter lessened. And for the first time, the sound of David mowing in the back yard could be heard. Hillary was the first to comment.

"I noticed your yard was freshly mowed when I came to the door," she said.

"Yes, but David's not quite through in the back."

"Who is David?" Hillary asked.

"Bethany's father," Cara said simply.

Twelve pairs of eyes turned instantly toward her. Twelve mouths dropped to an equal degree of shock.

"Oh, I've just got to have a look," Hillary said, and set her plate on the table without filling it and headed for the kitchen.

Eleven other women followed suit without waiting to see if Cara minded that they were trooping through the kitchen where she'd been preparing the food. She smiled to herself and followed, thankful that almost everything she'd been cooking with had been cleaned up and put away or was in the dishwasher waiting to be washed.

But when she got to the kitchen, she couldn't see outside. Every window in the room was lined with women who seemed too dumbstruck to move.

"That's him?" Hillary asked, and did something quite unlike herself and smeared the glass when she put her finger against the window to point.

Cara peeked over Hillary's shoulder.

"Yep, that's him."

"Have mercy," someone whispered. "He looks like that actor…oh, what's his name? He was in that movie *Sniper* and a whole bunch of others."

Someone offered the name Berenger.

"Yes! That's it! Berenger! He looks like Tom Berenger."

Then they all turned and stared at Cara as if they'd never seen her before—then turned again, their faces glued to the sight.

Cara crossed her arms as she watched them, resisting the urge to laugh. In spite of all her cleaning and cooking, a bare-chested man had been the hit of the day. And she couldn't blame them for gawking.

"Um, Cara?"

It was Susan Hanover, the banker's wife, who was standing near the door and waving her hand to be seen in all the shuffle.

"Yes?"

"Is he that, uh, *fit* all over?"

The eleven other women turned, all but salivating as they awaited the answer.

Cara smiled politely, as if they'd just asked for the recipe for her cake, although she knew her cooking was no match for David, naked or dressed. And the fact that he wasn't wearing a shirt and that his shorts were riding low on his hips didn't hurt. That hard, flat belly and that beautiful face were hard to ignore.

"Yes."

"Oh…my… God," Susan moaned, and leaned against the wall as if pretending to faint.

The question broke the ice of curiosity. The questions began coming at her from right and left.

"What does he do? Where has he been? Is he going to stay? Are you going to marry him? Is he going to come inside?"

Cara just waved away the questions.

"Food's getting cold," she said, and went into the dining room.

One by one, courtesy demanded that they follow, but when they finally all sat down to eat, they were looking at Cara with new respect. And as they chewed their first bites, they were thinking of their respective husbands, most of them soft, overweight and going bald.

After a few minutes, they seemed to settle down and as they talked and ate, they actually settled on most of the planning committees that they'd come to put in place. It wasn't until Cara was serving cake that she heard the back door slam. David was obviously through mowing the yard.

Again, twelve women froze; in the act of putting cake in their mouths, they seemed to hold their breaths, hoping against all hope they would get a closer glimpse. David gave them way more than they bargained for.

Still bare-chested and carrying his T-shirt in his hands, he stuck his head into the room. Everywhere he was bare was glistening with sweat, and his thick, dark hair was spiky and damp.

"Cara, I'm through with the back yard. I'm going to shower before I eat." Then he gave the woman an all-encompassing smile. "I sure hope you pretty ladies saved something for me."

Having dropped the verbal bomb in their midst, he sauntered off, giving them an all-too-generous view of his tight buns and long legs.

Susan, the banker's wife, laid her fork on her cake plate and covered her face with her hands.

"Lord, forgive me for my thoughts," she muttered.

They all burst into laughter, glad that she was the one who'd said what they'd all been thinking.

They lingered through coffee. Some even ate a second piece of cake just to prolong their presence in the house. When David finally emerged from the bedroom, he was dressed in slacks and loafers and a blue knit shirt.

"He looks good in clothes, too," Susan muttered, as he passed them by on his way to the kitchen.

David heard her and grinned. Well aware of the fuss that he'd caused, he didn't know whether to make himself scarce or go say hello.

Cara saved him the trouble of deciding by following him into the kitchen.

"We saved you a piece of cake," she said.

"Sure you want me in there?" he asked.

She sighed and then shrugged. "You'd have to be blind, deaf and dumb not to know that they're quite taken with you."

"Oh?"

"Yes. It started when they saw you naked."

"Naked?"

"Honey, when a man has nothing on but a pair of

shorts and wears them as well as you do, women can figure out the rest."

He grinned.

"So you may as well come in and finish them off."

His grin widened as he followed her into the other room.

"So, you did save me some cake after all," David said.

"Here! Sit here!" one of them said, and jumped up from her chair and gave him her seat.

"Oh, no, but thank you," he said. "A gentleman never sits in a room full of ladies. You sit yourself right back down. I'll eat my cake standing up. That way I can eat more."

Just the knowledge that the cake they'd been eating was now going into his stomach was all it took for twelve pairs of eyes to stare at his shirt, remembering the hard, washboard surface of his belly underneath.

"Have you finished?" David asked.

Twelve startled women looked at his face and then at their plates.

"With your meeting, I mean," David said.

Cara laughed. He was playing them like a fiddle.

"David Wilson, you are awful," she said. "Stop teasing them this minute, do you hear?"

He grinned and then leaned over and kissed her square on the mouth before taking another bite of the cake.

Twelve sighs of appreciation rose in accompaniment.

Cara smiled to herself.

Her luncheon had been a success.

Chapter 8

David woke up before sunrise, savoring the quiet of the room and the warmth of the woman snuggled against him. It was Friday and his time with Cara was already almost gone. Bethany and her family would be home the day after tomorrow and he would be in D.C., and he still hadn't told Cara he was leaving. Truth was, he was scared to tell her. They'd fought horribly the last time he'd announced his exit from her life. He didn't want it to happen again.

His thoughts scattered as Cara sighed and rolled onto her back. He watched her eyelids fluttering slightly and knew she was waking. Unable to wait, he leaned over and kissed her the rest of the way awake.

Cara stretched, then wrapped her arms around his neck.

"What a wonderful way to wake up," she said.

"Are you good and awake?"

She smiled. "I think so, why?"

"I don't want it to be said that I took advantage of an unconscious woman."

She laughed as he pulled her nightgown over her head and tossed it aside, then rolled over on top of her, pinning her to the mattress with the weight of his body.

"Are you paying attention?" he growled.

Another laugh bubbled up her throat.

"Woman… I'm trying to be serious here."

Suddenly, the laughter was over. Cara had her legs locked around his waist and her arms around his neck.

"How serious?" she whispered.

"Oh, baby, let me show you the ways."

Without foreplay.

Without sweet-nothing whispers.

Without warning.

Between one breath and the next, he was inside her.

Cara would look back on it later and realize that there was as much desperation in the act as there was love. But for now, she had no focus save the man above her and the hard, rhythmic pounding of his flesh against hers.

One minute spilled into the next and then the next and just when Cara thought she would die from the intensity, it shattered within her, splintering the power and flooding her body with a bone-melting ecstasy. She lay within his arms, her eyes closed, her heartbeat little more than a ricochet of its normal rhythm, while savoring the sensations from the act of perfect love.

She didn't know it wasn't over.

David paused, raising himself above her on tightly tensed arms, as if judging her expression. She groaned then sighed.

At that point, he seemed to shift gears.

She opened her eyes and looked up.

One slow, sensuous stroke after another, David started again, and all the while, he was watching her face. In her entire life, Cara had never felt so vulnerable or so loved.

A long minute passed, and then another, and time seemed to stop. There was nothing in their world but the sensual body-to-body hammer, seeking that fleeting and volatile burst of sweet pleasure. Sweat beaded across David's forehead and dropped into the valley between her breasts as, again, they danced the dance of love.

One moment Cara was aware of David above her, and then her mind suddenly blanked. Clutching his forearms, she arched beneath him, her eyes wide, unseeing. Shattered by the force of her climax, her moan became a scream.

It was the sound as much as the spasms of her body that sent David over the edge, spilling forty years of loneliness and denial into the woman beneath him.

Moments later, he collapsed with a gut-wrenching groan and then rolled, taking her with him so that she would not be burdened any longer with his weight. What had just happened was so perfect, he didn't even feel twinges from the stitches on his shoulder. So they lay locked within each other's arms, awaiting the end of the world or a steadying heartbeat, whichever came first.

Sometime later, she groaned and raised her head.

"David… I…"

He arched an eyebrow. "You're welcome."

She snorted lightly beneath her breath and teasingly pulled at his hair.

"Are you going to brag?"

He grinned. "Honey, after that, if I could walk, I'd be strutting."

She laughed. It was the most perfect sunrise of her life.

"Authorities are still searching for the perpetrators of the ongoing tri-county crime spree. The trio struck again around midnight last night, robbing the clerk at an all-night quick stop and beating him unconscious. The clerk, a thirty-two-year-old father of two, is in the intensive care unit of Burney Hospital. He is in critical condition."

Cara paused in the act of putting on her makeup and stepped out of the bathroom into the bedroom where David was watching the news on the wall-mounted television opposite her bed.

"That poor man…and his family," she added. "I can't believe they haven't caught those awful people yet."

David nodded without answering, his thoughts in a whirl. This wasn't something that SPEAR got mixed up in, yet his sense of justice was being sorely tried. Unless he'd missed a report, this was the third incident in the area since he'd arrived at Cara's house and the sixth in less than two weeks. That was close to one robbery a day. He knew how criminals like that thought. They were cocky now, confident of their ability to get away with anything, even murder. Besides the countless assaults, there were two deaths attributed to the criminals. If this young man died, it would make three. Unconsciously, his fingers curled into fists and his expression darkened.

Cara leaned over his shoulder and pressed a kiss on his cheek.

"You can't fix everything, darling," she said softly.

The gentleness in her voice touched him. He turned, pulling her into his lap and nuzzling the side of her neck before giving her a long, silent hug.

Cara sensed something was bothering him and suspected it wasn't all connected to the broadcast they'd just heard.

"Is there anything you want to talk about?" she asked.

He froze. Damn, she *was* good. There was plenty he needed to say, but now was not the time.

"No, honey…at least not now." He lifted his head and made himself smile. "You look good enough to eat, but I'd settle for a hamburger instead."

"Okay, David, I'll play your game. I'll be the silly, airheaded blonde who's blindly unaware of underlying currents, and you be the big, strong hero who needs to protect the little woman from herself."

A startled look crossed his face before he could hide it. She'd read him right down to the bone, and it shamed him that he couldn't deny it.

In a moment of blinding pain, understanding came to Cara.

Ah, God, he's going to leave me. But instead of crying, she slid off his lap and straightened her slacks and shirt. "Just remember that games eventually come to an end. At that time, I expect the truth. Deal?"

She fixed him with a steely gaze and held out her hand.

He sighed and then stood.

"Deal," he said, enclosing her fingers in his grasp.

Fear shifted within her, but she wouldn't give in. Not now. Not when they had precious little time left.

"Are you ready to go into Chiltingham?" David asked.

She nodded. "I just need to get my grocery list from the kitchen."

"I'll meet you out front," he said.

"Want to take my car?" she asked.

He hesitated, then shook his head. "No, let's take mine. I need to get gas, anyway."

Cara couldn't look at him yet. More proof he was getting ready to leave. Again, her heart twisted, but she refused to comment.

"Be right there," she said, and walked out of the bedroom before she made a fool of herself.

All the way to the kitchen she was blinking back tears, but by the time she walked out of the house, her emotions were under control. David was standing at the passenger side of his car, the door ajar, waiting for her to enter.

"Why, thank you, sir," she said, as she slid into the seat.

"My pleasure," he countered, as he closed the door and then circled the car to get in. He started the engine and then drove out of her drive onto the blacktop road. "Where to first, ma'am?"

"I'd say Hawaii, but I don't think you have enough gas."

He heard the desolation in her voice and reached over and squeezed her hand.

"Not this time around, I don't, baby. But maybe soon. Have you ever been to Hawaii?"

She sighed. "No, but I've always wanted to see if the water is as blue as they say."

"It is."

She smiled sadly. "I should have known you'd already been there."

He thought of the drug runner he'd chased for six

weeks before cornering him in an inlet off the eastern coast of Oahu.

"It wasn't a vacation," he said softly.

"Oh."

"When do you want to go?" he asked. "This fall? Next spring? You name the time and we're there."

Her eyes widened. "Are you serious?"

He pulled over to the side of the road and put the car in park, then took her in his arms.

"Yes, I'm serious. I'm committed. I'm in love. And I was going to wait until tonight to ask, but something tells me the time is now."

"Ask what?" she said.

"If I'm able to come back…and I will do everything in my power to come back…will you marry me?"

It was the last but best thing she would have expected him to say. Good sense demanded more time with the man before committing the rest of her life to him, but the good sense she'd used before had cost her forty years without him. She wasn't going to do it again.

"Yes."

David was all ready to plead his case. Her positive, one-word answer took him aback.

"You will?"

She nodded.

"Just like that? Without knowing if—"

She put her hand over his mouth, silencing the rest of what he'd started to say.

"Don't say it aloud. Don't give the words power, David. Just do what you have to do and come back to me when it's over."

"Ah, God," he groaned, and took her in his arms. "You won't be sorry, I swear."

"I told you no the first time and have regretted it for forty years. I'm not about to make the same mistake twice."

"Hallelujah," he muttered, and kissed her hard on the mouth.

A speeding car passed them by as they embraced, the driver blaring his horn as a taunt to the lovers.

Cara jumped at the sound, and David groaned and pulled back.

"Who was that?" David asked, as he stared at the disappearing taillights of the car.

Cara sighed. "Um, I'm not sure, but it looked a bit like Harold Belton's car."

David grinned. "Hasty Harold?"

"The same. And wipe that satisfied smirk off your face."

David put the car into gear and then pulled onto the highway.

"I wasn't smirking."

"You were smirking."

"It was more of a—"

"You were smirking, David. Have the grace to admit it."

He glanced at her, his eyes glittering darkly, a wide grin on his face. At that moment, Cara saw the young boy that he'd been. She couldn't help but smile back.

"Okay, I was smirking," David said.

"I know. Thank you for being honest."

"I was smirking because I got the girl and he didn't."

"True," Cara said. "But you had an unfair advantage coming in."

"What? You mean Bethany?"

"No. A flat belly and a dynamite kiss."

His smile widened.

"You're smirking again," Cara warned.

"You just keep on talking like that and by the time we get to town, I'll be ready to do that strut I promised you earlier."

She threw back her head and laughed. God, but she loved this man.

A short while later, he pulled up in front of the supermarket, but he didn't kill the engine.

"Aren't you coming in?" Cara asked.

"Not right away. I need to run a quick errand. It won't take me long. I'll be back before you finish, okay?"

"Sure. Just look for me in the aisles. I'll probably still be shopping. I want to get some food to make a special meal for Bethany and her family on Sunday." Her face lit up. "Oh, David, she's going to be ecstatic about you… and about us."

Sunday. He wasn't going to be here on Sunday. Damn. He had to tell her, but not now.

"I'll find you," David said. "Count on it."

She flashed him a smile. "I love you very much, you know."

"I love you, too, now scoot or I'll be tempted to dash your reputation even more by kissing you again." He pointed to the people going in and out of the store. "And we're not exactly alone this time."

"So what," she said, and gave him a quick kiss before getting out of the car. "If I finish before you get back, I'll wait for you inside where it's cooler, okay?"

"I'll be here before you're through, I promise."

She nodded and then shut the door behind her.

David watched her until she was inside the store, then he backed up and drove to the main street. If memory served, he distinctly remembered a jewelry store a couple of blocks down on the corner. He wasn't leaving Cara again without his ring on her finger.

Ten minutes later, Cara had yet to get down the first aisle. Two women from her church had stopped to ask her if it was true that Ray wasn't Bethany's father. Before she could answer, they'd followed that question with another. Was it also true that the real father was staying at Cara's house?

Cara had answered truthfully without elaborating and told them goodbye, knowing the moment she turned the corner they were going to rake her reputation over the coals. Instead of being bothered about it, she just smiled. She wouldn't trade David's presence in her life for anything, not even a perfect reputation. Besides that, she was more than slightly amused at being thought of as a loose woman. It certainly beat the loneliness and tedium of the last three years of her life.

Glancing over her shoulder, she saw the two women huddled together at the end of the aisle and looking her way. Impishly, she waved. They scurried away like flushed quail.

Still chuckling to herself, she continued with her shopping and was halfway up the next aisle when she heard a commotion at the front of the store. Remembering the large display of canned goods near the door, she assumed someone must have knocked it over and gave it no more thought.

Then she heard a woman scream and another start to cry. Those sounds changed everything. Afraid that someone had surely been hurt, she hurried toward the front of the store, but it wasn't an accident, as she feared.

As she rounded the corner, she found herself face to face with an armed trio of men. The store was being robbed!

Instinctively, she pivoted and started to run when someone grabbed her by the arm and dragged her toward the group of shoppers they'd already corralled.

"Get over there and shut up," the man said.

"Ow," Cara cried, as he twisted the flesh on her arm.

"Shut up, woman, or I'll give you something to cry about."

Cara flinched as he shoved her toward the others. She did as she was told. And even though she was standing here, watching three armed men tear through the cash registers for the money, the reality of the situation had yet to sink in. It wasn't until one of the armed men shoved his gun in the manager's face and demanded he open the safe that it hit her who they must be.

Less than an hour earlier, she'd been horrified by the television broadcast of the poor clerk who had been robbed and was in critical condition, and now she had become one of their latest victims.

Anxiously, she glanced out the window, praying for David's return. She knew he would come, and she also suspected that he was, quite possibly, their only hope.

"Move!" one of the robbers suddenly shouted, and as he did, the other two armed men herded the hostages toward the back of the store.

Cara's panic renewed. *Dear God, don't let this be the day I die.*

David slapped a credit card down on the counter, smiling to himself as the jeweler slipped a small velvet box into a sack. It was, without doubt, the most important purchase he'd ever made, and it had taken him less than ten minutes to make up his mind.

"I think your lady is going to be quite pleased with your selection," the jeweler said, as he handed David his credit card.

"So do I," David said, and hurried out of the store.

He got into the car, the smile still on his face. But by the time he was pulling into the supermarket parking lot, a sense of urgency had replaced his glee. It was that same hair-raising, flesh-crawling feeling that he'd had so many times before, and it didn't make sense until he tried to get into the store.

When he realized the front doors were locked, he began to frown. As he cupped his hands against the window and peered inside, he saw the drawers of the cash registers were all ajar. Added to that was the fact that not a shopper or clerk was in sight. It was gut instinct that made him go back to the car for a lock pick and his gun.

A woman drove up just as he was heading to the store.

"Do you have a cell phone?" he asked.

She nodded.

"Then call nine-one-one. The store is being robbed."

She looked askance, staring wildly at the gun he was holding and then at his face.

"Not by me," he said shortly. "The doors are locked and the cash registers are open. I'm going to try and get in, but I need you to help me, understand?"

She nodded, her expression startled.

"After you make the call, drive your car to the street and keep everyone else away. We don't need any innocent bystanders getting hurt, do we?"

"No! Oh, my! I can't believe..."

"Lady! Just make the call and then get the hell out of the way."

She bolted for her car.

Satisfied she would do as he'd asked, he headed toward the front doors again. He wouldn't let himself think of what might have already happened. Instead, he palmed the lock pick and with a few deft strokes, opened the door and quietly slipped inside.

He stood against the wall, his gun raised, listening for something that would tell him where everyone had been taken. The silence was more horrifying than any scream would have ever been. When he finally heard angry shouts coming from the back of the store, he closed his eyes momentarily, recalling the layout of the floor plan from his earlier visit, then started to move.

"Damn it, Travis, shut that woman up now or I'm gonna do it for you," Darryl Wayne shouted.

Cara flinched as the short man, the one who was shouting, grabbed a can of peas from a shelf and threw it at the hostages. Cara ducked, covering her head as the can sailed past her ear, only to hit one of the grocery clerks on the head. The woman never saw it coming, and when it hit her, it knocked her out cold. She dropped to the floor in a slump.

Cara scrambled over to her side, trying to staunch the flow of blood with the tail of her shirt, and was backhanded for the trouble.

"I told you people not to move and I meant it."

Pain-filled tears blurred her vision as she grabbed the side of her face. Already it was beginning to throb.

"Please," she begged. "Her head…it's bleeding badly."

Darryl grabbed her by the hair and yanked her to her feet.

"Look at me!"

Cara stared, too frightened to move.

"Can you see my lips?"

She nodded, wincing when he tightened his grip on her hair.

"I'm telling you for the last time, don't move. Can you do that?"

She nodded again.

He shoved her hard. She fell backward over the unconscious woman's feet, then onto the floor. From where she was lying, she could see the third man in the office with the manager, holding a gun to his head as the manager opened the safe. Never in her life had she been so certain she was going to die. The moment that safe came open, they were all expendable.

Oh, God! Oh, David! Where are you?

"Hurry up with that safe!" Darryl shouted. "We ain't got all day."

The third man stepped out of the office. "He says he can't get it open."

"Bull!" Darryl yelled, turned toward the hostages and fired at the nearest one, who happened to be the Methodist pastor's wife. The bullet tore through her shoulder and ricocheted against the concrete wall behind her. She slumped over without a sound. "One down, ten to go," he yelled. "Now see how fast he can open that safe."

The third man grinned and stepped back into the office. A horrified silence permeated the area. No one dared look up for fear they would be next. And because their heads were bent, they didn't see the man who slipped through the open door of the loading area and disappeared behind a stack of wooden pallets.

David's gut was in a knot. He'd been only feet away from the door when he'd heard the shot, and even though he knew there was bound to be other hostages, his heart sank. All he could think was, *Please, God, don't let it be Cara.*

A second later he was peering through the half-open door. He counted eleven hostages, two unconscious, maybe dead. When he saw the top of Cara's head and realized she wasn't one of the bodies on the floor, he said a quick prayer of thanksgiving, then slipped into the room behind a stack of pallets.

Two gunmen had their backs to him, and they were still talking to a third, who he figured must be in an office somewhere nearby. He glanced at his watch, trying to figure out how long it would be before the sound of police sirens alerted the men to their arrival. He'd been inside for more than four minutes, and if the police were on the ball, he didn't have much time.

Suddenly, a third man came into view, holding another at gunpoint. David froze. With less than five feet between them, he could have reached out and touched the back of the gunman's head.

"I got it!" the gunman shouted. "Let's get the hell out of here now."

David held his breath. If they would just leave, it would be the safest move for all concerned. Unfortunately, the short, stocky one who seemed to be in charge had other ideas.

"No witnesses," he said abruptly, and took aim at

the people on the floor as calmly as if he was about to squash a bug.

To David's horror, Cara was the closest to the gun. There was no time left to wait.

David coldcocked the man closest to him on the back of the head, then grabbed him before he fell, using him for a shield as he took aim. He fired twice in rapid succession, hitting the short man first and the next man as he was spinning around.

A stunned silence momentarily enveloped the hostages, and then they erupted into a melee of shouts and screams. Several started to run. David stopped them all with one shout.

"Wait."

They froze.

He looked at Cara, who was on her knees, trying to stop the blood pouring from the shoulder of one of the victims.

"Cara!"

She looked up, her eyes filled with tears, but there was a look on her face that told him she was all right. He yanked his T-shirt over his head and tossed it to her.

"Use pressure, honey. Help is on the way."

One of the stock boys followed suit and removed his T-shirt for her, as well. She nodded, quickly folding the shirts and pressing them against the front and back of the wound. The woman who'd been knocked out was coming around. To David's dismay, he realized it was the young cashier he'd teased only the other day. The one who had welcomed him to Chiltingham.

"See about her, too," he ordered, and immediately, a couple of the other hostages began to attend to her.

David motioned to the manager.

"I hear sirens. Go up front and meet the police and the paramedics. Make sure they know everything is under control. We wouldn't want anyone to be mistaken for a bad guy, would we?"

The manager nodded, still wide-eyed and shaking, unable to believe the ordeal was over. He bolted for the front of the store without looking back.

The man David had hit was moaning at his feet. He grabbed some reinforced strapping tape from a nearby shelf and quickly bound his hands and feet, then checked the two that he'd shot. They were dead.

Confident now that danger was past, he moved toward Cara, needing to touch her. When he knelt beside her, she looked up.

"I knew you would come."

He cupped the back of her head and pulled her to him, kissing her quick and hard.

"Let me help," he said quietly, and took over the job of keeping the pastor's wife alive while Cara rocked back on her heels and started to cry.

"It's all right, baby," he said quietly, as he inspected the woman's wound. Satisfied that it was a through shot and high enough that nothing vital had been hit, he kept pressure on the makeshift bandages and waited.

As they waited, the young clerk who'd been knocked out began to sit up. Looking around in stunned confusion, she saw Cara's face and then the blood all over the dress the preacher's wife was wearing and started to cry.

"Hey!" he said quickly. "Look at me!"

She blinked as recognition dawned.

"I know you," she whispered. "You're the new guy who moved to town."

"And it's a good thing he did," one of the hostages said. "They were going to kill us. He saved us all."

"Oh, my," she said, and then clutched her head and closed her eyes.

"Are you feeling sick to your stomach?" David asked.

She nodded.

"Put your head between your knees," he said, and then pointed with his chin toward a couple of the young grocery sackers. "Isn't that an ice machine over there?"

They nodded.

"Get a plastic bag, fill it with ice and put it on her head."

They did as he ordered, thankful to have something to do besides stare at the blood pooling beneath the two dead men.

David looked at Cara and the mark upon her face.

"Bring two of those bags of ice, will you? Give one to Mrs. Justice so she can put it on her face."

Cara tried to whisper a thanks, but she knew if she talked, she would scream. The horror of what had just happened was finally sinking in.

When one of the boys suddenly thrust the cold, wet plastic into her hands, she laid it against her face in mute thanksgiving.

n't need anything but David."
k, could you make this kind of quick?" David
f there are any details you need to fill in later,
reach me at Cara's. I'll be there another day

leaving town?" Foster asked.
elt Cara stiffen in his arms, but there was no
hat had to be said.
t only for a few days."
uld you tell me…briefly, of course…exactly
involved in this?"
e Cara a quick, gentle squeeze as he settled
within his embrace.
to a brief, but concise account of what had
t down to the moment he made the deci-
first shot.
stocky perp had already shot one hos-
ed another unconscious. When he said
d turned his gun on Cara, he lost what-
ight have given him."
said, then picked up David's gun, turn-
hands and casually eyeing the weapon.
ood shot."

gun like this before. Where did you

"That's because there's not another

David had only answered half his

Chapter 9

Moments later, they heard shouts at the front of the building, then the sounds of running feet. Suddenly, the back room of the supermarket was overflowing with uniformed officers as well as medical personnel.

"Here!" David called. "This woman is hurt the worst. She has a clean shot all the way through the shoulder but she's lost a lot of blood." Then he nodded toward the young clerk who was holding a bag of ice against her head. "She was knocked out for a short while. Might have a concussion."

"What about those two?" one of the paramedics asked, looking toward the two men on the floor.

"They're dead, and it's a better fate than they deserved," David muttered, then got to his feet and got out of their way.

A second later, Cara was in his arms, her face pressed

against his chest, the melting ice clutched tightly in her hand. David could feel the cold against his bare back, but didn't give a damn for the discomfort. Nothing mattered but Cara's welfare.

"It's all right now, honey," he said softly, holding her tight. "It's over."

"You saved us, David. You saved us all," she muttered.

"Yes, God bless you, mister," someone said, and patted him on the back, their hands warm against his bare flesh.

One after the other, the hostages thanked him, some hugging him, some unable to do anything but touch him as they were led away.

Just when David thought it was over, another set of officers arrived. These were in suits. He sighed. Detectives. Now the questions would really commence. But how to answer? Identifying himself and not giving himself away could be tricky, especially since he'd only left them with one live body to take to trial.

"So where's this Rambo they're all talking about?" one of the men asked.

"It was him, Robert! That's the man who told me to call the police."

David turned around. It was the woman from the parking lot. He looked back at Cara, assessing her condition. Her face was swollen where she'd been hit and she was still shaking. He needed to get her out of the building, but it wasn't going to happen. Not yet.

The detective looked first at David, then at the woman in his arms. Surprise spread over his face.

"Mrs. Justice, is that you?"

Cara looked up. "Oh… Robert, I should have ex-

"Interesting. How did you come by it? Did you design it?"

"No, I'm not that skilled."

"I don't suppose you stole it? I wouldn't want to hear something like that, especially since you're going to be the hero of the hour."

David sighed. "It's not stolen. Look, just run the serial numbers through the computer along with my driver's license number. It will explain itself."

Foster nodded. "That sounds simple enough," he said.

"Can we go home now?" Cara asked.

David looked at the detective.

Foster nodded reluctantly. "You say you'll be at Mrs. Justice's house for another day or so?"

"Yes."

"Then I'll just run the numbers on your gun and bring it out to you later this evening, if that's all right?"

"I'll be there," David said.

Cara slid out of his lap. "I can walk," she said.

David pulled her into the shelter of his arms.

"I know, but if you need to, just lean on me, honey."

Cara leaned. Not because she particularly needed to, but because she still could. She'd heard it from his own lips, even though it hadn't been said to her. Within a couple of days, he would be gone, maybe walking into something far worse than what she'd just witnessed, but she swallowed her fears and kept on walking.

The parking lot was a mess. Ambulances were coming and going and from the appearances of the police on the scene, they'd had to call in their reserves. Some weren't even in uniform, but were doing their best to keep curiosity seekers at bay.

When David and Cara emerged from the store, a

smattering of applause sounded from some of the bystanders. Obviously, word had already spread that he was the hero of the day. When he saw a television crew pulling into the parking lot, he kept his head down, tightened his hold on her hand and kept on walking.

"Hurry, Cara, I can't have my face splashed all over the news."

Cara looked startled, only then realizing the consequences of what he had done. By saving them, he'd blown whatever cover he'd had left. No one in the world would recognize him as Jonah, but Frank would damn sure recognize him as the man he sought.

With the help of a couple of the officers, the police cruiser blocking David's car was quickly moved. As soon as the car was free, he sped away. Only when they were on their way out of town did he breathe a sigh of relief.

"Thank God, that's over," Cara muttered, as she leaned back against the seat and closed her eyes.

David glanced at her, but didn't comment. If she only knew, it was probably just beginning. The moment Detective Foster ran the serial numbers of that gun through NCIC, it was going to set off so many bells in Washington that they'd probably hear them in heaven. And then there was Frank. David couldn't depend on anonymity any longer. He needed to start laying a trail for his brother to follow that would lead him as far away from Cara as possible.

A short while later, they arrived at Cara's home. She staggered as he helped her out of the car, then weakly apologized. He glared at her for apologizing again, then scooped her up in his arms. This time, she didn't argue. By the time he got her into the house, she was sobbing.

The tenderness in his voice was even more of her undoing.

"That's all right, baby. Go ahead and cry. Lord knows you've earned a few tears after the morning you've had." He set her on the side of her bed and began helping her take off her bloodstained clothes. "There was a time or two when I felt like crying, myself."

She hiccuped on a sob and tossed her bloodstained bra onto the floor. Gently, he cupped the side of her face, wincing at the bruising already taking effect.

"The son of a bitch," he muttered, and then kissed her there. "If I could, I would have killed him twice."

She sighed and leaned forward until their foreheads were touching.

"Oh, David, if you hadn't come back for me when you did, today would have been the day I died."

He shuddered. "Don't! Don't play that if game. It'll make you crazy. I know."

She wrapped her arms around his neck and hugged him fiercely.

"Before today, I hated what the government had done to you, but now..."

A sad smile came and went. He knew what she meant. He and Cara had been cheated out of a normal life, but because he knew how to kill, he'd saved her—saved them all—to live another day.

"Let's get the rest of these bloody clothes off of you," he said. "Can you stand on your own in the shower, or do you want to take a bath?"

"Shower, please, and yes, I can stand."

When she dropped the last article of her clothing in the pile on the floor, she kicked it aside with her toe.

"Throw them away."

"All of them?" he asked.

She nodded. "I don't ever want to wear them again."

He gathered them up in his arms and started for the door, then hesitated.

"Cara?"

"What?"

"The clothes will wash."

"But I—"

The despair on his face confused her, then suddenly she understood. David not only had blood on his clothes, but blood on his hands. And if she was so disgusted by something as inconsequential as bloody clothes, then what must she think of a man who had shed blood?

She made herself smile. "You're right. I just over-reacted. Besides, those are my favorite slacks. Maybe if you just tossed them in the washing machine in cold water and let them soak for a while?"

A rare smile of approval appeared on his face, before he turned and walked away.

A couple of hours later, they were in the kitchen eating some sandwiches David had made for them when the phone began to ring.

Cara looked at David.

"Want me to answer?" he asked.

She sighed. No use running from something she would inevitably have to face.

"No, I'll get it, but thanks anyway."

She picked up the portable, eyeing the caller ID screen, then rolled her eyes.

"Hello."

"Oh, my God, Cara, we just heard."

"Hello, Debra. Looks like news travels fast."

"Are you serious? It isn't gossip, honey! The whole thing is on the news."

"Now?" Cara asked.

"Yes, now."

"The television," Cara whispered, pointing to the living room. "Debra says the incident is on TV."

David bolted for the living room. Cara followed, still talking to her friend. To her dismay, she realized it wasn't a local news show, but a national network broadcasting live from the scene, where police were still working the area. She quickly disconnected and then slipped into the seat beside David.

"This isn't good, is it?" she asked.

"They don't have any tape of us. It should be all right."

At that moment, someone blurted out his name.

"Oh, no," Cara moaned.

David's expression darkened perceptibly. She was right. It wasn't good. Even though there were probably thousands of David Wilsons in the United States, there wouldn't be many who could have pulled off the rescue of eleven hostages single-handed. Hooray for the training he'd received at SPEAR and to hell with any anonymity he might have hoped to retain. When she clutched his hand, he slipped an arm around her and pulled her close, shoving all thoughts of Simon from his mind.

Less than ten minutes later, the phone rang again. This time, Cara handed the phone to David with a pleading expression.

David took it unwillingly.

"You could unplug the phone," he said.

"Please?"

He smiled, then answered.

"Justice residence."

"Is this David?"

He flinched. He'd only heard her voice once, but it was as firmly etched in his mind now as was Cara's face.

"Bethany?"

"Yes! We just saw the news about the supermarket in Chiltingham being robbed."

"Yes, so did we," David said. "Here's your mother."

"Thanks. Oh, David..."

"Yes?"

"Nice talking to you."

He found himself smiling. "Nice talking to you, too, honey."

He handed the phone to Cara and then started to get up and give her some privacy, but she grabbed his hand and pulled him back down beside her.

"Hello?" Cara said. "Bethany, darling, how are you?"

"We're all fine," she said. "I just had to call, though. It was so weird, seeing our little hometown on the evening news. Isn't it awful? They said someone was shot. Do you know who?"

"Yes, it was Margie Weller, the Methodist pastor's wife."

Bethany gasped. "How horrible! Was it serious? Is she going to be all right?"

"Yes, it was terribly frightening, but last word we had, she was in surgery and her prognosis was good."

"Thank goodness," Bethany said. "I guess you never know about things like this, but who would have thought it could happen at home, right?"

"Right," Cara said.

"They said there were eleven hostages and some guy named Wilson saved them all."

"Yes, he did," Cara said, wanting so badly to tell Bethany that it was her own father who'd been the hero that day. But telling her something like that over a phone was unconscionable.

"Is he new to the force?" Bethany asked.

"He isn't a member of the police force."

There was a moment of silence and then suddenly Bethany's questions took on the feel of an inquisition.

"Mother, is there something you aren't telling me?"

Cara sighed. "Everything is fine. We'll talk about it when you get home."

"Mother! Please God, don't tell me you were there?"

Cara's hesitation was enough to send Bethany into hysterics. She could hear her daughter screaming at her husband on the other end of the line. She looked at David and rolled her eyes.

David patted her leg. "It's to be expected, honey. It would be enough to scare the hell out of anyone, never mind that it's your mother."

"I guess," Cara said, then put the phone back to her ear. Bethany was shouting her name. "Yes, darling, I'm still here. Are you through screaming?"

Bethany was crying now. "Mother, my God…are you all right?"

"I'm fine."

Bethany moaned. "I can't believe this."

Cara tried to laugh, but it sounded awkward, even to her. "I know how you feel. It's a bit hard for us to believe and we were there."

There was a long moment of silence on the other end of the line and then Bethany spoke.

"He was there, too?"

"By he, I suppose you mean David? Oh, yes. Actually, he's the man of the hour in Chiltingham. I wouldn't be surprised if they name a street after him."

Now David was the one rolling his eyes.

"Is he the one they're talking about…the man who saved all of you?"

"Yes."

"I want to speak to him," Bethany said.

"Just a minute," Cara said, then covered the mouthpiece with her hand and looked at David. "She wants to talk to you."

David nodded, gearing himself for the sweet sound of her voice.

"Bethany, I promise your mother is fine."

At first she didn't answer and he thought he could hear her crying.

"Honey…are you there?"

"David, whoever you are, I just want to tell you that I'm so sorry for everything I first thought about you, and I will never be able to thank you enough for saving Mother's life."

"You're welcome," he said softly, and heard her sigh.

"I want to apologize to you," she said.

He smiled. "For what?"

"For thinking you were some kind of con man who was after my mother's money. It's not like she's rich or anything, but she has her home and Dad's retirement and…well…you know what I mean."

It hurt to hear the word *Dad* come out of her mouth and know she was referring to Ray Justice, but it was a title Ray had earned.

"I understand, and I don't care that your mother doesn't have a lot of money, because I do, okay?"

Cara's mouth dropped. "What on earth is she saying to you?" she whispered.

"She thought I was a con man after your money," David said.

"Oh, my word," Cara muttered. "Give me that phone." She took it out of David's hand with a yank. "Bethany Gail, you might be an adult, but you will never get old enough to question my behavior, is that understood?"

"Yes, ma'am."

"All right then," Cara muttered. "As long as we understand each other on that count."

"We're coming home a day early," Bethany said. "We'll see you tomorrow sometime after noon. Our plane is due in at Canandaigua around ten in the morning."

Cara hesitated. "Well, I'll be glad when you get home, but please don't shorten your vacation on my account."

"Mother, after this, do you think any of us could find a way to forget what happened to you and have fun? We want to come home…all of us."

"Then come," Cara said. "And have a safe trip."

"We will," she said, then added, "tell David goodbye for me."

"Tell him yourself," Cara said. She handed the phone back to David.

"Hello?"

"David, thanks again."

He smiled. "You're welcome."

Then she added, "David?"

"Yes?"

"I'm looking forward to meeting you."

He sighed and closed his eyes. "I'm looking forward to meeting you, too."

"Well…goodbye then."

"Yes, honey. Goodbye."

The line went dead in his ear. He handed the phone to Cara and then took her in his arms.

"My God, I don't think I've ever been this scared in my life, except maybe when that bastard put his gun in your face. Not even in Nam. She has every right to hate me."

"She doesn't have a right to hate anyone," Cara said. "She didn't do without a single thing in her entire life. She was loved from the moment of her birth, by both Ray and me. She had loving grandparents on both sides, and siblings, as well. She has known all her life that Ray Justice was her adoptive father. Knowing that you're still alive will be just as big a joy for her as it was for me."

"Swear?" David asked.

"I swear."

He smiled, and then leaned back on the sofa, eyeing the woman who'd given him something he thought he'd never have again—hope.

"You remember this morning…before we got to town?"

She grinned. "You mean when you proposed? Yes, I remember it, so don't think you can change your mind now."

"I don't want to change my mind. I want to make sure you don't change yours," he said, and then pulled the little velvet box out of his pocket and got down on one knee.

Suddenly, Cara was looking at him through a blur of tears.

"Oh, David."

"This is where I went when I let you off at the store.

You know I have to leave again, but I pray it won't be for long. I love you so much, and I owe you so much. A war cheated us out of a lot and I want to give you everything, all at once. I can't make any guarantees about the future, so you'll have to settle for just this, right now."

Her hand was shaking when he slid the ring on her finger.

"It fits," she said, more than a little surprised.

"Yeah, I'm a pretty good judge of things like that."

She shook her head and then threw her arms around his neck. "You're good at a lot more than that," she said. "I can't wait for the day when we can start living our life…for us."

"Me, too. Do you want to—"

Before he could finish, the doorbell rang. Cara jumped at the noise and then glanced at the clock. It was after nine. Surely it wasn't well-wishing friends coming this late?

"I'll get it," David said, and then strode to the door.

It was Detective Foster. Then he looked past Foster to the two dark-suited men behind him and sighed.

"Gentlemen, come in. I've been expecting you."

Chapter 10

Robert Foster glared at David as he stepped inside. He was still sweating from the unexpected confrontation he'd just had with these two federal agents.

All he'd done was what he'd been hired to do, which was investigate crimes. He'd entered the serial numbers from David's gun into the computer, and then proceeded to finish his report while he'd waited for the program to run.

Half an hour later, two strangers in suits had walked into the room as if they owned the place. Flashing their badges, they tossed him a hard copy of the file he'd sent through NCIC and demanded he bring them to the man who owned the gun.

Now, here he was, still reeling from being treated like an underling. No courtesy from one officer to another. No nothing. He didn't like it. He didn't like it one damned bit.

He turned back to the agents, still pissed and glaring. “Happy now?”

They looked at David, comparing this man’s physical description against the one they’d been given. They didn’t know who the hell he was, but when they got orders direct from the President, they knew enough to respond without question. Convinced that they had their man, one of them stepped forward and handed David his gun while Detective Foster continued to fume.

“You knew this would happen, didn’t you?” he said, giving David a share of his anger.

“Knew what?” David asked, eyeing the two men who followed Foster inside.

The detective turned, waving his hand toward his uninvited escorts.

“That Tweedledee and Tweedledum would show up and try to eat me for dinner.”

David stifled a grin. The man’s description of the two men who were with him was funny, but it wasn’t in his best interests to laugh.

“They don’t bite,” David said, and then added, “Unless maybe if I asked them to.”

The federal agents looked surprised as their curiosity grew, but they knew better than to voice it.

Foster was over his head and he knew it. He threw up his hands in defeat.

“Look, I don’t know what’s going on here, and I’m thinking it would be in my best interests not to ask.”

“Cara said you were bright,” David said.

Foster shifted nervously. “You’re someone special, aren’t you?” Then he shrugged. “Hell… I already knew that when you walked into the supermarket and took down three armed men. What I’m trying to say is…you have that damned gun back, and whoever you are, it's been a pleasure meeting you."

David shook the young detective's hand. "Likewise."

"David, is everything all right?"

All of them turned, acknowledging Cara's arrival into their midst.

"Mrs. Justice, I trust you're feeling better?" Foster asked.

"Much." Then she looked at the two men accompanying the detective. "Detective Foster, are you going to introduce your friends?"

"If I knew their names, I might," he muttered.

"They're here for me," David said.

It was the quiet, resolute tone in his voice that made her heart sink. She turned to David, silently begging him to deny what she feared. To her dismay, he shook his head.

"It will be okay," he said. At that moment, the two agents stepped forward, one of them handing David a phone.

"Sir, I'm Federal Agent Thomas Ryan, and this is Agent Patrick O'Casey. In less than a minute, the President will be calling you. We have instructions to await your orders."

Cara gasped and Detective Foster muttered, "Lord have mercy," beneath his breath.

Seconds later, the phone David was holding rang. He answered abruptly.

"Sir?"

"I must say, when you take a leave of absence, you don't do it quietly, do you, son?"

David almost relaxed. He'd expected a dressing down for getting mixed up in public matters.

"It was a choice I made. I would do the same thing again," he said.

"And I would expect you to," the President replied. "Now to more important matters. Our people have been monitoring your old contact station. You are receiving e-mail from the quarry."

One moment David's face was animated and the next expressionless. Cara shivered. It was like looking at a stranger. She took a step backward, unconsciously distancing herself from the fear that came with it.

"Sir, I'm assuming this line is secure."

A soft chuckle rippled in David's ear. "Yes. Feel free to speak your piece."

"The messages, what do they say?"

"He wants a meeting."

David pivoted sharply and walked into the other room alone.

"Can you see that he gets an answer?" David asked.

"Just a minute, son, I'm putting someone else on. Tell him what you want sent. It will get done."

"Yes, sir, thank you, sir."

Seconds later, another voice was on the line. It didn't matter to David who it was. If the President had him standing by, then he was okay.

"Ready to transmit," the voice said.

"Just tell him… Washington D.C."

"Got it. Anything else?"

"No."

Moments later, the President was back on the phone.

"Is there anything we can do for you?"

David thought of the hundreds of agents who could be instantly at his disposal and knew that their presence would do nothing but drive his brother further underground. It was time for all of this hate to end.

"No. I'll let you know when it's over."

There was a hesitation on the other end, and then a softening in the tone of the President's voice.

"Just make damn sure the call I get is from you, personally, do you understand me, son?"

David almost smiled. It was as close as the President would come to saying "be careful" without actually voicing the words.

"Yes, sir, I understand."

"All right then. Those men I sent are there to help you in any way that they can. Use them or send them home. It's up to you."

"Yes, sir, and once again, sorry about the fuss."

"There was a need. You made the right decision. Now go do your thing."

David disconnected, walked into the other room and handed the phone back to Agent Ryan.

"Thanks for escorting Detective Foster out to see me. You men have a safe journey home."

For the first time, the agent's composure was rattled.

"But sir, don't you—"

"No." Then he softened the answer by adding, "But thanks."

They nodded, ignored Foster's presence and smiled courteously at Cara. "Ma'am," they said, and then stepped aside, waiting for Foster to make his excuses.

He quickly took his cue. "Mrs. Justice, if you need anything, you know where to call." Then he looked at David. "Why do I feel the urge to tell you good luck?"

A wry smile tilted the corner of David's mouth. "Probably because I'm going to need it."

Moments later, they were gone, leaving David and Cara alone in the hall. She bit her lower lip to keep from crying, but he saw the gesture and opened his arms.

"Come here to me," he said gently.

She walked into his arms.

"I'm not going to cry and I'm not going to beg, but so help me God, if you get yourself killed, I will never forgive you," she muttered.

"I'm not going to die on you, baby. I spent too much money on that ring to let it go to waste."

"That isn't funny," she muttered.

"Oh, I don't know about that. I'm smiling."

She looked up. "You're crazy, you know that?"

"Oh, yeah, crazy in love. What do you say we call it a night?" He touched the side of her face where the bruising was starting to show. "I have this sudden need to just lie down beside you and listen to you sleep."

Cara knew he was trying to reassure her that there would be no lovemaking this night because of the trauma she'd suffered.

"We can do more than sleep, if you want," she said.

He shook his head. "Maybe you could, but I don't think I can. I'm still trying to get past the sight of that son of a bitch holding a gun in your face." He hugged her again, this time almost desperately. "When I think how close I came to—"

"But you didn't, and I'm still here. Let's go to bed."

Together, they locked the doors and turned out the lights before walking hand in hand up the stairs toward the bedroom.

A small lamp she'd turned on earlier lit the way as they went. It was a moment in time that was neither remarkable nor different, and yet Cara knew it would be in her heart forever. Small things she might never have noticed became things to remember.

Like the warmth of his hand as it enfolded hers.

The steady clip of his footsteps beside her.

The scent of his aftershave and the tick of the grandfather clock standing in the entryway.

The rush of cool air against her skin as she undressed.

The crisp, clean sheets on the bed as they slipped between the covers.

The way he pulled her into the curve of his body and then promptly fell asleep, as if girding himself for the trauma to come.

Unwilling to waste her last hours with him by sleeping them away, she lay without moving, savoring the rise and fall of his chest behind her.

Sometime after midnight, exhaustion claimed her. When she woke the next morning, there was a rose on her pillow with a note beneath.

Don't be mad at me for not saying goodbye. I did it once and look how things worked out. This time, I'm saying I love you, and please wait for me.

David.

Cara covered her face. To her surprise, her cheeks were already wet. She'd been so certain that the pain she was feeling was too terrible for tears. It would seem that she'd been wrong.

In another part of the country and at the same time they were going to bed, Frank Wilson was lying on top of his covers, smoking his last cigarette of the day and watching TV. But his mind wasn't on the programming. He was going through scenario after scenario, plotting all the different ways he could enact his revenge. A few minutes later, he stubbed out his cigarette and turned off the TV and lights and closed his eyes. Within seconds, he was asleep.

It was the first football game of the season and Frankie was almost ready to go. At sixteen, his voice had deepened to what would be his normal pitch and he'd finally grown into his feet. And he had a girlfriend. At least, in his mind, he did. The fact that Ellen Mayhew had yet to acknowledge he even existed was beside the point. He liked her, therefore he must be in as close a vicinity to her as possible without giving himself away.

He started out the door, his hair combed into a perfect ducktail, his sideburns just brushing the lobes of his ears. He thought he looked a little like Elvis.

"Frankie, you get your little brother back here by ten. School tomorrow," his mother said.

He froze, his hand on the doorknob, and then turned abruptly.

"Why do I always have to have that brat tagging along? How am I ever going to have any friends if I'm always baby-sitting with him?"

Davie leaned against the sofa, his gaze beseeching his brother to relent, yet a little afraid that if he did get to go to the ball game with Frankie, he'd pay for it later.

"Friends are fine," his mother said. "But brothers are family. Brothers are forever."

Frankie glared at the little brat, ignoring the fact that Davie wasn't so little anymore and that the kid's body was probably going to be more muscular than his own when he reached full growth.

"If you go, you're not sitting with me and my friends, you hear?"

Davie nodded. "I won't, Frankie, I promise."

"And I don't want to have to go looking for you when the game is over. You be waiting for me by the ticket gate, you hear?"

Davie nodded again. "I hear. I'll be there."

Their mother hugged them both. "That's fine then. You two go and have a good time, but remember, home as soon as the game is over, and Frankie, Davie's care is in your hands."

"Damn," Frankie muttered, and shoved his kid brother out the door ahead of him.

"I'm sorry, Frankie," Davie said. "I won't be any trouble, I promise."

Frankie muttered a curse word and hoped to God that Ellen Mayhew didn't see him walking into the grandstands with Davie in tow.

Two hours later the game was over. Davie Wilson stood by the ticket gate, watching anxiously for a sign of his big brother's face. Families filed past him, laughing and talking about the big win that they'd had tonight, and with each group that passed, Davie was certain that Frankie would be in the next group to come along.

But he wasn't.

When the gatekeeper and a couple of teachers came by, he slipped into the shadows, unwilling to be questioned as to why he was still at the field.

The lights went out. The last car drove out of the parking lot. Davie was alone.

He could have walked home by himself and would have, except then Frankie would have been in real trouble for abandoning him. So he waited, knowing they would be in trouble for being late, but at least they would be in trouble together.

A half hour passed, and then another. It started to rain. He pulled the collar of his jacket up around his neck and hunched his shoulders against the downpour. Everything that had been so familiar under the lights on the playing field now took on ominous tones. Familiar buildings became sinister shapes, waiting to morph into swamp monsters and ghouls. The only benefit to the downpour was that it hid the continuous stream of tears running down his face.

"Hey, kid."

He spun, his heart in his mouth. Frankie was standing before him with a sheepish expression on his face.

"I waited, Frankie, just like you said."

It was one of the few times in his life that Frankie Wilson was truly ashamed. Gently, he cuffed his little brother on the side of the head and then gave him a brief, bearlike hug.

"Yeah, kid, you sure did. I'm sorry, okay?"

Davie smiled. It was going to be okay. Yeah, they were going to catch hell from their folks, but it didn't really matter. Whatever happened, they were in it together.

"What are you gonna tell Mama?" Frankie asked, as they walked through the rain toward home.

"Nothing," Davie said.

Frankie felt even worse. "She's gonna be real mad at us."

"Yeah, I know."

Frankie paused beneath a streetlight, staring at the rain running out of Davie's hair and down his face.

"You aren't gonna snitch?"

Davie frowned and shook his head.

"Why?" Frankie asked. "I probably would."

Davie shrugged. "You're my brother."

An ambulance sped by the Chicago hotel with sirens blaring. Disoriented, Frank bolted from bed, his heart racing with the image of his brother's face in his head. Just for a moment, the magnitude of what he'd been planning to do overwhelmed him and he let out a cry and covered his face. The sound shattered within him, bringing him to his knees. He could hear his mother's voice as clearly as if she was standing by his bed.

You are your brother's keeper.

Thou shalt not kill.

Blood is thicker than water.

He moaned. Could he really do this? The first time had been in the heat of the moment, wrapped up in the day-to-day combat and the anger that had dragged him into a war he didn't understand. And he'd fueled that anger all these years with the need for revenge. He wanted to destroy him, that was certain. He wanted him defiled as he'd been—his reputation in shreds as his had been. But could he rip the heart from a man who was his blood?

Then he fingered his scars, remembering why they were there, and that his little brother had set him on fire. It didn't matter to Frank that David had thought him dead—that he had been trying to hide the evidence that would mark his brother a traitor.

He stood abruptly and strode to the wet bar, pouring himself a very stiff drink. He tossed it back without hesitation then poured himself another. By the time the liquor hit his stomach, his brief moment of uncertainty had passed. He moved to the window overlooking the city and to his surprise realized it was raining. Too restless to sleep, he turned on the television and then lowered the volume as he surfed through the few available stations. With nothing but CNN and some pay-per-view movies for company, he retrieved his laptop and decided to check his messages.

Using the bed for a desk, he crawled onto the mattress and centered the laptop between his legs. The television was on mute on the other side of the room, and only now and then did he even bother to look up to see what news-worthy event CNN was covering. When the You've Got Mail sign flashed across the computer screen, he refused to anticipate the contents of the box. With a click of the mouse, e-mail began to download. As it did, he glanced at the television screen across the room and then hit the mute button to reinstate the sound.

A spokesperson for some local police department was making a statement regarding the deaths and capture of suspects involved in a week-long crime spree somewhere in the state of New York. He was reiterating the well-being of one of the victims when the laptop signaled the end of the download.

Immediately, Frank hit mute again and looked at the screen. As he did, he missed hearing the location of the incident and the name of the man who was credited with the rescues. He didn't know it yet, but fate was already dealing him a handful of bad cards.

He scanned the list of messages, and as he did, his heart skipped a beat. Quickly deleting all but the one from Reunion, he began to read. As he did, a cold smile spread across his face, puckering the burn scars on his cheek and neck.

"At last, little brother, you finally got some balls."

He fumbled for the remote and turned off the TV. There were things to do and arrangements to make. He rolled out of the bed, dragged his suitcase from the closet and began to pack.

It was almost over.

But Frank Wilson was due for some more delays. He caught a few hours sleep and by daylight was on his way to the airport. By the time he got to Chicago O'Hare, it was just before seven in the morning and the gentle rain of the night before had turned into violent storms. Planes were grounded until further notice, and the airport was a melee of angry and unruly travelers.

Cursing the weather and people in general, he bought himself a cup of coffee and a doughnut, then settled down to read his newspaper. Time was still on his side.

The small Canandaigua Airport was a madhouse of voices and people. David stood at the windows overlooking the runway, watching the big silver plane coming in for a landing. As the wheels touched down, his heart skipped a beat. His daughter was on that plane, and for the first time in his life, he was going to see her in person.

Shifting nervously, he watched the plane as it began to taxi toward the terminal. A voice over an intercom announced the arrival of flight 447 at gate 9, and people began gathering, anxious for that first sight of their loved ones. David wondered what it would be like to stand with those people—to see the look of recognition on Bethany's face and feel her arms around his neck as she greeted him with delight. But as he'd learned long ago, he kept his thoughts to himself, masking emotion behind an expressionless exterior.

A few minutes later, the first of the passengers appeared at the gate, then more and more, until a steady stream of travel-weary travelers straggled from the ramp into the terminal.

He shifted his position so that he could better see the faces, his anxiety growing as the line continued and still no sign of the woman he'd seen in Cara's pictures.

Then suddenly she was there, walking beside a tall, sandy-haired man who was carrying one sleeping child while Bethany held hands with the other. Her shoulder-length hair was dark and straight like his, and she was taller than he'd expected. She was slim and graceful and when she smiled, he could see the beginnings of a dimple in her left cheek.

Without thinking, he moved toward her, wanting to hear the sound of her voice. Although there were at least a dozen people between them, he could hear her talking to her husband about how good it was to be on firm ground and laughing at something her oldest daughter just said.

God in heaven, he didn't think this would be so hard.

He paused a few feet away and watched as they passed by. As they did, a small stuffed rabbit fell out of the oldest girl's backpack. He pushed through the passengers and snatched it from the floor, then caught up with them a few feet away.

"Excuse me," he said, and briefly touched Bethany's shoulder. "This fell out of her backpack."

Surprised, Bethany turned, saw the rabbit in the stranger's hands and smiled.

"Oh, my! Thank you so much, that's Rachel's favorite toy." Then she looked down at her daughter and lightly touched her on the head. "Rachel, would you like to thank the man for finding Henry?"

David felt himself smiling as the little girl nodded.

"So, his name is Henry?"

She nodded.

"Well, it's a good thing I saw him jump out, right?"

Her eyes widened appreciably as he handed her the toy.

"He jumped?"

Without breaking a smile, David nodded. "It looked like it to me. Better hold him tight."

The child clutched the rabbit against her chest.

"Thank you so much," Bethany repeated. "Losing Henry would have been nothing short of disastrous."

"You're welcome," David said. Resisting the urge to touch the children, he nodded a goodbye to her husband as well as Bethany and disappeared into the crowd.

Bethany looked at her husband. "That was fortunate, wasn't it?" she asked.

Her husband nodded, still looking in the direction that the man had gone.

"You know, he reminded me of someone, but I can't think who," he muttered.

Bethany shrugged. "Come on, Tom. I'm anxious to get home and check on Mother."

"Yes, you're right," he said, and then headed toward the baggage claim.

A short while later, they were on the road home, unaware that the man they'd just seen was on a plane of his own and bound for the nation's capital.

Chapter 11

All day, Cara found herself listening for the sound of David's voice, although she knew that he was gone. Never in the three years she'd been widowed had she felt so alone. A gut-wrenching fear had settled itself in the pit of her stomach, and she couldn't find a way to get past it. She could only imagine what he was going to have to face, but could not wrap her mind around the truth of it. His brother wanted him dead. Dear God, how much more was he destined to withstand?

She'd prayed for him until her mind was spinning and the words numb upon her lips. She had nothing left to do but wait, and it was the uncertainty that was driving her mad. In desperation, she cleaned her house from top to bottom, even preparing some extra food, knowing Bethany and her family would arrive before the day was out.

During the cleaning, she'd run across the envelope of

pictures she'd taken on their day at the lake. It had almost been her undoing. Looking at the images of a happier time and wondering if they would be all she had left of him had sent her into another wave of weeping. Unwilling to put the pictures away, she searched out some empty frames and framed the best of the lot, adding them to the mantel with the others of her family. Only after she stepped back to look at them as a whole did the pain begin to subside. It was as if the pictures had given credence to his reappearance into her life.

Then she rubbed the diamond solitaire he'd put on her finger, shamed that her faith was so shallow. The pictures were wonderful, but she didn't need them, or the ring, or any tangible reminder that David Wilson was alive. As long as her heart beat, he would never be forgotten. With one last look at David laughing and holding up a very small fish, she blew him a kiss and walked away.

Four hours later, Bethany was at the door.

"Darling, how wonderful to see you again," Cara said, as she stepped aside to let her daughter in.

Bethany took one look at the spreading bruise on the side of her mother's face and burst into tears.

"Oh, Mother, your poor little face."

Cara quickly embraced her daughter. "Honey, it's not as bad as it seems, I promise."

Bethany was forty years old and almost a head taller than her mother, but at that moment, she felt like a child again. The horror of knowing how close she'd come to losing her was too horrible to contemplate.

"I can't believe that this has happened," she said, as

her gaze searched the familiar contours of Cara's face. "Are you sure you're all right? Is there anything I can do?"

"Yes, I'm fine, and you can come inside and sit down with me. I want to hear all about your trip." Then she looked over Bethany's shoulder, suddenly realizing the rest of the family was nowhere in sight. "Where are Tom and the girls?"

"They'll be along later," Bethany said. "I left them at home unpacking." She traced the curve of her mother's cheek with her fingertip, barely grazing the purpling flesh. "I couldn't wait to see you."

Cara smiled and did a dainty pirouette.

"Well, you see me. How do I look?"

Bethany frowned. "Actually, except for that awful bruise, you look wonderful." Suddenly, she remembered the man named David and looked around. "Where is this David person? I want to meet him."

Cara's smile slipped, but she wouldn't give in. Not now. Not in front of Bethany.

"And you will, but not today," Cara said. "He was called away on business quite suddenly. Actually, he left very early this morning, so you've just missed him." Then she remembered the pictures she'd put on the mantel and took Bethany by the hand. "However, I can show you a picture. I took some when we went fishing the other day."

Bethany followed her mother into the living room and was startled to see that her mother had put up not one, but three snapshots of the man on the mantel—and right in the middle of the family grouping. For once, she kept her thoughts to herself and smiled as her mother handed her the first one.

"This was taken last Tuesday at the lake…or was it

Wednesday?" Then Cara smiled. "Oh, I don't remember, but we had the most marvelous time."

Bethany scanned the image and then started to look at the others when something about the first one clicked. He hadn't been smiling when she'd seen him, but she would bet her best pair of earrings that she'd seen him before. She grabbed her mother's arm.

"Mom! You won't believe this, but I think we met this man!"

Cara turned. "When?"

"This morning. At the airport. Henry fell out of Rachel's backpack as we were getting off the plane and a man came out of the crowd and gave it back. I swear it was the same man, right down to those silver strands of hair over his ears."

Cara's heart started to pound. She should have known that David would find a way to look at his daughter's face—just in case he— She stifled a sob, unable to finish her own thought.

"Oh, Bethany, are you sure?"

Bethany looked intently at the other two snapshots, then nodded. "Positive." When she looked up, she knew something was wrong. "What?"

Cara hesitated.

"Damn it, Mother, I knew something was wrong from the start. Talk to me. Who is he? What has he done to you to make you cry?"

"His name is David Wilson, and I'm crying because I'm scared. The first time he left me to fight a war." She inhaled on a shaky breath. "And he left again because… because for him, that war has never ended."

Bethany's heart started to pound. She heard her mother's words, but they didn't make sense. She knew the man who'd been staying with her mother was named David Wilson. She'd heard her mother call him David, and they'd heard his last name when the incident had made the news. Her biological father's name had been Wilson, but he died in Vietnam. Hadn't he? What had her mother just said about the first time he left her? She started to shake.

"Mother?"

Cara felt guilty for the confusion on Bethany's face and when she heard the tremble in her voice, she reached for her hands, holding them close against her breast.

"That man…the man you saw in the airport…the man who saved my life…is your father."

Bethany's face crumpled and she staggered backward to a chair, her voice barely above a whisper.

"But you said he was dead."

"We all thought he was dead," Cara said.

"Where…why…?"

Cara sighed. "It's a long, terrible story, my darling, and it's not mine to tell. When David comes back, he will tell you himself."

Bethany looked up, the yearning there on her face for Cara to see.

"Will he come back?"

Cara smiled. "Yes, I believe he will."

"How can you be sure?" Bethany said.

Cara held out her hand. "Because he put this on my finger."

Bethany took one look at the diamond and burst into tears.

Cara knelt, cradling her daughter in her arms.

"Don't cry, darling. It's actually wonderful, you know. It's a miracle that David and I have been given a second chance for happiness."

"I'm not crying because I'm unhappy," Bethany sobbed. "I'm just crying, okay?" Then she clutched Cara a little tighter. "Oh, Mom, he has to come back."

Cara closed her eyes momentarily, refusing to give in to the fear.

"Yes, darling, I know just how you feel."

"Ladies and gentlemen, please fasten your seat belts and put your seats and tray tables in their upright positions. We will be landing in a few minutes and there will be personnel at the gate to help you with flight information should you be traveling on to other destinations. On another note, the time in our nation's capital is now one oh five p.m. The weather is hot and sunny, ninety-five degrees with a slight westerly breeze. Enjoy your stay and thank you for flying with us."

Ignoring the flight attendant's spiel, David glanced out the window as the plane began its descent. From where he was sitting, he could pick out several landmarks, the most noticeable of which was the Washington Monument. The spire was like a finger pointing the way to heaven—or away from hell. In this city, it was always a toss-up as to which one was in power at the moment. A sense of timelessness hit him as he looked down at the great white dome of the nation's Capitol. Since its inception, so many people had dedicated their lives to making certain that the nation maintained itself as a democracy, while others had spent fortunes trying to manipulate and control it. David had seen both sides and right now wasn't too enamored with either. All he wanted was to enjoy what was left of his life—and he wanted to do it with Cara. God willing, it would happen.

By the time the plane touched down, he had the entire situation mapped out in his mind. He would send Frank another e-mail. The meeting would take place. And he knew just where it would happen. A little bit of Vietnam—the place where it all began.

The park surrounding the Vietnam War Memorial was spacious and, at the right time of night, fairly deserted. There was plenty of cover. Plenty of places where a man could stand without being detected. Frank's name was on the wall. He wondered if Frank had ever seen it, but he knew it was a hell of a feeling to know that the rest of the world had given up and forgotten you. It was the closest a living man could come to knowing what it was like to be a ghost—that the only tangible evidence of your life on this earth was a name engraved on black stone.

But David had something more now than he did the last time he'd come to this city. He had Cara again, and he was going to have his daughter. Almost a year ago he'd come to D.C. and left a rose at the wall beneath his brother's name. Now he was coming back to kill him. It was a nightmare of unspeakable proportions.

God help me.

He shuddered, and as he thought of what lay ahead amended the thought to, God help them both. If only Frank would have a change of heart. If by some miracle he would simply appear and turn himself in, David would be ecstatic. There was nothing he felt he needed to prove—to himself or to Frank—and he so desperately wanted to be free of the past.

"Sir?"

David looked up. The flight attendant had her hand on his shoulder, smiling down at him.

"Yes?"

"I have instructions to tell you that you will be met."

It didn't surprise him. The President was doing his part to help bring an end to this, too.

"Thank you," he said.

"You're welcome, sir. As soon as the plane lands, I will escort you to the door of the cockpit. You will be the first to exit."

He nodded again, ignoring the curious stares from the other first-class passengers.

She walked away, taking her seat at the front of the plane and preparing herself for the landing, as well.

A minute or so later, the plane was on the ground and taxiing toward the terminal. His flesh crawled, much in the same way it had in the jungles of Vietnam.

It was beginning.

As promised, the moment the Fasten Seat Belt sign went off, the attendant was at his seat. He stood, retrieved his bag from the overhead bin and moved toward the cockpit.

A short, heavyset man who'd been sitting across the aisle from David grumbled just loud enough to be heard about some people getting privileges when they'd all paid to fly first class. But when he met David's gaze, the grumble stilled.

For David, that man was nothing more than a fly in the ointment of his life. By the time his foot touched the exit ramp, he was forgotten. David emerged into the terminal with his bag on his shoulder and immediately found himself flanked by another duo of suited men. He didn't know their faces, but he knew who'd sent them.

"Sir, Federal Agent MaCauley. May I take your bag?"

He lifted it from David's shoulder without waiting for an answer.

"I'm Federal Agent Matthews. This way, sir," the other said. "We have a car waiting for you."

David nodded. There was no reason to chitchat. They didn't expect it and he wasn't in the mood.

The ride to the hotel was smooth and silent. Every now and then he would glance out the window from his seat in the back of the car, absently admiring the lush, green beauty of the surrounding forests. When they crossed the river, his pulse accelerated. The closer he came to the Wardman Park, the closer he came to his destiny.

A few minutes later they reached the hotel. Before he could get out, the agent on the passenger side was out and opening his door while the other agent took his bag from the trunk.

"This is as far as you go, men," David said. "I can handle it from here. Thank you."

"Yes, sir. You're welcome, sir," they said, and then disappeared as quickly as they had appeared.

David turned toward the hotel and started inside, only to be met at the doorway by another man, this time an employee of the hotel, who promptly relieved David of his bag again.

"Sir, you've already been checked in. If you'll follow me, I'll escort you to your suite."

David had been here before and barely glanced at the elegant lobby or the open bar beyond. As they turned left at the hallway to go toward the bank of elevators, a woman suddenly jumped up from a nearby chair and grabbed his arm.

"Hey! Long time no see," she said, and tried to give him a kiss.

David grabbed her arms, gently but forcefully preventing the move.

"I'm sorry. You have mistaken me for someone else," he said, and tried to walk away, but she persisted.

"No need to act like that," she said. "I kept our little secret."

David frowned. He wasn't in the mood for this.

"Lady, I don't know who are you, so if you will please excuse me, I'm on my way to my room."

"Come on, Larry, this isn't funny," she muttered.

"My name isn't Larry," he said and pulled out of her grasp.

She frowned and then furtively glanced around before pulling a pair of glasses from her shoulder bag. The moment she slid them up her nose, her expression changed.

"Oh, my! You're not Larry. Larry's eyes are brown." Then she giggled. "Sorry. My mistake."

David was already walking toward the elevator.

"Everything all right, sir?" the man asked.

David nodded. "A case of mistaken identity."

As the elevator doors slid shut, David realized the woman was nowhere in sight. He frowned as a warning went off in his head and then moments later shrugged it away.

At the moment David was entering his room, the woman was in a stall in the women's bathroom with her cell phone to her ear, waiting for her call to be answered.

"This is Sheila. He's here." She waited, listening intently to the man on the other end of the line, then she smiled. "You're welcome," she said. "If there's ever anything else I can do for you…well, let's just say…you know where to find me."

She hung up, strode out of the bathroom and out of the hotel, hailed a cab. Having done her part, she disappeared from David's life.

* * *

Frank Wilson shoved his cell phone in his pocket, silently cursing the weather for causing the delays. He was still at the Chicago airport and David was already in D.C. He bolted up from his seat and strode to the window. Outside, the black wall of thunderstorms still hovered overhead, while intermittent flashes of lightning continued to strike. As he watched, one bolt suddenly came out of nowhere, striking so close he was momentarily blinded by the flash.

Covering his face, he turned away, his gut in knots, his body shaking. It was too reminiscent of the fire that had nearly consumed him. When he started to return to his seat, he realized someone had taken it, which just added to the unsettled mood he was in.

Cursing beneath his breath, he headed for a newsstand a short distance away. He bought another paper and then ambled toward a restaurant, finally finding himself a seat at the bar.

"What'll it be?" the bartender asked, as Frank slid onto the bar stool.

"I'll have a dark lager and a hamburger."

"Coming up," the bartender said, and walked away.

Frank opened the paper and began to read. A short while later, his food arrived. He ate for sustenance, not pleasure, hardly noticing that the meat was dry and the bread too soft. When it began to fall apart in his hands, he shoved the plate aside and sat sipping his beer instead.

It wasn't until the man at his right laughed abruptly and made a comment to a friend about a real-life Dirty Harry that he began to listen. As he did, he realized they were discussing a recent incident in a small town in upstate New York. At that point, memory clicked, and he remembered hearing part of it on the news the night before. But it wasn't the incident itself that had captured his interest. It was the name of the man who had been credited with the rescues. He continued to eavesdrop.

"Yeah, it was a hell of a deal," the man was saying. "Walked into this supermarket with a handgun and took down three thugs who'd taken eleven people hostage."

His friend made a comment Frank couldn't hear, but when the man next to him answered, the hair suddenly rose on the back of his neck.

"Oh, hell, isn't that the truth," the man said. "I got the same name as him, but I sure don't have the balls to pull something like that. But here's the kicker, Joe. You know what my wife said? If she'd married that David Wilson instead of me, she probably wouldn't fall asleep during sex."

Both men laughed, but Frank's focus had moved past the joke. Granted, David Wilson was a very common name, yet he couldn't help wondering how many men with that name could pull off such an incident and walk away without a scratch. That kind of skill came from combat—and special forces training.

He dropped the newspaper and strode out of the bar, his mind racing. Could it be? Would David do something so brash as to call attention to himself in this way? And why would he resume using his real identity?

The moment he asked himself the question, he knew.

Of course.

David had walked away from SPEAR. He would have had to anyway since his identity had been compromised. But why upstate New York? What could he have possibly been doing there if he was so focused on their meeting?

Frank's mind was racing. *What would I do if I thought I was going to die?*

I would want to see Martha.

The answer startled him. But David didn't have a Martha. He'd never married, and their parents were dead. To Frank's knowledge, he didn't have a personal tie on this earth.

At that point, he froze, then inhaled slowly. There was a flaw in that thought.

To his knowledge.

That's where Frank's mistake had begun. Just because he didn't know about any personal ties didn't mean they didn't exist. It occurred to him then that he'd never really explored that side of David's life. He'd been so busy trying to find him, then take him down from within SPEAR, that he'd never thought about investigating him from a personal angle.

He looked up, gazing blankly at the people passing by him and the others sitting glumly in their seats, as stranded by nature as he. Despite the fact that David had summoned him to D.C. and was already there waiting, Frank didn't want to pass up an opportunity to turn the knife after he'd plunged it into David's chest.

He turned, searching for a place where he could make some calls without being overheard, then realized there was no such place. Considering the small risk he would take in making the calls, he headed for a bank of pay phones, opting for one of the cubicles. He waited for one to vacate then slipped into the seat and took out his cell phone, pausing momentarily as he debated about who to call first. A few moments later, he punched in a series of numbers then waited for his call to be answered.

"Petroski Heating Oil, Pete speaking."

"I need a favor."

"Like what?" Pete asked warily.

"There was an incident in a small town in upstate New York yesterday. Something about a man rescuing a bunch of hostages from a supermarket."

"Oh, yeah, I heard about that. Some hotshot, huh?"

Frank frowned. "Maybe, but that's not the point. Is your brother-in-law still on the police force on Wykomis?"

"Yeah, but he ain't gonna go for—"

"Just shut up and listen to me," Frank said. "All I want is some information. I want to know the name of that town and what this David Wilson was doing there. I want to know how old he is, what he looks like, and was he just passing through or visiting. Get it?"

"Yeah, sure," Pete said. "I can do that. Give me an hour and I'll see what I can come up with. How can I reach you?"

"I'll call you back," Frank said, and disconnected.

He moved from the pay phones to a seat near his gate. This time when he sat down, his patience had taken itself to a new level. If there was a way to make David's life more miserable before he died, it would be Frank's pleasure.

Outside, the storms continued to hover over the city of Chicago, but it was the storm inside Frank Wilson's heart that was the most dangerous. Neither wind nor time was going to move it away. Only the sight of his brother's blood was going to put out the fire of his hate.

He sat without moving, his eye on a clock across from where he was sitting. When the minute hand finally ticked over for the sixtieth time, Frank took his cell phone from his pocket and made the call.

Pete answered on the first ring. "This is Pete."

"Talk to me," Frank said.

"David Wilson, mid to late fifties. Dark hair with some gray at the temples. A little over six feet tall and physically fit. They're calling him Rambo or something like that. He was picking up this woman and when she didn't come out, he went in after her."

"What woman?" Frank asked.

"Her name is Cara Justice. Gossip has it that she had his kid way back when. He was staying at her house when the incident occurred."

A slow smile began to spread across Frank's face, crumpling the scars and pulling the flesh until the smile turned into a grimace.

"The name of the town, please."

"Chiltingham, in upstate New York. It's up by the Finger Lakes region. Nearest airport would be at Canandaigua."

"Your check is in the mail," Frank said softly, and disconnected.

Then he stood abruptly and strode to the check-in desk.

"I want to change my flight," he said.

"But sir, none of the planes are taking off now," the clerk said.

"I know that," he said softly. "But when they do…"

The clerk felt herself resisting the urge to shiver as the man thrust his ticket across the counter and continued.

"I need to reroute from D.C. to Canandaigua, New York."

"Yes, sir," she said. "You do know there will be an extra fee for—"

"Just do it," Frank said. "Money is no object."

Chapter 12

It was just after nine the next morning when Frank's plane landed at Canandaigua Airport. He disembarked without notice, just one of the twenty-three passengers to arrive, and proceeded through the terminal to rent a car. Within the hour, and armed with a map of the area, he drove out of the airport toward Chiltingham. He had no plans beyond finding Cara Justice's home. After that, he would let impulse lead him.

A couple of hours later, he entered the city limits and was surprised by the quaint New England charm of the small country town. Saltbox houses abounded, some painted a pure robin's-egg blue with white trim, others in varying shades of pastels and whites. Lawns and hedges were neatly trimmed and the flower boxes at the downstairs windows of the houses overflowed with splashes of color.

He tried to picture the man known as Jonah living in a nondescript place like this, but the image wouldn't come. He reminded himself they'd grown up in a place not unlike this. He sneered. So little brother was trying to return to his roots. Too damned bad.

His stomach grumbled, a reminder that he hadn't eaten since yesterday afternoon, so he pulled in at the curb in front of a small café and went inside.

The scent of frying bacon and coffee only increased his hunger as he took a seat in a corner booth. Before he could reach for the menu resting between the napkin dispenser and the salt and pepper shakers, a waitress was at the booth with a pot of fresh coffee.

"Coffee, sir?" she asked.

He nodded and turned over the cup already at the place setting.

"Do you know what you want, or would you like a little time to look at the menu?"

"Bring me a couple of eggs over easy, bacon and hash browns and some whole wheat toast."

"Yes, sir. Would you care for juice?"

Frank looked up at her and smiled. "Sure, why not? How about grapefruit?"

The waitress nodded, although her attention had been transferred from the order she was taking to the mass of scars on the side of his face.

"It isn't catching," Frank said, taking some satisfaction in her embarrassment as she hurried away.

But the incident only served to remind him of why he'd come.

An hour later he drove out of town with a full belly and the directions to Cara Justice's home. It was relatively easy to find. His confirmation that he was at the right place was the name on the mailbox at the end of the drive.

Justice.

He smiled. How ironically perfect. That's what he'd come for—some justice. He paused at the mailbox to look at the house, making a quick assessment of the layout of the grounds. Since there was no need advertising his presence yet, he would come back after dark. As he put the car in gear to drive away, a woman came around the corner of the house with a garden hose in her hand. He hit the brakes, his eyes narrowing as he watched her watering the shrubs next to the house.

So, you take good care of what belongs to you. That's good. My Martha was a woman like that.

Suddenly angry with himself for even thinking of Martha and this woman in the same breath, he accelerated angrily and sped away.

At the sound of flying gravel, Cara turned, noticing a tan sedan as it sped past her house. She shook her head as she returned to her task, thinking that some people should never be allowed to drive.

As the water began to flow, a small fly buzzed at the corner of her eye and she turned to brush it away. When she saw her reflection in the windows above the shrubs, she couldn't help but flinch. The bruise on the side of her face was huge now, a dark, purplish-green. It was also the main reason she'd skipped going to church services this morning. If she'd gone, she would have had to talk about the incident at the supermarket and she wasn't in the mood. And there were bound to be questions as to why David wasn't with her, and where he had gone, and she darned sure wasn't in the mood to talk about him. So she was here, watering her plants and fussing at flies as if those were the only important things in her life, when in reality she wanted to scream. At least she would have Bethany and her family as dinner guests tonight. The vitality of their growing family should be enough to keep her mind off of what was happening with David, if only for a while.

A short while later, she went back inside and began making a strawberry tart for tonight's dessert.

Frank had always liked the dark. Even as a kid, he'd felt safe within the thick velvet shadows. It gave him a feeling similar to that of being cosseted beneath a warm comforter on a cold winter night. Tonight, he had the added adrenaline rush of a foray into new territory. He'd driven his car off the road into the woods about a quarter of a mile below Cara Justice's house and now he stood at the edge of the clearing, watching as she bid her company goodbye.

From the way they were all behaving, he took them to be family—a man, a woman and two young girls. He moved closer, staying within the tree line but wanting to hear what was being said. When he heard Cara Justice call the woman Bethany, he flinched. By God, two birds with one stone. If he had a rifle, he could fix it right now. David's woman. David's child. The perfect justice. If he popped both of them, he might just walk away from baby brother and let him live with the hell of knowing he was the cause of their deaths.

Then his flights of fancy settled. No need to make hasty decisions. The only certainty in his life was meting out a justice of his own. He leaned forward, listening intently as the people bid their goodbyes.

"Dinner was great, Mom," Bethany said.

"No, it was fantastic," Tom added, and Cara chuckled.

"I sent you the rest of the strawberry tart, so you don't have to keep bragging," she said.

Her son-in-law laughed. "You don't think I laid it on too thick?"

"Well, yes, but it was unnecessary. You were going to get the leftovers anyway."

Cara leaned in the back seat of the car and blew kisses to her two granddaughters.

"You're going to have to come spend the night with me at least one more time before school starts," she said.

"Oh, Nanny, don't even mention school," Rachel said.

"No school," her little sister, Kelly, echoed, although she wouldn't even attend preschool for another year.

Cara laughed and then stood back as they drove away, waving until the taillights of Tom's car disappeared.

Rubbing her arms with her hands and wishing David was here to hold her close, she took a deep breath and looked at the sky. The night was clear, the sky littered with stars.

"I'm here, darling, under the same sky, looking at the same stars. Just come home safely," she said softly, then dropped her head and said a brief, silent prayer.

An owl hooted from a nearby tree and she turned to look, hoping for a glimpse of the nighttime visitor, when something told her she was no longer alone. She turned abruptly, raking the area with a nervous gaze, but saw nothing to cause her alarm. Still the notion wouldn't go away. Uneasy, she hurried inside, locking the door behind her, then quickly moved throughout the rest of the house, making sure all the windows and doors were locked. Only after she'd set the security alarm did the hackles on her neck begin to settle. By the time she had turned out the lights and was moving toward her bedroom, she had almost convinced herself she'd been imagining things.

Almost—but not quite.

A short while later as she lay in bed, drifting between restlessness and sleep, the feeling came back. But it was too brief to hang on to. Exhaustion claimed her, and she slept.

Frank had the license number of Bethany's car. It would be simple enough to hack into the DMV and find her address. She would come later, after he'd dealt with her mother.

He waited until Cara had turned out the lights before making his move, still impressed by the fact that she'd sensed his presence. That wasn't something he'd expected. But then he thought of the man David had become and decided he wouldn't have settled for any ordinary woman. Jonah had to have a mate comparable to his talents.

A frisson of anticipation rippled through Frank's body. It stood to reason she would be perceptive enough to sense something amiss in her world. Would she sense him again—when he was standing at the foot of her bed?

When more than an hour had passed, Frank was satisfied that enough time had passed. He started toward her house, thankful that she didn't own a dog. He hated dogs.

For more than half an hour, he moved around outside, looking in windows, peering into the place where David had left his heart. From the little he could see, the house looked warm and inviting, and again he thought of Martha and ached. People lied when they claimed the passage of time made a loss easier to bear. For him, it was the opposite. The longer he was without her, the emptier his world became.

When he discovered the windows to Cara's bedroom, he ran his fingers along the edges, just to check and make sure they were locked, which they were. It didn't stop him from watching her through the part in the curtains. He watched for several long minutes until he was certain she was soundly asleep, then he headed for the electrical box he'd seen on the backside of the house. He knew the house was protected by a security alarm, but for a man who'd hacked into top secret computer files of the United States government, bypassing a personal security system was simple.

A few snips here, a couple of connections there and he was in. After that, he picked the lock on her front door and walked inside.

Once in, he stood for a moment, letting his vision adjust to the absence of light, until he could easily make out shapes of furniture as well as a hall leading toward the back of the house.

As he began to move, he smiled at the thickness of the wall-to-wall carpeting. Perfect covering to mask his steps, should she be a light sleeper.

He took a small penlight from his pocket and raked the walls with the tiny beam, more out of curiosity than anything else. He'd seen what Cara Justice looked like. Now he wanted to know what turned her on. Did she like bright, vibrant colors, or was she as subdued as she appeared?

As the light fell on the mantel, he saw the pictures she'd displayed and moved closer. From what he could tell, she had three, not just one child as he'd first believed, and she'd obviously been married to someone other than David. Two of the children looked like the stocky blond man standing beside her in one of the pictures. But it was the tall, slender woman with dark hair that Frank was interested in—the one who looked like David.

Bethany.

Nice name. Probably a nice enough woman. Damned shame his brother's blood ran in her veins.

He moved the penlight along the mantel, and when it fell on the snapshot of David with the fish, he caught himself from grunting aloud. It was a kick in the gut feeling of déjà vu that made him sick to his stomach.

David was laughing, making fun of the size of the fish on his line, and before Frank thought, he was grinning, too.

Stupid little shrimp of a fish. Why the hell would he want to have his picture taken with something like that?

And then he jerked as if he'd been slapped, reminding himself of why he was here. He was wondering about David when he should have been asking himself what the hell was wrong with him. He didn't give a damn about what David liked to do for recreation. It didn't even matter that David had looked so happy, or so at peace. He set the picture back on the mantel and turned away.

It, by God, does not matter.

Making himself focus on why he had come, he headed for the hall, remembering the direction of Cara's bedroom as he went. It should be the one at the far end of the house. Sure enough he was right.

He stood quietly just outside the doorway, listening to the soft, even sounds of her breathing, and checked his pocket for the knife that he carried. He favored knives over guns, two to one. They were swift and silent killers, much cleaner than a gun. Bullets always tore up the body. A knife, when used properly, could empty a body of blood within a minute, often less.

Confident that she was still asleep, he took two steps to the right and then one forward, then smiled.

He was inside her bedroom.

He could tell she was above average height and quite slender, although she lay on her side with her back to the door.

A dim glow from the outside security light pierced the gap in the curtains, highlighting the hair spilling across her pillow. From where he was standing, it looked like gossamer, and he had a sudden desire to see if it was as soft as it looked.

Resisting his carnal urges, he moved to the foot of her bed instead, and then slowed his breathing as he watched her sleep. Her breasts were full, her skin firm. She was a woman in every sense of the word. As he stood, watching her sleep, his palms began to sweat. It had been a long, long time since he'd lain with a woman like that.

She shifted in her sleep, quietly sighing and then rolling over onto her back.

He froze. Only when he was certain she was still asleep did he shift position again, this time moving slightly toward the doorway for a better view of her face.

God. She was beautiful.

He shivered with sudden anger, unable to believe that a woman other than Martha could awake any sort of emotion. His hands curled into fists and he tried to make himself move. In one single leap, he could be in her bed, lying on top of her, hearing her scream. He could have her with ease, savoring her panic as he whispered what he was going to do to her and her lover. It would be easy, so easy.

As a jealous lust for what was David's gained momentum, he leaned forward. Then he heard her take a deep breath and exhale on a sob. He paused again, frustrated by his hesitation.

So she's grieving. So what? So am I.

He took another step forward, his fists uncurling, his fingers itching to encircle the fragility of her neck.

Frank... I'll always love you.

He jerked as if he'd been slapped. Martha's voice was as loud in his head as if she was standing beside him.

His eyes narrowed. He wondered what she would think if she saw him now. Would she still love him, or would she look upon him with loathing for what he'd become?

As he watched, a tear rolled down the side of Cara's face then he heard her whisper a name.

David.

He cursed silently. Damn her. Damn her to hell. Fingering the blade of his knife, he started across the floor.

Bethany sat up in bed.

One moment she'd been sound asleep, and the next she was wide awake and cognizant. It was a skill she'd perfected after the birth of her first child, and it had yet to prove her wrong.

Glancing over at Tom, who was still sound asleep, she smiled to herself and then slipped out of bed. The roof could fall in and he wouldn't hear it. Out of habit, she reached for her robe as she left their bedroom.

As she entered her daughters' bedroom, she instinctively moved toward Kelly's bed first. As the youngest, she was still prone to more of the childhood illnesses than her sister, Rachel, who was almost ten.

But a quick check of her daughter's cool forehead eased her worries. Obviously, it wasn't Kelly who'd awakened her. She turned then, moving quietly to Rachel's bedside, but she, too, was resting quietly and fast asleep.

Frowning, she left their room, pausing momentarily in the hallway to listen. The house sounds were normal.

A clock ticking.

A tree branch scratching at the eaves of the house.

The intermittent sound of Tom's occasional snore.

Nothing that should have awakened her in such a manner.

Shivering now from nerves rather than cold, she wrapped her arms around herself and thought about waking Tom. But he had to go to work tomorrow and she resisted the notion. Telling herself that she must have been dreaming, she started toward their bedroom.

No sooner had she begun to move than she heard the faint sound of a board squeak, and when it did, her heart skipped a beat. There was a loose floorboard beneath the kitchen linoleum that squeaked just like that as she stood at the kitchen sink and another by the doorway leading into the living room.

Now she was scared.

Bolting into the bedroom, she shook Tom awake, then put her hand over his mouth and whispered in his ear.

"I think someone is in the house."

Tom's eyes widened. Without speaking, he rolled out of bed and hurried toward their closet. Taking a box down from the top shelf, he unlocked it, took out a loaded handgun and motioned for her to call 911.

"Yes, I know," she said softly. "I'm going to get Kelly
we're going to go to Mother and Daddy's room, un-
stand?"
The confusion on her daughter's face turned to fear
ner voice started to shake.
'Mommy…what's wrong?"
'Maybe nothing," she said. "Daddy's just checking
house." She scooped Kelly up in her arms and laid
across her shoulder and then grabbed Rachel's hand.
me with me, baby, and don't talk anymore."
seconds, she was across the hall and inside her
oom. Quietly, she shut the door and then laid Kelly
on the bed, pulled Rachel into her lap and then
up the phone.
n back," she said.
e your children with you?" the dispatcher asked.
."
ere is your husband?"
any wanted to scream. Instead, she took a deep
nd made herself focus.
't know."
e doing fine," the dispatcher said. "Tell me…
your children's names?"
l and Kelly."
Howell? Is she in the fourth grade?"
ll be," Bethany said.
her. My son, Billy, is her age. My name is
My dad owns the bakery."
e of a familiar face to go with the voice on
of the line was somehow encouraging.
so scared."
ing really good," the dispatcher said. "The

"What about the girls?" she whispered.

"Call the police first and then get them," he mouthed back.

Bethany watched in horror as Tom slipped out of their bedroom, then bolted for the phone. Seconds later, the 911 dispatcher came on the line.

"Nine one one. What is your emergency?"

"I think someone is in our house," Bethany whispered.

"Ma'am, are you alone?"

"No, my husband, Tom, is here, too. He's gone into the front of the house to check. He has a gun."

"Is your address one oh seven Sunset Drive?"

"Yes. Please hurry."

"Yes, ma'am, please stay on the line while I dispatch the call."

Now Bethany's heart was pounding. She needed to be across the hall with her children.

"Hello? Hello?" she whispered.

"Yes, ma'am, I'm still here," the dispatcher said.

"I need to be across the hall with my girls," she whispered.

"Ma'am, I need you to stay on the line with me. There is a police unit in your area. It should be there in a couple of minutes."

"Oh, God," Bethany whispered. "That could be too late."

"Just stay calm and listen to me, please. What's your name?"

"Bethany Howell."

"Okay, Bethany, tell me what you hear."

"Nothing now. I don't even hear Tom."

She started to shake. What if something had happened to him? What if someone was already coming this way? She needed to get to the girls. She needed to get them out of the house.

"Please. I need to get my daughters. I need to get them out of the house."

"Ma'am. Please. I need you to stay calm and stay quiet. Your husband might hear you moving around and think you were the thief. We don't want any accidental shootings, all right?"

Lord. She hadn't thought of that.

"All right, but please hurry."

The moment the board squeaked, Frank flinched. Seconds later, he heard bedsprings give and then the soft pat-pat sounds of bare feet on tile. His fingers curled around the knife in his hand as he moved toward the doorway. Moments later, he saw the woman come out of the bedroom and walk down the hall into another room.

His eyes narrowed angrily. That woman was David's daughter—but she was also his niece.

A good mother always checks on the children first.

The thought came out of nowhere and then he realized it was something his mother used to say when she would come in to tell him and David good night.

Son of a bitch. Why am I dwelling on all of these people who are already dead? They don't matter anymore. I need payback, not a stroll down memory lane.

Moments later, the woman exited the bedroom and stopped in the hallway. Instinctively, he slid into the shadows, and as he did, another board squeaked. He rolled his eyes, wondering why the hell these people hadn't nailed down the floors like they should have done.

He stood there in silence, well aware he'd
Should he run, or just finish what he came

When she bolted into the bedroom, he h
moments before his decision was made.

Bethany stood at the window, the phon
ear, watching and praying for the police
that moment, she got a glimpse of flashin
ping the hill just beyond their house, the
peared behind the trees.

She started to cry softly.

"They're here. They're here," she w
"Ma'am, are you saying the police a
"No, but I saw their lights on the h
"Don't go to the door, ma'am. Wait
okay? They'll search the outside of
for signs of entry before they atten
"Yes, all right," she said, her he
that she knew help was here.

Seconds later, she heard the
car pulled in the drive.

"They're outside now," she
"Just stay with me, ma'am
"Yes, all right," Bethany w
ror, she heard her oldest dau
"Mother! Mother!"
"My daughter is awak
get her before she walks
but I'm going after them

Without waiting for
room and down the ha
rubbing her eyes.

"Mother, there's a

police tell me they're going to your front door. Is there someone there to let them in?"

"Tom. Tom should be there."

"All right. Just stay with me a minute until I know they're inside."

Bethany could hear the faint but unmistakable sounds of someone knocking at the door. She caught herself holding her breath, praying that the sounds would stop, because that would mean that Tom had let them inside. They knocked again. Tears were rolling down her face.

Please God, don't let anything happen to my husband.

"No one is answering," the dispatcher said. "The police are asking me to tell you that they're going to come inside."

"The door is locked," Bethany said.

"They know. Just stay where you are, okay?"

"Yes," Bethany said, then dropped her head and started to sob. Something was terribly wrong.

David paced the floor of his room—from the bed to the windows and back again. He couldn't sleep. Every instinct he had told him something was wrong. What if Simon saw the broadcast of the robbery? What if he put two and two together and went looking for answers? Then he relaxed. No way! Simon never even knew about Cara, so he couldn't know about Bethany either.

Damn it to hell, but he hated being cooped up in this place. He was no better than a caged rat, waiting for someone to open a door so he could make a run for the cheese. Only the cheese in this maze was his brother, and his brother was taking his own sweet time about answering the e-mail that had been sent out.

Damn him, David thought. *Damn him to hell.*

He started for the phone, the need to talk to Cara uppermost in his mind, but then stopped. It was after three in the morning. Just because he couldn't sleep didn't mean he needed to disturb her rest. He hoped she'd taken a sedative to help her relax. The kidnapping and the assault were so recent, he knew she would still be suffering from the memories of the incident. Even worse, it galled him to know that just when she needed him most, he'd left her alone.

Damn Frank Wilson to hell and back. Why had he survived? What possible good had his existence proved?

Then he thought of Frank's daughter, Lise Meldrum, who by now was probably Mrs. Russell Devane. Her life was proof that there had still been some good left in Frank—that he'd at least been capable of loving a woman long enough to father a child. From what he knew, Frank's wife had been dead for years and Lise had been running their Australian cattle station in her father's absence. If Frank had died in that fire all those years ago, then Lise would never have been born.

David dropped onto the side of the bed, his shoulders slumped with fatigue. He glanced at the clock one more time and then rolled over onto his side. The least he could do was close his eyes and rest.

Within minutes, he was asleep.

Chapter 13

It started to rain just as Frank reached his car. Hurrying before his clothes got all wet, he opened the door and jumped inside. But he didn't bother looking back to see if he'd been followed. He'd already been out of the house and into the woods before the police cruiser had even pulled into the yard. As he locked the car door, he took a gun out of his pocket and laid it beside the knife he'd been carrying.

He paused a moment, resting his forehead against the steering wheel and letting the adrenaline rush settle as his heartbeat shifted into a normal rhythm. When he finally looked up, he was smiling. The gun he'd taken from Bethany's husband was out of habit. He'd never left a weapon on a victim before and he wasn't starting now, but as he'd been running through the woods, a thought had occurred. Now that he was on his way to

D.C., how poetic would it be to kill David with his own daughter's gun?

He liked the idea. In fact, he loved it. But getting it on a plane could be a problem. He started the car and quickly drove away. Considering what he'd left behind, lingering in the area wasn't wise, but as he drove, his mind was still sorting through the possibilities that would yield him what he wanted.

The streets were deserted as he entered Chiltingham on his way to the Canandaigua Airport. Even though no one was in sight, he still took great care not to speed or run any lights. The last thing he needed was to get caught with a stolen weapon.

On his way out of town, he passed a billboard advertising Fedex. About a half a mile later, the significance of that sign suddenly hit him, and a plan began to evolve. Now he knew how to get the gun to D.C. All he needed was a small box and some packing and the address of his hotel. With a little luck, it would be there waiting for him when he arrived.

It was mid-morning the next day when an envelope suddenly appeared beneath the door in David's room. Still in the shower and unaware of what had happened, he didn't notice until his breakfast arrived.

Later, as he was dressing, someone knocked on his door. Tucking a rugby shirt into the waistband of his slacks, he went to answer it, and as he did, he noticed the envelope and picked it up.

"Who is it?" David asked.

"Room service," a man answered.

Although he was expecting the food, he still looked through the peephole before opening the door. A bellhop smiled a good morning as he pushed a food-laden cart into the room.

"Where would you like this, sir?"

"On the table by the window will be fine," David said, as he signed the check and handed it to the bellhop, along with a generous tip.

"Thank you, sir. When you've finished, ring guest services and we'll come and remove the dishes. Enjoy your meal."

When he was gone, David sat down before the food, surprised to find he was actually hungry. He laid the letter aside for the moment and spread some jelly on his toast before tackling the first bite of his eggs. When he had partially satiated his hunger, he took a drink of coffee and then picked up the letter. Curious, he leaned back in the chair as he slit the flap, unprepared for what was inside. Abruptly, he sat up with a thump and reached for the phone.

"Front desk. How may I help you, Mr. Wilson?"

"Someone left a note under my door this morning. I want to talk to who put it there."

"Let me connect you with the mail office."

A few seconds later a woman answered. David repeated his request. There was a slight pause, as if she was checking her records.

"I'm sorry, Mr. Wilson, but we have no record of a letter being sent to your room."

"Are you sure?"

"Yes, sir, I'm sure. I've been on duty since six this morning. I would have known."

"Thank you," David said, and hung up.

His food no longer appealed, his appetite completely gone. Damn it to hell. Frank had once again regained the upper hand. He'd found David, had some flunky deliver a message and walked away without notice. As he reread the letter, his stomach knotted.

O two hundred hours tonight, little brother. At the Wall.

David laid down the note, his gut in knots. How ironic that it was both their intentions to meet at the same place. The Vietnam Memorial, otherwise known as the Wall, was fitting. A symbol of where it all began.

He stood abruptly, gathered his room key and wallet and then picked up his tray and set it in the hall. He would meet Frank at 2:00 a.m. as he'd requested, but he had some reconnoitering in the area that he wanted to do first and he needed to rent a car.

The day was hot, the wind brisk, and still they came. From the steps of the Lincoln Memorial where David was standing, hundreds of people could be seen milling about the grassy mall. Some were taking pictures, others laughing and talking, pointing with excitement at the surrounding monuments. Teenagers abounded in groups and he remembered that age—the awkwardness and lack of respect for anything or anyone older than themselves.

As for the veterans, they were easy to pick out. They were the ones who stood the longest, spoke the least and quite often left with tears in their eyes. And then there were their widows and families, tenderly stroking stone and marble that had been set in their loved one's honor because it was all they had left to touch.

The long, crystal-clear waters of the gazing pool that lay between the Lincoln and the Washington monuments reflected the surrounding treetops, as well as a clear, cloudless sky. At the north end of the pool, David watched a flock of circling pigeons as they landed on the greens and then proceeded to the water for a drink. The setting was idyllic—a picture-perfect day. It seemed obscene that before the night was over, either he or Frank would most likely die in this place.

Abruptly, he adjusted his sunglasses and took the steps downward, angling to the left as he went. He'd been at the Wall many times before, but never with the need to lay out an ambush.

As he approached it, a wave of guilt washed over him. That he was actually coming to this place with such a heinous plot in mind seemed sacrilegious, yet he'd been given no choice. Even if he'd been inclined to change the game plan, it was too late now. The wheels of his destiny had been set in motion. All he had to do was make sure he wasn't run over and killed in the process.

Anxious to get this over with, he sidestepped a couple pushing a stroller, then moved past a group of teenagers. As he neared the Wall, he came up behind an elderly couple trying to negotiate the downward incline. The old man was using a walker and his wife was trying to hold it upright, since it had a tendency to roll faster than either of them could walk.

At that moment, the last thing he wanted was personal contact with anyone, but his conscience wouldn't let him ignore them.

"Need some help, sir?" he asked, and then gripped the front of the walker and proceeded to slow it down so the old couple could keep up.

The woman's face was pink from exertion and the smile she gave David was enough to make him sorry he'd even hesitated to help.

"Oh, thank you, son. We didn't know this was so steep. Matthew's walker was about to take him for a ride."

Her youthful giggle surprised David, and he caught himself smiling back.

"Have you been here before?" he asked.

Her smile crumpled. "No. We always meant to, but we live so far away. We're from Idaho, you know. Our son Dennis's name is here. Matthew wanted to see it before—"

She didn't finish what she'd been going to say, but David knew what she meant.

"Got cancer," the old man suddenly offered, as he scooted along under David's guidance. "I reckon I'll die of old age before I die of the cancer, though."

David didn't know what to say. Their optimism in the face of such adversity shamed him.

"We never know what life's going to hand us, do we?" he finally said, and then changed the subject. "Do you know what section your son's name is in?"

The old woman gave him a scrap of paper she'd been holding.

"The lady back at the information booth gave that to us."

He read the name, the section and row and then turned toward the Wall, checking to see how far along they'd come.

"It's a little bit farther down," he said. "Can you make it?"

"Me and Shirley made it this far. I reckon I can go a little farther," Matthew said.

A few yards down the slope, David stopped.

"Just a minute, sir. It should be right along here."

The old man turned his walker so it would no longer roll, and then stared at the Wall, suddenly overwhelmed by the expanse of names that seemed to go on forever.

"We sure weren't the only ones who grieved, were we, Shirley?"

His wife leaned her head against his shoulder, tears streaming down her face.

Then David turned. "Here. His name is here."

They stared at the name, as if trying to conjure up an image to go with it, but he could see their eyes were blurred by tears.

"It's been such a long time," Shirley said. "I thought I'd cried myself out years ago."

"Yes, ma'am," David said softly, and handed her his handkerchief. "I know what you mean."

Matthew looked at him then, judging him with all the wisdom of his eighty-plus years.

"You got kin on this wall, too?"

"Yes, sir."

"Damn shame, that's what it is," he muttered, and then took out his own handkerchief and blew his nose while his wife began fumbling in her handbag. When she pulled out a camera, David knew what she intended.

"Ma'am, if you would allow me, I'd be glad to take your picture."

"I want to stand beside my boy's name," Shirley said, as she patted at her hair, trying to smooth down the white, flyaway fluff that the breeze had disturbed.

"The names don't show up too well on photographs," David said. "But if Matthew will turn just a little bit this way," David said, easing the old man and the walker a little closer to the wall, "and if you'll stand on this side, you can put your hand on your son's name. That way it will be easier for you to see it when the picture is developed."

Shirley nodded, but as she reached toward the name, her gnarled fingers tracing the letters, her little face crumpled. David looked away, waiting for her to contain her emotions.

"I'm ready now," she announced.

He took a few steps backward and lifted the camera to his face.

The image caught within the parameters of the lens almost sent him to his knees.

A dying father.

A grieving mother.

And all that was left of their son was his name on a wall.

He made himself focus and then took a deep breath.

"On the count of three," he said. "One. Two."

He snapped the picture.

"Take one more," Shirley said. "Just in case."

He took the second one, and when he handed her the camera, she gave him back his handkerchief and then gave him a hug.

"Thank you, son," she said. "And we're sorry for your loss."

David nodded, but there wasn't anything he could say. His loss? For years, he believed that he'd lost much more than a brother. Until last week, when Cara Justice had taken him back into her life and her heart, he'd almost lost his faith in God.

David started to help them along when Matthew shook his head.

"It's uphill the rest of the way and I can push better than I can run. We'll make it from here."

They meandered away, talking with animation, delighted that their quest was complete, and as they walked, David noticed that when one of them faltered, the other was there on which to lean.

A knot rose in his throat, swelling and burning until he thought he would choke. When he turned back to the Wall, he found himself looking through a thick blur of tears. Instead of looking for Frank's name, he bowed his head and closed his eyes.

And so he stood within the silence of his own heart, absorbing the peace of the monument and giving homage to the men who'd fought, those who'd died and those who were forever lost. He lost all track of time, freeing his mind of everything and feeling a cleansing from within that he'd never known before.

Finally, he lifted his head and as he started to leave, the hair on the back of his neck suddenly crawled. The sensation was old but familiar. He knew he was being watched.

Remembering the letter he'd found under his door, he turned, eyeing everyone who passed, but saw no one who set off any internal alarms. Convinced he wasn't imagining things, he began scanning the surrounding area. Again, no one person stood out in the crowds that should cause this alarm.

Still uneasy, he began to walk toward the east, coming out of the walkway and up onto the sidewalk. At the crest of the hill, he paused again. The feeling was still there.

A woman screamed loudly off to his right, shrieking her disapproval at her children. Instinctively, David turned toward the sound, and as he did, he caught a flash of movement within a cluster of trees a couple of hundred yards to his left.

There. That's where it was coming from.

It had to be Frank.

He lifted his head, his chin thrust forward in a gesture of defiance.

Frank smiled derisively as he watched his little brother playing Boy Scout to the old man and woman. When they finally moved on and he saw David bowing his head, he sneered.

"Pray, you son of a bitch. You're going to need all the help you can get."

When David suddenly looked up and then turned in place, he realized something had spooked him, but what? Adjusting his binoculars, he began to scan the area, too, searching for answers. When he looked back, David was no longer in sight. A slight spurt of panic came and went as he stepped out from behind a cluster of trees for a closer look. A few seconds later, David emerged from the walkway, pausing at the crest of the hill. As he did, Frank breathed a sigh of relief. It wasn't as though he was going to do anything here—too damned many witnesses, but he liked being the one in control, and being the observer gave him a sense of power.

He moved a step backward, and as he did, he saw David's focus shift. Cursing his carelessness, he retreated behind the trees, then lifted the binoculars, adjusting the focus to make up for David's new location.

When his brother's face came into focus, he jerked as if he'd been shot. David was looking straight at him. His heart started to hammer. His hands started to shake.

"You bastard…you arrogant bastard."

Through the lens, David stood tall and straight, his chin thrust forward in a dare-to-take-me attitude—his feet slightly apart, as if bracing himself for battle. Frank knew that he should move, but he couldn't tear his gaze away. At that moment, the truth of who his brother had become finally hit. Intellectually, he'd known David had been the omnipotent Jonah for several years, but looking at him now, he realized what that entailed.

The man he saw was a modern-day warrior, broad-shouldered and lean, hardened by the years and by life. The word invincible came to mind, but he shoved it aside, because that meant unbeatable, and Frank Wilson wasn't a man who accepted defeat.

To his utter dismay, as he watched, David took off his sunglasses, smiled directly at him, then turned his back and walked away. For Frank, it was a slap-in-the-face gesture he couldn't ignore.

"You'll pay, little brother, and I'll be curious to see how wide you smile when you see your daughter's gun pointed at your head."

Seconds later, he was gone.

David was calmer now than he'd been since this hell began. By this time tomorrow, it would be over. Instead of ordering room service, he decided to go down to the hotel restaurant for dinner. He came out of the elevator and past the bar with nothing but a medium-rare steak on his mind when he suddenly flashed on Cara's face. He was seeing her as she'd looked on the morning he left her sleeping, her hair in gentle disarray, her hands cupped beneath her chin as if she was praying. He wanted to hear her voice—to say something witty that would elicit that throaty chuckle. But if he called her now, before this was over, she would take it as a defeated farewell, rather than the selfish gesture it actually was. So he told himself to suck it up and kept on walking.

A short while later, a hostess seated him at a table for one and laid food and wine menus on the table. He ordered a glass of wine and then opened the menu. A small note was attached at the top, with one word printed in bold, black ink. *Bang.* Anger followed shock as he bolted from his table and headed toward the door, grabbing the hostess by the arm and spinning her around. It wasn't the woman who had just seated him.

"Where is she?" he yelled.

"Sir?"

David saw the fear on her face and immediately regretted his actions as he turned her loose.

"I'm sorry. I didn't mean to frighten you, but I need to talk to the other hostess. Where did she go?"

"There is no other hostess, sir. I'm the only one on duty tonight."

David lowered his voice when all his instincts made him want to scream.

"Not two minutes ago, a woman was standing right where you're standing. She picked up the menus and took me to that table in the back near the windows."

She looked at David as if he'd gone mad.

"Two minutes ago, I was in the kitchen. There was no one else here."

David slapped his leg in frustration and bolted out of the restaurant, then stopped about ten feet from the door. There were at least four different directions she could have gone, and each one of them led outside. As he stood, a sense of calm began to settle. He shook his head and then almost smiled. That was so like Frank. Always wanting to have the last word.

Refusing to let Frank's antics psych him out, he turned and walked into the restaurant, sat down at his table and ordered his meal. When it came, he ate slowly and with relish. Words on paper were nothing but mind games that he wasn't going to play.

Afterward, he went to his room. Debating with himself about what he wanted to do, he hesitated twice and then said what the hell and made the calls, leaving messages at each one.

About fifteen minutes later, one of his calls was returned. He took down the information without comment then sat on the edge of the bed, staring at the numbers. Finally, he picked up the receiver and made one more call, leaving one brief message before hanging up.

He left a wake-up call for midnight, took off his clothes, then laid down and went to sleep.

Frank's confidence had slipped another notch after watching David ignore his latest stunt. Still in his disguise, he'd been at the bar across from the restaurant sipping a drink when David had come running out. He'd been pleased by the anger and confusion he'd seen on David's face. And then he'd seen his brother smile.

It had unnerved him to the point that he'd ordered a second drink. But he'd come to his senses before he drank it, tossed a handful of bills onto the table and left without looking back. He kept running through scenarios all the way to his hotel.

Should he shoot him in the back and get it over with, or follow his urge to confront him first by toying with his mind and watching him come undone?

He thought he would prefer the latter.

When he reached his room, there was a message light

blinking on the phone. He frowned. No one knew he was here. He picked up the receiver and punched in the code to the mailbox, listening as the automated voice came on the line.

Mailbox 1077 has one new message. Message received at 8:05 p.m.

Frank's fingers clenched as a man's deep voice slid into his ear.

You missed.

His eyes widened in disbelief as he slammed the phone down. Damn it all to hell and back, how had David found him? He hadn't registered under his own name. He had not even shown his real face. He'd stayed in disguise from morning to night, removing the facial prosthetics only when he went to bed.

The son of a bitch!

Panic spread as he turned out the lights and then moved to the windows. Were they watching his room—just waiting for him to make his move? Was he going to be arrested before he even had a chance to pay David back for the hell he'd put him through?

He stood in the dark, peering into the streets below, trying to sort through the traffic for a sign of something suspicious.

There in the parking lot! Behind the wheel of that car on the end. Someone was sitting in the dark behind the wheel. He could see the end of their cigarette glowing in the dark.

But as he watched, a woman suddenly appeared within his vision, and as she did, the driver of the car emerged and went to meet her. They embraced briefly, then got in the car and drove away.

Frank cursed beneath his breath and moved his attention to some people on foot, certain that he was being watched. Yet each time he thought he'd zeroed in on a target, it would prove him false.

Every time he heard footsteps in the hallway, he expected a knock upon his door, and each time the footsteps went away, he went limp with relief. Finally, his nerves shot, he packed his bag, put on a new disguise and slipped out of the hotel, confident he had not been seen.

So he'd go to the meeting place early. There were plenty of places he could hide without being seen. He had yet to be beaten at his own game.

Even when he'd been shot.

Even when he'd been set on fire.

Even then, he had survived.

Tonight wasn't going to be any different.

Satisfied that he'd gotten away unobserved, Frank got in his car and drove away. He had Bethany's gun, his favorite knife, a one-way ticket to the Florida Keys and was already planning what kind of place he would buy. Something small but comfortable and close to the water. He liked the water. He liked to fish. That's what he would do. By the time he got to the area and parked, he was already planning what kind of furniture he would buy. He started to cross the greens and then paused and went back to the car. He opened the trunk, removed a bag and quickly removed his disguise. When he met David face to face, he wanted him to see the real damage that the fire had done. He needed to see the guilt and the shame on his baby brother's face—right before he killed him.

David rolled over and opened his eyes, wide awake and rested before his wake-up call came. When it did, he was already into the preparations for what lay ahead.

His pants were black and fit close to his body, leaving no loose fabric to catch on anything. A black shirt—lightweight but long-sleeved, to cover any white flesh that would show in the dark. Black, flat-heeled, rubber-soled shoes, soundless on any surface. In the bag that he carried was a handgun—the same one he'd used to free the hostages—a knife that he'd carried since Vietnam and a cell phone that was, for the moment, turned off. He tossed a small tin of camouflage face paint into the mix and then zipped the bag.

Exiting his room, he decided against the elevator and made his way to the stairs, taking the six floors down in less than a minute, retrieving his car from hotel parking without being observed, and was on the street within seconds—a true credit to being Jonah. He drove through the streets of D.C., parked on a side street beneath a broken streetlight and quickly disappeared into the night.

Although it had been a long time since he'd actually been on any missions, it felt normal, even comfortable to blend with the shadows. He'd learned long ago that darkness could be a friend, and in his business, he had few friends he could claim.

As he moved through the area, he felt the differences in the air out in the open as opposed to that beneath the trees. Even at night, there was a difference in temperature. It even felt thicker, although he knew that was a fanciful thought.

Once, he paused near a cluster of shrubs and glanced at the sky. What heavenly bodies had been visible were now all but obliterated by a growing bank of clouds.

On the horizon, he could see the faint threads of distant lightning, although the storm was too far away to be heard. He glanced at the digital readout on his wristwatch and then resumed his trek.

It wouldn't be long now.

Would Frank be waiting where he'd said he'd be, or would he be lying in wait, waiting to shoot him in the back as he passed?

David couldn't assume that his brother would do anything honorable. Not at this point. He didn't know what to expect, but he did know that whatever it was Frank had planned, he would most likely have a slim-to-none chance of survival.

Although he didn't like the odds, it was the *slim* that he focused on, rather than the *none*. He'd survived a lot worse with a lot poorer odds, so he hastened his steps, moving quickly now, anxious to get there. Anxious to get it over with.

By the time he got within seeing distance of the Wall, he was moving with extreme caution—always staying within cover until he was confident of the area before him. Dressed like the shadows within which he moved, he got as close as he could.

David stood quietly for long, silent minutes as time continued to pass. The closer and closer it came to 2:00 a.m., the more certain he was that Frank was nearby. But there was no way he could get to the Wall without being seen, so he stood and he waited, praying for something to change. When it did, he took it as a positive sign that God might be on his side.

It started to rain, first a whisper of mist, and then, within seconds, a blinding downpour. He was instantly drenched, but it was the first time in his life he could ever remember being glad to be this wet. The heavy rainfall afforded him the best cover he could possibly have achieved. And, although he was fairly certain at this point that he could have walked up on Frank without being seen, he wouldn't abandon all caution.

He dropped to his stomach and started to crawl.

Chapter 14

Despite the dark, overcast sky, the lights from the surrounding monuments kept the night at bay, and even though the hour was late, an occasional tourist could be seen meandering on the path leading to the Vietnam Memorial. Frank figured them as vets by their army surplus clothing and the way they lingered at the Wall, as if standing at attention. They didn't stay long, but the intermittent appearance of strangers kept him nervous. What if their presence kept David away?

With each passing hour, Frank felt himself coming unwound. This moment had been too long in coming. Instead of being tensed and focused, he felt weary and old. Hell, he was old in the ways that counted.

The fact that he'd been here at the monument far longer than he'd planned to be wasn't making things any easier. Within an hour of leaving the hotel, he knew that he'd overreacted, but it was too late to go back. So he had walked the area until midnight, searching for the best place to hide, finally settling among a thick stand of shrubs beneath a cluster of trees. Sheltered from most of the lighting and from any passersby, he began his watch.

Now he'd been here for hours. It was well after one in the morning, his knees were hurting, and the overcast sky had started to come undone. What had begun as a faint, drifting mist was escalating into an all-out thunderstorm, seriously diminishing his view. From where he was hiding, he could no longer see the Wall. If and when David showed, he wouldn't know it. If the rain didn't stop, he would have to move, well aware that when he did, he would give himself away. So he watched the time, hoping the storm would pass.

It didn't.

Thirty minutes later, the rain was still coming down and it was time to end that which had been left undone. He emerged from the bushes, completely soaked. Although the gesture was futile, he swiped his hands across his face to clear his vision, then checked his weapons.

His knife was still in his vest and the gun he'd taken from Bethany's husband was on his hip. The familiar shape of metal against his palm was comforting to a man who had lived his life by the sword.

Once more, he glanced at the digital readout on his watch. It was exactly 2:00 a.m. He straightened his shoulders and started to walk, no longer concerned about staying concealed. Face to face was how it had begun. Face to face was how it would end.

He moved past the statue of the nurses honoring the women who'd served in Vietnam, staying on the footpath that would bring him in at the east end of the Wall. Although the lights still burned, the Wall itself was a dark blur within the downpour. He felt the ground beginning to slope and knew he was moving downward on the right path. Every sensory nerve that he had was on overload as he listened, trying to decipher sounds that didn't belong to the storm. By the time he reached the apex of the memorial he was in knots, damning his brother and damning this rain.

It took David several seconds to realize that one of the shadows he'd been watching had started to move. Only after he blinked did he realize that it wasn't the shadow that was moving, but the man who was passing through.

His pulse jerked, but it was the only thing about his body in motion. He lay flat to the ground and watched, confident that Frank could pass right by him and never know he was there. He also knew that if he wanted, he could shoot Frank right now, without a word, without having to look at his face.

And it had to be said that he considered it. He wanted this over with in the very worst way, but he could also subdue and arrest him. It wouldn't be hard. That would leave the mess with Uncle Sam. It would, however, also endanger SPEAR, and that couldn't happen.

He knew Frank well enough by now to know that if he wound up in jail, there wasn't a cell in solitary strong enough to stop him from talking. With a few well-chosen words to the right—or wrong—people, SPEAR's benefit to the world would be null and void. And so David lay in the rain, struggling with his conscience and with what he knew he would have to do, all the while watching as Frank came closer and closer.

Frank was jumpy enough, but when a shaft of lightning suddenly struck nearby, shattering what was left of his control and striking close enough that he ducked, he hit the ground with a curse. Momentarily blinded by the flash, he covered his eyes. When he finally struggled to his feet, David was standing less than ten feet away. Adrenaline kicked like a mule as he went into a crouch, grabbing the pistol, swinging it toward his brother's chest.

"Hello, Frank. Long time no see."

Frank was pissed. He was the only one holding a weapon and yet once again, his brother seemed to have taken the upper hand. He straightened, unwilling to be the one who'd first taken a defensive stance.

Rain pelted both men, running down their faces and onto the ground between them, culminating in an eddying swirl that disappeared into some underground drain.

"You son of a bitch," Frank snarled.

David stared, trying to find the brother he'd once known in the tangled flesh of that man's face.

"We came from the same woman, Frank. Be careful what you say."

Frank roared. The rage came up and out of him without warning, diluted by the rain and tempered by the power of the storm.

"You set me on fire! What kind of a brother would do something like that? Answer me!" he screamed. "I want to know! I need to know!"

"I didn't set you on fire to harm you. I was trying to hide the shame of what you'd done from everyone, including the military. Besides, I thought you were dead."

Forty years of anger overwhelmed whatever caution Frank Wilson had left.

"Bull!" he screamed, and started walking toward David, the gun aimed right at his face.

But David didn't move—didn't even back up. Instead, he extended his arms to his sides, and for a moment it looked to Frank as if David was offering himself up for crucifixion.

"So…you're going to shoot me again, are you, brother?"

Frank stumbled. "What the hell do you mean…again?"

David stared at him without moving, unflinching beneath the onslaught of the storm and the dark, ominous barrel of the gun in his brother's hand.

"You shot first, you sanctimonious bastard," David said. "The gunrunner's money was worth more to you than I was, remember?"

Frank's heart skipped a beat. His gut started to burn.

"Shut up," he yelled. "Just shut up and say your prayers."

"I've already said them earlier today," David said. "Don't you remember?"

"Yeah, I saw you playing Boy Scout for that old man," Frank yelled. "You cared more for him than you did for me. I had a good thing going there in Nam and you screwed it up. We would have both been set for life when the war was over. But no, you had to play Boy Scout then, too, didn't you?"

Anger pushed back at David, and he started to talk, raising his voice with every word until at the end he was shouting at Frank through the rain.

"You were selling our guns to the enemy, Frank. How do you justify that in your sleep? How many ghosts haunt your dreams every night? How many men did you put on this wall?"

Frank shook his head. "You're changing the subject. Stop changing the subject!"

"No," David shouted. "You *are* the subject. Your whole life has been selfish. No one ever mattered to you. No one ever counted but you. You've spent the last twelve months trying to bring me down, and still you couldn't do it. You didn't give a damn that you were ruining good people's lives, or that you had put our entire country in jeopardy. All you wanted was revenge. But it's not going to happen. It's over, Frank. Even if you kill me, you're finished. You'll never get away."

Frank blinked, suddenly aware that his brother might not have come alone, after all. He glanced over David's shoulder into the darkness, waiting for the shadows to move. Desperate to get this over with, he took aim again.

"I will get away, just like I've always done." Then he smiled.

David hid a shudder when the scars on Frank's face twisted the smile into a demonic grimace.

But Frank didn't give a damn about how he looked and he wasn't through turning the knife in his brother's heart. If David loved Cara Justice as much as Frank thought he did, his little trump card would drive David insane. The idea was good. He wouldn't wait any longer to lay it down.

"She's pretty, you know. You always did have good taste in women."

David's mind went blank. He couldn't think past the gut-wrenching fear and the smile on Frank's face.

"She's even pretty when she sleeps," Frank continued, and then laughed, a low, cunning chuckle that made David's flesh crawl.

Oh, God. Oh, Cara. "What the hell have you done?"

Frank's smile grew wider. The fear on David's face was what he'd been needing. Now he was back in control.

"Done? Why, nothing you wouldn't have done in my place," he said.

David flinched, his mind racing.

"As for your daughter, she's a fine-looking woman, too. This is her gun, you know. Consider it justice that your child's possession will be the thing that ends your life."

Frank cocked the hammer on the pistol.

He never saw the knife David palmed until it was imbedded to the hilt in his chest. Oddly enough, there was no pain, only a rapidly spreading weakness. The gun slid from his fingers as he reached for the knife, trying to pull it out with both hands. Instead, his legs went out from under him and he fell backward and face up in the rain, his thoughts scattering as quickly as the blood ran out of his body.

This isn't fair. It wasn't supposed to happen this way.

David bolted, grabbing Frank by the shoulders and shaking him where he lay, the fear inside him so great, he could barely make himself heard.

"What did you do to Cara! Tell me, you son of a bitch. If you hurt her, I swear to God I'll follow you to hell."

Frank's eyes rolled back in his head. He wanted to laugh. He wanted to tell what he'd done, but words were beyond him. He sighed, and the sound came out in bloody bubbles. Like most of his life, it was a wasted effort as he died in David's hands.

David rocked on his knees and lifted his face to the storm.

"No!" he raged, and then pushed himself upright, fumbling in his pocket for a phone then punching in a quick code.

Seconds later, a voice answered. David's orders were painfully brief.

"This is Jonah. I need a cleanup crew at the Vietnam Memorial and I need it now."

"Yes, sir! In less than five."

David disconnected, then quickly dialed Cara's number.

It rang.

And it rang.

It rang while his heart began to shrivel.

It rang as he watched Frank's blood going down the drain with the rain.

It rang when he picked up Bethany's gun and put it in his belt.

It rang as he turned his face to the Wall and wanted to die.

He disconnected, then took a slow, sickening breath and dialed another number, unable to even pray.

It rang twice.

On the third ring, Bethany answered.

"Hello?"

The startled sound of her voice was a blessing. He took a deep breath and tried to speak, but the words wouldn't come.

"Hello? Is anyone there?"

"Bethany."

He heard a hesitation, and then a catch in her voice.

"Daddy...is that you?"

Suddenly blinded by more than the rain, he staggered away into the darkness, his chest swelling with a pain he couldn't ignore.

"Yes...it's me...your mother... I can't—"

"She's here," Bethany cried, and he heard her calling Cara's name, then she returned to the phone. "Someone broke into our home and injured my husband, Tom.

He's in the hospital. It's only a mild concussion but they wanted him to stay. Mother's been here with the children so I could be with him during the day."

Ah, God...she was alive. They were both alive.

He started to cry, hot, burning tears that tore up his throat, leaving him both mute and blind.

"Are you coming home soon?" Bethany asked, unaware her voice had taken on the tone of a hesitant child.

He looked behind him and moved deeper into the shadows. Some of his agents were arriving on the scene. He was still struggling to be able to speak.

"Yes… I'll be home soon."

"I can't wait," Bethany said, and then she added, "Mother wouldn't tell me anything about where you've been. She said it was your story to tell." Then she added quickly, "Mother's here now. I'm glad you called."

"So am I," he said gruffly, then held his breath, waiting for the sound of Cara's voice.

"David?"

He felt weak. Just his name on her lips was all he needed to hear—to know that it was going to be all right after all.

"Yes, baby, it's me."

He heard a catch in her breath and then she whispered, as if she didn't want Bethany to hear.

"Is it over?"

He closed his eyes, wondering if the nightmares would ever go away.

"Yes, it's over."

"Are you all right? I was so worried."

"I was worried about you, too," he said softly. "Bethany said someone broke into her house. Do they know who it was?"

"Not a clue," Cara said. "We've been afraid to close our eyes for fear he would come back."

David hesitated, but leaving them in fear was unthinkable, especially when he knew all the answers.

"Tell her not to worry anymore. He won't be back."

"I don't understand," Cara said. "How could you possibly—"

He heard her gasp, then he heard a soft moan.

"David…my God…are you saying that it was—"

"He said you were beautiful when you slept."

There was a long, startled silence. He couldn't see, but he knew then that she was probably crying.

"He was here?"

"Is Tom missing his gun?"

"Yes."

"I think I have it. I'll bring it back when I come."

"Oh, my God."

"He didn't touch you? He didn't hurt you in any way?" David asked.

"No, my God, no! My security alarm didn't go off or anything."

"Have an electrician look at it tomorrow…or rather today," he said. "It was probably bypassed."

"I will. I will." Then she lowered her voice again, only this time not in fear. "When are you coming home?"

He almost managed to smile. "Soon, baby. Soon."

"You're not in any kind of trouble or anything… I mean because of—"

"No."

"You're sure?"

This time he did smile. "I'm sure. I have…clearance… for this kind of thing."

The hesitation was longer this time before she answered, and he knew she was absorbing the fact that the man she loved had a license to kill.

"David?"

"Yes."

"I love you very much."

He closed his eyes as the last of his anger washed away with the rain. She made this all worthwhile.

"I love you, too," he said softly. "Have you been picking out that wedding date like I asked you?"

"No."

"Why not?"

"Because you're part of this act, so we're going to do it together. Is that okay?"

"Yeah, that's okay."

"David?"

"Yes, baby?"

"I'm so sorry."

He looked back at the Wall. There was no one in sight. Nothing to prove that he or Frank Wilson had ever been there at all. And even if someone had seen what had happened, it wouldn't have really mattered. A man can't die twice. And Frank's name was already on the Wall.

"Yes, Cara…so am I."

It was after four in the morning when David walked into his hotel room, hanging the Do Not Disturb sign on the doorknob as he went. He walked straight to the bathroom, leaving behind a trail of water from his clothes. The moment he was inside, he began stripping them off, leaving them in a sodden pile on the floor as he got in the shower.

It might have seemed odd for a man who'd been so wet for so long to feel the need to wash, but he felt tainted to the soul by all that had transpired. The only saving grace had been in knowing that Frank would never be able to threaten or harm anyone again.

Bracing himself against the walls, David leaned into the spray, lifting his face and then bowing his head to the power of the jets. He stood that way for what seemed like an eternity before he reached for shampoo. Methodically pouring a dollop of the creamy liquid into his hand, he worked it into his hair and rinsed, then picked up the soap bar and did the same for the rest of his body. He scrubbed until his skin was tingling and the bar had dissolved. Weary in body and heart, he crawled out of the shower and grabbed a towel from the rack, halfheartedly drying as he went. With a bone-deep groan, he collapsed facedown in the middle of the bed and closed his eyes.

It was four-thirty in the morning.

At noon the next day, his phone rang. He rolled over on his back and reached for the receiver without opening his eyes.

"Hello."

"I'm calling to express my sympathies for the way things went last night."

David recognized the President's voice and sat up in bed, rubbing the sleep from his eyes.

"Thank you, sir. I'm sorry I didn't call you right after it—"

"Not necessary. I got the word. I'm also wondering if it would be possible for you to come to my office… say around four?"

"Today?"

A soft chuckle sounded in his ear. "Yes, if you don't mind."

David scooted to the side of the bed. "Of course not, sir. I will be there."

"Thank you." Then he added, "It's almost over, isn't it, son?"

David slumped, his head dropping between his shoulders.

"Is it ever, sir?"

"Look at it this way. We all have crosses to bear. He *was* yours, but he's in God's hands now."

Oddly enough, hearing someone else verbalize what he'd been trying to convince himself of made it a little easier to accept.

"Yes, sir. You're right."

"Of course I am." He chuckled. "I'm the President. Now you go have yourself a good meal and think about that pretty woman who's waiting for you back home."

David smiled, and in that moment, he knew that whatever else had yet to happen, he was going to be okay.

"Yes, sir."

The line went dead in his ear.

David replaced the receiver then pushed himself off the bed. There were things to do before he went home to Cara. He had to arrange for his personal belongings to be shipped to Chiltingham and buy some presents for his family.

And then he suddenly stopped in the middle of the room and just smiled.

Family.

He had family.

There was a woman who loved him and a daughter who was willing to give him a chance. He even had a son-in-law and granddaughters to formally meet. Granted, they'd seen each other in the airport, but this time it would be different. He would be able to touch them and hold them, and if God was merciful, they would learn to love him.

He took a suit off the hanger, laid it on the bed and went to get a fresh shirt from the drawer. The least he could do was look respectable when he turned in his resignation.

"Sir...the President will see you now."

At the secretary's bidding, David stood abruptly and walked into the Oval Office. The President rose as David entered, and circled his desk, coming toward David with an outstretched hand.

"Glad you could come," the President said, and led him into an adjoining room. "I thought we would be more comfortable in here," he said. "Please sit down. Would you care for something to drink? Coffee? A cola?"

"No, thank you, sir," David said, and unbuttoned the jacket of his suit as he took a seat in a wing chair opposite the one the President had chosen.

For a few moments, David bore the President's silent scrutiny and then someone knocked on the door and the President looked up.

"Catherine, would you hold all my calls for a while. I don't want to be disturbed."

David knew the precision it took to keep a country running as smoothly as this man had done. He owed him a lot for keeping the faith during the security crisis that Frank had caused, yet he waited for him to speak first.

The President cleared his throat and then leaned forward, resting his elbows on his knees and reducing the meeting to that of one man to another.

"You probably deserve a medal for what you've done," the President said. "At the least a commendation." Then he sighed. "You know you'll get neither."

"This job was never about notoriety, sir."

The President nodded and then leaned back in his chair.

"Are you going to be all right?"

"Yes."

"Have you been debriefed since the incident?"

"Yes, sir. I finished about an hour ago."

"That's fine, just fine."

"Sir…if I may speak freely?" David said.

"Yes, of course. What's on your mind?"

"If I had ever been hired, this is where I would hand you my resignation."

The President grinned, amused by David's wry brand of humor.

"Yes, anonymity is a bitch to tackle, isn't it?"

David smiled back. "Yes, sir, considerably so. And… considering the damage that Frank has done to SPEAR's security, you and I both know my effectiveness is over. Besides, it's time I stepped down."

The President nodded. "You're going to be a hard man to replace."

"But you've already done it, haven't you, sir?"

Again surprised by David's intuitive humor, he laughed aloud.

"Actually, yes."

"And he can take control immediately, I hope?"

"He's already in flight."

An amazing weight lifted from David's shoulders. Surprised by how wonderful it felt, he leaned back in his chair and briefly closed his eyes.

"You did an amazing job for us," the President said.

"It was my honor, sir."

"I assume you've taken care of your personal belongings."

"Yes, sir."

"Again, I'm so sorry that I cannot publically acknowledge your unselfish contributions to this country's safety and security, both here and abroad, but there is a tidy little severance package in your name that I hope will soften the blow."

David smiled. He'd already received the paperwork that would net him more retirement money annually than he could have imagined.

"Let's just say it didn't hurt my feelings," David said.

Again, the President laughed, then stood, signaling an end to their conversation.

David stood as well, readying himself to leave.

"Is there anything I can do for you?" the President asked. "Anything at all?"

David hesitated, and then thought, *What the hell. The man asked. All he can do is tell me no.*

"Yes, actually there is," David said.

"Name it."

"If there are any military planes heading toward the state of New York, I'd like a fast ride home."

The President beamed. "I can do you one better than that," he said, and reached for a phone.

Chapter 15

Cara ran a brush through her hair one last time and then did a quick turn in front of the mirror.

"You look beautiful, Mom."

Cara turned. Bethany was standing in the doorway, smiling.

"Except for this lovely bruise, which isn't quite so vivid thanks to pancake makeup, I'll do. As for looking beautiful, so, my dear, do you."

Bethany fidgeted with the neckline of her dress.

"I feel a little bit like I did the first time I went on a date," she said, and then smoothed her hands down the front of her pink summer sheath. "I want him to like me and I want to like him, but I don't really know him."

Cara thought of what David had gone through with Frank, and with the last forty years of his life.

"But you will, darling, in time. Right now, all he is

asking for is a chance to get to know you. He isn't trying to take Ray's place in your life, or anything like that."

"I know…but, Mom…he's my father. My real father."

Cara stared, a little surprised by the tone in Bethany's voice.

"Why, honey, I never knew you felt anything less from Ray."

"It had nothing to do with the way I was treated, Mom. Please don't believe that. But think about it. Tyler and Valerie are shorter and blond like Ray. I'm taller than everyone in the family, including you. My hair is dark. My eyes are brown. In the family pictures, I looked like the cuckoo's child."

Cara felt like crying. To think Bethany had kept this to herself all these years was heartbreaking.

"I'm so sorry," she said, and hugged her daughter close. "I wish you'd said something to me."

Bethany smiled and shrugged. "What could you have done?"

Cara sighed. "Nothing, I guess, but it might have helped if you'd just talked about it."

"I wasn't sad. Just accepting," Bethany said. "It wasn't like I was the only kid whose father was dead." Then her eyes widened. "That's what makes this so special! It's nothing short of a miracle that he's back in our lives, and as for you marrying him…"

"So you're happy about that, too?"

"No. Ecstatic would be a better word."

Cara sighed. "I called Valerie and Tyler yesterday and told them a little about David."

Bethany frowned. "Surely they weren't upset?"

"I suppose a more accurate description would be puzzled. I'm not the impulsive type, you know, but here I am, engaged within a week to a man I hadn't seen in forty years. I think Tyler wanted to hire a private detective to investigate David's background."

Bethany chuckled. "It would be interesting to see what they came up with, wouldn't it?"

Cara smiled. All Bethany knew was that her dad had worked in a high-level branch of the government that dealt with security. She had no idea of the scope of David's duties or the life that he'd led, and in Cara's opinion, the less said the better. All she wanted was for David to have the life with them that he'd never had.

She wanted him to be able to make new friends and go fishing whenever he wanted. To look forward to rainy days and lazy mornings, and holidays with big family dinners. She wanted to know that, with time, the nightmares he lived with would fade. That's what she wanted for him and for her. God willing, it would happen.

"Where are Tom and the girls?" Cara asked, suddenly realizing the house was too quiet.

"He took them out back for a walk in the woods. I think he wanted to keep them occupied so that we'd have a little time alone together."

"Is he up to that?" Cara asked.

"Yes, I think he'll be all right. I don't know who was happier that he was released yesterday, him or me."

"I knew there was a reason I loved that man," Cara said.

They both laughed.

Suddenly, the back door slammed and they could hear both children shrieking at the top of their lungs. Bethany was out of the room first, with Cara close behind.

"Mommy! Mommy! Come look! Come look! There's a big hepacopter up in the sky."

"Helicopter," Bethany corrected, as she let Kelly lead her outside by the hand. Then she turned toward Cara, smiling. "I can't imagine why all this fuss. You'd think she's never seen a helicopter before."

Cara could hear it, too, and followed them out.

Tom was standing on the porch, shading his eyes from the sun with his hand. He looked a little lopsided with the hair they'd cut away from his wound, but Cara thought he was a hero for standing between his family and a killer and had told him so more than once.

"It's a military chopper," Tom said. "And I think it's going to land."

Cara started to smile. There was only one reason a military helicopter would be landing in her back yard—and he was getting out right now.

She walked off the steps, unwilling to wait a moment longer to feel his arms around her. About ten feet from the back yard fence, the chopper lifted off in a swirl of leaves and grass, leaving the man who'd disembarked to make his own way to the house in the distance.

The distance between Cara's steps increased, and by the time she cleared the gate, she was running.

David ducked his head and closed his eyes as the chopper lifted off. When he turned around, he saw Cara running toward him. The last of his old fears took wing, following the chopper's ascent. He dropped his suitcase and started toward her. Moments later, he was swinging her off her feet and into his arms. This felt so good—so right—and when he thought of how close he'd come to losing both her and Bethany, it made him sick. To this day, he didn't know what had stopped Frank from killing them, and he wasn't going to try to second-guess a man who'd lost his mind.

"I missed you," he whispered, and buried his face in the curve of her neck.

She laughed aloud and then kissed him soundly without care for the quartet who was watching.

"There's someone else who needs a welcome hug," she said softly.

David looked over her shoulder, then put her down.

Cara heard his breath catch and saw the fear in his eyes as Bethany came toward them.

"It will be all right," she said, and gave him a gentle push in the middle of his back.

He went to meet her—this daughter he'd never known—and when they were so close he could see his reflection in the color of her eyes, he reached toward her hair, fingering the dark, silky texture that was so like his own.

"My mother…your grandmother…had hair this color."

For Bethany, he couldn't have said a more perfect thing. This man who was her father was giving her roots to a family she'd never known.

"Was she pretty?" Bethany asked.

David smiled. "Not as pretty as you." Then he held out his hand. "Bethany, I'm really glad to meet you."

Her chin quivered. "I'm really glad to meet you, too." Then, ignoring the handshake he offered, she wrapped her arms around his neck and started to cry.

Two weeks ago, holding a crying woman might have undone him, but not anymore. He had a whole new set of responsibilities, and with so many females in his new family, he suspected that getting used to tears should be first on the list.

Cara came up behind them and put her arms around them both, willing herself not to cry.

David felt her presence and reached for her, pulling her into the family embrace.

Up on the steps a distance away, Bethany's two daughters stared intently at their mother and grandmother being hugged by the stranger. Finally, it was Rachel who spoke.

"Daddy, who's the man hugging Mommy?"

"Honey… it's her daddy."

"I thought Grandpa Ray was her daddy."

Tom sighed. "It's complicated to explain, but trust me, he's her daddy, too."

Rachel frowned. "I think she's crying."

Tom smiled. "Probably."

"Is he hurting her?" she asked.

Tom shook his head and then cupped the back of both his daughters' heads, unable to imagine what David must be feeling, to be holding his own daughter for the very first time.

"No, she's not hurting, she's happy. See how she and Grandma are smiling and talking."

Rachel leaned against her father, uncertain of all this grown-up stuff and even more uncertain where she fit into the mess.

"Is he going to hug me and Kelly, too?"

"I don't think so—at least not yet," Tom said. "But one of these days, I think you're going to want him to."

"Why?"

"Because he's also your grandfather, and grandfathers are really good things."

Rachel looked interested now. She loved Grandpa Joe. He always did lots of stuff with them, like riding bikes and playing tennis with them. She thought of the picture they'd shown her of this man—the one Nanny had on her mantel.

"Do you think he might take us fishing sometime?"

Tom grinned. No matter how young the woman, they always seemed to feel the need to plan a man's life.

"You'll just have to ask him, okay?"

"Okay."

Rachel stood, watching as they started toward the house—her mother, her nanny—and that grandfather she didn't know. And the nearer they came, the quieter she got, almost holding her breath and waiting for that first moment of eye contact between them.

David nodded at Tom and then they shook hands before he turned his attention to the girls.

Granddaughters. Lord in heaven, he had granddaughters. And they were so beautiful—and they looked so confused. He squatted, putting himself at their level.

"Are you Kelly?" he asked, as the little one leaned against her father's leg.

She nodded and then smiled as only an innocent child could.

David's heart melted. He reached behind her ear and pulled out a gold-colored coin.

"You better be careful about washing behind your ears," he teased. "Look what I found back there."

She laughed aloud as he handed her a newly minted dollar.

Rachel held her breath, wondering what he was going to do next. Curious, she tested behind her ears just in case, but there was nothing there.

David saw what she did and stifled a laugh.

"And you're Rachel, aren't you?"

She nodded.

"I remember your rabbit, Henry. I trust he hasn't hopped away anymore?"

Her eyes widened. This was the man who'd found Henry at the airport!

"I know you, don't I!" she cried.

He hesitated briefly, then knowing he was courting rejection, still held out his hand.

"You will, honey. You will."

Rachel glanced at her mother, who nodded an okay. Slowly, she laid her hand in the middle of David's palm, thinking as she did that he was bigger than her daddy and that his eyes were brown like Mom's.

David was a goner, and he knew it. All the ugliness of the past forty-eight hours withered and died in this little girl's eyes.

"I saw your picture on Nanny's mantel," Rachel said.

"You did? What did you think?" David asked.

She frowned in deliberation, wanting to be fair without actually asking the favor.

"I think you can fish."

He smiled. "Yes, I can. Do you like to fish?"

It was the opening she'd been waiting for.

"Oh, yes, I do. And if you will take me sometime, I will show you how to catch a much bigger fish."

David rocked back on his heels and burst into laughter.

Rachel looked a little startled, not quite sure what everyone thought was so funny, but glad they were happy.

David stood and wrapped his arms around Cara.

"Thank you, darling," he said softly.

"For what?" she asked.

"For letting me know what it feels like to come home."

Epilogue

July 4, 2001

The day was hot and still. In the distance, the United States Marine Band was tuning up as people continued gathering on the mall between the Lincoln Memorial and the Washington Monument. In a few moments, David would join his family for the festivities, but there was something he'd left undone. Something he'd done at the Wall every Fourth of July since its inception.

He started down the pathway in front of the memorial, trying not to think of what had happened here only a few short days before. With the sun beaming down on his bare arms, he should have been sweltering, but his mind was locked into a storm, and the rain pouring down—and his brother pointing a gun at his chest.

Dozens and dozens of people lined the path along the

Wall, each paying their own tribute to a loved one on this day of independence. The rose he was carrying felt heavy in his hand—a burden he didn't want to bear. Unconsciously, his fingers clenched, and as they did, a thorn pricked. He winced, but considered the pain as no less than he deserved.

Ten, maybe twelve steps more and he would be there—at the place where Frank had died. He couldn't look down—wouldn't look down—yet when he got there, his gaze automatically fell to the place where Frank had fallen.

He paused, staring at the concrete until his eyes began to burn. Finally he sighed.

Nothing.

They'd left nothing behind—not even a bloodstain marred the place where he had died.

He turned, searching the Wall for Frank's name and then moving through the crowd to touch it, tracing each letter with his fingertip, as if the simple act might resurrect and save a man who'd most likely gone to hell.

"Family?"

He turned. A stately, gray-haired woman dressed in black was standing at his side.

He nodded.

She pointed with a long, perfectly manicured fingertip. "That's my husband's name right below."

He looked. "Anthony C. DeFranco," he read, only afterward realizing that he'd read it aloud.

"I called him Tony," she said, and then dabbed a handkerchief beneath the lenses of her sunglasses. "We'd been married six weeks when he got drafted." She sighed. "I never saw him again."

"I'm very sorry," David said.

She sighed. "Yes, I know. We're all sorry, aren't we? But it happened and all I could do was go on." She shrugged, as if to indicate it was out of her hands. "What could I do? I was still alive, wasn't I?"

Then she walked away, leaving David with her simple truth.

He turned again, this time looking at Frank's name with new emotion. The woman was right. Even though Frank had died only days ago, technically, he'd been dead for forty years and God knows, David had grieved for him more than most.

It was time to move on.

After all, he was still alive.

He laid the red rose at the base of the wall, touched Frank's name one last time and then turned, looking back up the path at the way that he'd come.

Cara was there, as were all of her children. They'd taken to him in spite of themselves, and God willing, they had years and years left to learn to love.

He started to walk, moving against the stream of people who were still filing down—through a group of teenage girls, past a couple arm in arm, then behind a solitary man in an outdated uniform—until Cara was in his arms.

He held her there without speaking beneath the heat of the sun, cherishing the beat of her heart against his chest.

"Okay?" she asked quietly.

He made himself smile, and as he did, realized that for the first time in years it felt right.

"Yes, okay."

"Then let's go home."

They walked away, losing themselves and the past in the gathering crowd.

* * * * *

USA TODAY bestselling author **Rita Herron** wrote her first book when she was twelve but didn't think real people grew up to be writers. Now she writes so she doesn't have to get a real job. A former kindergarten teacher and workshop leader, she traded storytelling to kids for writing romance, and now she writes romantic comedies and romantic suspense. Rita lives in Georgia with her family. She loves to hear from readers, so please visit her website, ritaherron.com.

Books by Rita Herron

Harlequin Intrigue

A Badge of Honor Mystery

Mysterious Abduction
Left to Die
Protective Order
Suspicious Circumstances

Badge of Justice

Redemption at Hawk's Landing
Safe at Hawk's Landing
Hideaway at Hawk's Landing
Hostage at Hawk's Landing

The Heroes of Horseshoe Creek

Lock, Stock and McCullen
McCullen's Secret Son
Roping Ray McCullen
Warrior Son
The Missing McCullen
The Last McCullen

Visit the Author Profile page
at Harlequin.com for more titles.

COLLECTING EVIDENCE

Rita Herron

To Jamie, a brave and courageous young girl—
may all your dreams come true!

Prologue

Special Agent Dylan Acevedo pressed the blade of the knife against Frank Turnbull's fleshy neck.

"Go ahead, kill me," Turnbull muttered.

Dylan jabbed the blade into his skin, a smile curving his mouth as a drop of blood seeped to the surface. He should just do it.

The man deserved to die.

The images of the women the serial killer had brutally murdered—all young Native Americans in their twenties—flashed into Dylan's head in sickening clarity. Their delicate throats slashed, bodies left exposed in the rugged terrain of the desert, blood dripping as if to lure the wild animals to feed on their remains.

Young lives lost for no reason except to fulfill the sick cravings of a demented mind.

Dylan glanced down at the knife in his hand. The

knife that had belonged to Turnbull. The same kind he'd used to cut the women's throats.

It was only fitting he die by the same instrument.

With his throat sliced open by a Ute ceremonial knife made from white quartz and Western Cedar, the kind of knife used to cut the umbilical cord of a newborn or to harvest herbs for sacred ceremonies.

Another important component of Turnbull's MO was his calling card—he'd left a piece of thunderwood by each victim. Another dig to the Ute people who had a religious aversion to handling thunderwood a piece of bark from a tree struck by lighting. The Utes believed that thunder beings would strike down any Ute Indian who touched it.

Turnbull's swollen eye twitched with menace and a dare. A challenge to Dylan to feel the thrill of the kill, Turnbull seemed to say silently.

Dylan clenched his jaw. He wanted to see fear in Turnbull's eyes. Wanted to hear him scream as his victims had. Hear him beg for his life.

Instead Turnbull laughed, a hideous deep growl that punctured the night like a wild animal just before it tore into a smaller one's carcass.

"You're just like me," Turnbull mumbled. "I can see the evil in your eyes."

Dylan's fingers tightened on the knife handle. At that moment he did crave the kill. But his need was driven by revenge and justice, not depraved indifference.

"Dylan, don't…."

His brother Miguel's voice rumbled from behind him. Miguel, who was a saint compared to him. He'd been an altar boy while Dylan had been the troublemaker.

They hadn't always gotten along, but as adults they'd

forged a bond and developed a healthy respect for one another's differences. Miguel was a forensic scientist, and they often worked together on cases, relying on each other's expertise.

Miguel's footfalls echoed on the ground as he approached. "Come on, Dylan. We've got him. Let's take him in and make him pay for what he did. Make him face the families of the victims."

Dylan's hand trembled as his gaze once again locked with the monster. Then he saw the fear in the man's eyes. Turnbull wanted him to kill him.

Because he didn't want to face the families.

Miguel was right. Having to look into the pain-filled eyes of the parents of the women he'd hurt would be his worst punishment.

His hand slipped, caught the skin just enough to cause a flesh wound, then he gestured for Miguel to cuff the bastard.

Hours later, after their debriefing and a press conference to announce they'd finally arrested the ruthless Ute killer, Dylan walked into the Vegas bar. All he wanted was to purge his rage, and drown out the images of the girls he hadn't been able to save.

Just like he hadn't saved his fifteen-year-old sister, Teresa, when she'd been gunned down in a gang-related drive-by.

Suddenly, the most exotic creature he'd ever seen approached him. Long black hair that hung down to her waist swayed seductively as she walked, her dark chocolate eyes raking over him appreciatively.

She was Ute, fit the profile of the victims he'd fought so hard to obtain justice for. Could have become number eleven on Turnbull's kill card. Yet here she was, alive and smiling at him.

"Agent Acevedo," she said in a purrlike voice with the faint accent of her heritage. "I saw you on the news. Thank you for arresting that killer."

He shrugged. "I only wish we'd caught him sooner."

Wise, sympathetic eyes met his, along with a sultriness that made his body go rock hard and achy.

He was mesmerized by her beauty, wanted her naked and in his bed, soothing the heat and rage in his soul.

When she finished her shift, they talked for hours. Her name was Aspen Meadows. She was working as a cocktail waitress while earning a teaching degree.

Finally he escorted her to her apartment. Before he closed the door, she was in his arms and he was tearing off her clothes. He took her on the floor, against the wall, on the bed and in the shower.

A week of lovemaking couldn't assuage the pain or guilt in his chest. He didn't deserve her. Didn't deserve to be loved or soothed when he'd failed so many.

But he stole the hours and days anyway, desperate for a slice of heaven to ease the hell he lived with daily.

He knew it wouldn't last, *couldn't* last, though. A phone call the following Friday night reminded him too well.

Another murder. An undercover assignment.

He had to go.

He kissed her goodbye and left while she was sleeping. He wouldn't see her again. He couldn't.

His work put anyone he cared about in danger.

And he had enough dead girls haunting him to last him forever.

Chapter 1

A year later

Aspen Meadows had been missing for nine weeks now. Nine weeks of wondering if she was dead or alive.

Nine weeks of wondering if he could have done something to save her.

Dylan stared at Aspen's cousin, Emma Richardson, fearing the worst. He'd left Aspen last year to keep her safe, yet now she might be dead.

Possibly murdered by the same hit man who'd killed his fellow agent, Julie Granger. The FBI's theory—Aspen had witnessed Boyd Perkins and Sherman Watts disposing of Julie's body.

The case that had brought them to the Southern Ute reservation.

Emma pressed a hand to her head as if to clear her vision. "Aspen is alive."

His chest tightened as hope speared him. He didn't often trust a psychic, but Emma's visions had proven right before, and his brother, Miguel, who'd obviously fallen for the woman, believed her wholeheartedly.

And he trusted his twin brother more than anyone in the world.

Still, he had to swallow to make his voice work. He'd prayed for this news ever since he'd heard Aspen's car had been found crashed into a tree near the San Juan River.

But something about the tortured look on Emma's face disturbed him. "Are you sure she's alive?"

Emma nodded, although she swayed, her face pale, her eyes gaunt. Miguel rushed to help her to the sofa. She leaned her head back and closed her eyes with a shudder.

"What did you see?" Sweat beaded on the nape of Dylan's neck. He was terrified that Aspen had died and that he'd lost her forever.

Just as he'd lost almost every woman he'd ever cared about. His little sister, Teresa. Then his friend Julie.

Miguel rubbed Emma's arms, his voice low and worried, "Emma?"

"I…don't know. The vision… I just know she's alive, but she's scared." She opened her eyes and looked up at Dylan, cold terror streaking her expression. "And she's in danger."

Dylan paced across the room, his heart pounding as Aspen's son, Jack, cried out. The sound shattered the air as if he'd heard Emma and understood that his mother might be in trouble. Emma started to rise to go to the baby, but Dylan waved her off. She looked as if she might faint if she tried to stand.

He strode over to the bassinet and picked up the

squirming baby. Jack flailed his tiny fists, his face red, his nose scrunched as he continued to bellow.

"Shh, little man," Dylan said, jiggling him on his shoulder as he paced the room. The poor little fellow must miss his mother terribly. In the first few weeks of his life, he'd been in a car accident with Aspen, abandoned and left with Emma.

He patted the baby's back, cradling him closer. The scent of baby powder and formula suffused him.

If Aspen was alive, why hadn't she come back for her son?

The Aspen he'd known loved children more than anything. During their short affair—the best sex of his whole damn life—she'd told him her plans to return to the Ute reservation and teach.

Baby Jack kicked and screamed louder, a shrill sound that added to the tension thickening the room, his dark skin beet-red, contrasting to his thick black hair. He had Aspen's high-sculpted cheekbones, her hair, her heritage. It made Dylan long to see her again, to reconnect and hold her. To see if they could pick up where they'd left off and possibly have more than just a week of mind-boggling sex.

But she had a son now.

Everything had changed.

He rocked Jack back and forth, lowering his voice again to calm him. "Shh, it's all right. We'll find your mommy. I promise, little man."

Jack quieted to a soft whimper and Dylan turned him to his back, cradled him in his arms and gazed into his eyes. Eyes so blue that for a moment he felt as if he was looking in the mirror.

Suddenly a wave of emotion washed over him, sending his mind into a tailspin. He studied Jack's features more closely while he mentally calculated the baby's age, and the time lapse since he'd last seen Aspen. A little over a year ago, they'd met and fallen into bed. A week later he'd left and hadn't heard from her again.

Aspen had been missing now for nine weeks.

Jack was fifteen weeks old.

Dear God, could Jack possibly be his son?

The baby suddenly cooed up at him, his chubby cheeks puffing up as he gripped one of Dylan's fingers in his tiny fist.

Dylan's chest swelled. "Is it true, Jack? Are you my little *mijo?*"

And if he was, why in the hell hadn't Aspen told him?

The nightmares taunted her.

Every night they came like dark shadowy demons with claws reaching for her and trying to drown her in the madness.

If only she could remember her name, what had happened to her, how she had wound up near death and here in this women's shelter in Mexican Hat.

But the past was like an empty vacuum sucking at her, imprisoning her in the darkness. Only at night in her dreams, memories plucked at the deepest recesses of her mind, trying to break through the barrier her subconscious had erected.

Terrifying memories that she wasn't sure she wanted to recall.

She forced herself to look into the mirror, to probe her mind for bits of her past. She knew she was Ute—her high cheekbones, long black hair and brown eyes screamed Native American heritage.

But those eyes were haunted by something she'd seen, something that lay on the fringes of her conscience.

Her head throbbed, tension knotting her stomach. She rolled her shoulders to stretch out her achy muscles, but exhaustion was wearing on her. In the weeks since she'd come to the shelter, she'd recovered from her physical injuries, the hypothermia and bruises, but she still hadn't regained her strength.

The other women and children had gathered after dinner for a support group session in the common room. Sometimes she gathered the children into a circle on the floor for storytime, but tonight one of the mothers was teaching them how to string Indian beads to make necklaces.

Grateful to have some time alone, she gave in to fatigue and crawled onto her cot by the far wall. Dusk was setting, the hot sun melting in the sky, gray streaks of night darkening the room. She closed her eyes, pulled the thin sheet over her legs and turned on her side. But a hollow emptiness settled inside her. She had felt it the moment she'd awakened in the shelter, freezing and delirious. She'd known then that she'd lost something. Something precious.

A loved one maybe.

Tears trickled down her cheek, but she angrily wiped them away. Remembering what had happened could help her return home. But what if she was right?

What if she'd blocked out the memory because someone she loved had died and she couldn't bear it?

Finally, exhaustion claimed her, but the nightmares returned to dog her, dragging her under a rushing wave of darkness, smothering and terrifying.

Someone was chasing her across the unforgiving

land, toward the deep pockets and boulders. She tried to run but her legs felt heavy, her body weighted, and she skidded on the embankment, rocks tumbling downward and pinging off the canyon below. She tumbled and rolled, the sharp edges of the stones jabbing her skin and scraping her flesh raw.

Then his hands were on her, fingernails piercing as they bit into her shoulders. She fought back, swinging her hands up to deflect his blow, but he hit her so hard her head snapped back and stars danced in front of her eyes. Another blow followed, slamming into her skull and pain knifed behind her eyes, her breath gushing out as she tasted blood. She tried desperately to focus, to crawl away, but he yanked her by the ankles and dragged her across the rugged ground, the stones and bristly shrubs tearing at her hands and knees and face as she struggled to grasp something to hold on to.

God help her—he was going to kill her….

Somewhere close by, the river roared, water slashing over jagged rocks, icy cold water that would viciously suck her under and carry her away from everyone she loved.

No, she had to fight.

But the hands were on her again, this time around her throat, punishing fingers digging into her skin, gripping, squeezing, pressing into her larynx, cutting off her oxygen. She gulped and tried to fight back, swung her arms and kicked at him, but her body felt like putty, limp and helpless, as the world swirled into darkness.

Her heart pounding with terror, she jerked awake, disoriented and trembling. She'd only been dreaming; it had been the nightmares again….

She was safe.

But as she exhaled and her breathing steadied, a deadly stillness engulfed the pitch-dark room, the kind of eerie quiet before a storm that sent a frisson of alarm through her.

Then a breath broke the quiet.

A wheezing, whispery low sound. Someone was in the room.

Praying it was one of the sisters coming to check on her, she clenched the sheets and glanced across the space. The tall silhouette of a man stood in front of the open window in the shadows, the scent of sweat and cigarette smoke rolling off of him in sickening waves.

Pure panic ripped through her. Was it the man who'd tried to kill her in her dreams? One of the male abusers the women in the shelter were running from?

His hand moved to his waistband and the shiny glint of metal caught her eye.

She froze, body humming with adrenaline-spiked fear. A knife was tucked into the leather pouch attached to his belt.

She had to run.

Slowly she slid off the bed to escape and yelled for help, but he moved at lightning speed and trapped her. His big hands covered her mouth to silence her screams. She bit his hand, then clawed at him and cried out, fighting with all her might to throw his weight off of her.

Suddenly hall lights flickered on and footsteps clattered toward the doorway, doors banging open. The man's gaze shot sideways and he cursed, then lurched up, ran to the window and jumped out.

The sisters and three other women poured into the room, baseball bats in their hands, ready to attack.

The light flew on, throwing the room into a bright

glare that nearly blinded her. Sister Margaret rushed to her, pulled her into her arms and soothed her. "He's gone now. You're safe, child."

It took her precious seconds to stop trembling, then anger ballooned inside her. She was tired of running, of hiding, of not knowing. They'd all assumed that whoever had hurt her had been a violent boyfriend or husband she'd been running from.

But she couldn't go on living like this. She had to know the truth. If her attacker was a boyfriend or husband, he'd found her. And she refused to be a coward.

Somewhere she had a life she'd left behind. And she wanted it back. Wanted the man who'd hurt her to pay.

And the person she'd lost—she had to face that truth, too.

"We should call the police," she whispered. "Send them my picture, Sister. I want to find out who I am and who's trying to kill me."

Once the idea that Jack might possibly be his son entered Dylan's mind, he couldn't let it go. The baby shifted against him, finally falling back asleep, but Dylan didn't want to put him down. If the child was his, he wanted to know.

Dammit, he deserved to know.

Memories of his father taking him camping and fishing rolled back, and he saw himself doing the same thing with his own son one day.

When he'd first heard Aspen's baby had been found in her abandoned car, he'd assumed she'd moved on with her life, that she'd forgotten him, and had become involved with another man, someone on the reservation.

Because they'd been careful. And he'd trusted Aspen,

trusted that she would have told him if she'd gotten pregnant with his baby.

But looking at Jack's big blue eyes now, he didn't know what to believe.

He settled into the rocking chair while Miguel made Emma herbal tea. Color returned to her cheeks as she sipped the hot brew, although distress still lined her face and her hand trembled slightly as she set the teacup back onto the saucer.

"Emma," he said quietly. "I have to ask you something, and I want you to be honest."

Her gaze met his, and she nodded, although she fidgeted with the afghan Miguel had draped around her shoulders. "I told you all I saw."

"It's not that," he said gruffly.

Her eyes softened as she watched the baby, indicating how much she loved her nephew.

"Emma, who is Jack's father?"

Emma bit down on her bottom lip and glanced away.

"The truth," he said, knowing if Aspen had confided in anyone it would have been her cousin. When Emma was a teenager, her mother's abusive boyfriend had set fire to the house, killing himself and Emma's mother. Emma had moved in with Aspen and her mother, Rose. After that, the girls had been more like sisters than cousins.

"I don't know," she said in a low voice. "Aspen never told me."

He arched a brow, a muscle ticking in his jaw. "Are you sure? You're not keeping some secret?"

Miguel squared his shoulders and draped a protective arm around Emma. "If she says she doesn't know, she doesn't."

"It's important," Dylan said, his throat thick. "Was she dating someone?"

Emma frowned. "Kurt Lightfoot, a builder from the reservation, was interested in her. They went out a few times. But... I'm not sure he fathered the baby." She hesitated. "He certainly hasn't claimed paternal rights."

"Where are you going with this?" Miguel asked. "Are you thinking that Jack's father might have been the one who attacked Aspen? That it wasn't like we suspected, that Boyd Perkins and Sherman Watts tried to kill her because she saw them dump Julie's body?"

Dylan hissed between clenched teeth. "I'm just considering every angle. And knowing Jack's father is important."

"Why is it so important to you?" Emma asked with odd twitch of her lips that made him wonder if she had a sixth sense about this, too.

He traced a finger over Jack's cheek, then decided that Emma might confide more if he came clean. "Because I might be the father."

Surprise flickered in Miguel's eyes, although Emma gave him a sympathetic look. "I honestly don't know," she said gently. "Aspen simply said that the baby's father wasn't in the picture. I assumed that he didn't want to be and didn't push her on the subject. It seemed to upset her too much."

Dylan's jaw snapped tight with the effort not to defend himself. He would have wanted to be in the picture. And if he discovered Jack was his, Aspen wouldn't get rid of him, either. Above all things, Dylan valued family and believed in a father's duty to take care of his children.

"You and Aspen?" Miguel asked.

Dylan gave a clipped nod. "The timing is right. We

met in Vegas when I'd just come off that serial-killer case." God, the images of the dead Ute girls Frank Turnbull had killed still haunted him.

"Aunt Rose had just died then," Emma said quietly.

Dylan nodded. "I guess we both needed someone."

And he needed Aspen now and so did her baby… Possibly *their* baby.

Dammit, where was she?

Emma said she was in danger. Had Perkins or Watts found her?

Another possibility, one they hadn't considered, nagged at him.

If he wasn't the father, who was? Jack had been in that car when Aspen had crashed. He could have died, too.

If another man had fathered the little boy, had he tried to kill Aspen to keep his paternity a secret?

Chapter 2

Dylan's cell phone cut into the tense silence in the room, jarring Jack from sleep. He whimpered, and Dylan reluctantly handed him to Emma and connected the call.

"Acevedo speaking."

"Dylan, it's Tom Ryan. Listen, we just caught a break."

Dylan's pulse pounded. "What?"

"I'm at the Bureau now, and we received a fax from a women's shelter in Mexican Hat. It looks like we've found Aspen Meadows."

The blood roared through Dylan's veins. Trembling with relief, he muttered a silent prayer of thanks and crossed himself. "Is she all right?"

"She's alive. According to the sister I spoke with, she was brought in with injuries and has been healing there."

Fear gripped him again. "What kind of injuries?"

"I'm not sure. We didn't go into it. But I thought you might want to go to Mexican Hat and talk to her."

"Thanks. I will." In a brief moment of emotion, he'd confided in Tom that he had been involved with Aspen, that finding her was personal.

"I need to call Emma and tell her that we found her cousin."

"I'm with Emma and Miguel right now," Dylan said. "I'll let her know, then I'm on my way to Mexican Hat."

He disconnected the call, and turned to see Emma and his brother waiting with anticipation.

"They found Aspen?" Emma asked.

He nodded. "She's at a women's shelter in Mexican Hat."

"Thank God." Emma sagged in relief, although a second later, her nose wrinkled in confusion as she rocked Jack. "But if she's alive, why hasn't she called any of us? Why didn't she come back for Jack? She loved this baby more than anything in the world."

Dylan gritted his teeth. "I don't know. Only Aspen can tell us that. I'm going to bring her home."

"You want me to go with you?" Miguel asked.

Dylan shook his head and glanced at the baby. "No. Take a DNA swab from Jack and send it to the lab. And stick close to Jack and Emma. If Aspen is still in danger, her son might be, too."

Miguel agreed and Dylan rushed to the door, then outside to his sedan, worry knotting his stomach. Had Aspen been injured so badly she couldn't contact Emma? Had she been trying to protect her son by not returning?

He started the engine and raced away from Emma's house on the outskirts of Kenner City, anxious for answers.

If Jack was his son, he wanted to know why in the hell she hadn't trusted him with the truth. Not that he'd tried to contact her....

The little boy's baby blue eyes flashed into his head, and he grimaced. Jack had to be his—he knew it in his gut.

But as that possibility sank in, guilt assailed him.

If he'd been with Aspen and the baby, he could have protected them.

"According to the FBI agent who phoned, your name is Aspen Meadows," Sister Margaret said.

Aspen clenched her hands together, weighing the name on her tongue. "Aspen..." Yes, that sounded right. Familiar.

Yet a sense of dread filled her as she waited for more information. "What else did he tell you?"

Sister Margaret stroked her arms to soothe her. "Just that your car was found crashed near the San Juan River, and that you've been missing for nine weeks. He's sending an agent here to talk to you and take you back to your family."

"Family?" Aspen jerked her head up, tears blurring her eyes. "I have family?"

Sister Margaret nodded with a smile. "I'm sure they've been worried sick about you. But don't fret now, child. You're finally going home."

Aspen bit down on her lower lip, more questions assailing her. If she had family, why didn't she remember them? And if she'd been running from an abusive boyfriend or husband, why hadn't she turned to her family for help?

A half-dozen scenarios raced through her head, fear

gripping her. Maybe her family hadn't been loving at all. Maybe someone in that family had abused her.

Something about the scenario felt all too real…a distant memory plucking at her subconscious? Or had her contact with the women in the shelter stirred her imagination?

Since she'd arrived, she'd heard horror stories of wife and child beaters, fathers who'd sexually molested their daughters, of stalkers and possessive men who threatened and intimidated the very people they professed to care about, men who treated their women like property.

Had she left her family to protect them from the man after her?

Twice she'd seen a tall Ute man lurking outside, lingering near the fence surrounding the shelter. A Ute man who'd watched her and the other women with intense gray eyes that chilled her to the bone….

Was he the man who'd sneaked into her room and attacked her? Had she known him before?

And if he wanted her dead, would this FBI agent be able to protect her?

Dylan's emotions pinged between hopeful anticipation and trepidation over what he might find when he saw Aspen. He couldn't imagine the woman he knew deserting her child or not contacting her cousin to assure her she was safe.

Which meant her injuries must have been serious.

That or she was too scared to call home. And if that was the case, what had changed her mind?

The landscape swept by him with its pieces of flatland mingled with red-and-gray rocks, some twisted into convoluted shapes that as children, he and Miguel had played a guessing game to name when their family had driven through Colorado and Utah on family vacations. His mother had stopped to photograph the children playing outside their Navajo Indian houses. They'd camped along the San Juan and Colorado Rivers, visited Goosenecks State Park with its view of the steep cliffs and terraces, parked along the overhang and watched rafters take the long boat trip to Lake Powell.

God, they'd had so much fun during those trips. Muley Point had offered another view south over the twisting entrenched canyon to the desert beyond, and Monument Valley and the Valley of the Gods had been other favorite stops.

Baby Jack's face flashed into his mind and he wondered if he'd ever get to take his son camping along the ridges. If he'd be able to drive through the eerie formations of the Valley of the Gods and watch Jack's reaction when he first saw the sixty-foot-wide sombrero-shape rock that had inspired Mexican Hat's name.

He scrubbed his hand over the back of his neck—jeez, he was already thinking like Jack was his. Hoping he was….

If so, he had to find a way to make sure he stayed in the boy's life. Nothing Aspen could say would deter him.

U.S. 163 led him straight into town, and he let his GPS guide him down a side road to the shelter, a nondescript adobe building surrounded by a ten-foot iron gate. Inside, a massive cross stood in front of the steel door as if to guard its residents and stave off evil.

Dust and a wave of heat engulfed him as he climbed from his sedan, the gray night sky casting the center in dark shadows. He glanced around the outside but saw nothing amiss, so rang the buzzer at the gate entrance.

A second later, a woman's voice echoed through the speaker. "Yes?"

He produced his badge, then identified himself. "Special Agent Ryan spoke with you about the photo you faxed to the Bureau, about the woman you have staying here. Aspen Meadows."

"Yes, just a minute." A buzz sounded, and the gate swung open, a nun appearing in the doorway to the building. She checked his identification before letting him enter, then led him to a small office to the right.

"I need to see her," he said without preamble.

Her eyes seemed to be assessing him. "First, we need to talk. My name is Sister Margaret."

He gave a clipped nod, noting the modest furnishings, a battered wooden desk and desk chair, two wooden Windsor chairs and a ratty plaid sofa that had seen better days. She gestured for him to take a seat, so he claimed one of the Windsor chairs, and she settled onto the sofa. But the pinched look on her face and the way she fidgeted with her habit spoke volumes about her mental state.

His gut churned with anxiety. "Is something wrong, Sister? Is Aspen all right?"

She pursed her lips and sighed, a sound that disturbed him even more.

"Did you personally know Aspen?" Sister Margaret asked.

He was accustomed to asking the questions. But this woman was as protective as a mother hen, so he knew he had to answer. "Yes. A while back. I've been investigating her disappearance for weeks. Her cousin is worried sick about her."

"Yes, about that..."

Dylan leaned forward, bracing his elbows on his knees. "Just cut to it, Sister. Is Aspen all right?"

"Yes, and no," the sister said. "When she first came to us, she was suffering from hypothermia, and multiple bruises and lacerations covered her body and face. Along with that, she had a couple of broken ribs, a fractured wrist, concussion and it appeared as if someone had tried to strangle her." She shuddered, and Dylan's mind raced with the visual image she'd painted.

"Can you tell me what happened to her?" Sister Margaret asked. "Who hurt her?"

Sweat beaded on Dylan's neck, and he took a deep breath, struggling to control his anger. "We don't have all the pieces of the puzzle yet. We believe she may have witnessed a murder. Either that or she saw the killer dumping a woman's body. When the killer realized Aspen had witnessed his criminal actions, he came after her. We found her car crashed along the San Juan River. Her son was inside."

"Oh, my." A horror stricken look passed over Sister Margaret's face. "Aspen has a son?"

"Yes, a baby boy named Jack. He's fifteen weeks old now." *And he might be mine.*

Sister Margaret pressed a hand to her pale face. "We thought she might be running from an abusive boyfriend or husband, but she never mentioned a child, so we had no idea. If we had, we would have reported her missing right away."

Dylan arched a brow, confusion clogging his head. "I don't understand. Didn't Aspen tell you what happened?"

"That's the reason I wanted to talk to you," Sister

Margaret said softly. "Aspen was unconscious when she was brought in. And when she regained consciousness… well, she didn't remember anything."

Dylan's chest pounded. "You mean, she didn't remember the car crash or attack?"

Sister Margaret shook her head sadly. "I mean, she didn't remember *anything.* Not about what happened to her, not even her name or that she has family."

Dylan sat back in the chair, trying to absorb the missing piece the woman had just revealed. Amnesia would explain why Aspen hadn't contacted Emma or returned home for Jack.

Or called him for help.

"What did the doctor say about the amnesia?"

Sister Margaret looked shaken. "That the head injury could have caused her memory loss, but that the trauma could have been a factor, as well."

"Basically, she blocked out the events because they were too painful," Dylan said.

"Yes."

"Will she regain her memory?" Dylan asked.

The sister shrugged, her hands twisting together in her habit. "Probably. But that may take time. And Dr. Bennigan advised us not to push her, that doing so might traumatize her even more."

Dylan stewed over that revelation, bracing himself to meet an Aspen who had no idea who he was. "So what prompted you to finally report her appearance to the police?" Dylan finally asked.

The sister shifted nervously. "Someone broke into the center earlier, into the room where Aspen was sleeping and attacked her. She told us to call the police."

Dylan fisted his hands by his sides. Dammit, had Perkins and Watts tracked down Aspen and broken into the shelter to finish the job?

Aspen sat on the floor with the children surrounding her, her voice low as she recanted the legend of the Sky People. "Manitou is the Great Spirit—he lived all alone in the sky. But he was lonely so he made a big hole in the sky and built the mountains, then sent snow and rain down to make the world more beautiful."

"Did he make the animals, too?" a curly red-haired four-year-old asked.

"Yes," Aspen said with a smile. "He made all the animals and the birds. But soon, like children and grown-ups do sometimes, the animals began to fight. So Manitou decided he needed a king to rule them all."

"Was it a lion?" a little boy asked.

"A dinosaur?" another suggested.

Aspen shook her head. "No, a grizzly bear." She reached up her arms and held them wide. "Now give me a big bear hug and say night-night."

The kids giggled and hugged her, and as they parted, she looked up to see Sister Margaret standing with a man in the doorway.

Her breath lodged in her chest in a painful surge. He was broad-shouldered and tall, so masculine with his wide jaw and chiseled features that her stomach fluttered with nerves. Thick black hair brushed his ears and forehead, long black lashes framing the bluest eyes she'd ever seen, eyes like the sky on a clear Colorado day.

Yet he looked dangerous and imposing, anger radiating off him in waves. And those startling eyes were intense, haunted, seemed to be trying to see deep into her soul, and made a chill skitter up her arms.

So did the scar that slashed his chin.

Although even that scar didn't detract from his good looks.

One of the mothers herded the children to the back rooms for bed, and Aspen stood slowly, her ankle still slightly weak from her tumble with her attacker.

Sister Margaret offered her a tentative smile and gestured for the man to follow.

"This is Special Agent Dylan Avecedo. He came to take you home, Aspen."

Fear slithered through Aspen as she met his gaze. Then he extended his hand and she placed hers inside his large palm, and a warm feeling of awareness shot through her. Something about those eyes seemed…familiar.

Had she met this man before?

But how would she have known a federal agent? Did he have the answers to her missing past?

And if he did, was she ready to hear the truth?

Chapter 3

God, Aspen was even more beautiful that he'd remembered. Seeing her sitting on the floor with those kids triggered childhood memories of his mother doing the same with him and his siblings.

And served as a reminder that Aspen had intended to help children before her life had been interrupted by a murder.

Her long dark hair hung in a thick braid over her shoulder, her chocolate colored eyes huge and so sultry that once again he lost himself in the beautiful depths.

They were also pensive, pained by her loss.

Damn, he could almost feel the turmoil inside her, the need to replace her missing past with the truth. Yet she instinctively knew the truth wouldn't be pretty, and she was frightened.

"Detective?" Her voice was pleading, searching his for answers. Answers that he didn't have.

He studied her for any sign of recognition, for any glimmer that she would welcome him back in her life. That she knew that he could be trusted to stay by her side.

But he saw no indication that she knew who he was… or that she'd ever melted beneath his hands and mouth like a wanton lover.

Instead she looked at him as if he was a perfect stranger.

That hurt. He wanted her to know him, to recall what they'd had together, to want his touch as much as he craved hers.

Her face flushed slightly as he clung to her hand, and the trembling in her petite body and flushed expression in her eyes offered him a seed of hope. Even if she didn't remember him, there was something there, a simmering, immediate attraction, just as the first time they'd touched and fallen into bed.

She was serving cocktails in that casino in Vegas, wearing a short little black skirt with a cropped T-shirt that hugged her breasts and exposed the smooth brown flesh of her flat stomach. Her voice had purred like a kitten, her movements fluid and seductive, her body so tempting that he had had to caress her bare skin.

That body he knew so well. One he'd tasted and explored and memorized.

One he'd wanted so often over the past few months that he'd fantasized about having her again and again.

Somewhere in the building, a baby cried out, and he thought of Jack. Along with relief that she was physically okay and the instantaneous heat that ripped through him at the sight of her, anger churned through his gut.

Dammit, if Jack was his, why hadn't she told him?

Finally, she retreated and pulled away, wiping her palm on the side of her skirt. “Sister Margaret said you know where my family is.”

A slight tremor laced her voice, and he tried to place himself in her shoes, to understand what it must be like to be lost and alone with no memory of what had happened, but obviously aware she was in danger.

“Yes, your cousin Emma is waiting at the Ute reservation. That’s where you live. She’s been searching for you ever since you disappeared.”

A frown creased the delicate skin above her huge almond-shaped eyes. “How could I forget my own cousin?”

The doctor’s advice trilled in his head like a warning bell, and Dylan forced an understanding smile. “You suffered a head injury,” he said, hating the distress lining her face. “Sister Margaret said in time you may remember everything.”

She shivered and wrapped her arms around her waist.

“Sister Margaret also said a man broke into your room. Did you get a look at your attacker?”

She shook her head. “No, it was too dark. All I saw was his shadow. Then he attacked me, and I fought back and screamed.” Her voice broke, her breathing rattling out as if she was reliving that horrible event. “Then the sisters and other women ran in, and he jumped out the window and got away.”

A fresh bruise darkened her cheek, and he gritted his teeth to keep from touching it and pulling her into his arms to comfort her. She looked so small and fragile and…vulnerable. “What else do you remember?”

She chewed her bottom lip. “He had a knife in a leather pouch attached to his belt.”

Dylan's blood ran cold. "How tall was he?"

She hesitated, rubbing her head in thought. "I don't know. It was just a shadow."

"Did you notice a distinctive smell?"

"Cigarettes," she whispered. "And sweat."

Watts used to smoke but had supposedly given up the habit. But perhaps the man had picked it back up. "Did he say anything?"

She shook her head. "No, he just grabbed me and shoved his hand over my mouth. Then I… I think I bit his hand."

Her feistiness might have saved her life. Twice now. "I'd like to look around that room and see if I find any evidence."

Sister Margaret nodded, and he went to the sedan to retrieve his crime kit. He flipped on a flashlight, waving it across the room in an arc as he searched the corners, the bed and floor.

With a grunt, he knelt and with his gloved hand, retrieved a loose hair that had fallen on the floor. It might belong to one of the other women or children, but he'd check it out. The hair was longer than Boyd Perkins's or Sherman Watts's—but still, it might be a lead if there was a third perp.

Continuing the search, he paused at the window, then used a pair of tweezers to pluck a small piece of fabric that had caught on a nail on the windowsill, and bagged it along with the hair to send for analysis.

Maybe forensics would turn up something to help them nail the bastard and make sure the charges stuck when they finally tracked him down.

Stewing over the circumstances, he carried the evidence bags to the car while Aspen said goodbye to the other women. Outside, he phoned Miguel to explain the situation.

"Amnesia?" Miguel asked.

"Yes. She didn't recognize me. I'm hoping that seeing Emma and Jack will jog her memory."

"I'll warn Emma about the doctor's diagnosis," Miguel said. "And tell her not to push, to give Aspen time."

Five minutes later, Aspen returned carrying a small paper bag holding the meager possessions she'd accumulated since staying at the shelter.

Sister Margaret gave him a concerned look as she escorted them to the gate. "Take care of her, Agent Avecedo."

He squeezed her hand with a nod. "Don't worry. I won't leave her alone until we find out who hurt her." He paused and lowered his voice. "And, Sister, I'm going to need the medical report from when Aspen was brought in. When we find out who did this, it will help with prosecution."

If he let the son of a bitch live that long.

"I'll speak to the doctor, but we'll need a release from Aspen."

"I'll talk to her about it," Dylan said.

Sister Margaret agreed, then thanked him, and he walked Aspen to the car. She settled into the passenger side and buckled her seat belt, the tension thickening as he drove away from the shelter.

"Sister Margaret said that you were injured when you arrived at the center. That you thought that someone, an abusive boyfriend, was after you."

She shrugged. "It seemed like a likely story, Agent Acevedo."

"Call me Dylan."

She gave him an odd look, then nodded.

"Did the abusive boyfriend idea come from a memory?" he asked.

She fidgeted, looking back at the center as if she wanted to return to the safe haven she'd found within that iron fence. "Not really. Just a feeling that I was running from someone." Her voice warbled. "And then there are the nightmares."

"Nightmares?"

She nodded, her brown eyes huge in her face. "Nightmares of fighting some man, of running, of hearing the river and being cold..."

She angled her head to study his face. "Can you fill in any of the missing pieces?"

"Some, but not all. We found your car smashed into a tree by the San Juan River." He paused, debating over whether to tell her that her son had been left in her car. "There was evidence of a struggle. Blood in the car. We didn't know if you'd survived or if you might have drowned in the river."

She made a low sound in her throat. "My cousin... She was worried?"

He nodded and gently placed his hand over hers in an attempt to calm her, although heat radiated through him. He wanted more, wanted to hold her and assure her everything would be all right.

Wanted to shake her for not telling him that they had a son together.

"Yes, Aspen, her name is Emma, and she's anxious for you to come home."

Relief filled her eyes, and she relaxed slightly. As

much as he wanted to press her, he forced himself to rein in his emotions and let her absorb what he'd told her.

"You look exhausted," he said. "Why don't you try to rest during the drive? I know Emma will want to talk when we arrive."

She gave him a wary look, but nodded. A second later, she curled up against the door and fell asleep, but even in sleep, her body seemed wound tight and braced for battle as if she expected her attacker to reappear any minute and end her life as he'd tried to do before.

The nightmares returned again.

Aspen struggled to wake herself, determined not to let them suck her into the darkness, but the heavy pull of fear yanked her back to the day she'd been running.

Running, but from whom?

If she could only see the man's face…

She crawled along the steep rocks, fighting to steady herself as the river raged below, the snow-capped ridges reminding her that the water would be dangerous and freezing. That although she was an excellent swimmer, there was no way she could survive the icy temperatures or strong current.

Then the hands were upon her, clenching, hitting, choking her, dragging her into the murky depths of death.

She screamed, snippets of her life flashing in front of her. The Ute reservation, the casino, the Trading Post, the children gathering for a Ute celebration. The Bear Dance in the spring and the Sun Dance at Mesa Verde.

Her mother teaching her the ways of the people. The childhood stories of the Sky People, the legend of the

Sleeping Ute Mountain, and the ghost stories her mother insisted she pass on about the sacrifices of their ancestors.

Then she was drowning, the icy water sucking her down to the bottom, the rocks beating against her skin, the whisper of death calling her name.

She jerked awake, shaking and disoriented. Suddenly she felt the agent's hand on hers again. "More nightmares, Aspen?"

She lifted her head, pushed a strand of hair that had escaped her braid from her eyes and tried to steady her labored breathing. "Yes." She glanced down at his hand, aching to cling to him for protection, but she hardly knew the man. Still, he made her feel safe as if he wouldn't leave her to the terrifying memories that hacked at her sanity, tapping at the fringes of her conscience yet evading her.

While she'd slept, the weather had changed. Dark ominous clouds hovered above the ridges, the mountain runoff filling the potholes and shoulder with rising water. A chill filled the car, the temperatures dropping as they neared the canyon.

The road was virtually deserted, the landscape colored with shadows, prairie grass and scattered rocks. In the distance, the sound of a coyote rent the air, the slap of the windshield wipers battling the light rain eerie in the silence.

Occasionally they passed a pueblo style house, the elements having beaten its beauty to a muddy brownish orange. The story she'd told the children earlier reminded her that this area was dangerous territory for the reemergence of the grizzly bear.

And the ghost town that had once been a miner's haven made her anxious to return to civilization.

A gust of wind that sounded like a freight train sent tumbleweed swirling across the road, then suddenly bright headlights appeared behind them, racing up on their tail.

Aspen tensed as Dylan swerved, the car bounced over a rut in the road and hit a wet patch. The car behind them rammed into their tail, sending the sedan fishtailing across the dark highway, skimming rocks and spewing gravel and dirt.

Dylan cursed in Spanish and steered into the skid in an attempt to regain control.

But the car raced up behind them, rammed them again, then swerved to their right and a gunshot pierced the side of the car.

Aspen screamed, and Dylan shoved her head down. “Stay low!”

Dylan sped up, weaving left then right, as if he intended to outsmart their attacker at his own game of cat and mouse. The sedan sent the other car sliding off the road toward the creek, which looked as if it was about to flood from the mountain runoff.

Aspen covered her head with her hands, leaning down so her forehead touched her knees. But a second later, the other car’s tires squealed and the vehicle slammed into them again. Another shot shattered the window on the passenger side, sending glass raining down on top of her.

She cried out again, and Dylan shouted another obscenity, losing control as the sedan careened off the road, bounced over shrubs and rocks and hit a tall rock formation. Metal screeched and gears ground together as they spun toward the ridge out of control. The car flipped on its side, rolled and landed upside down in the creek bed.

The air bag exploded, knocking the wind out of her and trapping her in the seat.

Aspen thought she might have passed out for a moment, and when she recovered, her breath huffed out in tiny pants as water began to seep through the window.

"Are you okay?" Dylan shouted.

They were both hanging upside down, the seat belt cutting into her neck. She glanced sideways and noticed blood dotting his hands, and felt it trickling down her arm where glass had pelted them.

"Aspen?"

"Yes, I'm okay," she rasped. "But water's coming in."

"I know. Hang on to the seat belt and side of the car while I cut you out."

She sucked in a sharp breath and braced herself with one hand on the roof of the car and another on the door. Dylan retrieved a knife from his pocket and sawed at her air bag, puncturing it. It deflated with a whoosh, then he sawed at her seat belt. The icy water gurgled and spewed through the window, dripping onto the roof and soaking her.

"Hurry!" she whispered hoarsely as déjà vu struck her. She'd been in another crash and had almost drowned....

Her dreams of running, of being cold—they weren't just nightmares. They had been very real.

"Almost got it," Dylan said between clenched teeth.

The belt finally snapped, and she slid downward, her head hitting the roof. "Try to climb out," he said. "I need to cut my belt."

Terror seized her. She didn't want to go out there alone.

"Go, Aspen!"

His sharp voice jerked her from the fear gripping

her, and she maneuvered sideways, then kicked the rest of the glass free with her feet. Water gushed inside the vehicle, and she held her breath, grabbed the seat and shoved her weight through the window. The freezing water swallowed her, and numbness claimed her, but her foot connected with rock, and she used it as a springboard to propel her. Teeth chattering, she waded to the embankment.

Dragging in huge gulping breaths, her limbs shaking, she searched the creek and finally saw Dylan wading toward her in the waist-deep cold water.

He crawled from the creek, carrying the crime-scene kit in one hand. Another gunshot blasted the rock beside her, and Dylan grabbed her hand. "Come on, let's go!"

Her legs felt like Jell-O as he yanked her to her feet and dragged her across the embankment. She stumbled over rocks, and her ankle twisted but she plunged on, ducking low to dodge another bullet.

She couldn't die now, not when she'd just found out her name, and that she had family waiting for her.

Chapter 4

Dylan stuffed the evidence box beneath a boulder, then buried Aspen in the crook of his arm to protect her from the gunshots as they raced in an upward climb into the mountains. The terrain was rocky and pitted with shrubs and brush, the jagged ridges posing their own danger.

It was also a good place to hide.

Another shot pinged off a stone jutting out from the ridge, and they ducked, dodging it as he pushed her behind a boulder. The dark sky and mixture of rain and snow added to the dangers, making their footing slippery. A second later, he steered her toward another indentation carved into the red stone, pushing her to climb higher as they dodged more bullets.

Dylan crouched beside her, removed his gun and braced it to fire. "Stay down," he whispered. "I'm going after the bastard."

She grabbed his arm. “No. Don’t leave me alone.”

The cold terror in her voice and eyes made his chest clench, and he hated the shooter for putting it there. All the more reason to catch the SOB.

He brushed his hand against her bruised cheek. “I’ll be back.”

Slowly rising behind the boulder, he searched the ridges and cliffs, then spotted movement to the right. He fired, a shot pinging over the shadow, and rocks skittered down the ridge as the man scrambled to escape.

Dylan gestured for Aspen to stay put, then lurched forward in chase. He fired again and saw the shadow moving at lightning speed around a boulder, then disappear. Dylan wanted to pursue him, but a low cry escaped Aspen and a faraway look glazed her eyes as if she was reliving the trauma that had caused her amnesia.

Her arm was bleeding, too, and cuts from the shattered window marred her hands.

The sound of a car engine sliced the night, and Dylan breathed a sigh of relief, then stooped down and gathered Aspen in his arms. She trembled against him, wet and shivering, and he hugged her to his chest, whispering low words of assurance.

Thank God they had survived.

But he’d find the man who’d tried to kill him and put that terror in Aspen’s eyes and make him suffer.

Aspen clung to the agent, memories of another crash and running for her life bombarding her. She survived, she reminded herself, and she would survive now.

At least this time she wasn’t alone.

“It’s all right, Aspen,” Dylan said. “He’s gone now and you’re safe.”

She forced a calming breath, then looked up at him. "But he'll be back. And how can I fight him if I don't even know who he is?"

"Sister Margaret said you would get your memory back," he assured her. "You need time. Just trust me for now."

She folded her arms. "It's just so frustrating and scary. I feel as if I'm living in the dark."

He stroked her back, soothing her. "I won't stop until the danger to you is over and the man responsible for the shooting and for your memory loss is in jail, or dead."

She took solace in his strength, relaxed slightly and pulled herself together.

He wiped the blood dotting her arm. "We need to take you to the E.R."

"No. I'm all right," she said. "It's just a few scratches." She pressed a finger to his forehead. "But you might need stitches."

He shrugged off her concern and slowly extracted himself from her arms. "I'm fine. But I need to call for help."

She nodded, then he removed his cell phone and made a call, thankful it still worked.

"Tom, it's Dylan. Listen, I was driving Aspen back to the reservation and someone ambushed us. My car is upside down in the creek and we need an extraction. Also, I want forensics to go over the car for paint samples and bullets." He gave him their location, disconnected the call, then turned to her and took her arm.

"Come on, let's head back down to the car. I need to retrieve the evidence box to send to forensics."

Aspen took his hand as he helped her down the slippery rocks, grateful the precipitation had stopped, although the wind rustled the brush and ruffled her damp hair. Her hands and feet were numb already, the chill inside her mounting. He paused to grab the crime scene kit with the evidence bags he'd stowed inside and hoisted it in one hand while keeping the other firmly on her arm to steady her.

By the time they reached the bottom, the sound of a helicopter echoed from above, its blinking lights sweeping the terrain and promising a recovery.

The helicopter touched down in the flatter part of the canyon and two men climbed out, the pilot and another big guy, an Indian, who frowned as he stalked toward them.

Dylan stepped forward. "Ryan didn't say he was sending you, Bia. But I'm glad he did." He gestured toward Aspen. "This is Aspen Meadows. Aspen, Special Agent Ethan Bia. He's an expert tracker with the Bureau."

The Indian nodded and glanced at Aspen. "Nice to meet you, Miss Meadows."

"Please, call me Aspen."

"Sure." He angled his head toward Dylan. "Ryan didn't know what we'd find, if the shooter was still hiding around here and you might be holed up in the mountains."

"I ran him off," Dylan said. "But we need to collect the bullet casings and take paint samples from my car. When we find this SOB, I want to make sure we have forensics to back up an arrest."

Ethan nodded. "Absolutely. I'll look for the bullet casings while the pilot flies you two back. Ryan's sending a team and a tow truck for the car. I'll wait on them and make sure CSI processes it."

"Thanks." Dylan shook his head, and curved an arm

around Aspen, coaxing her toward the chopper. "Come on, let's get you warmed up and to the E.R."

Aspen had never ridden in a helicopter but she was too cold and tired to argue, so she crawled in beside Dylan, accepted the blanket he offered and burrowed beneath it while the blades of the chopper whirled and they lifted off.

Her gaze fell to Dylan's car where it lay upside down in the rising creek, and she flinched. They could have died and they might not have been found for days or weeks.

The realization that that was the shooter's plan sent another shudder through her. She had to remember what had happened nine weeks ago.

Her life depended on it.

The next few hours were hectic and strained as the helicopter transported them to the emergency room in Durango, and doctors examined and treated them for scrapes and cuts. Dylan earned four stitches to his forehead, but thankfully Aspen didn't need stitches. Still, she was bruised and battered and had suffered minor lacerations on her hands and legs.

He phoned Miguel, explained the circumstances and suggested he take Aspen home to rest before she saw Jack. Miguel promised to leave a key to Aspen's house hidden in the mouth of the horse sculpture in her front yard.

Fatigue lined her face as he secured a vehicle, dropped the evidence he'd collected earlier at the Kenner County Crime Unit in Kenner City, and drove toward the reservation. It was early morning, the gray dawn sky filled with the shadows of another impending storm. Neither of them had slept for over twenty-four hours, and he desperately needed a shower and food.

"Where are we going?" Aspen asked.

Her labored breath as she pressed a hand to her chest indicated her ribs were bruised from the impact of the air bag. If she felt like him, every bone in her body ached.

"To your house for some sleep. Then we'll reconnect with your family. Your cousin dropped off some groceries earlier if you're hungry."

"But, Dylan—"

"Don't argue, Aspen," he said, cutting her off. "You've had a lot to deal with in the past twenty-four hours and need some rest before you face your family."

And so did he. Because he wanted to be prepared when she saw Jack for the first time. "The doctor warned that you need to take it easy and not push things for your own health."

Wariness dimmed her features, but exhaustion and trauma outweighed any protest as her eyes slid closed. He clenched his jaw, hating the bruises on her battered skin and the fact that she'd forgotten everyone she loved. That fact alone confirmed the extent of physical and mental trauma she'd suffered.

And as much as he wanted to question her about Jack's paternity, he had to refrain.

Earn her trust. Give her time to heal. To reconnect with her family and home and let her memories return on their own.

Or he could drive the truth deeper into her psyche.

Which meant it would be even more difficult to find out who had attacked her.

And he had to do that to protect her.

If Boyd Perkins and Sherman Watts had tried to kill

her, she'd have to testify so they could put the men behind bars.

Of course, they had to find the bastards first.

And if someone else was involved…well, he'd find that out and uncover their motive. If Jack wasn't his son and another man was in the picture…

No, he couldn't go there yet.

But he needed to brace himself for that possibility. Couldn't allow himself to get too close to her or the baby until he knew the truth.

Did she think he wasn't father material? Couldn't she contemplate a future with him?

Agitated, mind racing with questions, he drove onto the reservation toward Aspen's. He wasn't surprised at the small pueblo style house with its adobe colors and Native American look. During their one glorious week in Vegas together, she'd talked about life on the reservation, her love of her culture, and her desire to teach the children and instill in them the importance of their heritage.

Aspen was deep in sleep, so he parked in the stone drive, climbed out and grabbed the key, his instincts on full alert as he scanned the property.

Satisfied no one was hiding in the shadows of the trees, he left Aspen in the car while he went to search the inside. Darkness bathed the interior as he entered, and he paused to listen for sounds of an intruder.

First thing tomorrow, he'd install a security system in Aspen's home. One that went straight to him if anyone set off the alarm.

Slowly, he crept inside the dark entryway, flipped on a light, then scanned the foyer. Native American artwork decorated the adobe colored walls, collections of handmade baskets, beaded jewelry, pottery and other artifacts and books filled the built-in shelves. A picture of a native Ute on horseback was centered over a soft brown leather couch opposite a woodstove in the den, which opened to the kitchen.

He moved to the left and found a master suite and bath, decorated in earth tones with accents of red, yellow and orange, and more Ute art. He searched the closet, beneath the bed, then moved to the guest bedroom on the opposite side of the kitchen.

His lungs tightened at the sight of the nursery. A primitive wooden crib sat in the midst of the freshly painted baby blue room, which held an assortment of stuffed animals, children's books and infant toys.

Hissing a breath of relief that no intruder was inside, he stowed his gun inside his jacket, then went outside to the car and lifted Aspen from the seat. She moaned softly in her sleep, and snuggled against him as he carried her to the front stoop.

She was wrapped in the blanket, wearing the scrubs the nurse had given her at the E.R. when they'd removed her damp clothes, so he carried her to her bedroom, pulled down the covers and laid her on the crisp clean sheets. For a brief second her eyes flickered open, and she looked at him with glazed eyes.

He inhaled her sweet fragrance, the softness of her skin, and ached to crawl in bed beside her. To rekindle the heat between them.

"You're home now," he said gently, then pulled the quilt over her and brushed back her hair.

She tugged at his hand, and a hollow feeling of need gripped him.

"Where are you going?' she whispered in a sleep-laced voice that triggered images of the two of them in bed together, of her voice purring his name after a night of lovemaking.

"I know it sounds silly," she whispered, "but I don't want to be alone."

God, he didn't want that, either. He wanted to make love to her.

Instead, he brushed the pad of his thumb across her cheek. "I'll sleep on the couch," he said, his voice thick and hoarse. "If you need me just call."

She nodded, closed her eyes again and curled into her bed. He ached to drop a kiss on her cheek, then her mouth, but remembered the doctor's warning and forced himself to leave the room.

Still, his body hummed with arousal and a fierce hunger that could only be sated by Aspen.

A woman who saw him as a perfect stranger.

Chapter 5

Dylan was exhausted but on edge, too wired to sleep.

It was the first time he'd been in Aspen's home and he felt uncomfortable and intrigued at the same time. Her furnishings were exactly as he'd expected, reminiscent of her culture, yet the sight of the nursery made his chest ache.

How would she react when she saw the empty baby bed? When she saw Jack? Would she remember her son?

He yanked off his shirt and walked around the den/kitchen combination, wishing he was here under other circumstances. That Aspen had invited him into her home because she wanted to see him again.

He studied the Ute items in the room and was once again reminded of the road trips his family used to take when he was younger.

Once they'd stopped to observe a young Ute woman with a horde of children surrounding her as she taught them to weave baskets. His mother had photographed her, and he'd thought about that photograph when he'd first seen Aspen.

The Uncompahgre beaded horse bag on Aspen's wall was made from tanned mule deer hide. Thousands of glass trade beads and tobacco balls were stitched into the sides and rim. The bags were used to hold pipes, carvings and religious totems and were opened only for private ceremonies.

An Uncompahgre Ute Shaved Beaver Hide Painting hung above the fireplace, and ceremonial pipes of salmon alabaster and black pipestone sat on the mantle. Several ceremonial rattles made from buffalo rawhide that were used to call spirits in Ute ceremonies decorated a pine sofa table.

Some Ute still used peyote in healing rituals. He wondered if Aspen did, or if she would use a traditional doctor with their son.

Her *son—you don't know yet that Jack is yours.*

Still, his gaze was drawn to the photographs, and he walked over to study the scattering of pictures. The first photo showed Aspen cradling a newborn to her chest. Dylan touched the frame, memorizing the picture. The baby's eyes were squished closed, his lips pursed, his fists on his chest.

The next one had been taken a couple of weeks later. A smiling Jack was propped against a Mexican blanket. The scant few pictures chronicled his young life up until the time Aspen had disappeared.

Jack had only been four weeks old at the time.

Aspen had missed almost three months of her son's life because of the attack.

And if Jack was his, he had missed those months, as well.

Dammit, he would find out who'd stolen those weeks from her and make sure she and Jack were never separated again.

Hours later, Aspen woke from an exhausted sleep to the delicious aroma of coffee. Still groggy, she rolled over in bed and looked at her surroundings. A fog still hovered over her memories, but the room, the art, the scent of lavender seemed familiar and evoked a warm fuzzy feeling as if she was finally safe.

Then the events of the night before crashed back, shattering her peace. Her limbs throbbed as she swung her legs over the side of the bed. A sharp pain splintered her midriff from her bruised ribs, and she breathed deeply to stem the pain, gripping the edge until her legs steadied enough to support her.

She was still wearing the scrubs the nurse had given her in the E.R., and desperately wanted a shower.

Footsteps in the den sounded, and she hesitated, the fear that had clawed at her the last few weeks returning. Who was in the house?

That agent—Dylan? Or someone else?

A tremor rattled the windowpane, and she stood and walked to the edge of the door and glanced into the den. Dylan Acevedo was sitting at the table, drinking coffee and looking at an opened folder.

Relief surged through her, and she hurried into the bathroom. The warm water felt heavenly on her achy body and helped to wash away the scent of the river and soothe her aching limbs. After toweling off, she let her hair hang loose to dry, and dug through the closet, noting the long flowing Indian skirts and beaded blouses. She chose a bright blue skirt, pale yellow blouse and a pair of leather sandals and dressed, then walked into the den.

Dylan glanced up, his dark blue eyes raking over her and sending a tingle through her.

But his mouth was set in a firm straight line, and the sultry look she thought she'd seen suddenly died, an iciness replacing it.

"I can't believe I slept so long." She accepted the mug of coffee he offered, surprised when he automatically dumped a packet of sweetener in it as if he knew how she liked it.

She started to question him about that, but he cleared his throat. "Your cousin Emma has already called. I told her we'd let her know when you woke up. She's anxious to see you."

Nerves fluttered in Aspen's stomach. "What if I don't recognize her?"

His dark look softened. "Don't worry. She knows about your amnesia."

A helpless feeling engulfed her. "But how could I forget my own family?"

He took her elbows in his hands, then guided her to the table. "You will remember. Just give yourself time to heal. Now why don't I make you something to eat and then we'll call Emma?"

She nodded and sipped her coffee as he made himself at home and whipped up two omelets. Odd that Dylan seemed comfortable in the kitchen—and in his skin.

When he placed the plates on the table, he set the hot sauce on the table. She immediately reached for it, something niggling at the back of her mind. How did he know she liked hot sauce on her eggs?

"Any more nightmares?" he asked as he sprinkled salt and pepper on his food.

She pressed a hand over her forehead, struggling with the tiny snippets of life that flashed in front of her. Another man cooking for her, feeding her in bed…

His big body taking up all the space in the room just as Dylan's was now.

"Aspen, are you all right? You're not eating."

She blinked to clear her head and cut into her omelet. "I think I was too exhausted to have nightmares. Either that or I felt…safe for the first time in weeks."

His breath rushed out and their gazes locked, the moment stretching between them before he finally broke the strained silence. "I'm glad you felt safe."

She frowned. Her comment seemed ridiculous—how could she feel safe when they'd been attacked and nearly died the night before?

Because Dylan was watching over her, protecting her, guarding her house. Deep down, she sensed he wouldn't let anyone hurt her.

He was an excellent agent, took his job seriously.

But there was more. He'd promised to protect her. And somehow, she knew that he kept his promises.

Still, nerves pulled at her sanity. And a voice whispered inside her head that she couldn't grow dependent on the agent. That she needed to keep her distance.

That hollow ache clutched her insides again. She'd never be whole again until she found out the truth.

Time for her to meet her cousin.

The fact that Aspen felt safe with him helped to dissipate his anger over the awkward situation.

A knock sounded at the door and he gestured to her

that he'd get it. He checked the window and saw Miguel's vehicle, then heard the rumble of his brother talking to Emma through the door. His jaw tightened as he opened it and saw Jack cradled in Emma's arms.

"Come on in, Aspen is waiting."

When he glanced back at Aspen, she was standing in front of the mantle, studying the baby pictures, tears shimmering in her eyes.

Emma's expression lit with excitement, although nerves also shimmered in the depths of her eyes as Aspen turned to face her.

Miguel closed the door, and Dylan angled himself to watch the reunion, feeling touched, but out of place as if he was an outsider, an intruder in this family.

A family that should be his.

"Oh, Aspen…" Emma's voice choked as she walked over to her. "I've been out of my mind with worry."

Aspen raked her dark brown eyes over Emma and Jack. "Emma?"

"Yes, it's me. I'm so relieved to have you home." Emma gestured toward Jack, a loving expression softening the anxious lines on her face. "We've both missed you."

As if he understood, Jack whimpered, scrunching up his nose and Emma rocked him back and forth.

"My baby…" Aspen whispered.

Emma nodded. "Jack. They found him in your car after the accident."

Aspen paled, and Dylan hurried over and coaxed her to the sofa. "Take a deep breath," Dylan murmured.

She did as he said, then turned tortured eyes to him. "I abandoned my little boy?" Shock made her voice sound screechy. "I can't believe I'd do that. What kind of mother am I?"

"You were—are—a wonderful mother," Emma said firmly.

Dylan stroked her back. "You didn't leave him of your own accord."

"Then you know what happened to me?"

Dylan, Emma and Miguel exchanged a frustrated look, each questioning just how much to confess. "We know that someone ran you off the road and attacked you," Dylan said. "That was evident from the injuries you sustained and were treated for at the shelter."

"I knew I was missing something," she said in a heart-breakingly agonized voice. "Every time I hugged one of the kids at the center I knew it."

"You love Jack," Emma said gently. "You would never have left him willingly."

"Who did this to me?" Aspen asked, her tormented gaze lingering on her son.

"We're not sure," Dylan said. "Miguel and I are both on the team investigating your disappearance."

Aspen nodded weakly, then pressed her hands to her thighs as if to dry the dampness from them, then reached up toward Emma. "Can I hold him? Can I hold my baby?"

"Of course you can, Aspen," Emma said softly. She moved closer then settled down beside Aspen and jiggled Jack to quiet him.

Aspen's chin trembled and a tear slid down her cheek as she took the squirming baby into her arms. "You are mine, aren't you, Jack?" Aspen whispered. "My God, I've missed you." She hugged him to her and Jack immediately quieted, a little chirp coming from his mouth as he gazed up at his mother. Aspen brushed a hand across his thick, dark hair, then lowered a kiss to his cheek.

"I'm home now, son." She nuzzled his cheek with her own and Jack cooed, reached out his tiny fist and pulled a strand of her hair. Aspen laughed softly, then kissed his cheek. "I'm so sorry I left you, Jack. You must have been so scared..." She lifted him to her chest and hugged him tightly. "I promise I'll never leave you again."

A tenderness warmed Dylan's insides, as well as protective urges that nearly overpowered him.

But once again Aspen looked at him as if he was a stranger and a pang ripped through his heart. He was already coming to think of Jack—and Aspen—as his.

Which he couldn't allow himself to do.

There might have been another man in her life since they'd parted a year ago, another man who'd fathered her child.

But if there was, why hadn't he stepped up to take care of her and Jack?

And if there was, was he responsible for the attack on Aspen at the shelter, or had that been Perkins or Watts?

Aspen's heart melted as she hugged her son to her. She finally felt whole again, as if she'd found the most important part of her missing life.

Yet frustration filled her as she studied her son's features and searched her memory banks for some semblance of details about his birth.

And the person who'd taken her away from him.

Dylan frowned, then asked Miguel to step outside, leaving her alone with Emma and the baby. Jack nestled against her shoulder, poked his thumb in his mouth and made sucking sounds..

"Are you really all right?" Emma asked.

"I will be," Aspen said, trying to sound convincing although questions swirled in her head.

Emma placed a comforting hand on her shoulder. "You know, I saw you," she said in a strained voice.

"What do you mean? Were you there at the accident?"

"No, not exactly." A shyness crept into Emma's blue eyes. "I forget that you have amnesia. I have psychic visions, Aspen. I saw you running from a man. I was terrified for you."

Aspen glanced down at Jack, who'd fallen asleep on her shoulder.

"Come on," Emma said, taking her elbow.

"Where are we going?"

"To put Jack back in his own bed."

Aspen followed her to the second bedroom, and a smile crept over her face at the sight of the nursery. For a brief moment, she saw an image of herself painting the room, of Emma helping her set up the changing table, of baby Jack watching the mobile twirl as it played a lullaby.

Another memory followed, this one of her and Emma playing together as children. Of Emma crying because a man had hurt her mother.

The memories blipped in and out of focus so quickly that she thought she might have imagined them. But they were so real, she knew they were truths pushing their way through the darkness that had consumed her the last few weeks. Those brief snippets gave her hope that she'd remember everything.

But the image of Emma crying disturbed her. Her father…no her mother's boyfriend had been abusive just as some of the women's husbands had been at the shelter.

She gently placed Jack inside the crib, then glanced at her left hand. She hadn't been wearing a ring on her finger when she'd been carried to the shelter. And there was no imprint indicating she'd ever had one.

She turned to Emma, debating over whether to ask, but she needed answers. The sisters had thought an abusive man might be after her. What if it was Jack's father?

"Emma, can I ask you something?"

"Of course, Aspen. Whatever you need."

Aspen tucked a yellow baby blanket over her son. "Who is Jack's father?"

Emma sighed softly and motioned for her to go to the den. After they settled on the sofa, Emma took her hand. "You didn't tell me, Aspen. All you said was that he wasn't in the picture."

"What about another friend? Is there someone else who I'd have told?"

"You're friends with Naomi Rainwater, another teacher on the reservation, but you told me that no one knew, and you intended to keep it that way."

Aspen frowned and glanced at the baby pictures on the mantle. Why wouldn't she have wanted anyone to know Jack's father?

Was he dangerous? Had she been running from him?

Dylan Acevedo thought he would trap him. Thought he would keep the Indian girl and her kid safe by hovering over them.

But he was wrong.

Acevedo and the other pigs had treated him like dirt way too long. Had hunted him like a dog and would keep on hunting.

But he was the hunter now. He was watching their

movements. Knew exactly where they were and what they were doing.

Because he was smarter than them all.

And the girl…killing her would serve his cause *and* torture Acevedo.

Pure pleasure bubbled in his chest as he flicked the cigarette butt to the ground outside Aspen's house and watched the embers spark to life on the brittle scrub grass, then slowly fade as the fire turned the blades a parched brown. He'd quit the cigarettes once, but his craving had returned.

No one knew he was here now or the reason why.

But they would soon.

Because the girl absolutely had to die.

A smile curved his lips.

In fact, he was looking forward to it.

Chapter 6

Dylan left Miguel to guard Aspen and Emma while he headed to the crime lab in Kenner City. But first he drove to Durango to his apartment to pack a bag to carry to Aspen's. He fully intended to stay with her until he was certain she was safe.

His mail had piled up, but he bypassed it and showered first, then packed his clothes and toiletries and stowed them in the rental car. His apartment seemed bare, quiet, empty. Lonely. As if no one lived there, not homey like Aspen's comfortable pueblo style house.

There was no baby here. No woman to love. No one to come home to or to care if he lived or died.

His chest ached, but he clamped a mental stronghold on his thoughts. He'd grown up in a loving home, but he'd gotten into some trouble as a teenager with a gang, but finally turned himself around. He'd told himself his job didn't fit with a wife and kid. That his work would put them in danger.

Although he'd stayed away, Aspen was still in danger.

And if he'd been around this last year, she might be safe now.

A brown manila envelope jutting out of the stack of mail caught his eye and he thumbed through the other pieces, then picked up the envelope with a frown. It was from Julie Grainger.

Ben Parrish and Tom Ryan had received packages from her with different medals inside. Ben had received the medal of St. Joan of Arc, the patron saint of captives, and seemed upset by the sight of it, Tom received a St. Christopher medal, the patron saint of travelers. Dylan wondered what his held and what the significance of each one meant.

Why had she sent each of them a gift? Had she known she was in trouble, that she might die?

Anxious to see if the contents led to a clue to the case, he ripped open the envelope and found a religious medal of Raphael the Archangel, the patron saint against nightmares.

He smiled at her choice.

Julie had known how much his sister's death and the Turnbull case had destroyed his nights. She'd tried to convince him to forgive himself, that he couldn't save them all, but dammit, he felt responsible.

His thumb brushed something else, and he dug deeper and found a photograph inside. An old black and white of a young Vincent Del Gardo and Belinda MacBride Douglas, Callie MacBride's mother.

What did the photo mean? That Del Gardo and Callie's mother had known each other years ago? That they'd been friends?

Or lovers?

Did Callie know they shared a past?

Hell, Del Gardo was a crime boss and their main suspect in Julie Grainger's murder. They also believed that Boyd Perkins had killed Del Gardo, which had brought Del Gardo's rival crime organization, the Wayne family, into the limelight of the investigation, complicating matters more.

Dylan would take the medal and photo to the crime lab, show them to Callie and see what she said. Maybe it was a missing clue of some kind.

He hurried to the annex building housing the Kenner County Crime Unit, took the elevator to the third floor and decided to check with ballistics before he talked to Callie.

Jerry Griswold, the crime lab's firearms expert, was examining a bullet as he entered and had several more shell casings spread on the table.

"Are those from the shooter who fired at my car last night?"

Jerry nodded and gestured toward the screen indicating the National Integrated Ballistics Information Network. "Bia did good. Looks like the bullet casings came from a .38. I checked NIBIN but didn't find a match. If I had the weapon, I could compare and verify if it belongs to the shooter."

Dylan rubbed his chin, then caught himself as his fingers brushed his scar. Boyd Perkins had a nine millimeter. Of course, he could have a whole cache of weapons, for all they knew. "I'll do my best to find it," Dylan said.

He thanked Jerry, then headed to the other part of the

lab. Callie, the head of forensics, glanced up from her microscope. "Hey, Acevedo."

"Hi, Callie. Have you had a chance to process the evidence from the Sisters of Mercy Women's Shelter in Mexican Hat?"

She called to Ava Wright, another forensics specialist, who appeared from a neighboring cube. "What's up, Callie?" She glanced at Dylan. "Hi, Acevedo."

He murmured hello. "Did you get the results on that hair I collected from the women's shelter?"

Ava nodded. "It belongs to a Native American male. That's about all I can tell you right now. Bring me a suspect and I can match it."

A Native American? "What about Sherman Watts?"

She shook her head. "Sorry, not a match."

He frowned, his mind spinning. "Did you get anything on the piece of fabric?"

"A denim shirt, cotton blend, inexpensive. The brand is one you'd find at the trading post or a dozen different stores, including online." She drummed her fingers on the table. "So far nothing distinctive about any of it, but I'll keep checking."

"How about the paint samples from my car?"

"We're still working on those."

He pulled the envelope from inside his jacket. "Callie, I stopped by my apartment and found this waiting. Julie must have mailed it to me before she died."

A wary expression made her lips thin. "What's inside?"

He hesitated, not wanting to upset her. After all, the man with her mother in the photo was a big-time criminal. But they had to know what the picture meant and if it was significant.

First though, he showed her the medal, and Callie examined it with gloved hands. "Why did she send Raphael the Archangel to you?" Callie asked.

"He's the patron saint against nightmares." Dylan scrubbed a hand over the back of his neck. "And during the Turnbull case, God knows I had my share of nightmares."

"We all had bad dreams about that one." Callie offered him a sympathetic look, then gestured to the medal. "I'll dust it for prints."

Dylan nodded. "There's something else."

Callie's brow pinched. "What?"

"Look inside."

She hesitated warily, but removed the photograph, her mouth twisting as she studied it. "It's my mother and Vincent Del Gardo."

He nodded, watching as the wheels spun in her head.

Finally a low sound of discomfort escaped her. "Oh, my God." Her gaze rose to meet his, shock settling in the depths of her eyes. "It looks like they knew each other. Like…"

Her sentence trailed off, and Dylan understood the dark place her train of thought had carried her. Del Gardo had his arm around her mother in the photo, and they were both smiling.

As if they had a personal relationship.

Before they could speculate further, Bree and Patrick Martinez entered the room. Patrick was the sheriff of Kenner City and Sabrina a Ute police detective. They'd struck up a romance while investigating Julie's murder and Aspen's disappearance.

"We heard you found Aspen," Bree said. "I'm glad she's alive."

Dylan explained about her amnesia and Bree sighed. "I'll try to stop by and see her. That poor girl and her baby have been through so much."

Patrick grinned and placed his arms around Sabrina's waist, pulling her up against him. "Speaking of babies. We're going to have one of our own."

"That's wonderful," Callie said. "How far along are you?"

Bree placed a hand over her belly. "Three months."

Dylan congratulated them, although a seed of envy stirred within him.

He hadn't thought much about being a father before, but now that he suspected Jack might be his son, he couldn't think of anything else.

His last encounter with Frank Turnbull flashed back, though, and he grimaced, doubt seeping into places in his mind he didn't like to visit.

Like—maybe he didn't deserve to be a father.

Maybe that was the reason Aspen hadn't contacted him....

She'd met him, *been* with him right after he'd arrested Turnbull. He'd been pent up, so full of rage that he'd admitted that he'd almost killed the man in cold blood.

That he had wanted to inflict pain on Turnbull, make the man suffer before he died.

Hell, he'd tried to pour all that anger and emotion into making love to her, into passion, but there were moments he feared it had bled through.

That he'd frightened her.

"Well, we have rounds to make," Patrick said with a sheepish grin. "Keep us posted on any new evidence. If Perkins and Watts are hiding out on Ute land or in Kenner City, we'll find them. It's only a matter of time."

"Yeah, let's just make that arrest before someone else dies," Dylan growled.

Murmurs of agreement rippled through the room, then they said goodbye.

When Callie turned back, Dylan saw the turmoil on her face as she glanced back at the picture.

But his mind was already straying to the unanswered questions regarding Aspen. He could continue living in a fantasy world, imagining that Jack was his son, or he could find out the truth. And the truth might lead to the unsub after Aspen.

Her safety was all that mattered.

"How about the DNA sample from Jack Meadows?"

Callie and Ava exchanged curious looks. "You think the baby's father might have attacked Aspen?"

He shrugged. "Just covering all the bases. If Watts or Perkins weren't at the shelter, then someone else is after Aspen, too."

"We haven't finished running the DNA," Callie said. "You know paternity tests take time, Dylan."

Frustration knotted his neck. "What if you had a sample to compare it to? Could you at least tell if it was a match?"

"That would help," Ava said. "Do you have one?"

Dylan hesitated, not sure if he wanted to divulge his personal reasons for wanting the test rushed. But he wanted answers. He *needed* answers. And who knew how long it would take for Aspen to remember.

He cleared his throat. "Yeah, mine."

Aspen felt antsy, as if she was crawling out of her skin. For some reason, having Dylan around had given her a safety net, and although she was comfortable with

Emma, the tension of struggling to recall details of her past was draining her. She kept imagining a faceless man attacking her, chasing her, trying to kill her.

Kept wondering who that face belonged to.

Miguel had moved to the porch with his computer and made himself scarce, obviously to give her and Emma privacy. She wondered about her cousin's relationship to Miguel and wanted to ask. Frustration filled her. This was yet another lost part of the past that everyone knew but her.

"You really don't remember anything that happened or how you wound up in that shelter?" Emma asked as they put together a light supper of pasta and salad.

Aspen shook her head, feeling inept, as if she was failing her son. "Not really. But when that car ran us off the road last night, I experienced déjà vu. And I've had nightmares for weeks...."

"I'm so sorry about all this," Emma said quietly. "It must be terribly frustrating."

"It is," Aspen admitted, wringing her hands together. "I don't even remember giving birth. How could a woman possibly forget one of the most important days of her life?"

Emma smiled with compassion. "Maybe you didn't want to remember the labor pain."

Aspen laughed softly. "Were you with me when I was in labor?"

Emma nodded. "Yes. The midwife on the reservation delivered Jack."

Aspen returned to the counter and tossed the salad. "Tell me the truth, Emma. What do you think happened? Why would someone want to hurt me?"

Emma hesitated, her words and tone measured. "How much did Dylan tell you?"

Aspen frowned. "Not much. Just that they thought I might have witnessed a crime."

"That's true," Emma said cautiously.

Aspen seemed to sense she knew much more. "Tell me," Aspen said, almost pleading. "I hate being in the dark like this. Everyone looks at me like I'm a freak."

"You're not a freak," Emma said gently. "But the doctor warned that we should let you remember on your own, not to push you."

Irritation gnawed at Aspen. "It's driving me crazy not knowing." She touched Emma's arm. "Please. I'm not as fragile as everyone thinks. I need to know the truth."

Emma studied her for a moment, then seemed to accept what she'd said and gestured to the kitchen table. "Then sit down, and I'll tell you what I know."

"Thank you." Aspen claimed a kitchen chair while Emma took the one opposite her.

Emma folded her hands on the table. "Dylan and Miguel are brothers. Twins actually. Dylan works for the FBI. Miguel is a forensic specialist for the Kenner County Crime Unit." She hesitated and inhaled a deep breath as if to fortify herself, and Aspen realized that her disappearance had deeply upset her cousin. But before she voiced her concerns and an apology, Emma continued.

"One of their friends, a federal agent named Julie Grainger, was murdered during the process of an ongoing investigation into Vincent Del Gardo, a major crime boss. The FBI believe that a hit man named Boyd Perkins killed Del Gardo and Julie." She paused as if weighing her words and Aspen encouraged her to continue.

"They found evidence that you might have witnessed a hit man, Boyd Perkins, who worked with a man named Sherman Watts, a local Ute man, dumping Julie's body. Apparently they saw you and chased you, causing you to crash. We thought you'd drowned in the river, but somehow you must have escaped."

Aspen massaged her temple, the horrific images of fighting the river current sending a shudder through her. "That makes sense. I've had dreams about nearly drowning and being chased."

Emma closed her hand over Aspen's. "I'm so sorry, honey."

Aspen squeezed Emma's fingers. "So how did you and Miguel get involved?"

A faraway look settled in Emma's eyes, one that indicated that Emma did see things more deeply than others. "When they found your car, Jack was inside. They brought him to me to keep until we found out what happened to you." Emma traced a finger along the hand woven placement. "Because of my visions, they had me visit the place where your car crashed. I sensed that you were alive, but I couldn't see anything specific to help."

Aspen's chest clenched at the frustration in her cousin's words. "I'm sorry. That must have been difficult for you, Emma."

Aspen swallowed. Moisture gathered in Emma's eyes. "Yes, it was. I was so afraid you were dead…."

"No, I'm all right. And thank you for taking care of Jack for me."

"I love him, Aspen. You two are the only family I have."

Aspen hugged her, the two of them bonding, memories of other times when she and Emma had shared problems surfacing. Aspen traced a finger over Emma's hair, pushing it back behind her ear. "So tell me about you and Miguel."

Emma dabbed at her eyes, then glanced toward the porch. "Miguel was working the case with Dylan. At first he didn't believe me, but then I led him to the gutter where we found a Native American leather necklace in the snow. That's how they connected Perkins to Watts and to you."

Aspen's mind raced. "So I was just in the wrong place at the wrong time?"

"I'm afraid so," Emma said. "Then…"

"Then what?"

Fear darkened Emma's eyes. "One night I had a vision and went back to the river, hoping to remember more. But Sherman Watts was there and tried to kill me."

Aspen clasped her hand. "Oh, my God."

Emma shivered. "I was terrified, but Miguel showed up and saved me."

"And he's been hanging around ever since," Aspen said with a smile.

Emma blushed and ducked her head. "Yes, we've grown close."

"I'm glad you found someone," Aspen said sincerely. "He certainly seems protective of you."

Emma blushed again. "Yes, well… Apparently the Feds think that Watts and Perkins are hiding out on the reservation somewhere. They're afraid he'll come back for me and for you." She glanced up at Aspen with terror streaking her face. "Apparently they did come after you."

The breath in Aspen's lungs tightened.

"But don't worry," Emma said. "Miguel will protect me, and I know that Dylan will stay with you until the men are arrested."

Aspen shifted, threading her fingers together. The thought of Dylan protecting her made her uneasy. He seemed angry, intense…and darkly sexy.

She was attracted to him in a way that she sensed she hadn't been attracted to another man before.

The sound of an engine jerked her from her thoughts, and Emma went to the door while Aspen glanced out the window. Speaking of the devil, the sexy agent was back. She could practically see the chords of muscle playing on his chest beneath that gun holster. Could feel the power radiating off of him.

Dylan met Miguel on the steps, both speaking in hushed tones that made her wonder what he'd learned at the crime lab.

A second later, a big black truck parked in the drive and a tall Indian climbed out, his sun-streaked ponytail accentuating a lean angular face. He was tanned and lanky, his body coiled with tension. "Who's that?" Aspen asked.

"Kurt Lightfoot," Emma said. "He works for the Weeminuche Construction Authority. He's very adamant about enforcing the code that all projects are performed on a merit shop basis with maximum use of Native American laborers and craftsmen."

"Do I know him?" Aspen asked.

Emma's face twisted. "Yes. You've gone out a few times."

Aspen's head throbbed with all the revelations. How well did she know Kurt? And how did she feel about him?

Dylan's stance turned protective, and he blocked the doorway, his arms crossed, his muscular legs spread wide. She imagined him interrogating Kurt and felt a margin of relief that he was present, that she didn't have to face this other man alone.

The tunnel of darkness into which she'd fallen seemed endless and growing deeper and more frightening every second. If she'd dated Kurt, why would she be afraid of him?

A tense heartbeat passed, then the three men stepped inside, Miguel and Dylan on each side of Kurt, like armed guards—or cobras ready to strike. "There's someone here to see you," Dylan said, although distrust and something even darker laced his voice.

Anger?

A smile broadened Kurt's angular face and he strode over and pulled her into his arms, then spoke in the ancient language of their ancestors. "Thank the gods, I'm glad you're home."

She studied him, trying to place him in her lost past. "What are you doing here?"

He cupped her face in his hands and kissed her briefly.

She forced herself not to react, waiting for some kind of response to shift inside her, for a pleasant memory to surface, for her to want this man.

But no sparks flew, no tingle of attraction or passion stirred as it had when Dylan Acevedo had first looked into her eyes at that shelter.

He pulled away slightly, examining her with narrowed eyes. "I came to see you and Jack," he said. "I've missed you both so much."

Distrust flooded her along with another disturbing thought. Could Kurt possibly be Jack's father?

And if so, why did she feel no attraction to him, only the need to put distance between them?

* * *

Dylan barely bit back a curse.

This big Indian in the suede-fringed jacket was the man Aspen had been dating? And he had just kissed her as if he owned her.

Pure rage ripped through him like an out-of-control brush fire, eating him alive. He fisted his hands and started to yank the man away from her, but Miguel caught his arm and gave him a warning look that reminded him of when they were teenagers after Teresa had died, and Dylan had been quick-tempered, spoiling for a fight.

Dammit. His brother was right. He was acting like a crazed, jealous husband, when he had no claims on Aspen.

But what if he wanted to have claims on her?

And what if Jack was his?

To fill the awkward silence, Emma rallied to explain about Lightfoot's work for the WCA, making his anger mount. Dammit, the guy sounded like a stand-up man.

But not everyone was as honorable as they appeared on the surface. Plus, the hair he'd collected at the shelter when Aspen had been attacked belonged to a Native American. What if Lightfoot had tracked down Aspen and broken into her room?

He'd have to get a warrant to compare his DNA.

And until he found the answers he needed, he'd stick by Aspen 24/7.

Aspen took a step back, and massaged her temple as if fighting a headache. "Jack fell asleep. I don't want to disturb him."

Lightfoot shoved his hands in the pockets of his faded jeans. "Of course. How are you feeling?"

"Actually I'm tired." Aspen's gaze flitted to Emma, then to him as if pleading for a way out.

"We had an accident on the way back last night," Dylan said, jumping in to circumvent a long stay by the other man. "The doctor gave her a clean bill of health, but she didn't get much rest."

Aspen nodded and rubbed at her head again. "Maybe we could visit another time, Kurt. I need to lie down for a while."

"I don't mind staying," Lightfoot offered with a shrug. "I can sleep on the couch and be here if Jack wakes up."

"That won't be necessary," Dylan cut in. "I'm Aspen's bodyguard until the threat to her is over and the men who attacked her are in jail."

Anger glinted in Lightfoot's eyes a second before he masked it. "Good. Nice to know the FBI is doing their job instead of ignoring us Utes."

Anger shot through Dylan at Lightfoot's implication, but again, Miguel held him in check with a forceful look.

Aspen excused herself and went to her room, and Lightfoot shifted uncomfortably, glancing at the nursery as if he wanted to go in. As if he had a right.

But Emma took him by the arm and diplomatically led him to the door. "Why don't you come back once she's had time to rest and adjust."

Dylan waited until she walked him outside, then went to Aspen's door, knocked and pushed it open a fraction. "He's gone. Are you all right?"

"Yes." Jack stirred and Aspen rushed to the nursery then returned, cradling him as if she'd never let him go again while Emma finished preparing dinner and set it on the table.

The meal was strained, and Aspen appeared fatigued,

so Emma and Miguel said good-night afterward. Dylan insisted on cleaning up while Aspen fed Jack, then he watched as she read him a story, sang a Ute lullaby to him and rocked him to sleep.

His chest grew hollow with the fear that this family wasn't his to have, an ache so deep inside him that he didn't know what he'd do if he had to walk away from her and her son.

Yet what if she didn't want him in her life when the investigation ended? What if there was another man, either Lightfoot or someone else, who had stolen her heart while he'd stayed away?

Jack fell asleep and she tucked the baby into the crib, then yawned, and Dylan encouraged her to go to bed.

But, dammit, he wanted to join her. If he touched her, held her, kissed her, would she remember what they'd shared?

Of course, he did none of that. He was working a case, and staying alert meant keeping his emotional distance.

And protecting his heart.

But after forty-eight hours with no sleep, exhaustion finally claimed him, and he stretched out on her sofa and fell asleep, dreaming about the night he and Aspen had met.

But sometime around 4:00 a.m., he jerked awake, his senses on full alert, his heart pounding.

Had he heard something outside?

A scream?

Aspen or Jack crying out?

He grabbed his gun off the coffee table, rose and checked Aspen's room, but she seemed to be resting. He tiptoed to the nursery, but when he peeked inside, Jack was sound asleep.

Nerves cramping his chest, he went back to the den, eased back the window curtain and looked outside. Darkness bathed the property, the stillness almost alarming in its own right. In the distance a motor rumbled, and a prairie dog wailed its call.

Dylan had to check outside.

Senses honed, he inched to the front door, unlocked it and slowly cracked the door open, the chain still intact. His gaze shot sideways, searching, scanning, his fingers gripping his weapon, ready to fire.

A stray cat trotted across the dirt, and dust swirled in a cloud from the road in the distance as if a car had just roared away. He glanced down at the porch and an icy chill rippled through his blood.

Frank Turnbull's calling card—a piece of thunderwood lay at his feet.

No…it couldn't be possible. Turnbull was supposed to be in jail….

Chapter 7

She was drowning.

The raging, icy current dragged her under, slamming her already battered body against the rocks. Pain shot through her limbs and head, and she battled for a breath but the water slapped her face and she choked.

She opened her eyes, saw the bottom of the river, felt the murky floor sucking at her feet, mud seeping into her shoes, the darkness swirling above her. Her head throbbed, her lungs aching as if they were going to explode....

What had happened?

A faint memory stirred. The car crash. Then the men chasing her...clubbing her in the head...then the black emptiness.

And now the icy river, her burial spot.

Her lungs squeezed, desperate for oxygen, and she

was fading, her energy waning. She wasn't going to make it.

Terror crawled through her.

No...she didn't want to die.

She was a good swimmer—she had to make her arms and legs work. Push away the numbness, forget the pain. One stroke, then another.

She had to survive. Someone was waiting on her. Someone important.

Determination raged through her, and she fought the waves, using her feet for momentum to push off the bottom and propel herself upward. Suddenly she was moving, swimming again. Her lungs begged for air, and her teeth chattered, but she ignored the burning ache and pushed harder.

One stroke, two, three, kick, kick, kick... She imagined the night sky above, the stars, a sliver of moonlight... Warmth.

So beautiful. She would see it again. She would feel warm and safe. Then she'd go home. Home to...home to something...

Finally she broke the surface, gasping for air. Light and cold air swirled around her, disorienting her as to which way to swim. She struggled to orient herself. The current tugged at her again, and she let it carry her forward.

Finally, through the shadows she spotted trees in the distance and kicked harder, aiming for the shore. Another stroke. Another. She could do it. She would make it to the edge and climb out.

Someone was waiting on her. Someone important. Someone who loved her and needed her to survive.

And then she was there, the riverbank only inches

away. She reached for the edge, lost her footing and slipped under again. But sheer determination spiked her adrenaline and she kicked to the surface. Her arms shook as she clawed at a tree branch and used it to drag herself to the bank. Coughing and spitting out water, she collapsed in a fit of exhaustion, shivering and shaking, too numb to move.

A second later, fear shot through her again.

But this time she was in the bed, and a man was lurching toward her. A knife glinted in the darkness.

She screamed, and kicked at him as he approached. She'd survived once, she could do it again.

His angular face filled the darkness, his breath hissing across her cheek as he grabbed her. A sliver of moonlight caught his profile. He had high cheekbones. Long hair.

He was an Indian.

But who was he? And why did he want her dead?

Dylan had just bagged the piece of thunderwood when Aspen's scream shattered the silence. He slammed the front door shut, grabbed his gun and raced to her bedroom, sweat beading on his neck.

What if Turnbull had escaped? What if he'd gotten in to Aspen's room?

Darkness bathed the room, so he flipped on the light, quickly searching for the intruder. But he didn't see one.

A quick glance at the window confirmed it was closed.

Aspen was sitting up in bed, trembling as she rocked herself back and forth.

He inhaled a steadying breath, stowed his gun in the

waistband of his slacks, then walked over to the bed. "Aspen..."

She jerked her head toward him, her terror-glazed eyes wrenching his heart.

"What happened?" he asked gruffly. "Are you all right?"

For a moment, she simply stared at him as if she hadn't understood what he'd said. Hating to see her in agony, he inched closer to the bed, wanting to console her.

"You're safe now," he said as he slowly lowered himself to the mattress beside her. "I won't let anyone hurt you again." He stroked her arms gently, aching to hold her. "Was someone here in the room?"

Her face seemed to crumple but she shook her head no, her teeth chattering. "I was running from a man, then he hit me over the head and threw me in the river. Then I was drowning," she whispered. "Drowning in the icy water. It was so cold...and I couldn't breathe."

"It was a dream, a memory of your attack," he said. "But you're safe in your house now."

She shoved a tangled strand of hair from her damp cheek. "I fought, had to swim, to escape. And then I was in the room at the shelter and that man was there. He had a knife and he came after me."

In light of the piece of thunderwood on her doorstep, her reference to a knife sent alarm down his spine. "Could you describe the knife?"

She frowned, her eyes narrowing as if in thought.

"Could it have been a Ute ceremonial knife? Was it made of white quartz and cedar wood?"

"I don't know. I didn't get a look at it," she said in a hoarse voice.

He tilted up her chin, forcing her to look at him. "What else do you remember, Aspen?"

"He was an Indian," she said. "I think I might have seen him before. Maybe hanging around the shelter."

Hope sprouted inside him. If she'd seen him, at least he'd know who to go after. "Was it the same man who threw you in the river?"

She clenched the sheet between her fingers. "No… I'm not sure."

Maybe he should show her some photos, see if they jogged her memory. But the doctor had warned him not to push. "Do you remember any more details, the color of his hair, his height?"

Her eyes were glazed as she stared up at him. "He had long hair, high cheekbones—I think he might have been Kurt Lightfoot."

He clenched his jaw. Maybe his theory about Lightfoot being Jack's father was on target. Maybe he hadn't wanted to claim the child and he'd tracked down Aspen at the shelter to silence her.

Then he'd shown up at Aspen's to test her to see if her amnesia was real.

Which meant he had to be nervous.

Dylan gave her arm a reassuring squeeze. "All right. I'll get a warrant for a DNA sample from him and run a background check. We can compare the DNA to the hair I found at the shelter."

He started to get up, but she grabbed his hand, clinging to him, and heat bolted through him. She was vulnerable now, not asking for a repeat of their Vegas week.

Although he couldn't erase the erotic images from his mind.

But if Jack is yours, she didn't tell you.

His anger returned, sharp and intense, and he steeled himself against feeling anything else. He had a job to do and he'd damn well do it.

"But what if I'm wrong?" Aspen said. "I don't want to accuse an innocent man of something he didn't do."

He frowned, wondering if she might have had feelings for the man. "Trust me to see just how innocent Lightfoot is."

Her big dark eyes studied him, probing, looking lost.

She finally nodded, and his breath whooshed out in relief. "I'm going to call and get a security system installed today. I want you and Jack to stay at Emma's while I go back to the crime lab."

"All right."

He stepped outside and phoned the warden at the Colorado State Penitentiary. Sweat beaded on his neck as he waited to be patched through to his office.

It seemed like an eternity before the man answered in a thick Hispanic accent. "Warden Fernandez."

"Warden, this is Special Agent Dylan Acevedo."

A long sigh echoed over the line. "You were on my list to call today."

That didn't sound good. "Really. About Frank Turnbull? Has he escaped?"

Another tense pause. "We're not certain. We think he may be dead."

Dead? God, he hoped to hell the man was.

"What do you mean, you *think* he may be?"

"Yesterday he was on a bus with three other prisoners we were transferring to the ADX in Florence."

The ADX, the Alcatraz of the Rockies, where the prisoners deemed most dangerous and in need of tightest control were locked away. The home of the notorious

Terry Nichols, Eric Robert Rudolph, Timothy McVeigh and Richard Reid, the shoe bomber.

The air in Dylan's lungs stilled. "And?"

"And the bus had an accident, caught on fire and exploded. There were six people on board—the driver, two guards and three prisoners. We found six bodies. So we're assuming Turnbull died in the accident, but the ME is studying the remains. That's going to take time, though. Wasn't much left but charred skin and bones. He's requested dental and medical records to verify the IDs."

"Tell him to rush it," Dylan said.

"You don't have to remind me. These were all lifers who needed maximum security."

Dylan pulled a hand down his chin. Two others as mean as Turnbull. Not good.

"We're investigating the accident to make sure it wasn't an attempted prison escape or sabotage from an outsider."

Damn, that would create panic.

"How did you find out?" Fernandez asked. "We've tried to keep it quiet so as not to frighten locals."

People needed to be warned. "I'm on the Ute Reservation, investigating the murder of one of our agents and working protective custody of a Ute woman. Early this morning, I found a piece of thunderwood on her doorstep."

"Turnbull's calling card," Fernandez muttered.

"Exactly." And Aspen fit the profile. Plus, Turnbull had vowed to get revenge on Dylan at his trial.

"Could be a copycat. Someone who knows you worked the case trying to yank your chain."

"I know. But we need to verify that Turnbull didn't

escape," Dylan said, trying to focus. "If he has, he's been planning it and may have had help from the outside. I want to look at all his prison correspondence. Because if he's out, he'll start his crime spree all over again."

And he had to stop him before any more women died.

Aspen managed to grab a shower, dress and make coffee before Jack woke up, although her muscles and limbs were still sore. The sound of her son cooing brought a smile to her lips, and she hurried to the nursery and stood over him, soaking in his features.

This was her child. Her little boy with the thick jet-black hair, brown skin and high cheekbones. He definitely had her Ute blood.

Except for those startling deep blue eyes…

He waved his hands and kicked his feet, and she picked him up and hugged him to her chest, savoring the sweet scent of baby powder and softness. "Good morning, little one. You're in a good mood today."

"Maybe because he's happy to have his mother home," Dylan said behind her.

Her chest squeezed. "Poor little guy must have thought I'd abandoned him."

"He seems resilient," Dylan said.

She carried Jack to the changing table and unsnapped the legs of his sleeper, laughing as he tried to put his toes in his mouth. "You silly boy, you. You can't eat your feet."

Dylan walked over and watched him for a moment, an odd look on his face. But a knock sounded at the door and he quickly left to answer it.

She finished the diaper change and snapped his jimmies, then carried him to the kitchen and retrieved a bottle while Dylan let two men from the security company he'd called inside to install the security system.

While they worked on the installation, she placed Jack in his baby seat, then made breakfast, pancakes with the fresh blueberries Emma had stored in the refrigerator.

Jack cooed and shook a toy rattle between his pudgy fingers while they ate, intrigued by Dylan when he turned to talk to him. But tension stretched between them, a silence filled with the questions she couldn't answer.

"Thank you for breakfast," Dylan said as he finished the stack of hotcakes and carried his plate to the sink. He rinsed it and placed it in the dishwasher, then started to clean up the pan.

"I'll take care of that," Aspen said, a warmth enveloping her. It felt oddly comforting to share breakfast with the man. Comforting and sexy…

And vaguely familiar, as if they'd done it before.

"Then I'm going to give Jack a bath before we go to Emma's."

Dylan nodded. "I phoned Miguel and told him you were coming."

"Thanks."

The workers finished with the security system, and Dylan explained how to set the alarm and deactivate it. "You need to leave it on at all times, even when you're home."

She nodded, picked up Jack and took him to her bathroom to bathe him. But anxiety plucked at her nerves. She didn't want to live in fear for the rest of her life.

She just hoped that Dylan found the person after her soon so life could return to normal. Maybe then her memories would surface, and she'd remember who Jack's father was and why he wasn't in her son's life.

After the security team left, Dylan drove Aspen and Jack to Emma's. Unlike, Aspen's house with its Native American look and feel, Emma's was a small ranch, the furnishings eclectic and more modern.

Aspen carried Jack inside and Dylan followed. Emma had set up a crib in the second bedroom along with baby paraphernalia, and eagerly welcomed her cousin and son inside. From the loving expression on Emma's face, she'd grown quite attached to Jack during their time together.

Aspen smiled gratefully as they settled in to visit, although her features were still strained.

Dylan gestured to the door. "Miguel, can I talk to you outside for a minute?"

Miguel nodded, his eyes narrowing as they moved to the front porch. "What's up?"

Dylan explained about the piece of thunderwood and his conversation with the warden.

"Good God," Miguel muttered. "You think Turnbull may have escaped?"

Dylan shrugged. "I don't know, but we have to consider the possibility."

Miguel grunted. "Jeez. This just keeps getting worse. Now we're not only hunting Perkins and Watts but possibly an escaped felon."

Dylan grimaced. "Yeah, and not just a felon, a man who likes to carve up Ute women."

Miguel's face paled. "I was on my way into the crime lab today for work. But I hate to leave Emma and Aspen alone."

"We can't," Dylan said. "If you need to go in, call the locals to dispatch a unit out here until I get back."

"Where are you going?" Miguel asked.

"Last night Aspen remembered that the man who attacked her at the shelter was Indian. The crime lab has a hair I found at the shelter. I want to get a warrant for a DNA sample from Kurt Lightfoot to see if it belongs to him."

"Did they compare it to Watts's?"

Dylan nodded. "No match. And the hair could have been there before. Or the man who came in could be one of the abusers another woman at the shelter was running from. But if it's Lightfoot's, then I can bring him in for questioning."

"I'll call Bree," Miguel said. "Ask her to watch Emma and Aspen. It sounds like the lab needs me now."

Dylan nodded. "Thanks, man. And if you don't mind, check with the state ME and see if he's ID'ed the bodies from the prison bus. We need to know if one of them is Turnbull's."

He studied the photo of Aspen Meadows, his hands twitching to finish her off. She should have died in that river, but she was stronger than anyone thought. Had fought her way out of the raging current and wound up being rescued.

Those stark features, her high cheekbones, long black hair, big brown eyes—the Ute woman had seen too much with those eyes.

The paper said she had amnesia. But her memory could return at any minute.

Then she'd squeal on him and he'd rot in prison.

No, he wouldn't get caught.

Rage shot through his blood, and he tensed and drew an X over the picture. Frustrated, he crumpled the paper in his hands and threw it against the wall.

Yes, Aspen Meadows had to die. The sooner the better.

And he'd make sure the end was painful....

Chapter 8

On the way to the Kenner County Crime Lab, Dylan phoned Tom Ryan and asked him to assemble the other agents and crime scene specialists for a meeting in the conference room.

Ben Parrish and Tom Ryan were the first to join him and Miguel, then Callie, Ava, Jerry Griswold and Bart Flemming appeared.

"Griffin Vaughn, his son, Luke, and new wife, Sophie, have come to Kenner City," Ben said.

"Interesting," Tom commented.

Everyone looked exhausted and frustrated as if they'd worked too many hours for too many weeks now with no hope of seeing the end in sight.

But he and Tom and Ben had been friends with Julie and had vowed to avenge her death.

And Aspen's safety was personal. *Very* personal.

Tom grabbed a cup of coffee and rapped his knuckles on the table to get everyone's attention. "Let's have an update. Any leads on where Sherman Watts and Boyd Perkins are hiding out?"

Ben shook his head. "No spottings. They could be anywhere." He paused with a hand gesture. "Or long gone by now."

Dylan grimaced. "I doubt that. With Aspen alive, they'll want to tie up loose ends. The fingerprint we found at the Griffin estate points to the fact that Perkins shot Del Gardo and that he's a hired gun with the Wayne crime family." Dylan gestured toward Jerry. "Griswold identified the bullet casings from my vehicle as coming from a .38. Could have been from Watts's gun." He glanced at Ava. "How about the paint samples from the car that ran me off the road?"

Ava consulted her notes. "They match the samples we found on Aspen's car, the ones that belong to Watts's vehicle."

Dammit. "So they are after her," he said, and everyone exchanged frustrated looks. So far Watts and Perkins had been as invisible as Ute ghosts.

"There's another complication," he continued, then gestured to the whiteboard where they were keeping lists of all the clues, evidence and suspects. "The hair I found in the room at the Sisters of Mercy Women's Shelter where Aspen was attacked belonged to an Indian, but not Watts. So we're also looking for another suspect."

"Why would someone else want to harm Aspen?" Ben asked.

Dylan added Kurt Lightfoot's name to the board. "We're not sure yet. But a Ute man named Kurt Lightfoot has shown interest in Aspen and her son." He hesitated then continued, forcing his emotions at bay as he glanced at Callie. "Do we have an ID on the baby's father?"

Callie shook her head. "Hopefully soon."

Dylan tugged at his shirt collar. "Apparently Lightfoot and Aspen dated for a while. I'm not sure how, or if the relationship ended but we need to check him out." He directed his attention to Bart, their computer analyst. "Lightfoot works for the Weeminuche Construction Authority. Dig up everything you can find on him."

"Will do," Bart said with a nod.

"And, Ryan," Dylan said. "I need a warrant for Lightfoot's DNA."

"You'll have it before you leave today," Tom said. "And, Bart, make that background check on the man a priority. I may need it for the warrant."

Bart stood. "I'll get on it now."

"Wait," Dylan said before he could exit the room. "There's something else."

Concerned looks floated around the room, then Dylan explained. "Frank Turnbull, the Ute Slicer, was being transported from the Colorado State Pen to the ADX Florence when his bus crashed and burned. Six charred bodies were found in the van. It appears Turnbull may have died, but the ME's analyzing the remains now to confirm. Until we have confirmation, we have to work under the assumption that he might have escaped."

"And you're basing that on what?" Ava asked.

Sweat trickled down the back of Dylan's neck. "On the piece of thunderwood someone left on Aspen Meadow's doorstep."

Startled gasps and low curses met his announcement. "Jesus, people will panic if this news leaks out," Ava said.

"Maybe we should issue a warning so the Ute women will be careful," Callie suggested.

Tom gave a brisk shake of his head. "Not until we know more."

"I'm going to push the ME," Miguel said. "See if we can get answers on that ID ASAP."

Callie gestured to speak. "I'll drive up there and offer my help. Won't hurt to have a set of our eyes on the investigation there."

"Thanks, Callie." Dylan felt marginally better knowing she'd be breathing down their necks. "I requested all of Turnbull's prison correspondence for analysis. I'm going to look at his visitors, letters, phone calls, e-mails, along with any inmates who might have befriended him," Dylan said. "If this so-called accident was the result of an attempted prison break, we need to find out."

"You think someone on the outside might have helped him escape?" Ben asked.

"It's possible. Let's face it. Turnbull didn't get away with ten murders before we stopped him because he's dumb. He's cunning, manipulative, well organized, a methodical cold-blooded killer. We all know the kind of violence he's capable of." He paused, wiping at his brow as he tried to banish the images of the dead girls from his mind. "And we all also know that some women get off on writing prisoners. If he has a fan club, I want to know about it."

"Good point," Tom said.

"And if Turnbull is dead?" Ben asked.

Dylan was sweating again. "Then we may have a copycat on our hands." He hesitated. "And Aspen fits the profile. With all the hype about her disappearance, and me working the case, he might come after her."

"All the more reason to smoke out anyone else who's after her," Ben mumbled.

Tom met his gaze, his brow pinching. "I agree. Dylan, I've been thinking about what you said. That Perkins and Watts won't stop until they kill Aspen."

A cold knot of anxiety clawed at Dylan's insides as tension thrummed through the room. "And?"

Tom's gaze turned to stone, and Dylan knew he wasn't going to like whatever Tom suggested.

"This mess has gone on way too long. We're all tired of chasing our asses and coming up with nothing." He planted his hands on the conference table and gave Dylan a dead-serious look. "I think we should consider setting a trap for the men. Flesh them out."

Dylan gritted his teeth. "How do you suggest we do that?"

Tom shrugged as if the answer was inevitable. "We use Aspen as bait."

Aspen fed Jack his bottle while Emma prepared lunch, a well of sadness engulfing her as she thought of the weeks she'd lost with her little boy. "The word *Ute* comes from the Spanish name for our tribe, Yuta," she said softly as Jack gazed up at her. "Most Utes speak English, but I'll try to teach you a few of the words of our Native language."

Jack splayed one little hand on the edge of the bottle and sucked vigorously. Apparently her son had a good appetite and seemed to be healthy despite the situation."The word *maiku* is a friendly greeting, and *tog'oiak'* means thank you." She stroked his thick black hair. “A long time ago our people lived in wickiups. They were small round houses shaped like a cone and made of a willow frame covered with brush. But times have changed and now we live in houses on a reservation.” She laughed as he squirmed against her, grateful she hadn’t forgotten her heritage. “A long time ago we traveled the rivers by building rafts. And we still like to hunt and fish. When you get big enough, I’ll take you to see the Bear Dance and the Sun Dance at Mesa Verde, and as you grow up, I’ll teach you more about the Ute ceremonies and how to use roots and plants for healing.”

Bree smiled at her from the kitchen where she was slicing fruit for a fruit salad. But the gun at the detective’s waist reminded her of the real reason Bree had stopped by.

“You’re a wonderful mother, Aspen,” Bree said.

Suddenly an image of her and Emma drifted into Aspen’s consciousness. The two of them as little girls playing with their dolls on the reservation. Then another, she and Emma skipping after her mother to the trading post. Her mother buying penny candy for them as a treat. Emma being quiet, shy, almost withdrawn at times. Emma finally confiding that sometimes she saw things she didn’t want to see.

Like her mother’s boyfriend hitting her.

And then her grandmother’s ghost…

She glanced up as Emma placed salads and herbal tea on the table. “Emma?”

Her face must have revealed her concern because Emma rushed to the table and sat down. “What is it?”

“A memory… I think.”

“Of the man who attacked you?” Emma asked, and Bree paused at the kitchen counter to study her.

Aspen shook her head. "No. Of you and me when we were young. What happened to your mother?"

Emma's face paled, and she knotted her hands on the table.

Jack was dozing so she eased him into the baby seat, then reached out and squeezed Emma's hand. "I'm sorry. I didn't mean to bring up a painful subject."

Emma sighed. "No, it's all right. It was a long time ago." She took a deep breath. "My mother's boyfriend abused her. One night they got in a terrible fight, and he set the house on fire. Both of them died."

"That's right. I had a memory about a fire," Aspen said.

"That's when I came to live with you and Aunt Rose."

Rose…her mother's name. An image of her face flashed back, bittersweet and painful because it felt as it was so long ago. As if it was another thing lost. Maybe forever.

"And my mother? She's dead?"

Emma's gaze met hers, tears glittering in her eyes. "Yes, Rose died last year of cancer. Right before you went to Las Vegas to finish school."

"And my father?"

"He was never in the picture. I think that's why you were so determined that you could handle raising Jack alone."

The rumble of a motor startled them all, and Bree held up a warning hand, indicating for them to wait, then removed her weapon from her holster and went to the window.

"Is it Miguel or Dylan?"

"Neither," Bree said. "Kurt Lightfoot."

Aspen tensed. Emma had said that she and Kurt had

dated. And she had wondered if he had been the man she'd seen at the shelter, the one who'd attacked her.

"Should we let him in?" Emma asked.

Bree shrugged. "I've known Kurt for a while. I don't think he's dangerous, if that's what you're worried about."

She opened the door, and Kurt's voice echoed from the porch. "I came to talk to Aspen. I figured if she wasn't at home, she might be with Emma."

"She is," Bree said, then gestured for him to come in.

Kurt shifted awkwardly as his gaze met hers. He was a handsome man, she supposed. Tall and muscular, and from what she'd been told, he was doing good things for the reservation by working for the WCA. But his gaze bore into hers as if she'd betrayed him by forgetting him.

And the dream of the Indian man attacking her haunted her....

"Can we talk in private?" he asked.

Aspen glanced at Emma, then Bree, and Emma gestured to Jack who'd stirred from sleep and was cooing at her. "Bree and I will take Jack out on the porch for a minute. If that's all right with you, Aspen?"

Aspen reluctantly nodded. If Kurt was dangerous, he certainly wouldn't try to hurt her with the detective and Emma present.

She dropped a kiss on her son's forehead, hating to let him go. She'd missed so much already. But Emma gently cradled him in her arms and whispered to him as she carried him outside, and Aspen took comfort in knowing that he was only a few feet away.

She'd never lose him again.

Kurt waited until Bree joined Emma before he claimed the chair beside her. "How are you feeling?"

"I'm doing all right, just frustrated that I can't remember my life." She twined her fingers together, nerves knotting her stomach.

"I'm sorry. I didn't come to push you," Kurt said in a deep voice. "I just wanted you to know that I'm here if you need me." He reached out and squeezed her hand, and a ripple of unease tripped through her.

"I care about you, Aspen. You may not remember it, but we were…are good friends." His lips curled into a smile. "In fact, we've been more than that."

Her gaze shot to his, probing, searching for the truth. "What are you saying?"

"That we talked about a future together, about marriage," he said quietly. "About me moving in and taking care of you and little Jack."

Confusion clouded her head as she struggled to recall that conversation and the relationship Kurt implied they'd had. Had she considered marrying Kurt? Had she been in love with him?

And if she had, why did she feel more drawn to Dylan Acevedo, the federal agent who was protecting her and Jack than Kurt?

"What about Jack's birth father?" Aspen asked. "Did I tell you who he was?" He stroked his thumb over her hand.

"No," Kurt said, glancing down at her fingers, which were curled into a knot. "But that doesn't matter to me, Aspen. I'll love Jack and raise him as my own."

She chewed over his words. "Did I say anything about Jack's father?"

A frown marred Kurt's face, causing wrinkles to crease across his forehead. "You said you didn't tell him about the pregnancy because you were frightened of him," Kurt said. "And that he'd never know about your son."

The front door squeaked open, and Aspen glanced up to see Dylan standing in the door, a thunderous expression slashing his chiseled face.

It took every ounce of Dylan's restraint not to lunge forward and rip Lightfoot's hands off of Aspen. Aspen had told Lightfoot she was afraid of the baby's father. Had she been afraid of him?

Or another man?

He folded his arms. "What are you doing here, Lightfoot?"

The Indian didn't budge, but Aspen slipped her hands down to her lap, twisting them together.

"I came to see Aspen and Jack," Lightfoot said with a scowl.

"About what?"

"I care about her," he said matter-of-factly. "I figured that she needed her friends now."

"She does need her friends," Dylan cut in sharply, "but I'm not sure you're one of them."

Lightfoot took a step closer as if he had no intention of backing down. "What makes you say that?"

Dylan held up the warrant. "The fact that we found a hair belonging to a male Native American in the room where Aspen was attacked at the women's shelter where she was recuperating."

A sarcastic expression curled Lightfoot's mouth. "In case you haven't noticed, I'm not the only male Indian in this part of the country."

Dylan shrugged. "Still, I'll need a DNA sample." His

tone challenged him to decline. "For elimination purposes, of course."

Lightfoot threw up his hands in warning as Dylan stalked toward him. "Wait a minute, you have no right."

Dylan smiled. The hell he didn't. "This warrant says I do."

"How did you obtain a warrant?" Lightfoot asked. "I've done nothing wrong, nothing suspicious."

The fact that he was all over Aspen was enough to make Dylan hate his guts. "The judge saw differently. Now about that sample?"

A muscle ticked in Lightfoot's jaw, then he growled. "You don't need to take a sample."

"Why not?" Dylan asked.

"Because I was there," Lightfoot admitted. "In Mexican Hat."

Chapter 9

"You broke into the room at the shelter?" Aspen asked.

Kurt reached for her but Aspen backed away from his touch. "It's not what you think."

"It sounds to me like you attacked her," Dylan suggested.

"No," Kurt said harshly. "You've got it all wrong."

"But you grabbed me," Aspen said. "I didn't make that up."

"I didn't attack you," Kurt argued. "I only wanted to talk to you, to make sure you were all right, but you panicked and started screaming. Then everyone ran in and I figured I had to get out of there before a dozen women pounced on me."

Aspen frowned, struggling to make sense of his explanation and debating over what to believe. She'd been terrified, having nightmares, and then she'd seen a man sneaking into her room.

Could she have mistaken his intent?

"We're not buying that story," Dylan said. "If you wanted to talk to her, you would have gone to the door like a normal person. Besides, how did you find her when the police hadn't located her yet?"

"I can explain." Kurt shifted nervously, one hand running over the length of that leather pouch. The one holding the knife Aspen had seen.

Dylan studied the man's body language, his senses on alert in case Lightfoot decided to attack. Kurt pressed his hand over the pouch.

"Don't even think about it," Dylan warned.

Kurt's gaze shot up. "Think about what?"

"About using the knife." Dylan gestured for him to remove the weapon and hand it over. Kurt muttered an obscenity, but gave him the knife.

Then he turned to Aspen. "Let me explain. Please."

Dylan pointed to the kitchen chair. "Sit down. And put your hands on the table in front of you where I can see them."

Kurt did as Dylan instructed, but gave Aspen a desperate look. "Please listen to me. I would never hurt you, Aspen."

Aspen frowned. "Then explain why you broke in my room and scared me to death."

"I'm sorry I frightened you." Kurt glanced at Dylan with wary eyes. "Aspen and I had been seeing each other for the last few months, ever since she moved back from Vegas to the reservation. But she confided that she was afraid of Jack's father, that he wasn't Ute, and that if he discovered he had a son, he might try to take Jack away from her."

The scar on Dylan's chin twitched with a frown. "So you aren't the baby's father?"

Kurt shook his head. "I offered to be, though." He glanced at Aspen with a soulful look. "I wish you remembered. I wanted to marry you and promised to raise the baby as my own."

Aspen massaged her temple. Kurt's words vaguely rang true and stirred distant memories of a conversation, yet the details didn't quite break the surface. Had she been afraid of Jack's father physically? Afraid he'd try to take her son off the reservation?

"Did Aspen say the man was physical with her?" Dylan asked.

Kurt shrugged. "Not in so many words. But he wasn't Ute, and Aspen wanted to raise her son in the Ute way. So, when she went missing, I was afraid that the baby's father might have gone after her."

Dylan drummed his fingers on the table. "But if he wanted the baby, why leave him in the car?"

A shudder coursed through Aspen as she thought about her little boy in that car for God knew how long, cold and hungry and alone.

Kurt ran a hand over his forehead, sweating. "I don't know. Maybe he was married or a politician or something and didn't want anyone to know he was Jack's father."

Aspen twisted her hands in her lap. Something about that scenario seemed wrong. She might not remember much about her past, but she didn't think she would have gotten involved with a married man.

Her gaze met Dylan's and once again she lost herself in those blue eyes. Blue eyes like Jack's…

But that was impossible. She must be imagining things.

She'd only met Dylan at the shelter after the attack. And there were other blue-eyed men. She must have known someone in Las Vegas when she was working there. Another student maybe. Or a patron from the bar or casino.

"Anyway," Kurt gave Aspen another pleading look before turning to address Dylan. "She told me that if Jack's father came looking for her, she'd go to a women's shelter and disappear. That she'd adopt a new identity and start over somewhere else. That's when I decided to start looking at the shelters around the area. I thought if she was alive, that she might seek help from one."

"But I would never have left Jack," Aspen said.

"I didn't think you would," Kurt said. "That's why I figured you were hurt. Or that you might be coming back to get him. And when I found you at the Sisters of Mercy, I assumed you were making arrangements for a new life, and that you'd somehow get Jack and then take off."

Aspen tried to follow his logic. It made sense, but somehow still felt out of place.

"That doesn't explain why you didn't go up to the door and talk to the sisters," Dylan pointed out.

"Are you kidding?" Kurt asked. "Those women don't trust any man. They would never have let me near Aspen." He turned to her, his brown eyes darkening. "I swear, Aspen. I saw you a few times out in the courtyard, but you looked at me as if you didn't know me. That's when I knew something was really wrong. I only slipped into your room that night to talk to you, to see if I could help. To tell you that if you wanted to go somewhere else, that I'd take you and Jack."

"If that's true," Dylan said, "then you won't mind giving me your DNA." He laid a warrant on the table. "And then I'll need to search your house."

A flicker of anxiety registered on Kurt's face but he quickly masked it. "What are you looking for?"

"A gun," Dylan said. "And anything else that might prove you're lying."

"I don't own a gun," Kurt said gruffly.

Dylan cut him off, then ordered him to open wide while he swabbed the inside of his mouth.

Dylan left Aspen, Jack and Emma with Bree again while he followed Lightfoot to his house to enforce the search warrant. Mentally, he sorted through the man's story, searching for the truth.

He wanted Lightfoot to be bad. Wanted to have a reason to get him away from Aspen.

But the man seemed to sincerely care for her. The fact that he'd offered to parent a child that he hadn't fathered was admirable.

Not that Dylan wouldn't do the same. He would.

But something else bothered him about Lightfoot. He said all the right things—maybe too right?

Or maybe you don't like him because he wants Aspen.

He wanted her, too.

Only wanting her had nothing to do with Jack. It had to do with the heavenly way she'd felt in his arms, in his bed. Her lips against his. Her body welcoming him inside hers. Her sultry voice whispering his name in the throes of passion.

"You're not going to find a weapon," Lightfoot said. "I'm a man of peace, not violence."

Dylan glared at him then proceeded inside the man's house, a simple wooden ranch that he assumed had been built by the WCA. The deer-hide rug, artwork and orange and yellow muted tones showed definite Native American influences.

It seemed Lightfoot and Aspen had a lot in common. Had she been in love with Lightfoot before the crash?

Worry gnawed at his gut. What if she hadn't told him about Jack because she didn't want him in her son's life? Lightfoot wasn't violent, claimed not to own a gun, worked for the WCA, whereas he was none of those things.

But he couldn't imagine Aspen leaving his bed in Vegas and jumping in bed with someone else so quickly.

Although she slept with you the first night you met.

But that was different. A hot, intense sexual chemistry had drawn them to each other immediately. And during that next week, the fire had only grown hotter.

He'd also learned more about her, found the woman beneath the exotic looks to be fascinating. Kind. Sincere. Intelligent.

And mesmerizing.

Lightfoot made a disgusted sound as Dylan rifled through his desk, but Dylan ignored him and searched the living area, closet, kitchen cabinets and pantry, then the bathroom before finally moving into the man's bedroom. A giant oak bed dominated the room with more Indian artwork. He grimaced as he checked beneath the mattress. Had Aspen ever been in this bed with Lightfoot? Moaned his name the way she'd moaned his when he'd made love to her?

Clenching his hands into fists and then unclenching them to regain control, he forced himself back to the job. He examined Lightfoot's dresser drawers, well aware Lightfoot watched with his arms folded angrily.

The closet came next, and he pawed through the man's suede jacket, buffalo-skin coat, jeans and the top shelf.

Dammit. No weapon. Nothing suspicious.

He stalked to the other bedroom and searched it, as well, and again came up empty. Nothing to incriminate Lightfoot at all.

"Satisfied?" Lightfoot asked through clenched teeth.

Dylan offered him a stone-cold expression. "Just because it's not here doesn't mean you haven't had a gun and dumped it."

"You're looking at the wrong person," Lightfoot snarled. "I told you I would never hurt Aspen, and I meant it."

"You'd better not hurt her," Dylan said. "Because if you do, you'll answer to me personally."

Dylan headed to the door. He would keep digging. If Lightfoot had any ghosts in his closet, Dylan would expose every last one of them.

By the time he arrived back at Emma's, Miguel was there and Bree was gone. She'd received a call to check out some trouble on another part of the reservation. He hoped to hell it was a lead on Watts and Perkins. He wanted them in jail so Aspen would be safe from their evil clutches.

Aspen and Emma were playing with Jack on a pallet on the floor, and the baby laughed and cooed as Aspen told him a story about a game they played as children.

Miguel met him at the door, his look when he gazed at Emma one of a man in serious lust.

Dylan wondered if his own expression when he looked at Aspen was just as transparent.

"What did you find?" Miguel asked.

"Nothing." Dylan ran a hand over the scar on his chin.

“I heard Ryan suggest setting a trap by using Aspen as bait,” Miguel said in a low voice. “Maybe you should consider it.”

Rage seared Dylan, quick and raw. “Absolutely not.”

Miguel shrugged. “It might be the only way to smoke out Perkins and Watts.”

He narrowed his eyes at his brother, unable to believe what he’d suggested. “Would you use Emma as a trap?”

Miguel’s face paled as he looked back at Emma. “No, I guess not. But I didn’t realize you were in love with Aspen.”

Dylan’s chest clenched. He was attracted to her, wanted her back in his arms and in his bed. Hell, he wanted to take care of her and Jack whether Jack was his son or not. But he wasn’t in love with Aspen.

Was he?

Aspen heard the protective tone in Dylan’s voice when he’d refused to use her as a trap, and something warm, mellow and sweet bubbled inside her. And what had Miguel said—something about Dylan being in love with her?

Had she heard him correctly?

No...he must have been talking about loving Emma. While they were gone, more memories of Emma had returned, and she was glad that her cousin had found someone special to care for her.

She was also tired of being in the dark, living in fear while everyone tiptoed around her as if she’d lost her mind, not just her memories.

Dylan and Miguel had instantly hushed as soon as she approached them, driving home her point.

"What did you find at Kurt's?" she asked.

"Nothing." Dylan's intense eyes skated over her with a dark look that sent a tingle down her spine. "But he could have dumped a gun if he had one."

"You really don't trust him?" Aspen asked.

Dylan shrugged. "I'm not sure. I know I don't want you alone with him."

Aspen shivered, his possessive tone arousing a deep need in her to be held and protected by this man.

But instead of reaching for him, she hugged her arms around her waist. "I can't go on like this. Everyone keeping secrets from me, afraid to talk, afraid I'll break." She injected conviction into her voice. "I'm *not* going to break. I want to remember what happened. I don't like suspecting my friends or people on the reservation. And I hate not knowing who to trust."

Dylan studied her for a long moment, indecision in his eyes. "All right," he finally said. "But I've told you all we know for now."

"You haven't shown me pictures of the men you think I saw disposing of that woman's body."

"Do you think you're ready for that?" Dylan asked.

She nodded, summoning every ounce of courage she possessed. "Yes. Maybe seeing their faces will trigger my memory. Then I want you to take me to the scene of my accident."

A troubled expression darkened his eyes as if he was mentally debating what to do, but also a seed of hope surfaced when he gave a clipped nod. They'd reached an impasse and needed her help. She'd prove she was strong enough to handle it.

Because she and Jack couldn't live in fear forever.

* * *

The woman's big brown eyes widened in horror as she realized his intent.

"Please don't kill me," she screeched. "I haven't done anything to you."

"I told you I need a place to hide out." He glanced around the modest little wooden bungalo. Not fancy but it would do. Just like the last place on the rez where he'd hidden.

But he had to keep moving. He couldn't get caught.

"You can stay here as long as you want," she whispered shakily as she tried to back toward the door. "I won't tell the police, I promise."

"Sorry, too late for that," he muttered.

He had to kill her. He couldn't leave any witnesses behind.

She tried to run, to escape, but he grabbed her by her long dark hair and jerked her back to him with a vicious yank. She screamed and flailed her puny arms, but he was stronger, and he slapped her across the face, then yanked out his knife and slashed her throat.

Blood spewed from her flesh and dripped down her pale neck, soaking her blouse in seconds.

Smiling, he dragged her limp body outside, weaving through the trees and brush, then tied rocks to her limbs and dumped her into the river.

Wiping sweat from his brow, he hiked back to the small cabin, went inside and scavenged through her refrigerator. A pizza, a six-pack of cold beer… His mouth watered. Damn, he'd hit the jackpot.

He'd kick back, get some rest, grab a shower and set up camp to watch for the right moment to kill Aspen Meadows.

Chapter 10

"Are you sure you want to look at those photographs?" Dylan asked.

"Yes," Aspen said. "The sooner I recover my memories, the sooner we can put this mess behind us and move on with our lives."

Then he could leave the reservation and Aspen….

That thought sent his gut into a churning motion, but he had a job to do and he had to focus. Finding the person or persons after Aspen was the only way to keep her safe.

And he couldn't live with her death on his conscience.

Not like his little sister. He rubbed his thumb over his pocket where he kept Teresa's photo. God, she'd been so young and trusting, so full of life, her future looming ahead of her.

All lost in a second.

Hardening himself, he headed to the door. "Let me get the files from the car."

Wind slashed his cheeks as he stepped outside, his gaze immediately scanning the property to see if anyone was nearby. The night sounds of the reservation, of animals in the distance, surrounded him, the silence eerie as if danger lay nearby.

Hoping Aspen was truly strong enough to handle the photographs, he retrieved the files then carried them inside.

Emma was feeding Jack peaches, and Dylan couldn't help but grin as the sticky orange goop dribbled off his chin. But his smile died when Aspen gestured for him to spread the pictures on the coffee table.

The last thing he wanted to do was to hurt or traumatize Aspen more. But she seemed determined to push herself and face this gruesome task.

Which hopefully was a sign she was healing.

Miguel's cell phone rang, and he stepped outside to answer it.

Dylan removed the picture of Boyd Perkins, and Aspen's fingers trembled as she reached out and traced his bald head.

"Perkins is a hired gun," Dylan said.

She swallowed. "His eyes are ice-cold and mean."

"Goes with the territory. He works for a crime family." Dylan shifted. "There are two major crime families in the area, the Del Gardos and the Wayne family," Dylan explained. "We believe that Perkins was hired by Frank 'the Gun' Wayne's nephew, Nicky Wayne, who has taken over his uncle's organization. He ordered the hit on Vincent Del Gardo, the father of his rival Mob team. We also think that Perkins was supposed to locate fifty million dollars that it's been rumored Del Gardo hid from the government. Perkins used Sherman Watts—" he paused and added Watts's picture to the table "—to help him hide out on the reservation. Watts has a sheet for petty crimes, but up until we made the connection between him and Perkins, the police didn't think he was dangerous."

Aspen narrowed her eyes. "He does seem familiar."

"Watts lives on the reservation, so you might have seen him before that night."

Aspen's gaze drifted from Perkins to Watts, who had scraggly black hair that hung down beneath a black flat-brimmed hat.

"Watts is pretty much a loser. He loves booze and women." Dylan paused. "And Perkins probably offered to pay him to help him hide out."

Dylan removed a photo of Julie, his breath tightening. "This is Julie Grainger, the agent Perkins killed."

Aspen glanced up at him with a curious expression. She must have heard the pain in his voice because sympathy softened her eyes. "Her death was personal to you. You were in love with her?"

Dylan frowned and shook his head, studying her for any sign that she'd recognized the men or him. But only a sliver of fear glinted in her eyes. "No, nothing like that. We were friends, we worked together. She…was one of the good guys and didn't deserve to die so young."

She shivered, and he stroked her arm. "You don't have to do this, Aspen."

"No, I want to. I *need* to," she said emphatically. "Please take me to the crash site now." She jutted up her chin, making his heart ache for her.

He had wonderful, erotic memories of the two of

them in bed. He wanted to make more of those memories, wanted to kiss her and alleviate the fear in her eyes.

But she was struggling to find her way back from the dark. And if taking her to see the place where her ordeal had begun might help her, he'd do it.

Then and only then could she tell him the truth about Jack and what had happened to her.

His cell phone vibrated on his belt, and he grabbed it and checked the number. Bree. Hell, maybe she'd found Watts or Perkins.

He hastily punched the connect button. "Acevedo."

"Dylan, it's Bree. Listen, I went to check out that trouble on the reservation and think I may have found out where Perkins and Watts have been holding up."

"Where?"

"It's a small ranch that belongs to the Running Deer family. They were on vacation for a couple of weeks and just returned to find the place a mess, food and dishes piled up, dirt tracked in, beds slept in."

"Any sign of Watts or Perkins?"

"Looks like they left in a hurry. But there were cigarette butts and booze bottles so we should get some forensics. CSI's on its way, and I've called Sheriff Martinez to issue an APB in case they're still close by."

"Good," Dylan said. "Maybe we'll get lucky and catch them this time." He paused and glanced at Aspen. "Call me and let me know if you do. I want to be there for the questioning."

Miguel had stepped outside but strode back in, his expression strained.

Dylan disconnected the call, his pulse racing.

Miguel had bad news.

* * *

Aspen thumbed her fingers through the tangled strands of her hair. "Did they find them?"

Miguel looked confused, so Dylan explained about Bree's call. "She thinks they may be close so she and Patrick are searching the rez near the Running Deer house."

"I hope to hell they find them," Miguel muttered.

Emma returned from the bedroom where she'd put Jack down for a nap. "What's going on?"

Miguel relayed the latest on Perkins and Watts. "Dylan, I just talked to the ME," Miguel said. "Maybe we should step outside."

"No," Aspen said. "Emma and I are a part of this. We deserve to know everything that's going on."

Dylan gave a reluctant nod, and Miguel shifted, looking uncomfortable. "It's about a past case. Frank Turnbull, the serial killer who killed all those Ute girls last year." He gestured toward Dylan. "Dylan tracked him down and arrested him. He's been in jail for murder for the past few months."

Aspen frowned, something about the case nagging at her. The Ute women had had their throats slashed. "What happened?"

"He was being transferred to APX Florence, and his bus crashed and burned," Dylan interjected, then turned to Miguel. "Do they have a positive ID?"

Miguel sighed. "The ME said they found a partial bridge plate that belonged to Turnbull. Matched it to Turnbull's dental records. But they're still working on the bones."

Dylan shifted on the balls of his feet. "That's good but not conclusive. After I drive Aspen to the crash site, I'm going to study his prison correspondence. We can't let down our guard until we verify that he's dead." And if he was, a copycat had surfaced. Maybe Turnbull had a fan who'd decided to imitate him.

Or what if he'd had an accomplice? Some serial killers worked in pairs. They'd considered that theory before but hadn't found any evidence to support it.

He glanced at Emma. "Do you mind watching Jack while I drive Aspen?"

"Of course not," Emma said softly. "I'll be glad to take care of him anytime you need."

Dylan placed a hand at Aspen's waist. "Are you ready?"

Aspen inhaled, determined to push forward. "Yes, let's go."

He ushered her to the car, scanning the property as they climbed in and drove off the reservation. Aspen sat in silence, her hands knotted, her gaze focused on the rugged terrain, steep slopes, ridges and brush. The scenery felt as familiar as her name had, and her love of the land returned, welcoming her home. Although it was May, in the distance, snow still capped the mountaintops, and a cool wind rattled the windowpanes, causing goose bumps to scatter along her arms.

The moon struggled to break through dark storm clouds that hovered above like winter ghosts taunting her with the threat of bad weather, the eerie sounds of the isolated area near the river echoing in the night.

Dylan bumped over rocky, dirt-packed ground and steered the vehicle toward an isolated area near the river, tucked in the shadows of the trees and foliage standing guard over the water rushing below.

He pointed toward a large tree across the way, its gnarled branches sweeping down as if to enfold them within its spidery dark hold.

She suddenly felt Dylan's hand slide over hers, the warmth of his body enveloping her as if he held her in his arms, as if he would keep the danger at bay.

"Aspen?"

"I'm ready," she said, mustering her courage and reaching for the door.

He opened his side and exited, then met her in front of the car. Her body trembled but she forced her feet forward until she stood in front of the tree. Even in the dark, she saw paint marks embedded in the bark that had been damaged from the impact of her car.

"This is where your car was found," Dylan said in a quiet but gravely voice.

An image of her red sedan flashed back then terror consumed her as snippets of that night returned. But other memories rushed to the forefront.

She was nine months pregnant, walking along the river when she'd spotted two men in the distance. One with scraggly black hair and a black hat, the other bald. They were dragging something.

Dear God, a body.

Her voice caught on a scream, and the men turned, searching through the trees looking for the source of the sound. A pain shot through her stomach, and she clutched her belly, a contraction hitting her full force. She leaned against a tree trunk and breathed through the squeezing torture, hiding behind the foliage. She had to get of there, get away.

If they'd killed someone, they'd probably kill her, too.

And her baby—she had to protect her child.

The pain slowly subsided, and she took off running, weaving through the brush and branches, checking over her shoulder to make sure they weren't behind her. By the time she staggered to her car, she was shaking and panting. She clutched the door handle, ripped it open and collapsed inside as another contraction seized her.

She leaned against the steering wheel, struggling to breathe through it, her thoughts racing. She should call the police, have them check for the body. Tell them what she'd seen.

But her vision blurred, and the events lost focus. What if it hadn't been a body? Maybe the men had shot a deer or elk...

And if she called the police, what if the men tracked her down and hurt her baby?

No...they'd be safer if she stayed quiet. Another pain caught her in its clutches, and she glanced at her watch. Only two minutes since the last contraction.

She had to make it to the midwife to help her deliver the baby....

"Aspen, are you all right?" A gentle hand stroked her back, soothing her.

She nodded, perspiration beading on her neck. "Yes, I remember seeing two men dragging a body. But I was scared…and having contractions." She heaved for a breath. "So I ran. I had to protect the baby."

"Of course you did," he said quietly. "Then what happened? Did the men see you?"

She clutched at him for support. "I wasn't sure. But later, after Jack was born, I heard about that agent's body being found. I knew then that I'd witnessed a crime…" Tears laced her voice. "I'm sorry, Dylan. I should have come forward sooner."

"You had a child to protect," he said with more understanding than she deserved.

He massaged her shoulders. "What happened after that?"

She closed her eyes, allowing the memories to come now. They were flooding her mind, rushing at her like a dam had broken.

She'd driven back to the scene, hoping to trigger details about the men to tell the police. But the men appeared out of nowhere as if they'd been watching for her.

She ran again, and quickly strapped Jack into the car seat. She had to get to the police.

Frantically, she cranked the engine, pressed the gas and tore down the graveled road. But a moment later, a dark car raced up on her tail and chased her off the road. Jack was screaming in the back, and she tried to soothe him with her voice, but fear clogged her throat, and she cried out as the car slammed into her and sent her flying into the tree. Tires had squealed, glass shattering, metal crunching, but the sound of Jack's distress wrenched her heart.

Dear God, her baby couldn't die...

With that choking thought, she'd fought her way past the air bag and ripped off her seat belt, desperate to reach him and make sure he was safe.

But rough, big hands dragged her from the car, yanking her by the hair. A fist slammed into her head and the ground clawed at her arms and legs. She screamed and kicked but another blow to her head made her legs buckle and the world spin into darkness.

By the time she fought through the nausea and the pull of unconsciousness, she was falling, falling, falling...

Through the dark space and into the icy water, her body slammed against the jagged rocks, the cold envel-

oping her until she was numb and knew she was going to die.

"Aspen?"

She didn't realize she was standing on the precipice of the ridge with the river raging below until Dylan suddenly jerked her back.

She was shaking and crying, the terror all too real as if she'd just been submerged into the frigid river again.

"Shh, baby, I'm here," Dylan whispered. "You're safe."

A warmth engulfed her as Dylan pulled her into his arms, and she burrowed against him, taking solace in his embrace and voice.

"Aspen, honey, are you all right?"

She nodded against him, and he literally felt her grappling for a breath, and sensed the terror in her trembling body.

"It's over now," he murmured into her hair. "I won't let them hurt you again."

"I was so scared for Jack," she whispered hoarsely. "They talked about killing him, but then decided he'd probably die in the cold anyway."

Dylan muttered a curse. Damn bastards would pay for leaving an innocent little baby alone to face the brutal winter elements.

"Jack's safe now, too," he whispered. "I promise they'll never harm either one of you again."

She turned teary eyes up to him, her lip quivering. "Why do you care so much? Why are you here protecting me and Jack?"

It's my job, he wanted to say. But she'd said she wanted the truth, not to be left in the dark. And, dammit, she was in his arms and he wanted to make her remember the time they'd spent together.

That her safety meant much more to him than any damn case.

He tucked a strand of her hair behind her ear, soaking up her features like a starving man. "Because I do care," he said quietly.

Her eyes searched his and for a moment, he thought he saw a flicker of recognition dawn in her eyes as if she remembered him. Her breath caught, her heart beating against his, and his body hardened, aching with the need to touch her, to strip her and join his body with hers.

To remind them both that she had survived.

Unable to resist, he lowered his mouth and pressed his lips to hers. Tentative at first. Testing. Tasting. Begging for her to recall what they'd shared. To invite him to explore her.

To take her the way he once had.

She moaned and threaded her fingers in his hair, all the invitation he needed to deepen the kiss. She opened her mouth, playing her own tongue along his, sending heat spiraling through him in erotic, torturous waves.

His hands slid lower, stroking her shoulders, her back, the soft column of her spine until he pulled her deeper into his embrace, her heat against his own, his thighs cradling her when her legs threatened to give way.

She moaned, the sultry sound indicating she liked the feel of his kiss, and that she wanted more. She clung to him, her hands needy and frenzied as she traced them over his chest and his arms.

Heat seared him, hunger bolting through his body at lightning speed.

Just like it had the first time he'd met her.

But suddenly a shot pinged through the air, whizzing next to his head. Aspen screamed, and he shoved her to the ground behind a large rock, shielding her with his body as he removed his gun and searched for the shooter in the dark.

He crouched on his knees, then crawled along the rocky embankment, his gun trained on Acevedo. He had to take the man out. Or at least impair him until he could get to the woman.

She was the one he wanted now.

But he'd be more than happy to kill the agent, too.

First, though, he had to make the woman suffer....

Chapter 11

Dylan cursed, scanning the woods as he grabbed Aspen's hand and led her through the trees toward the car.

Another shot grazed by her head, and she screamed as he jerked sideways to dodge the bullet. It hit the side of the car, and Dylan dragged her behind the rear bumper for cover.

Crouching down, he coaxed her to the passenger side and opened the door. "Get in and stay down."

She crawled into the car, burying her head beneath her arms. He shut the door, then circled back, searching for the shooter. A shadow of a man appeared in the distance, and he contemplated chasing him down.

He was tired of being the target.

But Aspen was in the car and he had to protect her. If this was Perkins and Watts, they might have divided up, might be watching, hoping to separate them so they could get to her.

Another shot hit the dirt beside him, and he inched around the back bumper to the driver's side, staying crouched and hiding behind the door as he opened it. Then he slid inside, turned the key and backed down the graveled drive, flooring the gas as another bullet spun toward them.

As he flew onto the highway, he reached over and stroked Aspen's hair, hating the way her body trembled. They had to find Watts and Perkins. She didn't deserve to live in fear, to have to look over her shoulder.

He grabbed his cell phone and called Sheriff Martinez. "Patrick, it's Dylan Acevedo. A shooter just fired at us from the site where we found Aspen's car."

Patrick hissed. "I'll send some units to the area immediately."

"Thanks. I'll stop by the crime lab and dig out the bullet in the car and leave it for ballistics," Dylan said.

He disconnected the call, but kept glancing over his shoulder as he raced away, relaxing only slightly when he didn't spot anyone behind them.

Finally he told Aspen he thought they were safe, and she crawled into the seat and strapped on her seat belt. "We have to do something," she said in a shaky voice. "I can't keep running."

"We're doing everything we can," Dylan said, although frustration hardened his voice.

"Are you?" Aspen asked.

He frowned at her. "What's that supposed to mean?"

"I heard you talking to Miguel. You said that one of the agents suggested you use me as bait to trap Watts and Perkins."

Emotions pummeled him. "Absolutely not."

She brushed a strand of hair from her cheek. "Why

not? I witnessed those men dump the woman's body. I remember them coming after me. I want to testify against them."

"I said no."

Aspen's eyes widened. "I don't understand. They're after me anyway, so why not take the proactive route and set them up?"

"Because they could kill you," Dylan said through clenched teeth.

"But you'll be there to protect me," Aspen argued.

"And what if I can't?" His tone turned razor sharp, the adrenaline from their earlier attack firing his temper. "What if I fail? I couldn't live with that…"

An odd look flickered in her eyes and she suddenly touched her lips. Was she remembering the kiss, the kiss that he'd wanted and had almost taken too far?

The kiss that had distracted him so that the shooter had gotten close enough to nearly kill them.

Aspen touched her lips, something about their conversation striking a familiar chord of recognition as if they'd had this discussion before.

His voice had cracked, almost as if protecting her was something more than a case to him, something *personal.*

But that was impossible…wasn't it?

Except that that kiss had stirred feelings inside her. Feelings of hunger and desire and need.

Feelings that disturbed her because they ran deeper than they should for someone she'd just met. Feelings that felt familiar.

"Dylan?"

His jaw was clenched, his hands wrapped around the

steering wheel in a white-knuckled grip. "I'm sorry," he muttered. "I can't take that chance."

"But it makes sense, and it may be the only way—"

"No. I care about you, dammit."

Her breath caught in her chest. He'd said that before. "What?"

He growled in his throat and ran a hand through his hair, then steered the car off the road and pulled behind a boulder as if to hide them in case someone was following. Then he turned to her, his blue eyes glittering with emotions she couldn't define.

His breathing sounded choppy in the ensuing silence. Then he clenched and unclenched his fists as if in a silent debate. "God, I'm not supposed to do this."

Aspen touched his arm, automatically feeling his strength seep into her, his heat warming her insides and sparking a fire low in her belly. "You're not supposed to do what?"

"I'm not supposed to push you. The doctor said to let you remember on your own."

"But I'm starting to," she whispered. "And I told you before I don't want to be left in the dark."

His gaze probed her. "But you didn't remember me when I kissed you, did you?"

"We knew each other before," she said in a low voice, then pressed her fingers to her mouth. "It's true, isn't it? That's why it felt so…familiar."

He gave a clipped nod, then reached for her arms and gently held her. "Yes, we knew each other. We met last year in Vegas right after I arrested the Ute serial killer."

"That's why I recognized the name Turnbull."

"Probably, although the case was major news. But we talked about it that first night." He sighed, looking tired and defeated. "I was upset. All those women had died, and for weeks I'd been looking at gruesome photos of Turnbull's murder victims, then I walked into that bar, and saw you and…"

"And what?" Aspen asked.

"And you were so damn beautiful that I watched you all night, then walked you to your apartment and stayed."

A fleeting memory tickled her conscience. Her in Dylan's arms, kissing, touching…stripping and falling into bed. "The first night?"

"Yes," he said, his voice cracking slightly. "We spent the week together, Aspen. A week in bed, making love to each other."

His words evoked erotic memories that aroused her and made her tingly inside. The first time she'd touched him at the shelter, she'd felt an electric chemistry between them. But she'd chalked her reaction up to fear.

Had thought she was drawn to him because he promised protection when she was grappling to plow her way back to the world she'd lost.

Another thought struck her. She'd wondered about Jack's bright blue eyes…

"I probably shouldn't have told you," he murmured in a tortured voice.

"No, I'm glad you did." Aspen gripped his hand. "Tell me what happened next."

Dylan's look turned pained, but he cradled her hand between his. "I was called away on an undercover assignment, so we parted. You told me your plans to return to the reservation to teach, and you obviously followed through."

Disappointment ballooned in her chest. "You're saying that we had a fling? A meaningless affair?"

Tension stretched between them then he finally sighed heavily. "I thought my job would get in the way," he finally said. "That you'd be safer without me in your life. Then Julie was murdered and you went missing, and I had to come here to find out who killed Julie." His voice cracked. "And I had to find you, to know if you were all right."

The pain and worry in his voice sounded far too real for her to believe that he hadn't cared. Still, she didn't know how to react. Because the truth was that he'd walked away without contacting her until the case had brought him back into her life again.

And had she just let him leave? Had he meant more to her than a one-week affair?

She struggled to tamp down the hurt eating at her and glanced at the road, suddenly anxious to set the trap, and catch the men after her.

She couldn't become too needy. Couldn't fall for a man who could walk away from her the way he had. She had a child to think of. Her irresponsible days were over, had ended with Jack's birth.

Another memory surfaced—this one of her mother. When Aspen's father had deserted her before she was born, her mother had guarded her personal life. She hadn't paraded a sea of men into their house because she hadn't wanted Aspen to get too attached. To call a stranger daddy then have him walk out on her.

Aspen had to safeguard her son the same way.

Dylan knew he'd admitted too much, but his emotions were bouncing all over the place.

Dammit, she could have died back there, and it would have been his fault. His hand automatically went to his pocket and he felt the folded edges of Teresa's picture taunting him.

Angry with himself, he started the car, checked the road, grateful not to detect a car hunting them down, then headed in to Kenner City to the crime lab.

"Dylan, please," Aspen said. "Call the other agents and let's set a trap. It may be the only way you can catch Boyd Perkins and Sherman Watts. I won't let Jack grow up living in fear."

"I don't want that, either," he said gruffly. Resigned, he phoned Tom and asked him to meet him at the crime lab.

Tension thrummed between them, questions left unspoken. He felt raw, exposed as if he'd finally confessed that she meant more to him than just a job, and it still hurt to know that she had no memory of the incredible week they'd shared.

That he still wanted her and she might not feel the same way.

A stiff wind battered the car as he crossed into the city and parked at the annex building. Senses alert, he scanned the outside of the building, then guided Aspen inside to the third-floor crime lab.

Tom met them at the door to the conference room, and Ava and Callie stepped inside, along with Bart Flemming. He introduced them to Aspen, then explained about the shooting, and Callie asked Jerry to dig the bullets from the rental car to compare to the others.

"We're glad you're safe," Callie said.

The others murmured agreement, and everyone settled into seats around the conference table.

"I'm still working on processing the evidence Bree and Patrick sent over from the Running Deer house,"

Ava said. "I identified Perkins's and Watts's prints inside, which confirms they were there."

"So they still are on the reservation?" Dylan said.

Callie shrugged. "As of a couple of days ago, it looks that way."

Bart piped up. "Well, I have something, too. Not to do with Perkins and Watts, but on Kurt Lightfoot."

Dylan's interest was piqued. "What did you find?"

"He works for the WCA and has done a lot of work for the Ute community, but I dug further into some of the contract jobs and suppliers and found something interesting." He paused. "There may be a link between him and the Wayne family."

"You mean, he's taking money for the WCA to help the reservation?" Aspen asked.

"Maybe."

Dylan chewed over that idea. "In exchange for what?"

Bart raised a hand. "I'm still looking."

"Maybe we should bring him in for questioning," Dylan suggested.

Bart tapped his pencil on the desk. "Give me another day or two and I may have something more definitive."

Dylan nodded and glanced at Aspen, his own need and hunger for Aspen warring with his logic. Setting a trap would definitely be the fastest way to smoke out their perps, but putting Aspen's life in more danger terrified him.

But he didn't have to speak up. Aspen did.

"We visited the crime scene earlier, and I remembered seeing Boyd Perkins and Sherman Watts dumping that woman's body." She paused, a strained look in her eyes. "I should have come forward immediately, but I was afraid," she admitted. "And at first, I wasn't certain what I'd seen. Then when I heard about a woman's body being found on the reservation, I knew I'd witnessed a crime."

Dylan spoke up, determined to cut her some slack. "Aspen was pregnant and went into labor," he said. "But later she decided to come forward, then Watts and Perkins recognized her. That's when they chased her down and she crashed into the tree."

"They tried to strangle me, then threw me in the river," Aspen said in a haunted voice.

"You guys know the rest," Dylan said.

Aspen cleared her throat. "I'm ready to testify. I overheard Miguel and Dylan talking about setting the trap for Perkins and Watts," Aspen said. "And I think it's a good idea. These men belong behind bars."

Dead silence met her declaration. Ryan and Callie shifted, then nervous glances crisscrossed the room between the agents and forensics specialists.

Finally Ben Parrish spoke up. "I think that's a smart move."

"I can contact the press immediately and let them know we have a witness and that Aspen is ready to testify," Ryan said.

Dylan planted a fist on the table. "We'll only agree to do this if I can move Aspen and her son to a safe house."

Murmurs of agreement rumbled through the room, along with excitement that they might finally be taking action.

As if in agreement, everyone stood. "I'll get back to processing the evidence," Ava said.

"And I'll finish that background check on Lightfoot," Flemming added.

Callie cleared her throat. “Dylan. Can I see you in my office for a second?”

Dylan’s gaze met Aspen’s, an intense heat simmering between them, his heart pounding so loudly at the thought of Aspen being used as bait that her words barely registered.

Then he jerked himself back to work. “Of course.” He glanced at Aspen. “I’ll be right back.”

He followed Callie into her office, shoulders tightening with tension.

Did she have the results of the paternity test?

Was Jack his son, or would he learn that another man had found his way into her bed and given her a child?

Chapter 12

Dylan braced himself as he entered Callie's office. "What is it?" he asked without preamble.

She raised a brow with a smirk. "You always are to the point, Acevedo." She indicated a folder on her desk. "The test results you asked for are in."

"Hell, Callie, you enjoy torturing a guy?"

She threw her head back and laughed. "No. But I'm not sure you want to hear this news. I guess that depends on how you feel about Aspen Meadows."

"She's just a case."

"Right."

He steeled himself against an outward reaction, resorting to the training he'd relied on to keep him stable and on task. "It doesn't matter. I just need the truth. Jack's paternity could prove to be a lead…or not."

"It's not," she said slyly.

A seed of hope slivered through him, and he jerked up the file, flipped it open and scanned the lab report.

Jack was his son.

The paternity test proved it beyond a shadow of a doubt.

A slow smile spread on his face as his breath whooshed out. He stumbled slightly, the exhilaration of knowing he shared a child with Aspen, that he'd known when he'd held him, drumming through his chest.

Emotions he hadn't expected to feel overpowered him. The thrill of knowing that his legacy would live on, that the time he'd spent with Aspen had been so strong that they'd produced a beautiful little boy with their physical bond.

On the heels of that joy, anger followed, the realization that he'd missed the first few months of his son's life.

That Aspen hadn't contacted him to inform him that he had a son.

And that Jack didn't have his name.

Lightfoot's comment that she'd claimed she was afraid of the baby's father taunted him. Why would Aspen have been afraid of him?

He gripped the folder with an iron fist and turned to go to Aspen and confront her.

But Callie planted herself in front of the door. "I know you're upset," she said in a low voice. "But stop and remember the situation, Dylan, and the doctor's warning about pushing Aspen too far."

"This is different," he ground out through the lump in his throat.

"No, it's not," she said gently. "She's still a witness

in our protection. And if you upset her, she could run. That would only endanger her more."

Callie's words made nervous sweat explode above his brow, and he dropped into the chair by her desk and lowered his head into his hands. She was right.

But, dammit, he didn't like it.

Still, the last thing he wanted was to see the mother of his son hurt.

Or killed because he'd gone half-cocked, scared her, and sent her running into the night, vulnerable and at the hands of the very men he'd vowed to protect her from.

Aspen stiffened as Dylan entered the conference room. His body language indicated something between them had changed. An air of fury radiated off of him that sent a chill through her.

Dylan rapped his knuckles on the table to get everyone's attention. "Let's work on the details of the trap. First, the press will leak the news that Aspen recovered her memory and is ready to testify." He angled his head toward her. "But you and Jack both remain under protective custody at all times. There will be no personal contact with anyone, not Emma or the other friends you made on the reservation. And when we stop by to pick up Jack, if Lightfoot comes by, we give nothing away."

Aspen nodded, although the thought of breaking off contact with Emma, the one family member she had left disturbed her. She'd felt isolated at the women's shelter in Mexican Hat. Now she'd be totally under Dylan's thumb.

And although she'd sensed different vibes coming from him—sometimes an intense heat that obviously had begun the year before—anger now tightened his jaw and hardened his words.

"Do you understand, Aspen?" he asked. "No contact with anyone. It's just you and me and Jack."

She twined her fingers together. "How long will we be…contained?" She'd almost said *imprisoned.*

His broad shoulders shrugged but his expression didn't soften. "Until Perkins and Watts are in custody, and I'm certain you're safe."

Her hesitation seemed to irritate him more. "Aspen?"

"Yes," she said, although nerves tinged her voice. Knowing that she and Dylan shared a past, that they'd slept together, made the thought of being totally alone with him for days—or weeks—almost shatter her resolve to set the trap.

But she looked into his eyes and a memory surfaced—Dylan tenderly holding her, caressing her, trailing kisses down her neck and breasts. His hands roaming over her, teasing, exploring, drawing an erotic response from her nerve endings until she begged for more.

Was she always such a wanton lover, or had she only been that way in his arms?

Dylan could barely look at Aspen. He wanted to shake her and make her tell him the truth about Jack.

He wanted to kiss her until she melted in his arms and welcomed him into his son's life.

And into hers.

But how would that work? He still had a dangerous job which would put her and Jack in jeopardy.

His cell phone rang, and he checked the number. Sheriff Martinez. He connected the call. "Acevedo."

"Dylan, you guys need to get over here. Bree and I found a body."

"Perkins or Watts?"

"No, it's a woman's. I've already called the ME."

An uneasy feeling clutched Dylan's chest. "I'll be right there."

He gave him the coordinates, and disconnected the call, then relayed the gist of the conversation to the others. "I'll stop and check it out on the way back to Aspen's to pick up her things for the safe house."

Ava and Callie jumped into motion to retrieve their crime scene kits to go to the scene.

Ben threw up a hand. "I'll set up the safe house in Mesa Verde."

"Thanks." Dylan took Aspen's elbow and guided her to the door. "Let's go."

"What's wrong?" Aspen asked.

"Other than a girl is dead and we're using you as bait for a killer?"

"I'm sorry," Aspen said in a contrite voice. "I just thought there was something else disturbing you."

He gritted his teeth to keep from asking about Jack.

The fact that Martinez had specifically requested him worried him, too.

The wind whipped the car as they climbed in, the windowpanes rattling as they drove across the reservation. Dylan's nerves were on edge as he constantly scanned the deserted roads and hiding spots for another attacker or car following them.

He parked on the ridge by Martinez's police car, and Callie and Ava parked beside him, climbing out with their kits in hand.

He pressed a hand on Aspen's shoulder. "Stay here and keep the doors locked. If anything happens, honk the horn and I'll be here in a second."

"I could go with you," Aspen offered.

Not knowing what he would find or the condition of the woman's body, he shook his head. "No. This is official police work. The fewer people contaminating the scene, the better."

She nodded in understanding, and he climbed out and punched the lock button before heading down the embankment to where Martinez and Bree were waiting. Bree met him at the bottom of the hill.

The scent of the murky water, vegetation and death swirled in the breeze as he approached the river where Martinez stood beside the local medical examiner. Dr. Pruitt, a fortysomething, gray-haired man with a cleft chin, was bent over the body, examining it.

Dylan braced himself to view another dead female body as he stepped closer. Martinez angled his head and moved to the side to give him a better view and Dylan's stomach churned.

Her hair was matted, skin pale white with fish and bug bites, her throat slashed from ear to ear.

"How long has she been dead?" Martinez asked.

"A day at least, but it's hard to tell with the decomp. The temperature of the water helped preserve her but the fish..." He shook his head. "Damn son of a bitch tied her down so she'd sink. But a couple of the knots slipped loose and she floated to the top. Some rafters found her caught between some rocks."

"You questioned them?" Dylan asked.

Bree spoke up. "Yeah, it was a couple of teenagers. They were pretty freaked out. I called their parents and they already took them home."

"Cause of death?" Martinez asked.

The medical examiner lifted the woman's head

slightly, and Dylan noted the slash mark on her neck. A slash mark that looked sickeningly familiar.

"She has a bruise on the back of her head and several on her body, but basically, her throat was slashed and she bled out. Forensics may be able to tell us more about the kind of knife the killer used."

The rope tied to the woman's wrist made bile rise to Dylan's throat.

At the end of the rope, he saw the chunk of thunderwood.

Dylan ground his teeth together. Callie muttered something under her breath, and Ava gave a small gasp.

"What do you think?" Martinez asked Dylan.

Dylan's throat thickened with fear. "You know what I think."

"It could be a copycat," Callie suggested.

Dylan met her gaze. "I know. Or Turnbull could have survived that crash and have started all over again."

"But it doesn't quite fit Turnbull's MO," Ava said. "Turnbull left his victims out in the open for us to find as if he was gloating about it. This time the body was tied and dumped in the river so we wouldn't find her."

Dylan stewed over that point. "Maybe he wasn't ready to let us know he'd survived the accident."

"Or Watts and Perkins did it and used the thunderwood to throw us off," Ava suggested.

"Find out who she is," Dylan said. "I'll phone Warden Fernandez to alert him of our suspicions." He'd also see if he'd sent over Turnbull's prison correspondence and take it with him to the safe house. Then he'd review it himself to see if Turnbull had orchestrated an escape or if they were dealing with a copycat.

Because this girl wouldn't be his last victim.

And the fact that he'd found a piece of thunderwood on Aspen's doorstep meant that the man would be coming for her.

Dylan had to be ready when he did. If he laid one hand on Aspen, he'd forget prison this time.

He'd kill the son of a bitch even if he had to go to prison himself afterwards.

The tension in the car as they drove back to Emma's made Aspen queasy. She'd returned home again, and now she had to leave her house, her cousin, everything behind. Worse, she had no idea how long she'd be gone.

Only that Dylan was going to be with her around the clock.

Under other circumstances, spending time with the sexy, handsome agent might be pleasant.

His gaze slid over her and her body tingled as she remembered the heated kiss earlier. She amended her thoughts. It wouldn't just be pleasant, it would be downright fun.

They might explore where that kiss could lead and recreate the passionate week he'd claimed they'd spent together when they'd first met.

He parked at Emma's and her heart sputtered with excitement at the thought of seeing her son again. How could she have forgotten him all those weeks? He was so much a part of her that she'd missed him the past few hours.

As soon as they entered, she smelled the scent of homemade stew and spicy jalapeno corn bread, and her stomach growled. Emma greeted her with a hug and Miguel stepped outside with Dylan.

"How did it go?" Emma asked.

Aspen explained that her memory had returned, and about the trap they planned to set for Perkins and Watts.

Emma's eyes widened in horror. "That sounds dangerous."

Aspen shrugged off her concern. "Dylan and Jack and I are moving to a safe house. Other agents will watch my house and if Perkins or Watts appear, they'll catch them. Then the danger will be over and Jack and I will be safe."

Dylan and Miguel came in wearing scowls. "You told Emma about the plan?" Dylan asked.

She nodded.

Miguel moved to stand beside Emma, a protective gleam in his eyes. "Did she tell you that Frank Turnbull may have escaped? That they found a Ute woman killed with the same MO?"

Emma leaned one hand against the table edge with a shudder, and Miguel took her in his arms. "That means you don't go anywhere without me, *Loca Linda*."

Emma nodded. "Don't worry. I don't intend to."

"I phoned the ME who's been analyzing the bodies from the prison bus crash and told him to put a rush on those bones," Dylan said. "If Turnbull has escaped, we need to put out the word. And if we have a copycat, we need to do the same."

Dylan's gaze met Aspen's. Fear glittered in his eyes for a brief second before he masked it.

Did he have reason to think that Frank Turnbull might come after her?

The Ute Slicer was legendary. Had earned fame and a reputation that would follow him into eternity.

He'd smiled as he'd watched from the top of the ridge as the Feds and police recovered the woman's body. He hadn't expected them to find her so soon, but hell, maybe this was a good thing.

The cops would be sweating. Sympathizing with the victim. Trying to figure out who he was.

While he was one step ahead of them.

The memory of slicing the woman's throat made his body go hard, and he mentally envisioned the knife piercing the girl's delicate flesh, then the blood gurgling and flowing down his hands.

The whites of her eyes had turned stark with terror when she realized her death was imminent.

Hell, yeah, it had been a rush he hadn't felt in a long damn time.

Let them shake in their shoes and stew for a while now. Try to figure out if Turnbull had survived or if a copycat had surfaced to mimic the man's crimes.

He held the knife up to the moonlight, the sharp blade glinting.

Meanwhile, life for some went on.

But for others, it was time to say a final goodbye.

Chapter 13

"Go pack," Dylan said as soon as they entered Aspen's house. "I want us to get out of here before the evening news airs."

Aspen cradled Jack to her as if he was afraid to release him. "He needs changing before we go."

"I'll take care of it," Dylan said. "Get your things together, then you can pack whatever we'll need for the baby." He hesitated, sensing her distress and reluctance to leave her home when she'd just found her way back. "Unless you've changed your mind." He grabbed her arm. "If you have, it's okay. I'll call off the whole damn plan."

She kissed Jack's forehead, her grip around the baby tightening as if she didn't want to let him go, but resignation lit her eyes and she eased Jack into his arms. "No. Those men have to be caught and put away."

He gently embraced the little boy, Jack's arms and legs kicking playfully. Aspen stroked the baby's cheek, then turned and rushed into her room.

Dylan released the pent up feelings he'd been holding in ever since Callie had given him the results of the paternity tests. Unbidden, moisture pricked his eyes as he pulled the blanket away from his son's face and gazed into his eyes.

His own blue eyes.

"My God, you are amazing," he whispered hoarsely. "You are my little *mijo,* my son, and I will never leave you now."

Jack grabbed his finger and curled his fist around it as if he understood.

Dylan's heart swelled with love. There was no way he could walk away from his baby or Aspen.

He'd die before he let anyone hurt them again.

Aspen blinked back tears as they left her house. Almost desperately she glanced back, memorizing the details of it as if she might forget where she lived once again.

"We're not going far," Dylan said, giving her hand a squeeze as if he sensed her distress. "We'll still be in Mesa Verde country."

Still among her people. She took some solace in that.

She squeezed his hand in return, grateful to know that he wouldn't leave her until they'd caught the men after her.

But then he would move on.

That realization sent an ache through her, an emptiness that reminded her of how lonely she'd felt the last few weeks when she'd been isolated and scared and had no one to turn to.

Jack gurgled from the back, and she turned sideways to comfort him. "It's okay, sweet one, we're just taking a little trip. An adventure."

Dylan gave her an odd look. "That was what my parents used to call it when we went on vacation."

She relaxed slightly. "Tell me about your family."

A wistful look passed across his face as he steered them toward Cortez. "My family comes from a long line of farmers who grew potatoes and alfalfa in the San Luis Valley. My parents were the first ones to go to college." A proud smile curved his mouth. "Papa is an attorney. He calls himself King Pro Bono. And Mama is an artist and teacher at Adams State College in Alamosa."

"You have other siblings?"

He nodded, although the scar at his chin twitched. "You met Miguel. I also have another brother and sister who are married with kids. And then there was Teresa." His tone lowered a decibel. "She died in a drive-by shooting when she was a teenager."

His story tapped at her memory banks as if he'd shared it before. "I'm sorry. That must have been horrible for your family."

He made a pained noise deep in his throat. "I was standing right there, only a few feet away. It should have been me."

She heard the agony in his voice, the guilt. "Her death inspired you to go into police work?"

He gave a self-deprecating laugh. "In a roundabout way." He sighed and rammed his hand through his hair, spiking the dark strands. "I was enraged, went looking for revenge. My father, Papa, was working the courts, my mother grieving. It was a rough time for all of us."

"And Miguel?"

"He was a damn altar boy. The smart, scientific one where I was the troublemaker."

"I'm sure that's not true."

"Oh, it was," he said with conviction. "Miguel toyed with being a priest. But he got shot defending his girlfriend and had a near-death experience. That changed him, and he decided to go into forensics and study medicine. He claimed that's what saved him. Although my mother always insisted that it wasn't the medical procedures that saved him but the healing soil of El Santuario de Chimayo and prayer."

"I think I'd like your mother," Aspen said softly.

A sultry smile softened his eyes as he turned to look at her. "You would. And I know she'd like you."

Aspen's heart melted at his words. His family sounded loving, honorable, spiritual, and reminded her of her own mother, and the role model she wanted to be for her son.

But what about a father or male figure for Jack to identify with?

She had managed without one. But was it different for a boy? Did he need a man in his life?

Aspen's questions about his family triggered bittersweet memories. The family trips, the camping, the cookouts, the normal childhood fights between siblings.

The empty hole Teresa's death had created.

The Christmas ornament they still hung on the tree every year in her honor—a graduation cap with her name on it and the date she would have received her high school diploma.

And then there had been the lectures from his family, the rules and consequences, the ones he'd balked at and fought.

The ones his parents had instigated because they loved him so much.

He'd do the same for little Jack.

Hell, he knew he'd make mistakes. But he'd do his damnedest to raise his son to be the kind of man his own father would be proud of.

They passed ranches and farmland, the open terrain, steep cliffs, ridges and deep canyons that made the majestic La Plata Mountains, the Sleeping Ute Mountain and the sharp-hewn silhouette of Mesa Verde a home for locals and a tourist draw for travelers far and wide.

Jack babbled noisily and Aspen turned to talk to him. "When you get bigger I'll take you to the Ute Mountain Rodeo," she said, and Dylan bit his tongue to keep from correcting her—*We'll take you to the Ute Mountain Rodeo.*

"And we'll visit the Cortez Cultural Arts Center so you can see the Indian dances and artwork of our people," she continued. "The Bear Dance is in June. Legend says it all began when a man went to sleep and had a dream about a bear. In the dream, he thought if he went up into the mountains, the bear would teach him something of great strength. And so he did."

She paused and Jack made a cooing sound as if he enjoyed the sound of her voice and understood the meaning of the story.

"The bear gave him words of wisdom and taught him the bear dance, so he came down and shared it with his people," she continued. "When you get bigger, we'll go to the Mesa Verde National Park to see the celebration.

They have a big balloon ride every year and you can watch the colorful balloons float across the sky. Most of the time our Ute people dress in regular clothes, in jeans and dresses, but a long time ago the women wore deerskin dresses and the men wore beachcloths. You'll see some of that at the festivals and dances."

By the time they arrived at the small house in the heart of Cortez, Dylan had learned more about the Ute history from Aspen than he'd ever learned in school. He'd developed a newfound respect for the plight of her people and her devotion to passing on the customs and stories of her ancestors.

The archaeology of the Mesa Verde cities was renowned and had inspired artists for years, the house where they were going to be staying was an adobe cottage that sat on top of a ridge and fit into the sweeping cliffs as if it had been carved naturally from the land.

Except this house had been fitted with a high-tech security system and a view of the mountainside to provide privacy and security for those who needed refuge from the world.

"It's beautiful," Aspen said as she carried Jack inside, and Dylan retrieved their luggage.

"I'm glad you like it." The space suddenly felt very intimate with the three of them inside. She offered him a tentative smile, and Jack cooed up at him from her arms. For a moment, Dylan savored the brief reprieve from the reality they'd left behind and imagined that this was their home.

That he and Aspen and Jack were a real family. That tonight they would put their son to bed.

Then they would fall into their own sanctuary together and make love until dawn.

And for once in his life, there wasn't a hit man or a serial killer lurking to destroy their happiness.

Aspen's skin prickled with awareness as Dylan watched her settle Jack into the infant seat in the Mexican tiled kitchen. She'd felt close to him in the car, admired the way he talked about his family and the affectionate tone to his words. He obviously loved them deeply.

What would it be like to be loved like that? To have a family unit who shared hopes and dreams yet still managed to maintain a close bond in the face of turbulent times?

Sadness welled in her chest. She missed her mother and Emma, and wanted her son to have the kind of family Dylan had described.

A family with a mother and a father.

But she had to be careful who she let into their lives.

Jack waved his fist at her and whimpered. He was probably hungry, so she stirred rice cereal into a bowl with the formula she'd heated from his bottle, making it soupy enough for him to swallow. Then she settled down in a chair to feed him.

He gulped down a few bites, spitting out half of it. She laughed. "I know it's not so tasty," she said, "but at least it's not grasshoppers." She scooped up another bite full and pressed the tip of the spoon to his lips, smiling as he sucked in the liquid mush.

"Tourists always ask what we Indians like to eat," she said softly. "Of course, we like modern food and fruits and vegetables. But they want to know about our past." She made a soaring noise with her mouth, swooping toward him with another spoonful as if they were playing a game. He followed the movement with his eyes, opening his mouth wide to slurp the cereal. "Years ago, it's true, that the Utes liked to eat grasshoppers and other insects. The Spanish thought it was disgusting, but they ate eggs and we thought that was gross, too."

Dylan moved up behind her and laughed as Jack puffed up his lips and blew bubbles, making cereal dribble down his chin.

"You'll like fish and meat better, little *mijo,*" Dylan said in a low voice. "Just wait and I'll teach you how to fish."

Aspen froze, her heart sputtering as she turned to look into his eyes. Why would he make a promise like that to her son when they both knew as soon as he caught Perkins and Watts, he'd be out of their lives?

Dylan realized what he'd said and had to back away. He'd allowed his love for his son and his dreams of fatherhood to destroy his concentration and had almost blurted out the truth to Aspen.

The fact that she didn't remember him or that he'd fathered her baby sent a white-hot rage through him. But the fact that she hadn't told him about their baby drove the pain deeper inside.

Jerking himself away from the table, he turned to retrieve the files they'd confiscated from the prison warden.

"Dylan?" Aspen asked softly.

"Just take care of the baby. I have work to do."

Her look of hurt and confusion added to his guilt, but his own emotions were too raw now for him to even try to explain. The Feds and local police were watching out for Perkins and Watts.

Better bury himself in the job and find out if Turnbull was alive, or if a copycat had surfaced.

He spread the files on the desk in the den, searching through Turnbull's visitor log. In the past year, he'd had a couple of visitors—a woman named Sally Ann McCobb, and his half brother, Freddy.

Freddy had been present in court. The man had looked so different from the shaggy-headed, tattooed, burly Turnbull that Dylan would never have put them in the same family. But during the trial, he'd learned that Turnbull was half Ute. His mother had married a Ute man and lived on the reservation with him, while Freddy had been born of her first marriage to a man in Utah.

He jotted down both names to follow up on, noting the dates of their visits. Sally Ann McCobb had visited two weeks before Turnbull had been transferred, the half brother only three days.

He'd check them both out.

Next, he scanned the phone calls and found both Sally Ann and Freddy on the list, along with two other women.

There were stacks of letters from other fans to sort through, so he put those aside to look over after Aspen and Jack went to bed.

Then he checked the list of inmates and friends Turnbull had acquired in prison. One name on the list made his blood turn to ice.

Larry Gerome Sawyer—aka the Slaughterer.

He had killed over twelve women in a bloodbath that had rocked the Northern Ute tribe.

Dylan had also worked that case. Like Turnbull, the con hated his guts.

His heart raced as he checked the list of prisoners being transported with Turnbull.

The pendulum of questions began to swing back and forth in his head. Dear God.

Had Turnbull and Sawyer been partners of sorts? Had one or both of them planned the escape and walked away alive?

He prided himself on watching the news. He kept up with politics, with the economy, the stock market, but mostly he had a fetish for the crime.

A chuckle rumbled from him as he watched the news anchor.

"Aspen Meadows, the Ute woman who was missing for several weeks, has been found and is safe and alive. Preliminary reports stated that she was suffering from amnesia, but recently her memory has returned. She admitted that she witnessed two men dumping federal agent Julie Grainger's body along the river. The men have been identified as Boyd Perkins, a man believed to be a hit man for a local mob family, and Sherman Watts, a local Ute man who has assisted Perkins in evading the law."

He pressed his hand to his chest and laughed. The damn Feds thought they were setting a trap, but he was smarter than them.

And he'd been lying low. He'd had time to plan.

Their scheme would backfire in their faces.

He looked down at the blood on the girl's neck and imagined Acevedo's face when he found her, her neck slashed, her eyes panicked in terror, her mouth wide-open in a scream.

He had to find a public place to dump her body, some place significant, some place that would mean something to Acevedo.

Some place he couldn't resist leaving Aspen to come to.

He knew the place.

Yes, Acevedo would find her and see her blood in his dreams for the rest of his life.

Then he'd feel vulnerable, guilty, unworthy, imprisoned by the people he couldn't save, as well as the ones he'd put behind bars.

So sweet that he would think the Ute Slicer was back.

Of course he wouldn't know his identity. Wouldn't know if it was Turnbull's knife that had killed the girl or someone who just admired his handiwork.

Not until it was too late and Aspen Meadows was dead.

Chapter 14

Aspen found the kitchen pantry and refrigerator stocked, as well as the nursery. After feeding Jack, she filled the baby bathtub full of warm water, stripped Jack and placed him inside with the rubber duck toy. He chased the little yellow duck as it floated around him as she bathed him, then scrunched up his nose in distaste when she soaped his hair with baby shampoo, then rinsed out the soap. But he seemed infatuated with the bubbles in the water and slapped at them with his hand.

"I'm glad you're taking this so well," she said. "You don't even seem to mind moving around."

While she didn't adjust quite so easily to change. She'd grown up on the reservation and, except for her college days, had never considered living anywhere else. Maybe that was the reason she hadn't kept Jack's father in the picture.

Or maybe he hadn't cared for Jack or her at all.

The water was growing cold, so she wrapped Jack in a bath towel, carried him to the dresser/changing table and laid him down. He kicked and swatted at the towel as she dried him off, then powdered his bottom and diapered him.

"You smell so sweet," she said as she wrestled with a little blue sleeper she found in the drawer. She snuggled him to her, then sat down in the rocking chair and read him a picture book, pointing out the simple objects on the colorful pages and smiling as he tried to grab the book and stuff the corners in his mouth.

A few minutes later, he dozed to sleep, and she rose and tucked him into the crib, covering him with a blanket. "Good night, little one. Sleep good." She kissed her hand, then pressed it to his cheek. "One day we won't be running," she whispered. "One day we'll be home to stay. And you can play with the other children on the reservation and learn to fish on the land. And we'll never have to leave home again."

When she turned to leave the room, Dylan stood at the door watching her, his gaze so intense that she froze. "What?" she whispered.

"You will be safe," he said quietly. "I promise you, Aspen. One day you and Jack won't have to look over your shoulders anymore."

The fact that he claimed they'd made love for a week taunted her. The kiss they'd shared proved the heat was still there, too, the embers of the fire simmering, waiting to be stoked.

She wondered if he was thinking about that week. If he ever regretted them parting.

And if being here alone with her and Jack might tempt him to come back to her bed.

Suddenly his look turned shuttered, as if he'd read her thoughts and had already answered them. And the answer was no.

Then he turned and left the room. She wanted to go after him. To see if they could rekindle whatever they'd had. But she couldn't.

She had to think of Jack and their future.

She didn't want to be left with a broken heart, or for her son to cry after a man who didn't want him.

Dylan left the room before he gave into temptation and kissed Aspen.

And admitted that he was Jack's father.

He wanted her to remember, dammit, and explain why she'd left him out of their lives. Why she'd indicated to Lightfoot that she hadn't considered him father material, and that she hadn't felt anything more for him than lust.

While he'd thought about her every day while he was away.

Damn. He had to focus. He had a stack of letters to Turnbull to check out. It was hard to believe that instead of being terrified of serial killers as one would expect, that some killers drew fans—groupies. That some women actually felt sorry for the bastards and thought their love could save the men's sorry souls.

Foolish, sick, dysfunctional—and a growing problem that still baffled him to no end.

He reviewed the names he'd collected so far. Sally Ann McCobb, the female who'd visited Turnbull in jail. Freddy, the half brother.

And Larry Gerome Sawyer—the Slaughterer.

He had to know if Sawyer had died in the crash.

Wiping his clammy hands on his jeans, he punched the number for the state ME. The man answered on the third ring.

"Hi, Doc, this is Dylan Acevedo with the Bureau."

"Yeah, I've been talking with your brother. I already told him I'd let you guys know when I finished the results."

Impatience gnawed at Dylan. "That means you haven't confirmed that Turnbull is dead yet?"

"The partial dental plate suggests it was him, but I'm conducting more tests to verify since the plate wasn't in the man's mouth."

"How about the other bodies?" Dylan asked. "Who have you identified?"

"For sure, the bus driver, the guards and one of the prisoners."

"Which one?"

"A guy named Barry Burgess—inmates called him Buffalo. Man wore a size seventeen shoe, so his remains were the most obvious. And dental records confirmed the rest."

"How about Larry Gerome Sawyer?"

"I'm working on his body and the one we think is Turnbull's now."

Frustration knotted Dylan's shoulders. "You heard that a woman was killed using Turnbull's MO. We need to act quickly. Let me know as soon as you get the results."

The ME gave a long, labored sigh. "Listen, I haven't slept in over twenty-four hours. I'm working as fast as I can."

Dylan hung up and rubbed the back of his neck, trying to massage away the knots. It was too late to visit Sally Ann McCobb tonight or go to the prison, but he would do both in the morning.

Still, he could do some background work tonight.

He tapped into the federal databases and plugged in the woman's name. A few minutes later, he had the scoop on Sally Ann.

She was in her thirties, had worked as a hairdresser for years, and recently gone back to school to study psychology. She'd first contacted Turnbull under the guise of research for a paper she was writing.

His interest piqued, he dug deeper. She had no record, no arrests, not even a parking ticket. Although she had been in counseling before she enrolled in the community college.

Counseling for spousal abuse.

The pieces fit with the general profile of prisoner groupies. He copied down her address, anxious to question the woman.

With Larry Gerome Sawyer on his mind, he accessed the files on his trial and crimes. The gruesome, bloody photos of a half-dozen women spilled onto the screen.

His stomach churned as he noted the details of his vicious attacks, stirring memories of the case. Memories he'd tried to banish.

Behind him, Aspen gasped. He stiffened, then turned to see her looking over his shoulder, her wide terrorized eyes glued to the photographs.

Dear God, he hadn't meant for her to see them or to know that another sick man just like Turnbull might be coming after her.

* * *

Aspen stared at the pictures of the bloody, naked bodies in front of her in horror.

She'd known Dylan was working but she'd assumed it had something to do with her and the trap they'd set for Perkins and Watts.

Yet he'd told her about the case he'd investigated before they'd met. Violent crime work was his job. Not just his job but his life.

"What are you doing?" she whispered.

He immediately shut down the file and stood. "I'm sorry. I didn't mean for you to see those."

She tried to recover, but she couldn't shake the images from her mind. "How do you do it?"

"Do what?"

"Investigate those crimes. Look at those dead women and not fall apart."

He reached out and stroked her arms. "I do sometimes," he said softly. Gently he lifted his hand and pushed her hair from her cheek. "The night we met. I was on the edge that evening. When I caught up with Turnbull, I wanted to kill him. Not lock him up but make him suffer the way he made those young women suffer." His tone dropped a decibel. "But then I met you and you brought me back to the brink of sanity."

Aspen's heart began to race. His touch felt so tender, but she heard the torment in his voice. "We talked about the case," she whispered.

He nodded. "I talked. You listened. You even thanked me for what I did." He gave a self-deprecating laugh. "I wasn't a hero that night, Aspen. I almost killed Turnbull in cold blood. Almost turned into a monster like him."

Aspen smiled, then reached up and pressed her hand

to his cheek. "You could never be like him. He viciously destroyed innocent people's lives. Not just the women's lives he killed but their families and loved ones. You are a hero—you sought justice for them when they couldn't speak for themselves."

He shook his head as if he still didn't believe her, and Aspen's lungs tightened. No wonder she had slept with him the first night she'd met him. He was the sexiest, most honorable man she'd ever met. After working grueling hours to catch a killer and protect lives, he'd needed someone to comfort him.

So he'd turned to her.

How could she have resisted?

How could she resist him now?

She couldn't. She slid her hand into his hair and pulled him toward her, then stood on her tiptoes and pressed her lips to his. He growled low in his throat and yanked her to him as if he'd been waiting on an invitation.

He tasted like coffee and strength and man, a tantalizing flavor that made her crave more. He probed her lips apart with his tongue, then slipped inside to tease her as he deepened the kiss. She moved against him, her body bursting into an erotic song and dance that begged to partner with him.

He slid his arms over her shoulders and back, massaging her as he pulled her into him. His erection pulsed against her abdomen, sending a torrent of sensations through her. His hand found her breast, stroking, teasing, making desire surge through her.

No wonder she had stayed in bed for a week with this man.

She wanted to drag him there now and make love to

him all night. To feel the pleasure his fingers and mouth evoked, to sate the burning need deep inside her.

He kneed her legs apart, pressing his hard length into the juncture between her thighs, and she grew moist with want. With a low groan, he dragged his mouth from hers and dipped his head to drop tongue lashes along her neck and throat, then downward until she arched her head backward and purred her delight.

A second later, his fingers traced her nipple through her blouse, and she groaned his name, hoping he'd follow the erotic touch with his mouth.

He didn't disappoint.

He slowly unbuttoned her blouse, parting the sheer fabric until he exposed the lace covering her breasts. His soft murmur of appreciation fueled her passionate response, and she reached for his shirt, anxious to feel bare chest against bare chest.

But he halted her movements by shoving her hands away, tugging her bra down and lowering his mouth to her nipple. He flicked his tongue over the pebbled bud, sending a spasm of need from her chest to her abdomen, then he closed his lips around the turgid peak, and she moaned. He wrapped his arms around her as her legs buckled, and he pulled the tip between his teeth, nipping, then suckling her until she thought she'd die from the pure pleasure of his wet tongue.

"Dylan, let's go to bed," she whispered, clutching him so her legs didn't give way.

Ignoring her, he moved his mouth to her other breast, loving it the same way, and heat shot through her, the yearning so intense that she slid her hand down to cup his sex. He was hard and full and ready.

She wanted him inside her, loving her, reminding her of the week they'd spent together, making her feel alive.

A sound jarred her from her euphoria. Jack. He was crying.

Dylan stiffened, slowly flicking his tongue over her one more time, then letting go to search her face. His eyes were glazed, his breathing erratic, the stark need in his eyes mirroring the frantic pounding of her heart.

But Jack whimpered again, and she gave him a look of regret. "I guess I'd better check on him."

He gave a clipped nod, and she left the room. Although when she glanced over her shoulder, he was still watching her, his eyes smoldering, and a warm tingling spread through her. Maybe later they could take up where they'd left off.

But as soon as she saw Jack, reality intervened. What in the world was she thinking? She couldn't get involved with Dylan, not when he would leave them both.

Not when she didn't even remember the past and the name of Jack's father.

Or whether he might resurface again and want to be a part of their lives.

His instincts warned Dylan it was better that Jack had awakened and stopped him from making love to Aspen. But his body betrayed all rational logic and throbbed in protest.

He wanted Aspen just as much as he'd wanted her the very first time he'd seen her.

No. He wanted her more.

He walked to the nursery door and saw her lifting Jack into her arms, and his heart swelled with longing. These two people could be his family.

Jack already was, although Aspen seemed to have no idea.

And until she did and explained why she hadn't told him he had a son, he couldn't take her to his bed.

His cell phone trilled, jarring him from the moment, and he forced himself to back away and answer it. "Acevedo speaking."

"Dylan, it's Martinez. You're not going to like this, but we found another body. A Ute woman, early twenties."

Dylan bowed his head. "Same MO as the Ute Slicer?"

"I'm afraid so."

Dylan cursed and glanced at the nursery door where Aspen stood holding Jack. His heart slammed into his ribs.

If this killer came after her, he'd have to go through him first.

Chapter 15

By the time Aspen rocked Jack back to sleep and returned to the living room, Dylan looked sullen. He was sorting through a stack of letters on the table and didn't even glance up when she stepped up beside him and placed her hand on his shoulder.

She wanted to pick up where they'd left off, but sensed he had withdrawn.

"Dylan?"

He stilled, dropped the envelope on the table and drew in a deep breath. "Go to bed, Aspen."

She felt the tension in his shoulder and rubbed the knot. "Why don't you come, too?"

His breath gushed out, but he didn't move to get up. Instead, he pulled away from her touch. "I have work to do."

Anger and confusion suffused her. "What kind of game are you playing?"

He finally turned and her breath caught at the intense expression in his eyes. Hunger was there, burning raw and bright, but also something akin to fear.

And maybe anger.

Déjà vu struck her. It was the same kind of dangerous look he'd had when she'd first met him. As if he was barely holding on to his ironclad control. As if he wanted to assuage the pain of the victims' faces that haunted him. As if he didn't deserve that reprieve.

"Please, Dylan," she said softly. "You've been working day and night."

His jaw tightened, and he finally stood and faced her, placing his hands on both of her arms. "And I'll keep working until I know that you're completely safe."

"We are safe here tonight," she said, hating to plead, but they both needed comfort.

"Maybe," he said in a deep voice. "But we just set the trap today. I have to stay focused and alert."

Disappointment made Aspen back away. She couldn't remember, but she didn't think she'd ever asked a man—begged a man—to go to bed with her.

She wouldn't do it again.

"Try to get some rest," she said, then she turned and fled to the bedroom before she forgot her promise to her son and convinced Dylan to make love to her anyway.

Refusing Aspen's invitation was one of the most difficult things Dylan had ever done. His body hummed with arousal, literally ached from wanting to join her in bed, but the phone call earlier had reminded him that Aspen was in more danger than even she thought.

That a madman, as well as Perkins and Watts, might be after her.

And all because of him.

He spent the next few hours going over the letters from the women who'd written Turnbull. The man had received hate mail along with letters from holy rollers who claimed they'd pray for his soul, and two other women who had offered conjugal visits. One from a lady in Nevada, another from a woman in New Jersey.

By 5:00 a.m., he called Ryan and asked him to contact someone in those states and check out the two women in case they'd recently been contacted by Turnbull or had helped him escape. He also asked Ryan to come and watch Aspen so he could follow up on the prisoners and Sally Ann McCobb.

Ryan was at the house by six. "I could go to the prison and talk to this woman," Ryan suggested.

Dylan shook his head. "No, I want to do it myself. Turnbull pledged revenge against me." Besides, he needed to put some physical space between him and Aspen.

Jack and Aspen were both still sleeping, so he left and drove to the prison first.

Warden Fernandez didn't appear surprised to see him. "I figured you'd show up sooner or later."

Dylan shook his hand and claimed the wooden chair across from the warden's desk. "I spoke with the state ME last night. It looks like both of your guards received wounds that suggest an attempted prison break. He's identified Burgess's body but is still working on Turnbull's and Sawyer's."

"Two of our most notorious," Fernandez muttered. "Frankly, I was glad they were being transferred. Both were cold-blooded psychopaths."

"Did either of them have any friends in here?"

"Friends?" Fernandez gave a sarcastic grunt. "I'm not sure either man knew what a friend was. Turnbull stabbed Sawyer and was in solitary the last few days before he was transferred."

"So they teamed up? That doesn't make sense."

He shrugged. "They were both tough bastards. Neither one showed any remorse."

And if the two of them had escaped and paired up—God help them all.

"Can I speak to Turnbull's former cell mate?"

"Sure." He punched a button on his intercom and ordered one of the guards to bring the man to a holding room, then gestured for Dylan to follow.

They passed through security, and Dylan stood by the wooden table in the interrogation room while the guard escorted Carl Tanner, a short, bald, robust guy in handcuffs and leg irons into the room.

Tanner was a doctor who'd killed his wife because she'd had an affair. Compared to Turnbull and Sawyer, he was a damn saint.

Although the snarl on his pocked face didn't look saintly.

Dylan produced his badge and introduced himself.

Tanner angled his head to the left. "What do you want?"

"I need to talk to you about Frank Turnbull."

A grin curled the man's lips. "Heard that son of a bitch died."

"That's what I want to discuss. There's a possibility he might not have been killed in the crash. That he could have escaped. Or that a copycat is imitating his crimes." He explained about the two murders following Turnbull's MO.

Tanner whistled. "So. What's it got to do with me?"

"You were his cell mate for a while. Were you two buddies?"

"Hell, no. Turnbull didn't make friends." Tanner yanked open the top buttons of his shirt, revealing a set of deep scars. "He did that with a fork. So, he definitely ain't no friend of mine."

That would work to his favor. "Did he talk to you about escaping?"

Tanner chuckled. "All the damn time. That and getting revenge on the man who put him in here."

"Did he ever mention a partner? Admit that he worked with someone to commit the Ute Slicer murders?"

Tanner shook his head. "Man like him wants control. He wouldn't have a damn partner—he likes to work alone so he can bask in all the glory."

Dylan's frustration mounted. He needed something new, concrete. "How about a name or a contact? Someone who would have helped him try to escape?"

Tanner leaned forward with his beefy arms on the table. "What you gonna do for me if I tell you?"

"What do you want?"

Pain flashed in Tanner's eyes. "To see my kid. I haven't seen him since I've been in. I want to tell him how sorry I am."

Dylan twisted his mouth in thought. "I'll see what I can do."

Tanner worked his mouth side to side. "Some bleached-blond bimbo used to visit him. Name was Sally Ann. He told me he hated the bitch but she'd do anything for him."

Tanner shook his head. "I don't get it. I get hate mail

for killing my cheating wife, and he murders girls for fun and women write him love letters."

"You're right, it doesn't make sense," Dylan agreed. "But a lot of crimes don't." He hesitated. "Can you think of anyone else?"

Tanner shrugged. "His half brother, Freddy. Seems he felt indebted to Turnbull for something but he never said why."

Dylan thanked him and stood. Maybe Freddy had paid off his debt by helping Turnbull escape.

Aspen stumbled into the kitchen to make coffee and was surprised to find Agent Tom Ryan sitting at the table instead of Dylan.

She frowned, grateful she'd thrown on a pair of jeans and sweater instead of wearing her pajamas. "Where's Dylan?"

Tom glanced up from his notes. "He wanted to pursue some leads, so you're stuck with me for a few hours."

She poured herself a cup of coffee and went to look out the window. Situated at the top of the ridge, she had a sweeping view of the land, the snow-capped mountaintops, the shrubs and grass in the canyon that would be turning green as soon as spring resurrected life back to the parched land.

Why had Dylan gone instead of letting one of the other agents pursue the leads?

Because he wanted to get away from you.

She sipped the hot coffee, renewing her vow not to push him again. Obviously whatever they'd shared when they'd first met had meant nothing to him. She was just a case now that he had to finish. A witness to protect.

Not the woman he loved.

"You shouldn't stand in front of the window," Agent Ryan said. "It's too dangerous."

A chill rippled through her at his warning, and she backed away, suddenly angry and claustrophobic. "I hate this," she muttered. "Hate being afraid. Hiding out. Wondering if or when someone might come out of nowhere and strike."

"We have agents watching your house. We'll get them."

She whirled around. "But it's so unfair. He has the control, the power."

"It'll be over soon, Aspen. You just have to hang in there and trust Dylan."

Trust Dylan? That was the ironic thing. She *had* trusted him from the moment he'd picked her up at the shelter.

Jack whimpered from the nursery, and she forced her thoughts about Dylan to the back of her mind. Her baby needed her.

And she would do whatever she had to do to protect him and give him a good life.

Her mother had raised her alone and managed. Somehow, she would do the same.

If only she could stop wishing Dylan would be a part of her life.

Dylan drove to Eagle's Landing to see Freddy, but the man wasn't home. He found a work address from the database and headed to the garage where Freddy was supposed to work.

A skinny man, probably midforties, wearing grease-stained coveralls and smoking a cigarette loped toward him. "What you want, mister?" He gestured toward Dylan's car. "Need some work done?"

"No." Dylan removed his ID from his pocket and flashed it. "Name is Special Agent Acevedo. I need to speak to one of your employees, Freddy Lakers."

The man took a drag of his cigarette and blew smoke through his nose. "Freddy ain't showed up at work for going on a week now."

Dylan frowned. "Has he called in? Anyone here heard from him?"

"Nope, not a word." The man puffed on his cigarette again. "But if he does show up, I'm gonna fire his ass."

Dylan gave him his card, told him if he heard from him to call him, then climbed back in his car. He checked Sally Ann's address and turned onto the street, then headed toward Crescent Canyon.

On the drive, his mind raced back to the night before, to the fact that Aspen had wanted him.

And not because she remembered their time in Vegas together.

A smile curved his mouth as a thought struck him. Maybe their time in Vegas hadn't just been a heat-of-the-moment affair. The fact that she wanted him again now meant there might be something deeper between them.

But how could they have a relationship with secrets and lies still between them?

He knew where Aspen Meadows was hiding.

He'd followed Acevedo and watched him escort the Ute woman inside that house on the mountain. He thought she was safe.

But none of the Ute women were safe.

Only Aspen could wait a few hours.

First he had to pay a visit to another woman. One he'd fantasized about reuniting with for the past year.

One he wanted to kill.

But first he'd make her suffer.

He stared at the battered old house with hate churning in his gut. Here, his first evil thoughts had been born. Here, he'd fantasized about murder.

Ducking low, he wove between the shrubs and bushes surrounding her small wooden house, memories of her cruel beatings and preaching returning.

The paint on the house had faded and chipped over the years, the windowpanes were dirty, the porch sagging and rotting. He'd heard that his stepfather had long ago run out on her.

Not that he blamed him. The damn bitch would kill any love anyone had for her.

The house was dark inside, the lights off, and a mangy dog lay sprawled in front of the porch steps. He stopped to scratch behind his ears, then the wood floor squeaked as he climbed the rickety steps and let himself inside the house.

He paused to listen. A low humming sound echoed from the back room. He didn't bother to hide himself or keep his footfalls quiet. He wanted to see the look on her face when she saw him.

A minute later, her humming stopped. She'd heard his footsteps. He stood in the den by the ratty plaid sofa and remembered being forced to his knees while she ordered him to pray after one of her famous beatings.

He smelled her before she entered. The lemony scent of floor cleaner and dusting spray that still had the power to nauseate him. Then her rail-thin wrinkled face appeared in the doorway. She'd aged drastically, but those sharp eyes were just as mean.

"My lord," she gasped.

He grinned and reached for the knife at his belt. "Hello, Mama."

Chapter 16

Sally Ann McCobb lived in an apartment outside Crescent Canyon. Dylan noted the weathered siding, the overgrown unkempt bushes and the broken-down car in the parking lot, frowning at the sight of a scruffy little boy riding a battered tricycle on the sidewalk.

Sally Ann lived on the bottom floor, so he knocked on the door. He'd considered calling first, but wanted the element of surprise on his side.

He paced while he waited, and when no one answered knocked again, and finally heard footsteps shuffling toward the door. A minute later, a bleached blonde with red puffy eyes, a swollen lip and a bruise on her left cheek squeaked the door open.

Dylan flashed his ID. "Special Agent Dylan Acevedo."

Her eyes widened perceptively for a brief moment of

panic before a resigned look settled over her features. "Yeah?"

"You're Sally Ann McCobb?"

She gave a slight nod. "I ain't done nothing wrong."

Dylan offered her a smile. "No one said you have. I just need to talk to you, that's all, ma'am." The wind whipped through him, swirling dust and a fast-food wrapper around his feet. "Can I come in?"

She hesitated, then seemed to decide she had no choice, and unfastened the chain and allowed him entry. The inside of her place was no more impressive than the outside, with cheap, worn furniture and a battered oak table in the kitchen/den combination.

He immediately scanned the room, searching for a sign that a man had been there. One coffee cup on the table, not two. Although an empty bottle of whiskey lay atop the overflowing trash.

Turnbull liked whiskey.

Sally Ann tugged a faded chenille housecoat around her plump shoulders. She didn't look like Turnbull's type.

"I think you know the reason I'm here," he said.

She twisted her mouth sideways, biting on her lip, then went to the coffeepot and poured herself another cup. "You want some?" she asked.

He nodded, not really wanting it but deciding to stay in her good graces as long as he could. She didn't ask if he wanted sugar or creamer, just handed him the chipped mug and he took a swig, nearly choking on the potent brew.

"You've been writing Frank Turnbull in prison?"

The nervous flicker of her eyes gave her away. "I was doing research for a class I'm taking." She tapped a pack of cigarettes against her palm, pulled one out and lit it. "I talked to several prisoners."

"But you continued writing Turnbull, didn't you? Personal letters? *Love* letters?"

She blew out a plume of smoke. "I guess you already know that. So why don't you cut to the chase. You're wondering why a woman would write love letters to a prisoner."

He gave a clipped nod. "You know how many women he killed?"

"Yes. But that was before he found Jesus."

And she'd bought that dog and pony show? "Do you know where he is now?"

"Heard he died in a bus crash being transferred to ADX."

His gaze met hers, that flicker of unease giving her away again. "That's what he wants people to believe, isn't it?"

She took another drag on her cigarette, then thumped the ashes into a foam cup on the counter. "That's what happened."

He made a low sound in his throat, deciding to change tactics. "So, Sally Ann, how did you get those bruises?"

"My ex beat me," she said matter-of-factly.

"I thought you were finished with him."

"I am."

"How about Turnbull? If he survived, would you help him?"

"If he survived that crash?" She gave a sarcastic cackle. "Hell, yeah. If I didn't, he'd kill me."

"But you're not his type," Dylan said.

"I know," she said in a pained voice. "That's what he told me. He likes Ute girls."

"Not for sex," Dylan said.

She shook her head. "Not for anything."

He walked over and picked up the bottle of whiskey. "You drink all this yourself, Sally Ann?"

A panicked look shot through her eyes. That look alone was enough to send a cold chill through Dylan. "He was here, wasn't he? And he gave you those bruises?"

Pain darkened her expression. "I loved him," she whispered hoarsely. "I really thought he'd changed. That he'd found the Lord and we could have a life."

Dylan gritted his teeth. "Did he say where he was going?'

"I told you he's dead." Sally Ann gestured toward the door. "But he had a groupie, some guy who wrote him and thought he was a god. Turnbull told me about him during my last visit."

"Did he give you a name?"

"He called himself Ulysses. Said he was going to make Frank's work look like child's play. And that he'd start the game all over again."

Dylan's mind raced. Was Turnbull alive? Or had this man taken on his MO?

"Did Turnbull mention having dental work done lately?"

She stubbed out her cigarette with an annoyed grunt. "Yeah, so?"

"So far, the only concrete evidence that Turnbull might have died in the crash was a partial bridge."

Her face paled.

Dylan's patience snapped. "What? You have to tell me if you know something. We can protect you."

A tense heartbeat passed between them before she replied. "I think that guy Ulysses was a dentist."

Dammit.

His stomach in a cold knot of dread, he grabbed the whiskey bottle with a handkerchief and carried it to his car to drop by the crime lab. If it had Turnbull's prints on it, they'd know for sure that he was alive.

He also had to track down this guy Ulysses. Find out where he lived.

If he was copycatting Turnbull or if they'd teamed up together.

And he had to do it before either one of them found Aspen.

A chill invaded him. If one or both of them had been watching Aspen and him, they knew she wasn't at her home. Could they have followed him to the safe house?

He'd taken every precaution. But still anxiety ripped through him, and as he drove toward the crime lab, he phoned Ryan to warn him to stay alert.

Aspen hated that Dylan had left her alone. Tom Ryan was a nice man, tried to be unobtrusive, but having a stranger guarding her drove home the fact that Dylan was only back in her life because of this case.

So did the news clip that aired on TV, a repeat of the earlier broadcast.

"Police have now confirmed that a missing Ute woman, Aspen Meadows, has been found safe and alive. Although preliminary reports stated that she was suffering from amnesia, Miss Meadows's memory has returned.

"The woman witnessed two men dumping the body of Special Agent Julie Grainger on the Ute reservation.

"Those men have been identified as Sherman Watts " the reporter paused while they flashed Watts's picture on the screen "—and Boyd Perkins—" another pause to show his photograph "—who is believed to be a hit man.

"Police have issued an APB for both men and a manhunt is underway.

"Meanwhile, Miss Meadows has agreed to testify against the men when they are apprehended. If you have any news about either Perkins or Watts and their whereabouts, please contact the FBI immediately."

Aspen shivered. There was no going back now. She only hoped that the two men took the bait and came after her at her house.

She spread a blanket on the floor and arranged several baby toys around Jack, turning the jack-in-the-box crank handle until the clown popped up. A laugh bubbled from her son's throat, and she pushed the doll down inside and cranked the handle all over again.

Agent Ryan's cell phone trilled, and he glanced at it, then connected the call. "Hey, Acevedo."

She tensed, her nerves on edge as she listened to the one-sided conversation. As soon as Ryan disconnected the call, she asked him what Dylan had said.

"He's following some leads on the Turnbull investigation, then stopping by the lab to check in. He should be back in a couple of hours."

Aspen wanted more details. But Ryan stepped outside with his phone, cutting off her question. She'd have to wait on Dylan. The Turnbull case had obviously gotten under his skin, the reason he'd personally left to do the legwork.

Would the Ute Slicer come after Dylan for revenge?

The idea of something terrible happening to him sent a shudder through her.

Jack grew fussy, and she picked him up and walked him around, talking to him to soothe him. But he was hungry so she fixed another bottle, cradled him in the rocking chair and fed him.

"He has to come back," she whispered as Jack fell asleep. "He just has to."

When Jack dozed off, she laid him in the crib and covered him with a blanket. The door squeaked open and she hurried to the living room, hoping Dylan was back. But Agent Ryan had stepped back inside.

"Is something wrong?" she asked.

"No, I was just checking the perimeter," he said. "And I phoned Agent Parrish to see if Perkins or Watts showed up at your house."

"Have they?"

"No," he said. "But they still might. They're probably waiting until dark."

She nodded, and glanced at the clock. That was hours away. Hours of waiting and pacing and not knowing. Hours of hoping and praying the two men got caught.

Hours of wondering if that psycho Turnbull would come after Dylan.

Worry needled Dylan as he parked at the crime lab and rushed inside. He met Callie at the door of her office and held up the whiskey bottle. "Can you print this and run it right away? I need to know if Turnbull's prints are on it."

Her brow furrowed. "Where did you get it?"

He explained about the prison mail and visitor log.

"Did she admit that he was alive?" Callie asked.

Dylan shook his head. "No, but I read between the

lines. I think he paid her a visit and she realized that his talk of redemption was bull."

With gloved hands, Callie took the bottle to her workstation, dusted it for prints then ran them through AFIS.

Dylan watched as she pulled up Turnbull's prints and the computer program worked its magic.

Seconds later, his fears were confirmed.

Turnbull had been at Sally Ann McCobb's house.

Which meant Turnbull was alive.

"Damn," Callie muttered. "How did that SOB walk away from that burning bus?"

"With help," Dylan said cryptically.

"Sally Ann?"

"No. Well, hell, she may have given him some money, but she's not bright enough or devious enough to pull this off." He hesitated, his mind working. "I couldn't locate his half brother, Freddy. I'm going to get an APB issued for him immediately. And Sally Ann McCobb mentioned that Turnbull had a fan. Called himself Ulysses." He snapped his fingers. "I probably have mail from him in that stack at the safe house, the pile I haven't gotten to. I'll analyze when it I get back there. Maybe it will lead us to his real name and address. My guess is that that corpse in the fire either belonged to his half brother or his fan."

Callie nodded and Dylan called the state ME to relay his findings.

"I did ID Sawyer," the ME said. "But there's something odd about the last body. Signs on the corpse indicate that the man suffered from a brain tumor."

"It's not Turnbull," Dylan said, then explained his discovery. "But you need to find out who he is." He told him to get Freddy's dental and medical records and to check DNA. And he needed to find out what this man Ulysses's full name was, if it was, in fact, his real name.

As soon as he hung up, his cell phone trilled. Bree. "Acevedo, you have to get over here. There's another woman's body. And you won't believe who it belongs to."

"Who?"

"Turnbull's mother." Her breathing sounded erratic.

Dylan disconnected, jogged toward his car and drove at a dead race toward the address Bree gave him.

When he climbed out, sweat beaded on his skin and he hurried up to the house.

As soon as he ducked below the crime tape, he met Bree. She was as pale as a ghost.

"It's bad," she said.

The metallic scent of blood and human wastes assaulted him as he entered. Then he saw the blood everywhere. Splattered on the walls and floor, the elderly woman's body sprawled on the kitchen tiles in a river of red where she'd been gutted.

Chapter 17

Sheriff Martinez took Bree by the elbow. "Go outside. Get some air. Agent Acevedo and I have this one covered."

Bree didn't argue. She hurried outside as if she desperately needed fresh air. Dylan remembered her pregnancy and understood Patrick's reaction.

If he'd known Aspen was pregnant, he would have been just as protective.

The crime techs arrived to process the scene, but Dylan studied it, seeing the dark rage Turnbull had had for his mother.

"Who do you think did this?" Patrick asked.

Dylan gave a bitter laugh. "Turnbull. He escaped the crash and he's out here."

Patrick muttered a curse. "Why the overkill?"

"His mother was the source of his rage." Dylan grimaced. "Unfortunately, the past year in the pen has probably fueled his anger. And judging from this bloodbath, the viciousness of his crimes will probably escalate."

"That's all we need," Patrick mumbled.

Dylan grimaced. "Yeah. And if he's going after the people he thinks hurt him, then he's on a personal vendetta."

Which put him at the top of the list.

But he knew Turnbull. He was cunning. He wouldn't just try to kill him.

Just as he had gotten inside Turnbull's head when he'd profiled and interrogated him, Turnbull had gotten into his head. He knew the case had gotten to Dylan.

He'd recognized the vengeance in his eyes when he'd nearly killed the killer.

Cold sweat dotted his body and his heart hammered in his chest.

He'd make him suffer by hurting another woman.

Aspen.

He didn't know how Turnbull had figured out that he cared about her, but he had.

And that was where he'd strike.

The piece of thunderwood he'd left on her doorstep had been a statement.

He had to go back to her now. Trust his fellow agents and the cops to do their jobs.

Nothing else mattered except keeping Aspen and their son safe.

The sun had faded behind dark storm clouds, night setting in. Aspen fed Jack and played with him on the pallet until he finally conked out again. She watched him breathing for a few minutes, still unable to believe she'd given birth to such a beautiful and wonderful child.

Finally the sound of a car engine split the tense silence, relief welling inside her as she looked out the window and spotted Dylan climb from the car.

Agent Ryan met him outside, and Aspen ached to join them, but Tom had given her strict orders not to go outside for fear someone was watching.

She felt like a prisoner.

How long would this confinement last? Would she have to look over her shoulder for the rest of her life? Live in constant fear that someone would try to kill her?

Tears threatened, along with a deep desperation, but she willed herself to be strong and not fall apart.

It seemed like an eternity before Agent Ryan left and Dylan finally came inside. As soon as she saw the solemn expression on his face, she knew something was terribly wrong.

"What happened?" she asked.

Although anger simmered below the surface of his guarded calm, his blue eyes glimmered with emotions she couldn't read. He clenched and unclenched his fists. "Nothing. No hits on your house yet."

He was lying. "There's something else, Dylan. What is it?"

He shrugged. "Is Jack all right?"

"Yes," she said. "Now stop avoiding me. I need to know what's going on."

"You just have to trust me," he said, then walked into the kitchen for a glass of water. But his brow was furrowed and damp, his body language perched for battle, his senses alert as he combed through the house checking windows and locks.

He reminded her of a big cat, like a panther, stalking the place as if in search of prey—or a predator.

"Do you think Perkins or Watts know we're here?" she asked, her heart starting to race.

"No," he said a little too fast.

"You do, don't you?" She grabbed his arm and forced him to look at her. "Did they follow you?"

"No, I told you not to worry. I'll protect you."

Instead of consoling her or pulling her into his arms, he seemed cold, distant.

Impersonal.

"Damn you, Dylan. I don't understand you. You're lying, something is terribly wrong. I'm not an idiot."

"I know that," he said in a clipped tone. "I'm just doing my job."

Hurt and bewilderment speared her along with bitterness. "So I'm just a job to you now?"

His gaze met hers, and for a brief second, something else flickered in his eyes. Hunger. Desire.

Fear.

"Tell me what's going on, Dylan. One minute you're hot and hold and kiss me like you want me, and the next you look at me like I'm a perfect stranger, just some woman you have to protect for your damn job."

He tried to pull away, but she clawed at his arm. "You say we spent a week together, a week in bed, and when you kissed me before and we almost made love, I felt something intense between us. A heat I've never felt before." Her breath feathered out, choppy with her frustration and desperate need. "But now you act as if you don't care about me at all. How can you be so cold?"

A muscle ticked in his jaw, and he reached up and covered her hands as if to pull them away, but his touch was so warm, and she needed it so badly, she whispered his name again.

"Don't you care, Dylan? Don't you care at all?"

Tension stretched between them, her question echoing in the silence.

"Dylan, please," she said, hating the pathetic desperation in her voice. "Please don't shut me out. I need you."

There, she'd said it. Bared her soul and shed her own protective barriers.

"It's not that I don't care," he finally said in a gruff voice.

"Then why pull away from me?"

His mouth tightened as if answering her cost him. "Because I care too damn much."

Her breath caught in her throat along with a painful surge of longing, prompting her to lift one hand to his cheek. God help her, but she wanted him.

"Aspen, don't," he murmured.

But that plea reverberated with suppressed desire. Desire that mirrored the hunger he had to see reflected in her eyes.

He might leave her when the case was over. But she needed him now.

And with death knocking at her door, the moment was all that mattered.

On some subconscious level, Dylan knew he was crossing the line, that he should remain alert and not allow his personal feelings to clutter an already complicated and dangerous situation, but he'd lost that game a year ago when he'd first met Aspen.

No, before, when he'd nearly killed Turnbull just because he wanted to see the man die.

Only Aspen had saved him back then. Aspen and her understanding. Aspen and her sultry looks, her tenderness and passion.

She'd reminded him that the world consisted of something other than ugliness and cruelty, that it could also be beautiful and loving.

Needing that reminder now, to hold on to the fact that she was alive and in his arms instead of in Turnbull's or this copycat's unmerciful hands, he dragged her into his arms and claimed her mouth with his.

Her lips tasted like ripe berries and sunshine and sweetness, causing his chest to clench with a warmth that helped to chase the chill from his body.

The chill that had dogged him ever since he'd found that piece of thunderwood on her doorstep.

The chill that had grown to insurmountable heights at the sight of the man's latest brutalized victim.

His mother.

Don't think about the case. Think about how wonderful it is to finally hold Aspen again. To finally be able to touch her and stroke her bare flesh and meld your body with hers.

She moaned low in her throat, and he delved his tongue inside her mouth, hungry and taking everything she offered.

He deepened the kiss, one hand plunging into her hair while the other one skated over her back, down to her waist, then her hips. He tugged her up against his hard body, his sex jutting against the fly of his slacks and brushing her thigh.

She whispered his name in a low purr as he tore his mouth from her lips and trailed kisses along the long slender column of her neck. His mouth watered for more, his length throbbing to be closer to her. He kneed her legs apart, and fit himself into the cradle of her thighs, then groaned when she arched her hips into him.

Raw need tore through him, and he slid his hand down to cup her breast, kneading the plump mound through her blouse until she begged him to remove her top.

One flick and buttons went flying. He ripped off the garment, her throaty sounds of approval spurring him on. Then her skirt came off, fell to the floor in a puddle, and he paused to drink in the sight of her beauty. Full breasts encased in ivory lace rose and fell with her erratic breathing.

"Dylan?"

"I'm here, baby." Dark fantasies sprang to mind as she reached for his shirt and hastily unfastened the buttons. Her fingers fired his flesh, enflamed him to the point that he thought he might explode with need.

Desperation turned the next few seconds into a frenzy as they yanked at each other's clothes, throwing them onto the floor.

Naked, she was a glorious sight to behold.

Her body was slightly rounder now she'd given birth, a soft lushness to it that, if possible, made him crave her even more.

He thought he'd memorized each inch of her, but as he explored the fine contours of her breasts, her hips and thighs, he knew his memory had failed to imprint her exquisitely soft skin or the exact dark brown of her nipples into his brain.

His senses sprang to life, soaking in her sweet feminine fragrance, his skin erupting with white-hot sensations as she traced her fingers over his bare chest and arms then lower to his abdomen.

He sucked in a sharp breath when she feathered touches on the insides of his thighs, and images of her on her knees pleasuring him flashed behind his eyes.

She had done it before. Tasted and tortured with him her tongue and lips, and he wanted her touch now.

But he had to taste her first.

Starved for her sweetness, he picked her up and carried her to the bedroom, then spread her on the bed to feast.

She moaned and clawed at his arms as he kissed her breasts, then pulled one hard tip into his mouth and suckled her. She arched her hips as if in silent invitation, but he forced her to wait while he loved her.

Teasing her thighs apart with his hand, he toyed with the soft curls at her center, loving her other breast until she pleaded his name.

"Dylan, please, I need you inside me."

"Soon, baby, soon," he whispered against her belly as he pressed kisses down her stomach to the treasure below.

He licked her folds, spreading her legs and jutting his tongue out to taste her heat. She whimpered, and tried to stop him, but he forced her still and fit his mouth over her core, sucking the heart of her desire until her honeyed juices flowed into his mouth.

She bucked upward, clenching and twisting the sheets between her fingers as she cried out her release.

Need enflamed him, his body aching with the relentless force of a man who needed to pump inside a woman.

And not just any woman.

Aspen.

The woman who'd soothed him a year ago, the woman who'd reminded him that beauty still thrived in this godforsaken world of killers.

A woman who'd stolen his heart and, he feared, his very soul.

Aspen closed her eyes, savoring the brilliant splash of colors sweeping her into euphoria.

The moment Dylan had touched her bare flesh, her inhibitions had fled like rain evaporating on a hot pavement.

Had it always been this way between the two of them? This explosive?

He rose above her, bracing himself on his hands. "Open your eyes, and look at me, Aspen." He nuzzled her neck with his lips and teeth.

"I want you to see me when I'm inside you."

Aspen did as he said, the pure raw passion glazing his eyes, sending spasms of erotic excitement through her.

Slowly he teased her center with his full hard length, back and forth in an exquisite torture that sent her over the edge again. She dug her fingernails into his arms and clung to him as he thrust deeper inside her, stretching and filling her until the memory of him binding himself with her flashed back, sweeping her into the vortex of desire that had robbed her breath a year ago, a hot yearning that had burned through her each time he'd touched her.

The present blended with the past, their dance of lovemaking familiar and overwhelming her.

He lifted her hips with his hands and thrust deeper, angling her so their bodies met so intimately that another orgasm rippled through her.

He hammered harder, faster, his own groan of satisfaction whispering in her ear as his release came, swift and potent.

For a long moment, he held himself inside her, their bodies quivering together as the aftermath of their passion ebbed and flowed.

And as the sensations overrode her earlier fear, another memory surfaced.

The moment she'd realized she was pregnant.

And that her son belonged to Dylan.

The realization rocked her world, and she froze as he turned her over in his arms and held her.

Her breath rushed out as she tried to piece together what had happened between them. She and Dylan had made a baby during their short affair. A beautiful little boy that she'd loved from the moment of conception.

But she hadn't told him he had a son.

And he was going to hate her for it.

Dylan crushed Aspen in his embrace, his chest heaving. He had needed her tonight, needed her sweetness, her loving.

Yet he felt her shutting down.

Only this time he refused to let her.

He pulled back slightly to look into her eyes. Dark brown eyes glazed with passion, and a hazy look of arousal that made him want her again.

But she stiffened in his arms and he felt her putting some distance between them just as he had last year when he'd guarded his heart.

"Dylan?" she said softly.

His chest tightened. "Yes?"

"I remembered something else."

"Something about your attack?"

She shook her head, and suddenly the truth dawned on him. "You remembered us being together?"

She nodded, a wariness filling her eyes.

"And what else?" he asked gruffly.

She clamped her teeth over her bottom lip and bit down as if debating on whether to confide in him.

"What?" he asked, his impatience mounting.

She sat up, tugging the sheet up around her, and he gritted his teeth, hating to do anything to encroach on the closeness they'd just shared.

But he had to know the truth.

"Tell me what you remember, Aspen."

She exhaled as if to steady her nerves. "I remember us making love last year. The week we spent together." A faint blush crept up her cheeks. "It was…wonderful."

He nodded.

"But then we parted."

"Yes. I got called away on an assignment."

"And I finished school and went back to the reservation to teach."

"That's right."

She hesitated. "And a few weeks later, I discovered I was pregnant."

His throat tightened as he waited, tension stretching between them. He wanted to prod her, shake her. "Go on."

Her gaze met his, the heat still simmering between them. But lies and secrets stood like a wall they needed to climb.

"Aspen, what else did you remember?"

Tears filled her eyes. "That you're Jack's father."

Chapter 18

Dylan's heart swelled with her words, an overwhelming protective urge slamming into him. He would protect her and Jack with his life.

Yet anger that she'd kept the truth from him made him grit his teeth. "I know. Why didn't you tell me you were pregnant?"

Shock widened her eyes. "What do you mean, you know?"

"For God's sake, Aspen. I put two and two together, and wondered, so I took a DNA sample."

Hurt strained her features. "Why didn't you tell me? Why go behind my back?"

Hell, she was turning the tables on him?

"Why didn't I tell you?" He wanted to shake her. "Why didn't you tell me? Why didn't you contact me when you first realized you were pregnant?"

She pressed her fingers to her temple, massaging her head as if struggling with the memories.

"I did," she whispered. "I tried to contact you a few times, but the Bureau said you couldn't be reached, that you were out of the country."

He closed his eyes on a hiss, and when he opened them, she was watching him. "You should have tried harder."

Tears glittered in her eyes. "Why? You left without telling me where you were going, without asking me to see you again." Pain laced her voice and any bravado she had wilted.

"So why not try when he was born? You could have left messages. If I'd known, I would have come."

She stood, grabbed her robe, put it on and knotted it tightly then walked to the window and looked out.

Anger and fear choked him. He wanted to know the truth, yet what if she said that she hadn't wanted him in their son's life? That he was too dangerous?

Aspen trembled, hating the anger in Dylan's voice. But how could she blame him? She'd deprived him of knowing his son.

And his question raised her own insecurities and resurrected other memories.

"Why, Aspen?" Dylan asked. "Why didn't you call me when he was born?"

"I didn't want to feel like I'd trapped you."

"It wouldn't have been like that," he said. "Besides, I had a right to know."

"I know that," she whispered. "But I was afraid," she admitted.

"Afraid of what?" He gripped her arms and spun her around, his eyes icy cold. "You were afraid of me? Afraid I would hurt Jack? That I wouldn't be a good father because I told you I almost killed Turnbull?"

The distress in his voice made her heart clench. Then her conversation with Kurt Lightfoot rolled back. He'd said that she was afraid of Jack's father, but that wasn't true. "I was afraid that you might try to take Jack away from me."

"What?" Hurt tinged his voice.

"I was afraid you'd want custody. That you wouldn't want me to raise Jack on the reservation." Her voice cracked. "And Kurt said that with your government job that you had power and money. That you probably knew people and could convince a judge to give Jack to you."

A sense of betrayal stabbed at him like a knife.

"You listened to Lightfoot instead of coming to me?" he said, his voice thickening. "You told him about our baby and not me. What did you plan to do, marry him and let him raise my son as his own?"

The very thought fueled irrational jealousy.

He had to get out of there. Couldn't look at her and think about her keeping his son from him and allowing Jack to call another man his father.

"No," Aspen whispered.

But he couldn't listen to her now. Couldn't look at her.

Couldn't stay in the room, wearing his feelings on his shoulder and knowing that she'd even contemplated such an idea.

Furious, he yanked on a pair of jeans and stormed from the room. He heard her calling his name, and he shouted for her to leave him alone.

He didn't look back to see her reaction. Instead, he stalked outside, slammed the door, jogged down the porch steps and glanced into the trees shrouding the ridge.

He leaned against a tree and closed his eyes, his chest heaving.

He had to regain his composure.

But suddenly a twig snapped behind him, and he opened his eyes, automatically reaching for his gun.

Dammit, he'd left it inside.

Before he could move to retrieve it, something sharp and hard slammed into his skull, and he collapsed on the ground, the world going black.

Aspen's heart ached. She hadn't meant to hurt Dylan but she obviously had.

But she had to be honest with him. She'd wanted him to know about Jack, but she also hadn't wanted to pressure him into marriage or taking responsibility for their son.

She'd wanted him to come to her because he cared for her and wanted to be a part of her life.

Her own mother had faced the same dilemma and had opened herself up to Aspen's father, but he'd walked away without looking back. He'd even accused her mother of lying and trying to use a baby to force him into marriage.

Aspen grabbed jeans and a shirt and dressed, then wrapped her arms around herself. She'd been afraid of the same thing.

Afraid to trust that Dylan might love her.

She had to make him understand that her fears stemmed from her past.

She hurried through the bedroom door into the living room, then to the door. But just as she opened it, she spotted Dylan lying on the ground, facedown, not moving.

Panic sent a bolt of adrenaline through her, and she screamed, and turned to run inside to phone for help. But a big, hard body tackled her from behind, and she pitched forward, then they rolled backward. Her knees hit the steps, her hands clawing for control and digging into gravel and dirt.

Two hands jerked her by the shoulders, and she scrambled to try to escape, but a hard whack on the back of her neck made her reel with pain. Her head spun, the world shifted in a drunken state of nausea, and an icy chill invaded her as the man dragged her up and threw her over his shoulder.

He stalked down the hill, rocks scattering and pinging off the ridge as he wove through the brush to an old van.

She kicked at him and pounded his back with her fists, but he threw her inside and slapped her across the face so hard that her eyes sank back in her head and she passed out.

Sometime later, she aroused from unconsciousness, terror sweeping over her. Her hands and legs were bound with tight-corded ropes, her mouth gagged, and the van was bumping over gravel and dirt.

Who was this man?

And where was he taking her?

Dylan slowly roused from the black sea where he'd fallen, swimming upward toward the light. He had to paw his way up, had to surface.

Aspen needed him.

He pushed up from the ground, his hands scraping the dry brush as he sat up and tried to regain his senses.

Then he spotted the piece of thunderwood.

Pure panic slammed into him. How long had he been out? Did Turnbull have Aspen or was it a copycat?

Fear made him shoot upward, and he staggered up the steps, and rushed inside, his gaze scanning the darkened interior.

Pausing to listen, he prayed that she was still alive. Still inside somewhere.

But he inched through the living room to the bedroom and found it empty.

Jack.

God, please don't let him have hurt the baby.

Trembling with terror, he raced to the second bedroom and held his breath as he checked inside. A whimper from the crib made his chest clench, and he flipped on the light and hurried toward the crib.

Jack had stirred and opened his eyes and was looking up at him as if he knew something was wrong.

He quickly checked the baby for injuries, but he appeared to be all right.

Though his mind raced with horrid images of what this man might be doing to Aspen, he shoved the images aside. He had to act fast.

Turnbull had kept his other victims for at least twenty-four hours. But what if this was the copycat?

And if Turnbull had killed his mother so violently and was escalating, what would he do to Aspen?

Cold sweat broke out on his brow.

"I'll be right back, Jack. I have to get help." His heart pounding, he raced to the bedroom and retrieved his gun and phone. Throwing on his shirt, he punched in Tom's phone number. Three rings later and Tom answered.

"Tom, it's Dylan. Either Turnbull or his copycat found us and he has Aspen."

"I'll call the locals and tell them to set up roadblocks and get some choppers in the air."

"We need to figure out where he'd take her. And I need someone to watch Jack."

"I'll call Miguel right now."

Dylan scrubbed his hand over his face, frantic. He had to think. Where would Turnbull take Aspen?

Dear God, please don't let me be too late....

Aspen's body ached from being tossed around in the back of the van as the vehicle careened over the rocky terrain. The interior was pitch-black, the smell of cigarette, sweat and booze an acrid stench that made bile rise to her throat. Was Dylan all right?

Was he alive?

Panic clogged her throat and she tried desperately to choke back the fear.

What if he didn't find her in time?

And what if he was dead and Jack was in that house all alone? No one would even know he was there.

Who would take care of him if she didn't survive?

Emma.

Emma would raise Jack as her own. Emma knew what it was like to lose a mother. She would tell him about Aspen and about how they grew up together on the reservation. She would share the stories that Aspen wanted so badly to pass on to her son.

And even though Emma was only half Ute, she would raise him in the Ute way.

Tears leaked down her eyes, but she was helpless to stop them. She didn't want to leave Jack again—she'd promised him she wouldn't.

She didn't want to die, either. She wanted to watch Jack grow up. Teach him how to ride a bike. Watch him grow into a man.

And she wanted to tell Dylan that she loved him.

She sobbed with the realization. Why hadn't she realized it before? Why hadn't she confessed her feelings?

Confess how terrified she'd been that he couldn't love her back? That that was the reason she had stopped trying to contact him.

She'd tried to convince herself that having Jack was enough. That she didn't need or want Dylan.

But she'd lied to herself for months.

And now it was too late.

The van suddenly screeched to a halt, and her stomach knotted with a sick fear as the sound of the driver's door opening and slamming rent the night.

Outside the van, footsteps shuffled against rock. Somewhere in the distance, an animal screeched.

Then hard bands of steel snapped around her wrists and dragged her from the van. She kicked again, determined to fight, but he slammed his fist against her cheek and she saw stars.

Then he dragged her across the rocky terrain toward some kind of small building a few feet away.

A church.

She blinked, trying to focus. It was old, weathered, deserted. Overgrown weeds and bushes shrouded the front. The smell of something rotten permeated the air.

And the scent of death floated to her, eerie and numbing as the sight of several graves caught her eye.

Then the shiny blade of a knife shattered the darkness as he tossed her against one of the cement markers staked in the dirt-packed ground.

Dylan had dropped Jack off at Emma's. She was terrified but Miguel had stayed with her to calm her, and he'd promised to call as soon as he found Aspen.

He only hoped he found her alive.

He raced into the crime-lab conference room to confer with the others.

"The ME confirmed that Ulysses Ramstead was the other dead man in the prison bus crash. He must have joined forces to help Turnbull escape, then Turnbull stabbed him in the back and left his body to burn so we would think he was dead. Turnbull left his dental plate to mislead us."

"Where would he take Aspen?" Dylan asked as he paced the room. "I would have thought if he wanted to get revenge on me, he would have just done it right there. That he would have even forced me to watch."

"He does want revenge," Ben said. "But his sickness has to do with killing Ute women."

"That's right," Tom said. "Remember his profile. He hated his mother because she raised him on the reservation. Because she was brutal and a religious zealot."

Dylan fisted his hands, his heart hammering. He had to climb in Turnbull's head. Think like the sadistic sick man he was.

Turnbull hated his mother and he'd killed her. He hated Ute women.

He hated the church.

His mind racing, he hurried to the table and opened up the files on Turnbull, quickly scanning them.

"Send someone to Turnbull's mother's house. Maybe he's going to take her there."

"I'll cover the house," Tom said.

Dylan hesitated, his mind humming with another possibility. "He knows we'll look there, though."

Dylan flipped the page, scanning the psychologist's notes. "This is it. The church." He glanced up at Tom with dread in his belly. "You go to his house, and I'll check out the church. He might take her to the very place his mother forced him to go as a child when she pounded religion into him."

Tom gave a clipped nod. "You might be right."

Both men sprang into action, Tom hurrying to his car and Dylan to his own.

He flipped on his siren, spread the map on the car seat and tore from the crime lab, weaving his way through Kenner City, out of town.

Bright lights nearly blinded him from an oncoming car, and he blew his horn, then sped past, careening around a curve, his hands sweating on the steering wheel and his breathing choppy.

It seemed like days, but was only a matter of minutes until he reached the small dilapidated, deserted church where Turnbull had been baptized.

He spotted a dark van, and his heart thundered. He had to be in time.

Aspen couldn't be dead.

He had to save her and take her home to their son.

Not bothering to slow down, he screeched to a halt, jumped out, his gun at the ready.

The blue lights twirled across the barren land, flickering across the terrifying scene in front of him.

Aspen was on her knees in the dirt by a marker, her hands tied, feet bound, while Turnbull stalked around her, preaching a sermon as he wielded the Ute ceremonial knife.

Chapter 19

Aspen shuddered at the sound of the crazed man humming in the ancient language. He didn't look Ute, but he seemed entranced at the moment, as some kind of demon had possessed his soul.

The scent of death, damp soil and fear invaded her. Her head throbbed where he'd hit her, and her wrists and ankles were raw from trying to free herself from the ropes biting into her skin.

She was going to die.

No, she'd heard the siren. The police were coming.

Dylan would find her and save her before this madman used his knife on her.

He leapt toward her, jamming the pointed blade at her throat, and she flinched as a droplet of blood seeped from her impaled skin.

Then a loud growl broke the silence, the sound almost inhuman, and she looked up and saw Dylan launch himself at Frank Turnbull.

She screamed, fighting to escape her bindings, fear clutching her as her captor swung the knife in a wide arc, then jabbed the point at Dylan.

Dylan shouted an obscenity, and threw his body against Turnbull's and the two men fell to the ground in battle.

It was so dark she couldn't see, but the scent of blood assaulted her, and Dylan's shout of pain rent the air.

Dear God, no. Dylan couldn't die. She needed him.

And so did their son.

Rage seared Dylan, more painful than the blade that Turnbull drove into his shoulder. Blood oozed from the wound, trickling down his arm, but he ignored the pain, and grabbed Turnbull's hand, then they fought for the weapon.

Turnbull must have been working out in prison, and had gained weight and muscle, but the images of the women he had brutally slain flashed back, fueling Dylan's fury and renewing his strength.

He karate chopped Turnbull's wrist and the knife flew to the ground. Turnbull scrambled to get it, but Dylan tackled him and slammed his fist into the man's nose. Bones crunched and blood spewed, but Turnbull wasn't giving up.

He rammed his head into Dylan's stomach, gripped his arm where he'd stabbed him and pain rocked through Dylan. He grunted and fought back, but Turnbull managed to escape and grabbed the knife out of the dirt.

Aspen screamed as the man ran toward her, and Dylan saw red.

Adrenaline surged through him, and he reached for his gun. He found it on the ground by a cement marker, picked it up and aimed.

The bullet pierced Turnbull in the back, and he howled, then twisted around with a shocked gleam in his eyes as if he'd never expected Dylan to actually win.

Then Turnbull dove toward him again and Dylan pumped another round into the man. His body bounced backward, and he collapsed on top of a grave.

A sinister smile tilted his lips and his mouth moved. "I knew you were just like me," he said in a croaked whisper.

"I'm nothing like you," Dylan growled.

Turnbull's body jerked, then he took his last breath and his body went still.

Dylan staggered to him, then kicked the knife from his hand. Aspen cried his name, and he turned to see her struggling to free herself from the bindings.

He stumbled across the dirt-packed grave, then fell to his knees.

Moonlight streaked her pale face, and rage shot through him again as he spotted the bruise on her cheek and forehead.

"Are you all right?"

She nodded, tears streaming down her face. "But you're hurt."

"I've had worse," he said. Then he cursed as he looked down at her bound limbs.

A fierce frown pulled at his mouth as he retrieved Turnbull's knife, cut the ropes binding her wrists, then hastily slashed the ones on her ankles.

She fell against him on a sob, and he wrapped his arms around her.

"You're safe now," he whispered hoarsely. Relief ebbed through him as his blood soaked her blouse and they clung together. "I'm sorry I left you. Sorry he got to you—"

She cupped his face between her hands. "Shh. No, it's okay. It's over now."

"Thank God you're alive," he said.

They clung to each other for a long time, but she finally insisted on calling an ambulance. While they waited, she helped him tie his T-shirt around the wound to stop the blood flow.

He leaned against her, his pallor gray and chalky, and fear clutched Aspen. She had to be honest with Dylan.

He had nearly died to save her life.

He might leave again, even if she did confess her feelings, but she had to take that chance. Whether he loved her not, she wanted Jack to know this courageous strong man.

She wanted him to have the father she never had.

"I love you, Dylan," Aspen whispered. "I'm sorry I didn't tell you about Jack."

He gazed into her eyes, a mixture of hurt and hope glimmering in his slow smile.

"I'm just sorry you didn't trust me," he said gruffly. "I would never have tried to separate you from our son."

Her heart fluttered with anticipation, love mushrooming inside her as he fused his mouth with hers.

"And I love you, too," he whispered. "I think I did from the moment I saw you."

Epilogue

Two days later, the team met in the conference room at the Kenner County Crime Unit to review the case.

Tom had located Turnbull's half brother, Freddy, who'd gone into hiding when he found out his half sibling could have escaped.

"We've identified the woman's body we found in the river. She was just an innocent Turnbull killed for fun."

Dylan gritted his teeth. "What about Watts and Perkins?" Dylan asked. "Do we have any leads?"

"They didn't take the bait and come for Aspen," Tom said. "Which makes me think that they've both left the reservation."

"They're probably long gone, in Mexico now," Tom said.

Dylan shifted, although his nerves spiked at the thought that they might return for Aspen. He wouldn't allow them to. Not now.

Not ever.

"We did link Lightfoot to the Wayne family," Ben said. "He admitted he took money to help his people, and that he was afraid they'd call in his marker. He's agreed to go into Witness Protection. I think he's afraid of what they might have asked him to do."

Dylan gave a clipped nod. He was glad to see the man go.

Not that he thought Aspen was in love with Lightfoot. In spite of the pain and stitches in his shoulder, the past two days had been bliss.

"Before everyone leaves," Tom cut in, "Callie and I have an announcement."

Callie grinned and took Tom's hand in hers. "We're engaged."

Congratulations erupted all the way around with hugs and handshaking.

"It looks as if my brother's getting married, too," Dylan said as he clapped Tom on the back. "He called earlier to say he and Emma have eloped to Las Vegas."

They wrapped up the meeting, and Dylan hurried toward his car and drove back to Aspen's. The sight of her pueblo-style house brought a smile to his face and a sense of peace over him.

Aspen had worried that he wouldn't want to live on the reservation and had surprised him by offering to move, but he wanted his son to be raised in his mother's footsteps and to appreciate his culture.

His heart warmed as he parked, walked up to the door and let himself in. She smiled at him and Jack cooed as he rushed over to give them both a kiss.

Aspen was right. This was home. But it had nothing to do with the house.

It was home because the two people he loved most in the world were here.

And soon he would make Aspen his wife, then his son would carry on his name. And no one would ever tear them apart again.

* * * * *

SPECIAL EXCERPT FROM

HARLEQUIN

INTRIGUE

Twelve years ago, a tragedy tore a small Georgia town apart. Now, as the new high school principal, Kate McKendrick does everything she can to put the past behind her, but someone has her in their crosshairs. It's up to firefighter Riggs Benford to keep her safe... no matter the cost...

Read on for a sneak preview of The Secret She Kept, *by* USA TODAY *bestselling author Rita Herron.*

Riggs battled the urge to kiss Kate. Her story had touched his heart.

In spite of his bad-boy reputation, he did not take advantage of vulnerable, frightened women.

And judging from the way Kate was avoiding eye contact with him, she wouldn't welcome his lips on hers.

That fact stung, but he wrangled in his libido. If he wanted her to think he was a better man than his father, or the lowlife everyone thought him to be for abandoning his pregnant teenage girlfriend, he had to prove it.

Act like a gentleman. Keep his hands to himself.

Even if it killed him.

Talk business. "Kate, other than Billy, is there anyone in particular who'd want to hurt you?"

She ran a hand through the long strands of that wavy auburn hair, making his hands itch to touch it.

HIEXP40999

"Probably half the folks at that meeting tonight. You heard them." She dropped her hand back to her lap. "The truth is I understand their feelings," she said, compassion flickering in her eyes. "Change is difficult. So is forgiveness."

True. "Have you received any threats lately?"

She worried her bottom lip with her teeth. "Not exactly," she said slowly.

He narrowed his eyes. "What do you mean, not exactly?"

Indecision played across Kate's face before she set her mug on the coffee table and retrieved her purse. She withdrew an envelope from inside and offered it to him.

He removed the invitation to the dedication ceremony, confused at first. Then he spotted the hand-scrawled message on the back.

It was your fault.

Anger tightened every muscle in Riggs's body. "When did you get this?"

"Today. It was in the mail at school."

The timing was definitely suspicious. She'd received a cryptic message the same day as the town meeting, only hours before her SUV had burst into flames.

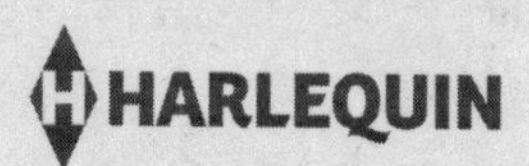
HARLEQUIN